Of Royal Blood
CAROLYN ZANE

In Pursuit of a Princess
DONNA CLAYTON

SILHOUETTE®
DESIRE™

*Silhouette, Silhouette Desire and Colophon
are registered trademarks of Harlequin Books S.A.,
used under licence.*

*First published in Great Britain 2003
Silhouette Books, Eton House, 18-24 Paradise Road,
Richmond, Surrey TW9 1SR*

The publisher acknowledges the copyright holders of the
individual works as follows:

Of Royal Blood © Harlequin Books S.A. 2002
In Pursuit of a Princess © Harlequin Books S.A. 2002

*Special thanks and acknowledgement are given to Carolyn Zane
and Donna Clayton for their contributions to the Royally Wed series.*

ISBN 0 373 04866 1

51-0503

*Printed and bound in Spain
by Litografia Rosés S.A., Barcelona*

Of Royal Blood
by Carolyn Zane

৩ ৵৵ ৫

Sebastian was claiming to be the missing heir to the throne of St. Michel?

Marie-Claire stood in the doorway, not sure that she'd heard correctly. His words hung in the air.

Why had he never told her this before? And, if he were the missing heir, wouldn't that make him the Crown Prince? And, if he were the Crown Prince, wouldn't that make him Philippe's son, which would then make him—

Marie-Claire's ears began to buzz. Her face caught fire and bile rose in her throat. Suddenly, the enormity of this moment hit her like a ton of bricks and she felt as though she would faint.

But it was her heart that refused to believe what he was saying. Because with the feelings she had for Sebastian LeMarc, there was no way he could be her brother…

* * *

Praise for Carolyn Zane

In Pursuit of a Princess
by Donna Clayton

ᕙ ᕗᕈᕗ

Etienne suddenly realised that he was falling hopelessly in love with this woman.

Sighing, he closed his eyes and tried to relax. But the notions eddying in his head made that next to impossible.

All of these realisations posed a huge problem for him.

He'd gone out seeking a wife. A princess. As the successor to the Rhineland throne, he knew his parents fully expected him to fulfil that goal.

Yet here he was at the top of Byron Mountain after having run away in the night with a woman who had no title, no fortune, no lands…not even a social standing to offer him and his country.

Had he totally lost his mind?

Or just his heart…

* * *

Praise for Donna Clayton

'Donna Clayton pens a cosy romance
with a lot of humour, heart and passion.'
—*Romantic Times*

Available in May 2003 from Silhouette Desire

A Man of Means
by Diana Palmer
(Texan Lovers)
and
The Millionaire's Pregnant Bride
by Dixie Browning
(The Millionaire's Club)

Cowboy's Special Woman
by Sara Orwig
and
For This Week I Thee Wed
by Cheryl St. John

Of Royal Blood
by Carolyn Zane
and
In Pursuit of a Princess
by Donna Clayton
(Royally Wed)

OF ROYAL BLOOD
by
Carolyn Zane

CAROLYN ZANE

lives with her husband, Matt, their pre-school daughter Madeline and their latest addition, baby daughter Olivia, in the rolling countryside near Portland, Oregon's Willamette River. Carolyn finally decided to trade in a decade of city dwelling and producing local television commercials for the quaint country life of a novelist. Though they seem to have bitten off decidedly more than they can chew in the re-modelling of their hundred-plus-year-old farmhouse. The neighbours are friendly, the postman actually stops at the door and the dog, Bob Barker, sticks close to home.

For Rita Dubenko, neighbour, friend,
one dang fast race-walker, and sister-friend
of whom it is said, 'She is faithful.'

Thanks to You, Lord, for Your amazing faithfulness.

Do not be afraid of sudden terror,
nor of trouble from the wicked when it comes.
For the Lord will be your confidence.
—*Proverbs* 3:25-26

Chapter One

Princess Marie-Claire de Bergeron—third daughter of Philippe de Bergeron, king of St. Michel, a small nation just north of France—squeezed between her two older sisters in order to better view the amazing physique of Sebastian LeMarc: playboy, aristocrat, successful import/export trade businessman. Clutching her sisters' arms to keep from falling too far back in the crowd, she watched with rapt fascination as he paused in his approach to the seventeenth hole to sign an autograph for a giggly young fan.

In St. Michel, Sebastian was a local celebrity. A good-natured philanthropist, a sex symbol and an all around hotty.

"Hotty, hot-hot," Marie-Claire murmured, loving faddish American slang nearly as much as she loved American movies, TV and cheeseburgers.

"Get away, Marie-Claire." Her oldest sister, the newly married Lise batted at her. "You are breathing down my neck."

Obligingly, Marie-Claire popped up over her middle sister, Ariane's, shoulder and allowed her gaze to follow the handsome Sebastian as he signaled his caddie.

In homes all over the globe, golf enthusiasts followed this action on a cable sports channel. Color and comment announcers strained toward a bank of television monitors and murmured, "He's approaching the tee…uh-oh." Muffled laughter.

"We seem to have a bit of a problem on the course. Sebastian LeMarc's caddie has taken a spill."

"That's right, Frank. Looks like it'll be a minute."

"From what we are able to gather here in the press box, LeMarc's regular caddie was under the weather…"

"Too much celebration after yesterday's rounds?"

More male laughter. Papers rustled.

"Rob, the caddie pinch-hitting for LeMarc today is, believe it or not, the son of the de Bergeron palace gardener, eighteen-year-old Eduardo Van Groober from St. Michel. Eduardo was on his high school's golf team last year and hopes one day to be the next Tiger Woods."

"Let's see if he can stay on his feet."

More chuckling.

"I think he was distracted."

"The king's daughters would do that to the most seasoned caddie, I'm afraid."

On television, cutaways of Marie-Claire and her attractive sisters filled the screen.

Marie-Claire watched as the flame-faced Eduardo fumbled with the golf bag, rushing to insert the clubs and frantically searching for one to offer Sebastian.

Sebastian found a club lying on the ground and, stepping over the still-flailing Eduardo, moved to the tee.

"Frank, Sebastian LeMarc looks to be using a seven iron, an excellent choice. With his powerful swing and ability to focus, this next shot could put his team in the lead."

Marie-Claire wriggled with excitement, but when a thoughtless member of the press obscured her view, she dropped down and poked her head under Lise's elbow, only to receive a glare of exasperation for her effort.

"Stop skulking around beneath us, Marie-Claire," Lise admonished in low tones. "Your hair is so filled with static, you look as if you've been electrocuted."

I feel that way, Marie-Claire thought, catching an exhilarating glimpse of her hero from between the reporter's lanky legs as Sebastian took a few practice swings.

"Ouch! What in heaven's name are you doing?" Ariane demanded as Marie-Claire's knees found the tips of her toes.

"Trying to see…him."

Ariane guffawed. "He's got to be what, twenty-eight? Twenty-nine?"

"Thirty-two."

"*Mon Dieu!* You're too young for him."

"I am not."

"Are too. Just look at you now."

"He's noticed me before."

Lise and Ariane exchanged droll glances. "When?"

Marie-Claire considered silence but their expressions spurred her to divulge. "It began five years ago. When I was sixteen, and we had a…moment."

"A…moment?" Lise asked.

"*Sixteen?* You are hallucinating." Ariane smirked.

"No. He remembers me, I know it."

"What kind of moment? Did you run over him in driver's training?" Pretty heads together, Lise and Ariane hooted. Marie-Claire pulled herself to her feet and, eyes blazing, attempted to tame her flyaway hair.

"He knows who I *am,* I tell you."

"He *knows* all of Papa's offspring."

"That's not what I mean. This is a special connection. You wouldn't understand."

Ariane snorted. "Marie-Claire, you are such a dreamer."

"Be that as it may, he carries a tiny place in his heart just for me." Marie-Claire turned her back on her skeptical sisters and focused on Sebastian, who in that moment, turned, caught her eye, and shot her a sexy wink. "See? Did you see that?" Her voice a tinny squeak, she yanked on her sisters' arms. "He winked at me!"

Lise lifted her nose. "He was not winking at you. The sun was merely in his eyes."

"The sun is *behind* his head!"

Ariane had to give her that. "Then he winks at all the pesky little kids in the kingdom. See? He just winked at Eduardo."

"And," Lise pointed out, "if I'm not mistaken, Eduardo just winked at you, Marie-Claire."

"He wants you, Marie-Claire." Ariane laughed.

"Shut up."

"Marie-Claire Van Groober. That's very pretty, don't you think?" Lise and Ariane made slobbery smooching sounds and then snickered into their hands.

Marie-Claire decided to ignore them.

Sebastian…*LeMarc.*

Marie-Claire *LeMarc.* Mentally, she traced the letters of his surname in her mind. For five long years he'd starred in her fantasy life, playing the part of her future husband and the father of their four yet-to-be-conceived children, three sons and a beautiful daughter.

Oh, that he would only notice her again, the way he had that night. She flushed, as those memories came flooding back. She knew he remembered. He must. How could he forget?

As he surveyed the fairway, she studied the confident curl

of amusement that seemed so permanently etched in his upper lip. She took in the slightly cynical, yet thoroughly charming creases that bracketed the corners of his mouth. The thick, dark-brown hair with the tiniest smattering of silver at the temples. The squarish, masculine chin that sported an angel's thumbprint. The velvety midnight-blue eyes and the come-hither look he seemed completely unaware he exuded from beneath the thick fringe of his lashes. Somehow, he looked more like George Clooney than George Clooney.

All around her, women were salivating, posing to attract his attention, applying lipstick and nudging each other. Marie-Claire's shoulders flagged. Her sisters were right. He had no time for her. Sebastian was an experienced, sophisticated man. And she? Well, at twenty-one, she was surely an overly sheltered case of arrested development. It was hard to become an independent, worldly wise woman with bodyguards and security cameras monitoring her every move.

Wildflowers need air. Light.

Hunkering low, Sebastian peered down his club, a thoughtful expression on his boyish mug. With a nod and a last murmured confab with Marie-Claire's father, King Philippe, he stood, pressed his tee into the grass and set his ball atop. Carefully, he positioned his feet and squinted once again down the fairway.

Oh, this was so exciting. Even the back of his head was enthralling. Sebastian was about to bring her father's team to certain victory.

Marie-Claire strained forward, knocking Ariane off-balance.

A hush descended over the crowd.

Sebastian laced his fingers over the handle of the club and, having lined up his shot, drew back.

On the down swing the words *"Go, Sebastian!"* pierced the hush and too late, Marie-Claire realized that the giddy shriek had come from the depths of her own throat. She wanted to die.

People turned to stare.

King Philippe rolled his eyes.

Buck teeth poking through his smile, Eduardo shot her the thumbs-up.

Her sisters' strangled giggles revealed their horror. Lise hissed, ''You're not supposed to yell at a golf tournament, you silly twit, have you lost your mind?''

Ears still ringing, Ariane gawped at her. ''It's no wonder he's noticed you. You're a loon.''

Much to his credit, Sebastian managed to execute a perfect shot, straight down the fairway, ending up a mere yard from the flag. The crowd went wild. Grins broad, King Philippe and Sebastian locked their hands overhead in a victory high-five and the paparazzi went nuts, scribbling on their pads, cameras flashing.

Through the throng, Marie-Claire felt Sebastian's eyes search her out as he turned and, once again, winked at her. Hands to face, her cheeks scalded the cool tips of her fingers and, in spite of her mortification, she smiled.

Their gazes met and clung, as they had, from time to time, over the years.

Around them, noises and colors swirled. Reality fell away. Marie-Claire's heart skipped several important beats and planet Earth seemed suddenly to be rotating backwards, so slowly was everything moving.

Sunlight glinted off the back of Sebastian's head, highlighting his dark hair in a glorious crown of burnished gold. He dipped his regal chin, his deep bedroom eyes never leaving hers and he arched a brow so loaded with questions that Marie-Claire knew.

He remembered.

* * *

Now that the tournament had ended, people were headed home to get ready for the victory celebration being held at the de Bergeron Palace that evening. A great ocean of humanity flowed past the clubhouse to the parking lot and gridlock was immediate. Impatient horns sounded and threatening shouts only added to the festive feel of victory.

Sebastian LeMarc watched his caddie as the lanky, flame-haired Van Groober lad stood staring after Marie-Claire. His freckled face wore the twitter-pated look of unrequited love. Sebastian knew the feeling. He'd been watching the stunning Marie-Claire de Bergeron from afar for half a decade now. Along with most of the male population of St. Michel.

But that was going to change.

Tonight.

She was twenty-one. Fully grown and fair game. And he had a good feeling that his interest was reciprocated. At least he hoped so. She was an amazing young woman. Full of vitality and as beautiful on the inside as she was on the outside.

Apparently, Eduardo thought so, too.

"She's something, huh, man?" Sebastian clapped the gangly lad on the back.

"Yes, sir. I mean no, sir! I'm not...I could never..." He tore his gaze from Marie-Claire's retreating form and stared up at Sebastian. "Have you ever been in love, Mr. Le-Marc?"

Sebastian took his golf bag from the skinny Van Groober and shouldered it with an easy move. "Yes."

"What happened?"

"Nothing." He squinted off into the throng. "Yet."

From where she stood in her suite behind the king's state apartment, Marie-Claire could hear the muted strains of a victory party gearing up from the grand Crystal Ballroom below. She pressed her nose to a balcony window to better see the headlights swinging around the circular drive at the front of the castle to the valet parking area.

For the umpteenth time, she wondered when *he* would arrive. She strained to make out his sleek Peugeot through the gloaming and almost thought she saw it parked in the family's private guest area. No doubt he was already downstairs, mingling. Though there were slated to be somewhere between twelve- and fifteen-hundred guests, for Marie-Claire, there was only one.

Sebastian LeMarc.

Light-headed with anticipation, Marie-Claire pushed the window ajar and music wafted in on the evening breeze. Every window in the palace blazed, and the gardens that unfurled from its rock walls were strategically lit to invite the fairy Queen Mab's dreamers, or young lovers in clandestine escape.

It was unusually warm for the first week in September, sultry, deceptively lazy, for the humidity lent an electric quality to the air, almost as if the thunderclouds looming in the distance might roll by and let loose with a wild abandon that would rival the emotional storm brewing beneath her breast.

Palms to the ornately carved window casing, she levered herself from her fascination with the arriving guests and moved to her vanity to give her gown a tentative twirl and to check her makeup one last time for flaws. After a breathless inspection, she deemed herself to be as ready as she'd ever be, and set off to find her sisters.

"How do I look?" Marie-Claire burst into Ariane's suite to find her helping Lise fasten a dazzling choker of platinum, gold and diamond baguettes about her neck. No doubt a gift from Wilhelm Rodin, Lise's husband of less than a month. Appearances were important to Wilhelm.

They both spared Marie-Claire a casual glance.

"You look quite grown up this evening," Ariane allowed. "Hoping to catch Sebastian in a weak moment and club him over the head and drag him by the hair to your cave?"

Fingers to lips, Lise pinched back her amusement.

"Yes, as a matter of fact, I am." With a grin, Marie-Claire waved off the sisterly jibe. "Any advice?"

Lise sobered. "Yes. Stay away from men."

"This from a newlywed?" Marie-Claire's own smile faded and she exchanged a concerned glance with Ariane.

"Wilhelm and I were never a love match, you know that."

"Yes, but we thought you were at the least very good friends."

Lise shrugged. "They say that even for lovers, the first year is the hardest. For friends, I imagine it to be…less appealing."

Marie-Claire ached for her sister. She could never imagine agreeing to a marriage of convenience. It was lucky Papa hadn't chosen her to create a political alliance between St. Michel and Rhineland because, though Wilhelm was handsome and charming, there was no warmth in the depths of his velvety brown eyes.

Not at all like the sexy twinkle that sparked in Sebastian's eyes when he caught her gaze and held it across a crowded room. Marie-Claire gave her head a slight shake. She would ponder Lise's marriage another time. Tonight, she had a date with destiny.

To Ariane, "What from you, dear sister? Any words to impart, to aid me in my mission?"

Ariane sighed. "Quite simply? Stay off the floor, *try* to

keep your hair pinned neatly to your head, and check your teeth for spinach, if you must eat. Speak when spoken to, and don't, under any circumstances, let on that you care. Play it cool. Men like that.''

Marie-Claire frowned. They *did?*

Always the practical one, Ariane had little time for whimsy.

But Marie-Claire was a much freer spirit. ''I'm off.''

''But we're not ready.''

''So?''

''You're surely not thinking of descending the stair by yourself?''

''Oh, pish, Lise. This is the new millennium. You don't have to do everything you are told to do, you know.'' Marie-Claire moved to the heavy double doors and swished through to the hall. ''Don't dally, or you'll miss all the fun.''

As Sebastian LeMarc watched Marie-Claire descend the grand staircase into the spectacular Crystal Ballroom— named for the priceless one-of-a-kind set of Austrian crystal chandeliers that shimmered fire the full length of the ceiling—he was transported back five years, to a night not unlike this.

His eyes caught hers and held and the age-old tightening kindled within his gut. Just as it had every time he'd caught her eye for the last five years.

Yes, it had been a night very much like this indeed. The second of September, to be exact. The air had been heavy that day, too. Muggy. Thunderclouds threatened harmlessly on the horizon, omitting an occasional distant rumble. The trees were only just beginning to turn into what would soon be a kaleidoscope of lemon-yellows, burnished golds, rusty oranges, and blood-reds.

It was that hour of the day just before the sun fell off its tentative perch on yonder hilltops and cast an ethereal glow over the land, turning raindrops to diamonds and ordinary leaves into a vibrant, translucent mass of color that would rival any pirate's treasure trove. Against the charcoal gray of the dramatic sky these colors came to life in a way that only the most talented old masters had been able to replicate on canvas.

Sebastian had been out riding with friends when he reined in his mount in order to bask in the glory of this magic view. His friends—royal consorts and visiting dignitaries deep in a political discussion—hadn't bothered to look up and rode on ahead for the palace stables.

The air held anticipation.

But of what? Sebastian couldn't pinpoint the source of the restlessness he felt burning deep in his gut. Perhaps it was the changing of the seasons. Or, the melancholia of saying goodbye to another warm sunny time of year and heading inside to spend months beside the fire.

Then again, perhaps it was the feeling that in three short years he'd be thirty. An age when people began to look toward producing a legacy of some sort. A marriage. An heir. To contribute to society in ways other than hunting with the boys and making the aristocratic social scene that had been handed him at birth.

For a long moment, Sebastian sat on his mount and pondered his universe as the sun began its nightly descent behind distant hills and the shadows grew long.

And then, just as he was about to turn homeward for the night, a blinding streak shot out of one of the royal stables farthest from the main compound. With a gleeful war whoop, this shrieking banshee took off across the meadow on a horse—or a bolt of lightning, Sebastian couldn't be sure—and headed toward the woods nearly a kilometer away from the rear of the stables.

Sebastian squinted into the setting sun. Where would a stable boy be charging off to at this hour? Unless he was up to no good.

Reining his horse around, Sebastian set off after the boy, knowing that King Philippe would never have sanctioned such after-hours escapades. The quickest way to ruin prime horseflesh was to ride at breakneck speeds in the dusk.

The wind whistled in his ears as he hunched low and followed the boy over the rolling hills of St. Michel to the edge of a great forest that was rumored still to harbor a fire-breathing dragon and a band of magical fairies. Well, Sebastian didn't know about that, but when he caught up with this kid, be might just breathe a little fire himself.

Upon reaching the forest, he had to slow dramatically to pick his way through the trees to avoid being clothes-lined by a low-lying branch. He could hear the horse and rider just ahead, crashing through the underbrush, and then the roar of falling water as a rushing river cascaded over a precipice at one end of the king's well-stocked fishing pond.

A poacher, no doubt. There to catch a few illegal fish for his undoubtedly lazy, thieving family. Jaw grim with determination, Sebastian stayed just far enough behind to keep this unsavory character in view, while at the same time taking care to avoid being detected. Slowly now, he wove amongst the dense foliage. It was darker deep in the woods, growing more so as the sun's rays began to fade.

Overhead, the sky rumbled an ominous growl, and Sebastian felt the first of several warm drops splat on his head and hands. Urging his mount forward, he peered through the branches and was instantly rewarded with a view that stole his breath away.

This was no boy, standing on an outcropping of rock, hastily shedding his clothes.

No.

This was a young woman!

Casually grazing, her horse was tethered to a tree near the water's edge, about a dozen or so feet beneath the spot where she stood silhouetted against a fiery backdrop of fir trees. Lit from behind as she was by the sun, dusty rays fanned out in a long star pattern as she moved, giving her an almost wraithlike appearance.

Unable to tear his eyes away, he watched as she snatched open her buttons and pulled her blouse free of her jeans. Next, she yanked down the zipper of her pants and eased them over her slender hips. An impatient kick sent them into a haphazard pile with her blouse to the shore below.

Clad in only a pair of lacy wisps that left little to the imagination, she stood and surveyed the way the setting sun shimmered like gold coins bobbing on the surface of the gently lapping waves.

Sebastian's breathing grew shallow. Who was this woman? She was no stable hand, this he knew, as females were never hired in such a capacity in this particular kingdom.

Her body was long and lithesome, yet curvy in all the right spots. Her thighs and calves were shapely, well muscled obviously from years spent riding, and her shoulder-length hair was wild, glowing gold with the slanting light of the setting sun.

Sebastian's mouth went dry. He knew he probably had no business standing there, staring at her this way, when she thought she was by herself, but on the other hand, she had no business being out here alone. It wasn't safe. Anything could happen to a young woman out swimming after dark.

Deciding to stay put, just in case she needed him for whatever reason, he watched as she moved to the edge of the outcropping of rock and surveyed the black water below. As if in slow motion, she balanced on her toes, crouched low, and then using the rock as a springboard, arched out over the water and executed a perfect, nearly splashless, dive.

Sebastian felt as if he'd swallowed a golf ball whole as he watched her disappear from view. When the water's ripples had calmed, his guts began to churn. Where the devil was she? She should have been up already.

He stood in his stirrups and craned in her direction, mentally preparing to go in after her. He waited another three or four seconds.

That did it.

She was in trouble. Likely hit a rock, or maybe she was caught by the hair on some branch beneath the surface of the water.

Throwing a leg over his saddle, he dismounted and hit the ground running in one fluid move. Just as he reached the edge of the pond, she burst forth from the water's surface, like a phoenix rising, her giddy laughter ringing out as she whipped her bra and panties in a circle over her head and flung them onto the beach.

Sebastian could only stand there and stare. His heart was beating ninety miles an hour and the battle he waged was whether to paddle this brat for scaring him so, or to kiss her because she was alive.

And beautiful.

In his life, the plastic, well-bred beauties that vied for his attention had jaded Sebastian. Aristocratic women could be so dull. Vain. In search of a trophy to call husband.

But this woman was different, he could tell. Her complete lack of affectation captivated him, and he found himself wanting to know more. Was she a commoner? If so, who was her father? What did he do?

Then reality struck.

Could she be taken? She certainly did not act the staid,

married matron. Her body and her carefree personality betrayed her youth and he judged her to be no more than twenty. Twenty-two at the most.

A perfect complement to his twenty-seven.

Watching her, he felt his world-weary cares begin to seep away. There was something mysterious about this mermaid. She inspired ridiculous thoughts. Flights of fancy he'd given up entertaining long ago. Thoughts of the magic of finding one's true love.

His heart began to pound and his blood rushed powerfully through his body. He flexed his hands, and watched her move to stand waist-deep at the opposite shore, her back toward him, wet hair tickling her shoulder blades. Hands cupped, she used them as a scoop to douse stray tendrils away from her face.

Then, as if she suddenly sensed that she wasn't alone, the woman slowly turned to face him, her arms snaking across her bare breasts just before she sank to her shoulders in the water.

"Who is there?" she demanded.

Sebastian stepped forward and their eyes locked for an infinite, supercharged moment before he spoke.

"Perhaps I should be asking you the same question, woman. This is the private property of His Royal Highness, King Philippe. You are breaking the law by stealing one of his horses and swimming in his pond after dark."

The woman did not seem daunted, and instead smiled. "I'm not afraid of him."

"Then perhaps you'd consider being afraid of me."

"And who, pray tell, are you?"

"I am Sebastian LeMarc, a friend of the royal family and, when I have to be, the nude-beach police. Who are you?"

She tossed back her head and sent throaty laughter into

the twilight. "You know, Sebastian LeMarc, you should probably join me. To cool that hot head of yours."

Sebastian stared at this cheeky sprite. Who the devil did she think she was? "If I have to, I'll come in there after you."

"Suit yourself. Or not. This is a suit-optional pool." She giggled, tickled with herself, and Sebastian couldn't help but smile as she dove beneath the water's surface, sending a spray of drops into the air.

What was he going to do with this woman? Dragging a slippery porpoise, one that had no intention of being caught no less, out of the water would be a challenge indeed.

She surfaced, this time nearer the waterfall and beckoned to him. "Come on in. The water's fine."

"Didn't your parents ever tell you not to play naked with strangers?"

She laughed. "Yes. But you are not a stranger."

"You know my name only."

"I know that my father trusts you."

"And who would your father be?"

"You really don't know?"

"If I did, would I have to ask?"

"I am the third daughter of Philippe de Bergeron, King of St. Michel, and owner of this pond."

Sebastian stared, mouth agape. That was impossible. Marie-Claire de Bergeron was a child! He wracked his brain, attempting to recall her age, but she was certainly no more than twelve or thirteen. He'd never given the king's young daughters a second thought, as over the years they seemed more occupied with the affairs of dolls and roller skates than with affairs of state. On the odd social occasion that he'd come in contact with the king's children, he'd been preoccupied. Concerned with the well-being of his date du jour, or the hour's political topic.

Languidly, she swam toward the beach where he stood and finding purchase on a submerged rock with her toes, allowed her shoulders to protrude from the water.

His eyes dipped to the cleavage she cradled in her arms. Seems he'd lost track of her birthdays. Suddenly guilty at the lascivious direction his thoughts had taken, he took a giant step back.

"Does your father know you are here?"

"Papa is too busy to keep track of me."

"Every father wants to know that his children are safe. Especially after dark."

"I am no longer a child," she argued hotly. "As of yesterday, I am sixteen years old. A royal debutante, of an age to begin dating."

Sebastian snorted, even as a keen disappointment settled in his gut. *Sixteen?* She was a child. "You are a royal pain, of an age to be spanked and I'm tempted to be the one to do it. Get out of the water now."

"Make me."

Sebastian arched a brow. "You are a brat."

"And you are a killjoy."

She aroused myriad emotions within him, and his jaw flexed as he pondered his next move. It was rare that anyone, let alone a teenaged girl, challenged his authority. And strangely, it exhilarated him.

For the longest moment, neither of them spoke. The only sounds were those of the rushing waterfall and the soulful cadence of the cricket's song. Somewhere in the distance, an owl hooted. The sun disappeared altogether, leaving the storm clouds on the horizon, silver-plated. The steady *plip-plop* of raindrops turned into an all-out shower, but still neither of them moved. Nor spoke.

At least, not with words.

Even so, they knew that what was passing between them

was life-changing, for them both. He waged a battle in his mind, but was far too ethical to take advantage of her foolishness.

You're too young.

But I won't always be.

I'll wait.

Do.

With a nod, Sebastian turned and easily mounted his horse and set off through the trees.

"Get dressed," he ordered over his shoulder. "I'll wait for you at the edge of the woods and escort you safely home."

This time, she did not argue.

Chapter Two

She'd turned twenty-one just yesterday. This Sebastian knew, as he'd etched the date on his brain five long years ago. And now, as the beautiful Marie-Claire de Bergeron descended the stair alone, all eyes in the steadily growing crowd turned to greet this vision with approval and, he noted with a swift glance about, some lechery.

A fierce wave of protectiveness washed over him and he excused himself from a conversation he was having with Lise's new husband, Wilhelm Rodin, and moved to stand at the bottom of the stairs.

As it had so often in the past, his gaze drew hers and they were locked in a world of their own making. Only now, they both knew she was a full-fledged adult, legal in every way and responsible for her own decisions in this life.

Seeming to sense the moment was perfect, the royal orchestra struck up a rousing waltz and Sebastian held his hand out to Marie-Claire.

"Dance?"

"*Oui.*"

Bashfully, she extended her hand and he suppressed the grin he felt surging up from his belly. She was such a conundrum. One minute, she was wildly cheering him to victory on the golf course and the next, a blushing innocent, struggling to exude sophistication. Though soft and small, her hand was strong, and she clung to him as he led her through the throng to the dance floor.

When they arrived, a number of couples were already sweeping about the gleaming marble. King Philippe danced with his wife, Queen Celeste; Philippe's mother, the Dowager Queen Simone danced with the prime minister, Rene Davoine; and a number of court consorts, celebrities and political acquaintances from different countries also whirled across the Russian imported flooring.

Sebastian drew Marie-Claire's lithe body against his own and it was like a homecoming. He breathed in the scent of her perfumed hair and rested his hand at the small dip in her lower back. Holding her this way was far more exhilarating than any dream he'd ever had. As he'd known they would, they fitted as if they were born to be together.

Shyly, she glanced up at him, and it was the first time ever he'd seen her at such close range. Her skin was the flawless stuff of youth, peachy smooth and the color of cream with a hint of cinnamon. Tonight, her sun-streaked hair was upswept, revealing the graceful length of her neck, and her almond-shaped eyes reflected the emerald sheen of the satin confection she wore. Shadowed by the ghost of a smile, her lips were slightly parted and Sebastian longed to press his mouth to them, to see if their kiss would be as explosive as he'd imagined over the years.

However, this was not the time or place for such a first. He wanted it to be perfect. And he wanted them to be alone. For now, he would settle for the joy of simply holding her in his arms. That, and the knowledge that he was the luckiest man in the room.

"Your twenty-first birthday was yesterday, no?"

Marie-Claire's gaze shot to his. "How did you know?"

"Math."

"Math?" Her smile was quizzical.

"On this day, five years ago, you had been sixteen for a whole day."

A charming flush crawled up her slender neck and settled in her cheeks. "You remember that day?"

"Vaguely." Someday, when they'd been long married, he'd confess how the memory had plagued him, ruining subsequent relationships and making sport of his sleep. "Happy Birthday."

"Thank you."

"What did you do to celebrate this time?"

"For one thing, I stayed out of the pond."

"Too bad."

Again, the endearing blush. "Papa took me to Paris for the day. I went shopping for this gown."

"Excellent choice."

"You think so?"

"Mmm. I think you are easily the most beautiful cheerleader in the room."

Marie-Claire heaved a heavy sigh and stared down at the floor. "So you heard that?"

Unable to restrain the grin that tugged at his lips, Sebastian ducked his head so that he could peer into her face. "Marie-Claire, thanks to the wonders of cable television, the entire world heard that."

"How singularly mortifying."

"I thought it was charming. Cute."

"Cute?" She made a face. "Now everyone thinks I have a schoolgirl crush on you."

He tipped her chin, forcing her gaze to meet his. "And do you?"

Suddenly seeming to forget her mission to prove herself the sedate lady, her candid laughter had his pulse surging.

"Well, since the entire world knows, I suppose there is no point in lying to you. I guess you could say I have an…infatuation, where you're concerned. But…" she held up a finger, smiled brightly and blathered on, "I'm struggling to overcome that. I'm thinking of joining a twelve-step program. Not that I'm a stalker or anything—"

"Don't do that on my account."

"What?"

"Don't abandon your…addiction."

She stumbled over his foot. "No?"

"No."

"Oh." She stared up at him and smiled.

He smiled back, and her heart took wing. This moment was perfect. The musical medley picked up pace and segued into a driving rumba. Marie-Claire loved to rumba.

"May I cut in?"

Marie-Claire froze.

Eduardo, his teeth pointing at Marie-Claire from behind his eager smile, tapped Sebastian on the shoulder. His wild, rusty head of hair had been tamed with what looked like an entire bottle of styling gel and his tuxedo was inches too short in the sleeve and cuff. Fingers itching, he fairly pried Marie-Claire from Sebastian's grasp.

She wanted to scream as Sebastian stepped aside and with obvious reluctance handed her over to the young Eduardo Van Groober's arms. Darn! Just as things were getting interesting. Eduardo clutched her close and her back already ached from the pressure he exerted.

"Save another dance for me?" Sebastian called as Eduardo jerked her away, rattling her teeth in the process.

Marie-Claire nodded dumbly and watched with longing as Sebastian backed across the room and straight into the voluptuous—and morally emancipated—Baroness Veronike Schroeder of Germany.

Before Sebastian had time to react, Veronike cast out her web, snared him, and then dragged him out to the dance floor for the kill.

Eduardo made an awkward attempt at conversation and Marie-Claire listened with half an ear. And, when he wasn't trying to impress her with his prowess on the high-school golf team, his nose was buried in her hair. Marie-Claire batted at him in a distracted fashion, straining to keep her sights on Sebastian.

And Veronike.

Euro-trash with pretensions to the Hapsburg dynasty, Veronike was a formidable personality and when she wanted something, she usually got it. And Veronike did enjoy the occasional dalliance with a handsome playboy.

Jealousy seared like a hot knife through Marie-Claire's heart. Compared to Veronike, Marie-Claire felt quite the underdeveloped adolescent. Insecurity assailed her as she watched Veronike swivel seductively to the pounding beat. Veronike draped over Sebastian like a skimpy chiffon window dressing, all fluttering lashes and fat, blood-red lips.

The dress the German siren wore tonight seemed less a gown and more a figment of the imagination. Smashed against Sebastian's firm chest, Veronike's ample bosom strained to be set free of its wispy confines and her hips ground against Sebastian's in a way that would have Marie-Claire's molars reduced to dust before the end of the evening if she didn't make a concerted effort to change her train of thought.

Ooo.

Wilhelm tapped Eduardo on the shoulder and cut in, no

doubt feeling it was time to put in the appearance of caring, Marie-Claire thought churlishly. Eduardo obviously hated to let her go and there was an awkward scuffle as Wilhelm dismissed the hormone-ravaged boy. Where Eduardo was chatty, Wilhelm was stony, allowing Marie-Claire to drift.

She winced as she retraced the inane conversation she'd made just now with Sebastian, and wondered if she wasn't better off eating her heart out over Veronike's physical charms.

I'm joining a twelve-step program for stalkers.

Her sisters were right. She was certifiable. During her next dance with Sebastian, she hoped—if there *was* a next dance with Sebastian—she'd be able to control her idiotic tongue before she blurted out that she wanted to snatch Veronike bald.

Oh.

Marie-Claire's eyes slid closed as she reflected on how unbelievably right it had felt to have Sebastian's arms around her. She knew he'd felt it, too. She moaned, and an involuntary shiver wracked her body. Head back, she clutched Wilhelm a little tighter at the memory of Sebastian's powerful body steering her around the dance floor. She immediately regretted the impulse as the rigid Wilhelm looked down at her with a curious frown.

"Stiff knee," she fibbed.

After a frightfully dull turn on the dreary Wilhelm's arm, her father at last rescued her, just before Eduardo could reach her again. The boy's disappointment was plain.

"You are looking well tonight, daughter. This gown suits you."

Coming from her father, this was high praise. Though King Philippe was not effusive in speech, Marie-Claire knew she was loved. Cherished. And, because she was the youngest of three daughters by his first—and now deceased—wife a tad favored.

"Thank you, sir. You're looking rather dapper tonight, yourself." She gave his satin cummerbund a playful tug.

"Oh, I know you're simply trying to put a bit of a bounce in an old man's step."

"Fifty-one is hardly old."

"I'm sure it must seem that way when you are just twenty-one. You know, I was Sebastian's age or thereabouts when you were born."

"Oh?"

His smile was gentle. "I see the way you look at him."

"I don't suppose my ladylike caterwauling on the golf course has anything to do with your assumption that I'm smitten."

A chuckle rumbled from deep within Philippe's robust chest, and Marie-Claire couldn't help but notice how handsome her father still was. The little cleft in his chin and the twinkle in his eye put her in mind of another of her favorite American actors, although Michael Douglas was perhaps not quite as tall. But the physical resemblance was something folks had remarked upon before. That and the fact that they both preferred young, beautiful wives.

Marie-Claire spared a glance in Celeste's direction, and noted the raucous laughter and phony social-climbing demeanor her stepmother had assumed with the prime minister. Her father was blind when it came to Celeste's rather lengthy list of foibles.

"I suppose you could do worse than Sebastian." Though Philippe's remark was offhand, as he looked at his daughter, his gaze roved her suddenly burning cheeks.

"Papa!"

He ignored her weak protestations. "You are a beautiful woman, Marie-Claire. Unfortunately for me, the time has

come to let go of you. To let you loose upon the world...."
King Philippe pulled Marie-Claire close, the gesture at odds
with his words.

"Heaven forbid!"

"You will do great things in this life, my dear. Always
know that I love you, and am so very proud."

Marie-Claire felt her throat tighten at his sweet words,
and impulsively stood on her toes to plant a kiss on his
cheek. This pleased the king and he blinked back the tears.

As the evening wore on, Marie-Claire and Sebastian were
obliged to dance with other people. Thankfully, Veronike
was a popular partner and had not been available for a second go at Sebastian. And, though they were not always in
proximity, Marie-Claire could feel Sebastian's proprietary
gaze and her confidence soared. Unable to tear her eyes
away from him for more than a moment, she found keeping
up with the task at hand nearly impossible.

"So," Charles Rodin, Wilhelm's twin brother commented, "I understand you are a fan of old movies. Have
you seen *Adam's Rib*?"

"I have never eaten there, though I do enjoy American
barbecue..."

"Oh?" Charles frowned.

Prince Etienne Kroninberg of Rhineland told her, "It is
my understanding that your sister, Ariane, is planning to
come to my country for a visit."

"No, Ariane is around here somewhere, I think. I just
saw her..."

Etienne opened his mouth as if to speak, then thought
better and shut it.

The prime minister said, "Your grandmother is looking
well tonight. The king's victory seems to have put roses in
her cheeks."

"Yes, she has ten green thumbs, at least."

More than once, she trod upon her partner's toe and had to beg pardon. And more than once, she caught Sebastian's smile of amusement.

After what seemed to be an eternity, Sebastian finally made his way back to her and solicited her hand from a stodgy third cousin and whisked her off.

"Is it hot in here, or is it just me?" Sebastian angled his head and cocked a playful brow.

"I think there is no chaste way to answer that question." Marie-Claire returned his grin.

Admiration for her wit flashed in his eyes. "Shall we set the tongues to wagging and head out to the verandah for a breath of fresh air?"

"Why not? The tongues have been wagging all day."

"Come on then. Let's give them some more grist for the rumor mill."

Marie-Claire's heart bounced about in her rib cage at the intimate quality in his voice.

The verandah outside the ballroom was nearly as large as the ballroom itself. Made of concrete, it sported a low railing with balustrades as broad as small wine kegs. Light poured from the palace windows and the music—a lilting Vivaldi piece—danced upon the gentle night breezes. In the air, there was a hint of burning leaves and the last fragrances of summer's flowers.

Never had Marie-Claire felt more vibrant. Alive. Pulsing with vitality. Sebastian's touch on her hand was warm and this warmth spread up her arm and burned and swirled in her chest, making it hard to catch her breath.

This was the moment she'd been dreaming of. A moment alone with a man with whom she'd bonded, once upon a twilight evening in her youth. And, though before tonight they'd only conversed on the most superficial topics, it was an unbreakable bond, for whatever magical reason. Fate. Kismet.

Destiny.

Didn't matter what one called it. Marie-Claire believed that God himself wanted them together and there was no use even pursuing other options.

A few dried leaves skittered across the patio's floor as a warm wind flirted with Marie-Claire's hair and skirts. A violent shiver wracked her body as anticipation rolled up her spine and settled in her throat.

"Are you cold?"

She swallowed against the excitement that burned in her throat. "No. Quite the opposite, actually."

Sebastian untied his bow tie and unfastened a collar stud with his free hand. "Same."

As they strolled, other couples, seeming to find the climate in the ballroom confining, began to wander out of doors looking for a bit of fresh air and some privacy. Inside the ballroom, Eduardo could be seen, bobbing about, peering out various windows, obviously searching for Marie-Claire.

"Come on."

Sebastian took her hand and tugged her into the shadows and down an immense stair. A sea of rolling lawn unfurled before them, and Marie-Claire bent to remove her high-heeled slippers so that she could better keep up with his rangy stride.

"So. Last time we were alone together, you were sixteen, and of an age to begin dating." He tucked her hand into the crook of his elbow and cast a disarming grin down at her. "Did you?"

"Did I?" Marie-Claire could barely think. The wool of his jacket made a pleasant swooshing sound against the verdant satin of her gown. "What?"

"Date?"

"Oh." How embarrassing. How could she couch the truth and exude the worldly persona she longed for Sebastian to see in her? Her mouth went dry and she touched her tongue to her lips. "Uh… Well, not right away. Actually, Papa caught wind of my plans and shipped me off to an all-girl boarding school."

"I know."

"You knew?"

"I may have inadvertently mentioned your intention to begin dating to him after I escorted you home that night."

Marie-Claire's jaw dropped, and a guttural gasp escaped.

"Apparently, your father was not aware of your plans." Amusement quirked in the corners of Sebastian's lips. "I didn't realize you meant to keep these plans secret."

"Oh, sure." Bristling, she stared at him through narrow eyes. "So. You are the reason I suffered through two years in that horrendously stuffy all-female boarding school?"

"Sorry."

"You should be. The experience was quite scarring."

Sebastian hooted. "I can see that it left you socially re-tiring."

To keep from being affected by his infectious laughter, she hiked her chin and ignored his teasing tone. "In any event, my dating career had to be postponed until…er… college."

"Ah, but you went to an all-girl college."

Her bravado flagged some. "Don't tell me. All-girl college was your idea, too."

"Of course not." Sebastian shrugged. "I may have had some input but the final decision was always your father's."

Bemused, she stared up at him. How was she ever going to convince him that she was worldly when—thanks in part to him—she'd been cloistered away like a cultured pearl?

Images of Veronike's seductive red lips, puffy and pouty, taunted her and she refused to let him go on thinking of her as some kind of inexperienced virgin.

Even if that's exactly what she was.

"Well, it may have been all girls, but there were men." She wracked her brain for the roster of professors. "There was, um, let's see…Alonzo, and Barnaby and uh, and umm." She frowned. What was his name again? "Cedric! And, uh—"

"An alphabetical accounting of your lovers?"

Her chin jerked up and she could make out the twinkle sparkling in his eyes by the light of the harvest moon. "You don't think I've ever even had a date, do you?" There was a heat in her tone that she struggled to squelch.

"I hope not."

"Oh, you do, do you? Why?"

"Because," he answered simply, as they reached an immense yet shallow reflecting pool, "you're mine."

Marie-Claire was dumbstruck. For a moment, everything went fuzzy, and little pinpricks of light danced before her eyes. Her heart palpitated, and a wild joy sprung from deep within the vicinity of her stomach and, like a flash fire, spread throughout her body.

"Oh." The breathy utterance hovered on the air between them.

"You're not entirely surprised." He paused and turned to face her, lifting her chin with his thumb and forefinger.

"No."

"There is something. It's been there since that night."

"Yes."

"Something special. It's almost as if we were…" He squinted off into the night sky and his Adam's apple bobbed as he searched for the words, "…somehow kindred spirits."

"I know," she whispered.

He dipped his head back toward her and they stood in a shaft of moonlight, regarding each other. Discovering the truth in each other's eyes. It was a powerful moment, fraught with a tension so palpable it generated heat that radiated between their bodies.

Marie-Claire could see that Sebastian was as stunned by the power of their chemistry as she was. For an instant, he seemed to lose his perennial confidence. There was vulnerability in his expression that endeared him impossibly closer to her soul than ever before.

In front of them, seeming to float on the vast surface of the reflecting pool, *Le cheval du roi*—a statue of her great-great grandfather's royal steed—reared, flanked on each side by two equally impressive mares. Years of weather had given the cool, dark metal a streaked green patina. The fountain was especially spectacular when it was lit for a party, as it was tonight.

Seemingly unable to endure the tension that shimmered between them, Sebastian abruptly turned and tugged her to the edge of the pool. He stepped up to the top of the two-foot high wall rim, then helped her up behind him. Off in the distance, strains of an orchestra sounded over the fountain's spray.

Sebastian stepped out of his highly polished wingtips and kicked them to the ground below. Then, reaching for the slippers that dangled from Marie-Claire's fingers, he dropped them on top of his own shoes. "I never did get another dance."

Marie-Claire lifted her arms and draping them over his shoulders, let her wrists dangle. "And so you did not."

"Shall we?"

"We shall."

Marie-Claire whooped in surprise as he took her by the waist and stepped into the pool's knee-deep water. Her gown ballooned on the surface before it sank to swirl about her ankles. Sebastian drew her close and they began to move about their watery dance floor.

Laughing, she leaned away from him so that she could better see his handsome face. This was a moment she would forever remember, she promised herself. Full of hope and possibilities. A veritable dream come to life.

Playfully, he swung her away from him and back again, then bent her low in a dip that had her giddy laughter ringing out. Their spontaneous hilarity caused those who loitered on the verandah to smile with indulgence as the king's youngest daughter frolicked in the fountain with St. Michel's most eligible bachelor. As the tempo of the music increased, so did their silly antics.

Sebastian lifted Marie-Claire in his arms and spun until they were both dizzy and in danger of tipping into the drink.

"You're going to soak us!" Marie-Claire clutched his neck for dear life and wished the ebullient feelings that bubbled into her throat would last forever.

Neither seemed to notice that the music had stopped.

"Don't look now," Sebastian set her down and pulled her up against the solid wall of his chest, "but we're pretty much wet."

Pretending to pout, Marie-Claire leaned sideways. She paused to study her voluminous skirts, hanging heavy against her legs. "I can't go back in now."

"We'd get the floor all wet."

"People might fall."

"You'll let me know if you're thinking of shucking your dress for a skinny dip?" Grin teasing, he cupped her cheek in his palm.

"Will I ever live that night down?"

"You haven't yet. Not in my mind." Their noses grazed as he looked deeply into her eyes. Marie-Claire could feel his warm breath against her lips as he spoke. "Even when you were gone away to school, you were never far from my thoughts."

"I know. It was the same for me."

"You were so young."

"Yes, I was." More than once it had occurred to Marie-Claire that Sebastian could so easily have taken advantage of her foolish crush when she was but a child. But he hadn't. He was an honorable man, and that was only one of the myriad qualities that attracted her. "But I'm not anymore."

"No. You're not." The muscles in his jaw worked as his thoughts seemed to race back over the years. "Waiting for you to grow up has been tedious. I knew any involvement for us before you were of legal age could have caused problems for your father. But—" On a heavy sigh, his eyes slid closed. "For so long, I've wondered…and wanted…."

By now, his lips were brushing hers as he spoke and so it was only a matter of allowing himself to finally indulge in the guilty pleasure of their heretofore forbidden kiss. Ever so slightly, he leaned forward until his lips covered hers in a touch so gossamer, Marie-Claire was tempted to wonder if she was dreaming.

That was all it took for the glowing embers to flare to life.

Immediately, the kiss became heated. Sebastian's arms circled her waist, pulling her closer as his mouth closed over hers. The years of waiting and wondering were over and it was with relief and complete exhilaration that their mouths, their bodies, their souls, came together.

The kiss deepened, and, laboring in sync, their lungs heaved, and their hearts pounded. They struggled to quench their insatiable urge to get closer to each other. To know each other. To learn what they'd wanted to discover for the past five years.

Marie-Claire wound her fingers into the silky soft hair at his nape as he bent to nuzzle her neck and kiss the spot where her shoulder met her neck. A hot blaze shivered down her spine and coiled deep in her belly. In great waves, gooseflesh raced across her body and she gasped at the onslaught. She could hear the thunder of her pulse and wondered how long her heart could take such exertion.

It felt so natural, standing here, being kissed by Sebastian LeMarc. It was as if they had some kind of history together that transcended time. And space. And logic. They were each one half of the other. Whole only when they were together.

And they'd known it that night, five years ago.

Sebastian held Marie-Claire's face in both hands and pulled his mouth away from hers, a fraction. "What are we going to do?"

"Marie-Claire!"

"We've been found out." Sebastian kissed her hard, then took a step back.

Marie-Claire groaned. "My sister, Ariane. Do you think if we ignore her, she'll go away?"

"Likely not. She sounds upset."

Marie-Claire bristled. "I don't know why. I'm old enough to take care of myself. No doubt she saw us and wants to remind me to appear disinterested."

Sebastian grinned. "She's too late."

"We could run," she suggested hopefully.

"Your skirts are too heavy. I'd have to carry you on my back. It would slow me down, but we might stand a chance if we bolt for it now."

Marie-Claire giggled.

"Marie-Claire! *Marie-Claire!* Come quickly! It's *Papa!* He's collapsed!"

Chapter Three

Six months later

It was wonderful to be home.

Marie-Claire had just finished unpacking and moved from her closet to her bedroom window to study the familiar view. It was incredibly warm for March and flowers were blooming early this year. Down below, a veritable army of gardeners swarmed over the de Bergeron Palace's grounds. Mowers roared, clippers hummed and the sweet scent of freshly shorn grass filled the air.

Marie-Claire swallowed against the ever-present lump in her throat. Spring was Papa's favorite time of the year. He'd liked to say it was a time for new beginnings. She stared, unseeing, at the fountain where she and Sebastian had last danced together. She hoped Papa was right. She was finally ready to put the shattered pieces of her life into the dustbin and take a stab at starting over again.

The small country of St. Michel was only just now beginning to recover from the shock of King Philippe's unexpected death. But Marie-Claire doubted that she'd ever fully mend from the mortal wound to her heart. Her heavy sigh fogged the windowpane.

Thank God for Sebastian.

During the much-publicized funeral, and in the frenzied days that followed, he'd been a rock. Though he battled his own grief—for Philippe had been like a father to him since Sebastian's own father had passed away when he was a boy—he was protective and solicitous of Marie-Claire. The tragedy had only strengthened their special bond and she loved him more than ever.

Even so, the overwhelming memories of her father seemed to haunt her healing process. She was an orphan now. Granted, she was a full-grown orphan, with the money, power and prestige that came of being born into royalty, but nonetheless, she felt cut adrift on an ocean of grief. That she'd been a favorite of her father's only made her anguish that much more acute.

A deep depression had absconded with Marie-Claire's usual carefree nature and left her weepy, exhausted and not caring if she lived or died. She'd known she wouldn't be fit company for anyone, let alone Sebastian, until she spent some healing time with her maternal grandmother, Tatiana. And so, a week after her father was laid to rest and she'd fulfilled all of her social duties as a member of a grieving monarchy, Marie-Claire listlessly packed her bags and headed off to Denmark to find comfort in the bosom of her mother's side of the family.

The last time she'd seen Sebastian was the day he'd taken her to the airport and kissed her good-bye. It had been an emotional kiss, fraught with promises and hope and sorrow and the terrible knowledge that separation, just as they'd finally come together, would be hard.

And it had been.

Marie-Claire was sure they could have paid much of St. Michel's national debt with what she and Sebastian had spent in phone charges. But it was worth it to hear his soothing voice. To hear news of home. To know that he still cared.

Tatiana had helped her through the worst of her struggles, talking late into the night, drying her tears, telling her stories of her papa's pride when she'd been born and giving her the benefit of years of living. She was a very wise woman. And for such a tiny thing, she was a tough old broad. Tatiana didn't have time to baby Marie-Claire and after a month, put her to work as a volunteer in a children's hospital in hopes of helping her to see that the rain fell on the just and the unjust.

It worked.

Immediately, Marie-Claire fell in love with the children and in her effort to comfort, was comforted. There was nothing like the sweet feeling of little arms around her neck to soothe her own emotional injuries and before long Marie-Claire had a new life motto and with a gentle push, Tatiana nudged her out of the nest.

"Life is too short to waste even a minute," Marie-Claire murmured against her windowpane. Off in the distance, *Le cheval du roi* came into focus and a sudden burst of happiness that she hadn't felt for half a year filled her breast. "Too short, indeedy." She turned away from the window, rushed to the phone and dialed.

"Hello, Sebastian? I'm home."

Sebastian pocketed his cell phone and, for the first time in ages, his smile was real. Marie-Claire was home. In less than an hour, he'd see her. Hold her. Kiss her. It had been an eternity. These last six months had seemed to drag on longer than the previous five years combined. Yes, waiting for Marie-Claire to grow up had sorely tested his patience, but once he knew the rapture of her kiss, staying away had been hell.

More than once he'd been tempted to barge in on old Tatiana and take what was his, but he knew Marie-Claire needed time. Truth was, he did, too.

Philippe's death had been a shock. Worse, for some reason, than when he'd been a little boy and lost his own father. For as far back as either family could remember, the LeMarcs and the de Bergerons had been close. And Philippe had always been good with Sebastian, possibly seeing him as the son he'd always longed for, Philippe had been a patient mentor, a listening ear, and a model of manliness.

Sebastian missed him. Nearly as much as he'd missed Marie-Claire.

Sebastian reached for his jacket as his mother swept into the over-decorated and cluttered parlor of her sprawling country estate.

"You're leaving? But you just got here." Claudette's face fell as she watched her only son shrug into his jacket and re-knot his tie.

"I'm sorry, Mère. The royal family has requested my presence at lunch today."

"Well, it's about time." Claudette bristled. She gave her short, wavy and, still dark at fifty-two, brown hair a smoothing pat and pursed her lips in dismay at her attire. "This will never do. I'll just be a moment."

"Mère," Sebastian said, suppressing a smile.

Claudette stopped in her tracks and without turning around, heaved a heavy sigh. "I'm not invited. Oh. Well. I see." She waved an airy hand and settled upon a settee as if she had no cares.

But Sebastian could tell she was hurt. Claudette had always been overly enamored with anything that smacked of aristocracy. The fact that she'd been slipping in the St. Michel social ranks since her influential husband had died was not lost on her. A lunch at the palace would surely boost her weight with her cronies down at the club.

"I'm sure it was simply an oversight."

"Of course." Claudette's laughter was brittle. "Why on earth would they invite *you* to lunch over *me?*"

"You see? A simple mistake. I'll give them all your love."

"Yes. Do that, darling. And be sure to tell them how deeply I've been affected by Philippe's death." Making odd faces, Claudette peered into a gilt mirror hanging next to the settee and checked the corners of her eyes and mouth for stray bits of makeup.

"Yes. I'll do that too."

"Good. Well. When can you come back? We barely had a chance to talk and there is something I need to discuss with you."

"What?"

"It's..." Claudette huffed in irritation. "It's financial. I can barely believe it, but I seem to be having some credit problems. I'm sure there must be some mistake down at the bank. Some silly twit or other has punched in the wrong number and left me practically penniless. Could you straighten this out for me?"

"Mère..."

Claudette took immediate offense to his censorious tone. "I've been as frugal as Ebenezer Scrooge himself, I'm telling you!"

"I'll take a look at your bank and credit statements, but I'm still guessing that you need to live a little less ostentatiously."

Claudette moaned. "Oh, how would that look to the

girls?'' Her hoity-toity social circle spent money as if it were something one harvested in a field.

"Most likely I can cover your debts. This time. But it's time for you to go on a budget.''

"A budget?'' Claudette stared blankly at him.

"Yes. Look it up.'' Sebastian turned and headed for the vast foyer of her country mansion. "I'll come by later tonight and we'll get started putting one together for you.''

Claudette followed him to the door and watched him slide into his gleaming Peugeot. "Bring me some of those Bavarian chocolates they serve for dessert.''

Sebastian waved goodbye.

Marie-Claire sensed that Sebastian had arrived even before she saw him. Hearing the slam of a car door had her flying out of the palace's service entrance and straight into his arms. He picked her up and whirled her about and they kissed as if they needed to sustain lip contact to survive.

"You're here!'' Marie-Claire was finally able to say, when they'd paused to gulp in a great lungful of air.

"Mmm.'' Impatiently, Sebastian angled her mouth back under his and went back for seconds. "Mm-hmm.''

Oh, it was so good to see him. To feel him. To smell him. To taste him. How she'd managed to stay away for so long was a testament to the depth of her heartache over her father's passing. For an endless moment, they stood, basking in the joy of simply being together. Their kiss slowly grew less frenzied and more soulful, and Marie-Claire was lost to this ecstasy. Was there anything more wonderful than falling in love? She didn't think so.

She ran her hands over the powerful planes of Sebastian's chest then locked them at his nape and hung on for dear life as he playfully ravaged her neck. Liquid laughter burbled past her lips. Though she nestled as closely as she could to him, she longed to be even closer, and knew that she'd never truly be happy until she and Sebastian became one forever in the bonds of holy matrimony.

That it would eventually happen, Marie-Claire had no doubt. They were meant to be together. Had been from the very beginning. Their eventual marriage was simply a matter of timing and politics. She closed her eyes and imagined herself in a wedding gown, and that she and Sebastian had just taken their sacred vows to love each other until death parted them. Sebastian's hot mouth on her neck and jaw had her toes curling with delight.

Her sisters could carry on the tedious royal traditions, and she and Sebastian could settle in their own house in his family estate in the country and raise those three little boys and that darling little girl with his striking blue-gray eyes, so eerily translucent and soul-searching. They would also inherit the darling dimples that bracketed the corners of his mouth. Marie-Claire lifted a finger and traced these curves and then ran her fingers down his jaw to the dimple at the apex of his chin. They would have thick, wavy heads of hair, and be filled with life and mischief and they would call her Mama, or Mère…that was cute…*Mère-Claire*…

"Marie-Claire!"

For heaven's sake, why did real life *always* seem to intrude? Frustrated, Marie-Claire's head dropped and she moaned against Sebastian's neck.

"*Marie-Claire!*" Ariane's voice reached them from the Ruby Salon on the third floor of the de Bergeron Palace. "Sorry to butt in…"

Marie-Claire fumed. "You most certainly are not," she shouted.

Sebastian laughed.

"Yes, I am." Ariane's own laughter blended with Lise's

and floated down to interrupt what had been a dalliance in paradise.

"Then say what you must and go away." Marie-Claire cast them a withering glance.

"Grandmama Simone wants everyone present at lunch for a special announcement. Hi, Sebastian." Again, their girlish giggles.

He waved.

"You are to be included in this meeting, Sebastian."

He groaned.

"What special announcement?" Marie-Claire demanded.

"We don't know. She won't say. But she insists that everyone meet her in the formal dining room in five minutes. She is there waiting now."

The formal dining room?

This was serious. Marie-Claire glanced at Sebastian, her disappointment keen. The Dowager Queen Simone was not one to be ignored, and the formal dining hall always meant a harrowing topic followed by endless and boring discussion.

With great reluctance, Marie-Claire took a step back and, clasping Sebastian's hands in hers, regarded him. "Will this be all right with you? I know you weren't expecting an impromptu meeting on our first day back together."

"It's fine. I'd sit through a presentation on time-share condos if it meant I could be with you."

"Somehow, I doubt it will be anything so painless."

As it was, Sebastian would rather have been gutted, grilled and served for lunch than suffer the tense scene that followed his all-too-brief reunion with Marie-Claire.

They were the first to arrive in the cavernous dining hall and find their pre-assigned seats. Soon after, other family members entered, glanced warily about, took in Queen Simone's dour expression from where she perched on a tall-backed chair at the head of the table, and then cautiously found their own places.

The bowling-lane-sized table was set for the kind of multi-course meal usually reserved for heads of state and very special occasions. A variety of tantalizing aromas wafted through the air ducts from the kitchen—a floor below—as a legion of domestics slaved over the stoves. The de Bergeron insignia blazed from the center of each platter, and the gold charger plates gleamed from a fresh buffing. Myriad pieces of monogrammed silver cluttered each place setting, along with crystal stemware of every size and shape. Sebastian frowned as he pulled his napkin across his lap. Clearly, everyone would need more than one glass of wine to digest the queen's latest bit of news.

The enormous dining hall was as silent as the first day of snow.

No one uttered a word, though it was obvious everyone was wondering about the nature of the dowager queen's command performance. Her stoic expression gave no hint of what was to come, and forbade any queries.

At seventy-five, she was thin as a whip, and it was rumored that she was proud of her skeletal figure and showed it off with expensively tailored garments, nipped in at the waist and snug over the hip. She disdained even a healthy amount of meat on the bones, declaring that it smacked of no self-control. And if there was anything that Simone hated, it was being out of control. Not even the hair on her head dared to defy its perfect coif, dyed dark to belie her age, and snipped short to save time and nonsense. Her eyes were twin chips of ice that rarely sparkled unless it was in irritation.

Lise sat alone, looking decidedly greenish about the gills in these early stages of her pregnancy. Sebastian wondered where Wilhelm was keeping himself, but wasn't surprised at his absence. Trouble had been brewing in paradise since shortly after they'd taken their vows. In a land as small as St. Michel, nothing was sacred, and the private lives and marriages of the royals were frequently discussed over the backyard fence. Or, in Sebastian's mother's case, the cocktail table at the country club where she and "the girls" pretended to play tennis every afternoon.

Ariane sat fidgeting across from her older sister, seemingly eager to dispense with the day's protocol and get on with her own rather guarded agenda.

King Philippe's stepchildren, Georges, twenty-six, and Juliet, twenty-two, and Philippe's fourth daughter, twelve-year-old Jacqueline, by their mother and his second wife, Hélène, all came in together and silently found their seats.

The last to enter was Queen Celeste, her belly burgeoning with the six-month pregnancy that King Philippe had died too soon to celebrate. With a performance worthy of the stage, Celeste, clutching the table attendant's arms, lowered herself into her seat, scooted hither and thither as she fussed with her derriere's perfect arrangement, and then sighed heavily and drummed her fingertips to make everyone aware that she was quite put out at having to sit in such an uncomfortable chair.

After an interminable silence meant to bestow proper ceremony upon the proceedings, Simone at last spoke.

"Thank you all for taking time out of your busy schedule to humor an old lady." A small smile twitched in the corner of her thin lips, and her blue eyes flashed with mystery. "As you all know, many of the legalities concerning my son's death are in the process of being concluded."

Everyone gave a stiff nod, but dared not murmur aloud lest they incur her well-known wrath.

"It is my feeling," she continued, "that sufficient time has passed for grieving. Now, we need to attend to some important issues that should have been addressed years ago. These are personal matters, concerning my son's marriages, and the particulars discussed here will be kept in this room. Is that understood?''

Again, all heads bobbed, and eyes shifted, but no one spoke.

Celeste frowned.

Sebastian fumbled under the tablecloth for Marie-Claire's hand, grasped it and pulled it into his lap. Though her smile was tight, gratitude filled her eyes and she squeezed back. This would be hard on her. She'd only been back for a day and they were about to delve into the private details of Philippe's too-short life.

After giving her throat a lengthy clearing, Queen Simone removed her glasses and seemed to stare off into the distant past.

''As you know, my Philippe was married more than once. But…what you may not know,'' she paused and refocused on Philippe's three oldest daughters, ''is that he was married once before he married your mother, Johanna Van Rhys.''

Ariane and Lise gasped and exchanged shocked glances with Marie-Claire. Sebastian felt Marie-Claire clasp their tightly laced fingers with her free hand as she braced herself for the rest of the story.

''When Philippe was but a boy of eighteen and crown prince, he fell in love with a very beautiful seventeen-year-old American girl named Katie Graham. She had come to St. Michel from her home in Texas with her father, Henry, who was here on business. He'd taken Katie out of school because her mother had recently passed away and he didn't want to leave her alone for the three months it would take him to complete his corporation's business. However, though he'd hoped to keep her from feeling abandoned, it seems he was not entirely successful.

"Henry was occupied most days and had business dinners some nights, so Katie had plenty of time to explore St. Michel all by herself. And one day, while she was out doing so, she met Philippe. It was immediate and deep love from the beginning and no amount of common sense imparted by King Antoine or myself could keep either of them away from the other."

Sebastian glanced at Marie-Claire and knew exactly how Philippe had felt.

"And so," Queen Simone continued, staring now out the window and over the lush, rolling hills beyond the palace walls, "without our knowledge of just how far things had progressed, they ran off to France and were married in a secret, civil ceremony. Needless to say, when Antoine and I found out, we where horrified. Katie's father was a middle-management employee, thus, Katie had no money and no social standing."

Marie-Claire bit her lower lip and, as her eyes slid closed, Sebastian could tell it was all she could do not to scream. Social status meant nothing to Marie-Claire and that was one of the things Sebastian loved best about her. Especially since he'd grown up in a household where aristocracy was everything.

Queen Simone perched her glasses at the tip of her nose, and slowly searched each face with her piercing gaze before she continued. "The magnitude of this misfortune only increased when we learned that the children had married because they were expecting a baby."

The entire room drew in a collective breath and held it.

Marie-Claire's jaw dropped. Ariane grinned in amazement. Looking decidedly ill, Lise covered her face with her hands. Philippe's second wife's children, Georges and Juliet, remained silent, as Philippe was not their real father, and this news did not particularly affect them. And Philippe's youngest girl, Jacqueline, was but twelve and the ramifications were over her head.

Celeste seemed to have forgotten her discomfort and stared at Simone with rapt attention. Jaw jutting, eyes glittering, she cradled her own unborn babe with protective arms.

Queen Simone fiddled with the soft fringe at the edge of her shawl and sighed noisily through her nose as the memories came flooding back. "Because St. Michel had been threatened with annexation by Rhineland we needed some clout and had hoped that Philippe would make a politically advantageous marriage. In fact, our very freedom depended on it. We had no choice, Antoine and I. We did what we thought best."

By this time, everyone was hanging on her every word. All eyes watched as the dowager queen pressed her thumbnails together, and searched for the proper words to best explain her actions of over thirty years ago.

"We...Philippe's father, Antoine, and I...we decided that it would be in the best interest of the children to tell them that..." Queen Simone's words grew halting with long-forgotten emotion. Hands shaking, she pressed the fringe of her shawl to her quivering lips and waited until she felt able to continue.

The tension in the room was so high, Sebastian believed it could power the chandelier. The wine stewards must have sensed this too and moved in with loaded magnums to fill the wine goblets.

Forcing herself to stay on track, no matter how painful, Queen Simone continued.

"Antoine and I told the children that their marriage was not legal because Katie was underage, and had not received her father's permission. Katie's father, Henry, did not know enough about French law to dispute our claim, and neither did the kids. We were afraid that if they tried to get an annulment, since they would both be required to sign, that one or both of them might refuse, so we did not press for that.

"Further, this would have revealed that the marriage *was* legal and would have given both Katie and her father the opportunity to take advantage of the situation. Then heaven only knows what would have happened. My husband, King Antoine, told Henry that if he told anyone about this scandalous affair that we would pressure his corporation—where poor Henry had been working for twenty years—to fire him. We knew that his company had a huge vested interest in doing business with St. Michel and other European countries related to St. Michel and that we had Henry over the proverbial barrel."

Simone leaned back in her chair, seeming to shrink and age considerably as she did so. Outside, a cloud eclipsed the sun and the room darkened perceptibly.

"So, we gave Henry a substantial amount of money to remain silent. Henry, who was very conservative, was not anxious to broadcast his daughter's 'shame' anyway, so he took the deal and the money. As far as we know, they went back to Texas. We have never heard from them again."

Simone tented her gnarled fingers before her lips for a moment, pondering what she would say next.

Marie-Claire glanced up at Sebastian, her cheeks pale, and eyes bright with myriad emotions that would no doubt be surfacing for days to come. He gave her hand a little squeeze and she leaned into him, drawing strength and comfort from their touch, much the way she had in the days after her father had passed away.

"All right." Queen Simone pushed herself up in her seat and hauled her rounded shoulders back into bony points. "The down side of all this—"

Marie-Claire stared up at Sebastian and mouthed the words *"down side?"* Apprehension filled her eyes, and Sebastian adjusted his position so that their arms and thighs touched, hoping the contact would calm her.

"—is that we were never sure that the marriage had been annulled. If, as we suspect, Katie and Philippe's marriage was never absolved, then Philippe's marriage to the Dutch princess Johanna Van Rhys was invalid, as well as his subsequent marriages."

She let that sink in a moment before announcing, "Which, of course, would make Phillipe's four daughters and unborn child illegitimate. The icing on this rather botched cake would be that we never did learn the sex of Katie's baby. If this baby was a boy...and if he is still alive...he would now be St. Michel's crown prince."

Chapter Four

"The reason I even bring this up now," Queen Simone explained to her dumbstruck family, "is that St. Michel's government is a monarchy based on primogeniture, which, as you all know, means that the throne passes through the male line. If there is no male heir to the throne, there is a very real threat that St. Michel will be…will be…" she faltered, swallowed and began again, "…will be absorbed by our neighbors in Rhineland, of which it was part until the seventeenth century."

Expression pensive, Simone hunched forward.

"In Rhineland, there is a faction that has been plotting to take over St. Michel. It's all economics. As you are all aware, we have the St. Michel River inside our border by a good kilometer. It's the only way to the North Sea from here. And…from Rhineland. They've grown weary of paying us for its usage. With the king's death, they have begun to make serious plans to gain control not only of the river, but of our government as well."

Slowly, Simone rubbed her gnarled knuckles with her thumbs.

"These people present a grave threat to the freedoms we enjoy as a small nation. So far, they have only issued idle threats, but make no mistake. These people are dangerous. There is little conscience to stop them from taking what they want, and so it is up to us to create a united, organized front, with an heir firmly in place before this goes any further."

Celeste stopped drumming her fingertips. No one moved. Silence fell like a coastal fog before dawn.

Horrified, Marie-Claire glanced up at Sebastian and could see the truth of her grandmother's words reflected in his eyes. She felt numb from head to foot. How could she, just six short months ago, have been leading such a carefree life? Before Papa died, her only concerns were catching Sebastian's eye and shopping in Paris.

Now, her whole world seemed to be shifting on its axis. The security of her homeland was being threatened, she had an older sibling she'd never met, and to top it all off, she was most likely illegitimate.

The sun was still hidden and now, ominous thunderclouds were rolling in, echoing the dark nature of what was happening here at the table today. Marie-Claire squirmed in her seat, feeling suddenly claustrophobic and desperate to get away. To run somewhere, anywhere with Sebastian and to cry and rage against life's little injustices.

And those not so little.

"We know," Queen Simone's wavering falsetto again captured all eyes, "that this faction in Rhineland has heard the news of our missing heir, but are not yet worried about this, assuming that either the heir will not be found, or she will be a girl, given Philippe's history."

Celeste could not stand being ignored another moment.

With a sudden explosion of fury, she battled her way out of her chair. Arms akimbo, face flaming, veins popping, she barreled, belly-first, toward the dowager queen.

"*My baby* is next in line for the throne! *My baby* is a *male!* My baby is legitimate! How *dare* you all discount *my baby,* who is Philippe's last gift to us all, and go off searching for some *fairytale heir* who was most likely *never even born!*"

Ever unflappable, Simone dismissed Celeste's outrage. "You won't have so much as an ultrasound, so how can we know if you are having a boy? This is your first baby. You have a fifty-fifty chance. I won't bet this kingdom on those dismal odds. Besides, how can we be sure that the baby you are carrying is even Philippe's? Philippe has been gone for as many months as you are pregnant. I find this last-second production of an heir suspiciously convenient."

Shaking like the tail of a coiled rattler, Celeste gripped the back of an empty chair as murder glittered in her eyes. "You will regret that insinuation, old lady."

"Perhaps you should go lie down, Celeste," Simone suggested placidly. "You're not looking so well."

Celeste hovered for a moment then thrust away the chair she clutched. A cold smile crept across her lips, but not into her eyes. "For the sake of the *true heir* to St. Michel's throne, I will rest now."

And with that, she turned and swept out of the room.

Queen Simone signaled for the dining-room attendants to begin serving the first course. While they bustled about, she lifted her goblet and everyone joined her in tossing back a deep drink of wine.

As she prepared to make her next announcement, she blotted her thin lips on a fine linen napkin and swallowed a delicate burp.

"I feel it is time for us to bring in an investigator from

the St. Michel Security Force, and the prime minister has recently secured a good man by the name of Luc Dumont to find Philippe and Katie's child and to determine if this child is indeed a male.'' She let this news digest a bit then asked, ''Any questions?''

Still shell-shocked from the bomb she'd just dropped, everyone simply stared, unseeing, deep in thought about how all this news would affect each of their lives.

Though the clouds that hovered over the western horizon were black and heavy with unshed rain, the air was unusually humid. The minute Marie-Claire and Sebastian stepped outside the palace and left the comfort of the climate-controlled rooms, Marie-Claire began to wilt. Thank God for Sebastian's strong arm. And, though the two glasses of wine on her still-empty stomach were somewhat fortifying, she was devastated all over again. She thought she'd spent the previous six months crying out the last of her tears, but here they were, hovering at the edge of her lower lashes again.

Sebastian pulled her hand to his lips and kissed her palm as they walked, and, unable to speak for fear she'd start crying and be powerless to stop, she swallowed and blinked and kept pace with him.

Together they strolled through the blossoming gardens in a comfortable silence. And though they had no particular destination in mind, they moved with purpose, past *Le cheval du roi* fountain, through the fabulous glass-walled greenhouses, around various gazebos and on down the gravel path that led beyond the rolling lawn toward the small valley that sheltered the stables from bad weather.

Sebastian moved with an easy masculinity that still thoroughly captivated Marie-Claire. He always seemed so calm. So sure of himself. Able to ride out even the wildest storm without a trace of damage. She glanced down at her hand, enveloped in his stronger, larger one and was bolstered at the sight.

The shadows were lengthening across the lawn and birds twittered from the acres of forest that edged the numerous manicured garden areas. Off on a neighboring farm, cattle lowed as they headed inside for their evening milking.

Just strolling along together was incredibly calming, and Marie-Claire realized that, for the first time in a long while, she felt safe. It was almost as if, with Sebastian by her side, she could face any obstacle life might toss her way. The knots in her stomach loosened some, and the burning lump in her throat began to subside. As if he understood, Sebastian kissed her temple and Marie-Claire was consumed with love for him.

The stables that loomed just ahead had been her favorite place of escape as a child. To her, they meant freedom. She'd learned to ride at an early age and before entering her teens had won a number of prestigious equestrian competitions. She felt as at home on the back of a horse as she did in a rocking chair and so it was natural that she'd unconsciously steer Sebastian to this destination, when she was hurting.

Together they entered the now-silent main stable. Though daylight poured through the doors and windows, the lights were burning in the broad hallway. Out in the paddock, trainers worked a number of horses, leaving Marie-Claire and Sebastian alone for the time being.

The pungent aroma of horse sweat, fresh manure and sweet hay, mingled with the musty scent of old wood and slowly drifting dust motes. Eyes closed, Marie-Claire filled her lungs and believed she could smell the medieval history radiating from the ancient walls and floor.

She paused, with Sebastian at her side, and listened intently, straining to hear the past, both distant and recent. The stomping hooves and impatient snorts echoed those from centuries gone by. The faint reverberation in the back of her mind came from a time when St. Michel had had to fight for its precious freedoms.

And the stronger sounds were born of times of peace— her papa's low laughter, a horse's eager whinny and the wind whistling as they flew.

Marie-Claire drew Sebastian past a dozen stalls till she reached her father's horse, Sovereign's Golden Boy. Low nickers rumbled forth as his thoroughbred head protruded from the stall to greet his visitors. Ears twitching, he watched their approach with soulful brown eyes. His nostrils flared and blew as he strained to reach them.

Marie-Claire buried her nose in the horse's neck and inhaled the serenity she always found here. "Hey, handsome. How about a kiss for your girl?"

Golden Boy lipped her cheek and snorted through her hair and after a bit of a slobber that could be construed by a creative mind as a kiss, he pulled back his whiskered lips and seemed to send Sebastian a challenging grin.

"Should I be jealous?" Sebastian wondered.

"Mm-hmm." With a coy smile, she nodded and reached for a carrot in the pail behind her. "He's mine now," she murmured. "Lise, Juliet and Ariane weren't interested, Jacqueline was too young and Papa knew I had loved him since he was a foal."

"Beautiful."

He was stroking the horse, but she knew his eyes were on her as she let Golden Boy lip the carrot from her palm. An exhilarating flutter of physical awareness bubbled in her belly. Unsettled by his blatant interest, she strove to appear as if the look in his dark, bedroom eyes had no effect on the strength of her knees or the steadiness of her hands. She touched her tongue to her suddenly dry lips and searched for a change of subject.

"I'm so sorry you were subjected to that..." Marie-Claire groped for the words as she pushed away from Golden Boy's neck and went to the tack room for a set of curry-combs, "that...scene at dinner." She was glad he couldn't see the flames of embarrassment that licked her cheeks. "Had I known that Grandmama was going to sort the dirty laundry at the dining-room table, I'd never have invited you for tonight."

"Marie-Claire, your papa was like a father to me, too. He always had a way of making me feel a part of his life. Of his family. And all families have their good conversations and their bad conversations."

"Yes, but seldom do the skeletons come flying out of the closet at such a rate without benefit of air-traffic control." When she emerged from the tack room she handed a brush to Sebastian and kept one for herself.

Sebastian chuckled. "I have to admit I learned a few things about your family tonight." Together, they tethered her horse just outside his stall and set to work brushing his satin coat to a high sheen.

"So did I." Her mouth curved in a rueful twist as she laid her cheek upon Golden Boy's smooth flank. "I wonder why Papa never mentioned Katie to any of us?"

Sebastian paused in his grooming of the horse's broad chest and shrugged. "It was a long time ago. He probably didn't think it was relevant any longer."

"Not relevant? Sebastian, they had a baby together! I'd say that might be worth mentioning."

Snuffing and blowing, Golden Boy swung his head down, and lipped Sebastian's hair. Good-naturedly, Sebastian patted his nose, then nudged him away and continued brushing.

"As king, your father was in a precarious position. Sometimes the hint of scandal in the tabloids can bring a country as small as ours to its knees.''

"Yes, but we're his *family*. I'd have liked to have known I had another sibling before now. After all, this person would have to be..." she did some mental calculating and stared at Sebastian, "...as old as you!" Her jaw sagged. "That's ancient."

"Sebastian, I'm trying to be serious here." She squinted at him. "You don't have any old wives and children that may come popping out of the woodwork any time soon, do you?"

Sebastian took a step and gathered her in his arms and rocked her playfully. "No wives and definitely no children. Although, I might be persuaded to get to working on that, if you were in the mood." He nuzzled her neck, sending great waves of gooseflesh sailing down her back and arms.

Marie-Claire reared back and, unable to help herself, laughed. "You are terrible." She stared into his mesmerizing blue eyes for a long time, and felt herself go limp. "I feel so sorry for Papa," she whispered.

"Why?"

"To have this...and then to lose it."

"We won't let that happen."

"Promise?"

"Mmm." He pulled her close and gently kissed her lips. "I promise."

"I don't understand how he could have married my mother, not knowing what had become of his first love and his baby."

"It was a more complicated time, back then. He had to fulfill his duty and bring an heir to the throne."

"We'll never know, now that they are both dead, but I wonder if that's why he really divorced my mother," Marie-Claire mused. Hands dangling behind his neck, she plucked at the coarse bristles of the currycomb she still held. "Siring three daughters was not the most auspicious start on his legacy."

"No, but I know he loved you without reserve."

Marie-Claire felt her throat grow tight. "I know. But I don't think he ever really loved Mum. She was too wild."

"Like you?"

A tiny smile teased Marie-Claire's lips. "More so. She wanted to be a freedom fighter. And a firefighter. And a bullfighter. She was an awesome woman. But she never should have been a mother. She died in a scuba-diving accident, somewhere near the Great Barrier Reef on one of her endless—and infamous—vacations."

"Philippe never mentioned that."

"Guilt, I'd imagine. Their divorce was a bit acrimonious."

"Still, you're spontaneous, like her."

Marie-Claire lifted a shoulder and cast him a lopsided grin. "Unfortunately true." Slowly, her hands traveled from his broad shoulders and over his powerful chest. Not trusting the sudden impulses she felt to unbutton his placket and to see if his chest was really as smooth and hard as she'd dreamed, she turned and began to vigorously brush Golden Boy's mane.

Sebastian set back to work himself. "Marriages of convenience are not unheard of even in this day and age," he mused. "Chances are he needed her for their positive political alliance, but probably wasn't in love with her."

"Or Hélène, for that matter."

He glanced over his shoulder. "I think there was probably some sympathy happening there, being that Hélène was his old friend's widow. But again, a political alliance was advantageous for everyone."

"That's just so...*sad.*" She wrapped several coarse

strands of Golden Boy's mane around her forefinger and, try as she might, could remember neither her father's divorce from her mother, nor his marriage to Hélène when she was only three. "I'm sure that had a lot to do with it. Papa felt sorry for Hélène and her children, Georges and Juliet." She finger-combed the horse's forelock and kissed his soft, whiskery nose. "Poor Hélène. She was so desperate to prove herself worthy by bearing Papa a son."

"That's how she died, isn't it?"

"Mm-hmm. The first baby boy was stillborn and that shattered her. When Jacqueline came along she fell into a terrible depression, and by the time she gave birth to her last baby, she simply did not have the strength. She and the boy both died within hours of one another. I'm not sure she ever even knew it was a boy."

A low sound of sympathy rumbled from Sebastian and he glanced at her with a look that spoke of his unconditional love. Of a love that transcended their stations in life and their age difference. A love that Marie-Claire knew would see them through battles both personal and political. A love that would overlook bad hair and cramps and graying heads and wrinkles.

Sweet and at the same time wildly exciting, it was the love Marie-Claire had craved her entire life. The kind of love her father had enjoyed for but a fleeting moment in his youth.

"Papa carried a lot of guilt for Hélène's death. That guilt and a healthy dose of mid-life crisis led him to Celeste, I think." Marie-Claire's laugh was mirthless. "I cannot imagine what else would have blinded him to her…her," she grimaced, "…imperfections."

"A beautiful face will lure a man into all kinds of trouble." He winked at Marie-Claire, and she responded with a cheeky smile.

Sebastian moved into the tack room and Marie-Claire could hear him rummaging. He returned with a saddle blanket, a saddle and a bridle. These he dropped on the ground, save for the blanket, which he tossed up over the horse's back.

"Still," Marie-Claire began, too lost in thought to really ponder his actions, then dropped to a bale of hay and tucked a straw into the corner of her mouth, "it's all very tragic. I'd be willing to bet that Papa never found true love again after Katie. I wonder whatever happened to her. To her baby."

Sebastian hefted the saddle up over the horse's back and reached under his belly for the girth. He was as comfortable in the barn as he was in the boardroom, she noted idly. She watched as, with deft fingers, he adjusted the stirrups. Oh, but he was handsome. And all male. Beneath his snug polo shirt, rugged muscles flexed and her eyes followed his smooth motions. He would age nicely, she decided, taking in the distinguished silver threads at his temples and the tiny lines at the corners of his eyes.

Just like her papa.

Sebastian and her father had a lot in common. A zest for life. A gentle, yet decisive nature. Above average height. King Philippe would have loved to have had him as a son-in-law, she just knew.

The sobering memories of her father had sudden tears stinging the backs of her eyes and a burning lump of emotion lodging in her throat.

Sebastian swung into the saddle and, as if he could read the direction of her thoughts, extended his hand.

"Come on," he instructed. She didn't hesitate and, in an inkling, she was seated in front of him. "Let's get away for awhile."

In his sparse apartment in St. Michel's capital city, St. Michel, Luc Dumont hung up the phone and sank to the edge of his lumpy bed. He'd just been on the line with the offices at Interpol, the international police force, and a few pieces of his latest puzzle were beginning to fall into place.

He scanned the fax they'd just sent of the thirty-three-year-old marriage certificate and the faded blurb in a small French newspaper announcing the marriage of Philippe de Bergeron and Katie Graham.

Luc frowned. Either Philippe had bought the silence of the county clerks, or they'd worn some sort of disguise, because the news of St. Michel's crown prince's marriage should have been the stuff of a front-page headline, not a brief mention buried in the milestones column.

Katie Graham, 17, student, Houston, Texas, U.S.A.,
and Philippe de Bergeron, 18, student, St. Michel,
were wed in a civil ceremony,
Tuesday, July 22, 1969.

There were no pictures, but Luc imagined that, as teenagers, they were baby-faced innocents. He stared, unseeing, at a crude watercolor of the Eiffel Tower that clung to his wall and wondered at the fate of this woman and her baby.

In a way, he could commiserate with this mystery child. He knew what it was like to lose a parent at an early age. This royal baby had never known his father. Luc, on the other hand, had lost his mother when he was only six.

He shook his head. Raw deal, but those were the breaks.

He reached for the phone and considered calling his father and telling him that he was working a big, prestigious case, knowing that Albert would be proud. It would be early morning, stateside. Albert's wife, Jeanne, would still be home. On second thought, Luc set the handset back in its cradle. Jeanne had never liked Luc. He'd always figured it was because he resembled his mother. Riddled with insecurities, Jeanne was the reason he'd grown up in boarding schools. Even now, he avoided contact with her whenever he could.

He'd call later, he decided. After Jeanne went to bed.

Sovereign's Golden Boy was surefooted and his canter smooth as Sebastian and Marie-Claire rode down the gravel road, away from the stables. Off in the distance, the setting sun peeked through a clear spot in the black thunderheads, causing a perfect—nearly neon in its intensity—rainbow to curve over the deep forest that loomed ahead. Wind whipped through Marie-Claire's hair, twining strands around Sebastian's neck as he held her firmly against his body.

Instinctively, Sebastian led them to the edge of the trees, and slowed, picking his way toward their pond. Marie-Claire twisted around and looked up at him with a smile that he was sure only he could understand.

After wending their way through the underbrush, they emerged at the outcropping of rock that protruded over the water's edge. Over the years, not a thing had changed. Even the weather was the same. Humid. Sultry. Charged with electricity. A rumble of thunder clapped beyond the hills and overhead, fat, warm drops spattered to earth. One at a time. For now.

The deluge was to come, Sebastian was sure. Of both rain and emotion.

Without words, Sebastian handed Marie-Claire to the ground. After he'd spent some time tethering Golden Boy, he turned and looked up to find her poised at the edge of the rock. His jaw worked and his mouth went dry at the sight. She'd removed her sandals and sweater, but still wore the filmy white sundress she'd worn to lunch. Seemingly the heavens had sent down an angel as the twilight sun set her hair aflame with a golden haze. The dark shadows of her long, shapely legs were backlit beneath her translucent skirt.

Sebastian felt as if he'd stepped back in time, only now, Marie-Claire was a full-fledged woman. Fire kindled in his belly and he stood watching her, unable to move. Her slow gaze traveled to his and locked. In silent communion, they stood, intrinsically knowing things about each other that no one else ever could.

He studied the emotions that flitted across her face.

He could feel the depth of her sorrow. Her feelings of betrayal, inspired by Simone's shocking news. And, the fierce devotion she held for him. These emotions seemed to war within until she was driven to escape.

Taking flight, she executed a graceful arc and dove into the pool below. This time, she surfaced immediately, shook her head and the poignant look on her face spoke of a loss of innocence. His throat tight, Sebastian mourned for that carefree girl, even as he fell in love with this evolving woman.

As she waded toward him, water ran in rivulets from her hair, over her face, landing in sparkling droplets on her full lips. Her thin sheath clung to her body, drawing him inexorably toward her.

Stripping off his shirt, he waded waist-deep into the water and pulled her into his arms. With the pads of his thumbs, he smoothed the drops—tears or water, he couldn't be sure—from her cheeks and lips.

"Don't worry," he whispered. His chin grazed hers as he spoke.

Gaze plaintive, she stared up at him, her arms locked at his waist. "I don't even know who I am anymore."

"I do."

"Who then?"

"The other half of me."

Her eyes fell shut and her sigh was sweet against his cheeks.

"It will all work out." He only wished he was as assured as he sounded. Feeling suddenly afraid that his words rang false, he pulled her close and kissed her with a fierce possession that rivaled any emotion he'd ever experienced before.

Though Marie-Claire was famished and chilled as they rode back to the stables on Golden Boy, the strong arms that kept her firmly in place in the saddle fortified her. Sebastian's chest was warm and solid against her back, and Marie-Claire nestled against him, cupping his biceps with her palms. The five o'clock stubble that shadowed his jaw caught strands of her hair, giving her an excuse to occasionally reach up and brush his lips with the hills of her knuckles.

He smiled down at her with a look that couldn't have felt any more intimate than if they'd made love, back there on the sweet spring grass. But they hadn't.

It would have been wrong.

As excited as they'd been, they both heard the powerful echo of her father's voice cautioning them to live up to the royal code of ethics and morals. To make him proud, even now, in his absence.

And since Sebastian was an honorable man, he'd mustered his last shred of willpower to tear his lips from hers and set her away from him. Even though his labored breathing told her that he'd been just as tortured to stop at kisses as she was.

Marie-Claire heaved a disgruntled sigh. She'd never listened to Papa when he was alive. Why start now? She peeked up at Sebastian's rugged jaw, hovering just over her shoulder and knew the truth.

Because this was more than merely important. Sebastian was her soul mate. The first time they came together, it had to be perfect. And right.

Soon, she promised herself. Soon enough, they would be man and wife. And they would spend whole days in bed together. Marie-Claire shivered at the vivid thoughts that exploded in her mind and—thinking she was cold—Sebastian held her tighter and kissed her neck, which only caused her to shiver again.

"We'll be home soon," he murmured.

"Mmm." Not nearly soon enough.

When they'd put Golden Boy up for the night, they rushed to the palace and sneaked in through the servants' entrance and into the kitchen. While they raided the pantry for leftovers, wearing terrycloth robes, one of the evening housekeepers dried their clothes. They made banal conversation, designed to convince the staff that there was nothing going on between them.

As they ate, Marie-Claire had to wonder at the success of their ruse. She could see the knowing glances and small smiles exchanged by the kitchen staff in the reflection of several large windows. No doubt rumors would be flying by morning. She didn't care. Sooner or later, the world would figure out that little Marie-Claire de Bergeron was all grown up and madly in love.

"I wish you didn't have to go," she murmured a short time later as they stood in the shadows just outside the servants' entrance.

"Me, too, but we've given them enough to wonder about for one night, don't you think?"

"You noticed the cooks whispering while we ate?"

Marie-Claire swallowed against the mirth that rose into her throat.

"No. But I think several of them are watching us now. Either that, or they enjoy standing at the window with their faces smashed to the glass."

"Where?" Laughter spurted past her lips.

"Shhh. Don't look, or they'll know we can see them."

"What should we do?"

"Depends."

"On what?"

"On what you want them to think."

"What are my options?"

"Well…" He rubbed his jaw and looked up into the night sky. "We could shake hands and I could pound you on the back, like a buddy."

Marie-Claire thrust out her lower lip. "That's no fun."

"Or, I could make an inappropriate advance, and you could slap me…"

"Definitely more interesting, but I'm a lover, not a slapper."

Sebastian groaned. He took a deep breath. "Okay, we could walk over to my car, where they can't see us, and I could give you a proper kiss goodnight. Let them wonder."

Marie-Claire's eyes dropped to half-mast as a tempest of elation rose and fell in her belly. "I choose that last one."

"Me, too. C'mon."

Every second that Sebastian lingered in the shadows with Marie-Claire, it became harder to leave. It was only the knowledge that the watchful eye of the security cameras could capture images that would make their private life a public circus, that enabled him to leave.

At times like this, he hated the fact that she was of royal blood and wished that instead she was the peasant girl he'd originally taken her for when she was sixteen. Then nobody would care about the stupid details of her life. She'd be able to be with whomever she pleased without having to pause and think about how her actions would affect a nation.

As he lifted his hand in a parting wave and pulled his car onto the circular drive, he rotated his head to dispel the tension. He considered turning around and coaxing her to disappear with him. They'd elope. Leave St. Michel forever and live life on their own terms. Surely, they'd be happier as paupers not having to deal with the idiotic protocol that went with living as a royal.

Sebastian could empathize with Philippe and Katie. The thought of bucking the system and living life on his own terms was powerfully seductive. Although not realistic. Their life was here. In St. Michel. Soon enough, they would be married. Living as one. Forever.

Overhead, a bolt of lightening split the sky and Sebastian had to turn on his windshield wipers as rain began to fall in buckets. The weather was the perfect complement to his foul mood. He squinted at the road, his mouth twisting sourly.

For propriety's sake, they would have to be engaged for at least six months before they could be married. And the time of mourning for King Philippe would be over as well. Until then, he'd have to endure being stalked by various and sundry security guards and chaperones and live for stolen moments.

Just ahead, the road forked, one way leading to his house, the other to his mother's. Sebastian passed a hand over his face and heaving a tired sigh, turned down the road that lead to Claudette's. He knew his mother would be anxiously awaiting details of his lunch at the castle, eager for juicy tidbits of royal gossip.

Lights blazed in every room of his mother's house and as Sebastian parked his car, he made a mental note to lecture her on the finer points of conservation.

Brandy swirled into matching snifters as Claudette poured from her private reserve. While she busied herself, Sebastian relaxed by the fire that roared in her magnificent hearth and allowed his gaze to travel over the eclectic décor his mother had foisted upon the once-clean lines of this elegant room. Clutter from every corner of the earth abounded, making the walls close in, leaving little open space. Expensive shelving units had been erected to hold all nature of bric-a-brac and collectibles meant to impress visitors with her taste and wealth. No inch went undecorated; the walls were covered with art, the tables with treasures and the floor with furniture and rugs.

Sebastian's gaze drifted about, noting new additions to the chaos, and he sighed. The likelihood that Claudette would learn to control her impulse spending seemed nil. No doubt she would land in bankruptcy court before she would part with a single treasure. The prospect of an evening spent sorting her scrambled records had his head suddenly throbbing.

Outside, the wind screamed over the countryside and rain poured in sheets down her windows. Inside, his eyes slid closed and he fell into a dreamy twilight filled with blissful thoughts of Marie-Claire until his mother's shrill voice startled him to wakefulness.

"Well? Are you going to just sit there, or are you going to tell me what went on up at the palace today?"

Sebastian sighed and took the glass that she'd thrust under his nose. "Of course. What do you want to know?"

"Everything!" She squinted at him. "But first, tell me why, now that Philippe is dead, were you invited to dine with the family? It's not as if you are intimate with any of them.''

"True enough." Amused, Sebastian felt a wry grin tug at his lips. Not just yet, anyway. Since his budding relationship with Marie-Claire was still far too private to share with anyone, let alone his meddlesome mother, he decided to steer her toward information he knew would become public knowledge within the next few weeks. "Perhaps they invited me because they know of my business ties with Rhineland.''

Claudette stared at her son, expression baffled. "What has Rhineland to do with anything?''

"You will hear this soon enough, I suppose." Sebastian took a thoughtful sip of brandy. "Since Philippe's death, there is a faction in Rhineland that is plotting to reabsorb St. Michel into their government. Simone wanted to ask me what I knew about the political climate over there and some of the nuances of negotiation with their government officials.''

Claudette huffed over the rim of her glass as she rested it against her ruby lips. Clearly this was not the kind of personal buzz she was looking for. "Why would we worry about Rhineland? We seceded centuries ago. Why the sudden fuss?''

"Because now there is no heir to the throne. And—'' though he knew he probably shouldn't confide anything more intimate than the weather report with Claudette, he continued in hopes of dousing the flames of curiosity with a thimbleful of information, "apparently Philippe may have another child. My age. Perhaps a boy. If they can find him, he would be crown prince.''

Lips pursed, Claudette's gaze darted to his and she swallowed. Hard. After a long, frozen moment she queried, "What?''

"Remember, St. Michel is a monarchy that passes through the male line." Sebastian leaned back in his chair and crossed his legs on top of the leather ottoman. "Aside from Celeste's baby, our only hope of remaining independent is finding this possible first-born son to ascend to the throne. It seems there is some question as to whether Celeste's baby is even Philippe's, let alone a male, which makes locating this missing heir even more important."

Claudette froze, eyes glazed, the wheels in her brain processing this new information. Finally, she touched her tongue to her suddenly parched lips and managed to croak. "Missing heir?"

"They've hired the head of St. Michel's security force to find him."

She stared at Sebastian, but her eyes saw only the images that whirled in her mind. Her breathing had become shallow, and her glass tilted, a bit of brandy spilled upon her lap. She did not notice. "This heir. You say...he would be the crown prince," she murmured.

"Mm. About my age."

"Yes. Exactly your age."

"Seems Philippe was married to an American teenager named—" Sebastian frowned, struggling to recall her name.

"Katie."

"Yes! That's—" Brow arched, he glanced at his mother. "How did you know about Katie?"

Claudette opened her mouth to speak, but could only emit tiny, guttural sounds, as if she were choking. Sebastian pulled his legs off the ottoman and leaning toward her took the glass from her hands and set it on a nearby table. Concerned, he watched the blood rush into her neck and cheeks. Tiny beads of sweat formed on her upper lip and she trembled.

"Mère, what is it?"

Hands to her cheeks, Claudette gawped at him, her mouth working, struggling to form the necessary words. ''I never wanted to tell you.'' Her eyes brimmed with tears.

Outside, thunder roared and seconds later a flash of lightning lit the room. The power failed and a sudden feeling of doom clutched at Sebastian's heart as the firelight flickered over his mother's tortured expression, and he forced himself to ask what he was quite sure he wouldn't want to know.

''Tell me what?''

Chapter Five

Claudette clutched Sebastian's hands till he was certain she'd drawn blood. Like a carp plucked from the lake and gasping for precious oxygen, she gurgled. He'd never known her to be so afraid of the dark.

"Mère?" Sebastian prompted. Claudette had always possessed a flair for the dramatic but even so, her rigid countenance and glassy-eyed stare was unusual. Unnerving.

Outside, the storm raged. Inside, Sebastian could feel one brewing. He disentangled his hand from Claudette's clutches long enough to fumble through an end table's clutter for some candles and matches. Once he'd lit these, his mother's face was less shadowed but no less contorted.

Wind screamed through the ancient window casings and thunder, like the rumble of an earthquake, vibrated overhead, rattling the decorative plates perched upon the mantle. Immediately following, a flash of lightning rent the gloaming, and, as Sebastian glanced out the window, he felt an uncommon chill snake down his spine. Against the blinding light, the trees stood stark, crooked branches beckoning like the bony fingers of the grim reaper.

Sebastian raked a hand over his jaw and snorted.

He was letting his mother's imagination run away with him. Even Claudette's master manipulation couldn't produce the squall outside and its colliding weather fronts. The electricity in the air was simply that, and had no deeper, evil nuances.

Whatever she was about to tell him was no doubt simply a tempest on the tennis court. Some local gossip that would have nothing to do with him. As soon as the lights came back on, he'd persuade her to gather her financial papers and a calculator and they'd begin wading through the mess that was Claudette's filing system.

He found their brandy glasses, topped them off and handed one to his mother. "Mère, try to relax. It's just a storm. The lights will be back on soon."

Claudette moaned and dropped her chin to her bosom. "If only it were that easy."

Sebastian rotated his head to ease the tension. And irritation. "What? If only what were that easy?"

Claudette's flighty gaze glanced to his face. Remembering the brandy she held, she tossed back a slug, wincing and shuddering as it blazed its way down her throat. Through her nostrils, she sucked in a deep breath and then dabbed her mouth on the back of her wrist. "I've kept this from you, because I felt it was for your own good."

Okay. Here it came. She'd bought ocean-front property in Antarctica or some other such lunacy. Impatient with her, Sebastian dropped into the club chair by the fire and crossed his feet atop the ottoman. Leaning back, he let his eyes slide to half mast, and exhaled his long day into the shadows. This was going to take a while.

"Go on."

Trembling, Claudette pressed her lacquered fingertips to her lips and spoke in muffled phrases. "I had to do it. Because I was protecting her. And him. Everyone."

"Her? Him? Who?"

"I was there. At the wedding. It's all true."

"What wedding? What's true?" He squeezed his eyes shut as a nebulous foreboding filled his belly. What was she up to now?

"She was pregnant. Her father was so angry. He was working class. A nobody. The boy's father and mother were horrified. There was nothing anyone could do. So they decided to have the baby quietly, and then give him up, to…to…to…"

"Mère, could you go back to the beginning and clue me in as to who the devil you're talking about?"

"…to…to a childless couple. A couple she believed could not have children of their own, though they were desperate for a baby…"

Another unnerving clap of thunder forced her to momentary silence. When she resumed speaking, the corresponding bolt of light that filled the room amplified her dry, raspy words and bleached her turbulent expression.

"That couple…was us."

"What the devil are you talking about?"

"You."

Sebastian moved not a muscle.

"*You!*" Claudette shrieked then began to blubber into her bejeweled hands. "You are that child."

Tiny hairs on the back of Sebastian's neck stood at attention and as he stared at his mother, realization slowly dawned. He stared at her for a long, electric minute, his mind attempting to make sense of her jumbled information. He filled his lungs and deliberately kept his voice low.

"Are you trying to tell me that I am not your son?"

They stared at each other until Claudette could take the strain no longer and, with a tortured moan, propped her elbows on the arm of her chair and buried her face in the great folds of her sleeves.

"You will always be my son! It's just…it's just that you…Katie…Philippe…I always wanted a baby, and she…well, she had no recourse. She was an American. So young. There was so much at stake. The reputation of the crown prince, the future of the monarchy…*Ohh*."

Claudette's ghoulish wails rivaled the wind that shrieked through the valley. She snatched a handful of tissues from a silver dispenser at her elbow and alternately blew and mopped.

"Mère, if you think this is funny, you are wrong."

"Sebastian, my darling, I have never…" her mouth worked, her eyes glazed, "I have never been more… more…*serious* about anything. I…I have proof. Documentation. With a few phone calls I'm reasonably sure I can get it for you in the morning."

The muscles in his jaw jerked and his eyes narrowed. "Why have you waited until now to tell me?"

Her lips were now a smeared slash of ruby red and fiery spots of guilt over this late-in-the-day admission stained her cheeks. Brackish rivers ran from her eyes, over her mouth and drip, drip, dripped onto her hands.

"I never *wanted* to tell you. Your father and I loved you as if you were our own flesh and blood. There was nothing more sacred to us than your happiness. We knew that growing up with the stigma of having been rejected by the royals would have been a horrible cross to bear for a little child."

Sebastian jumped to his feet, took several steps back and could only stare at this woman he thought he'd known all his life. It was almost as if she were speaking a different language, so foreign were her words.

"And it didn't seem to matter that you were of royal blood. After all, Philippe has many children that could ascend to the throne."

"All female."

"Yes. Girls." Claudette lifted hands of supplication, imploring him to understand. "But until you just reminded me, I'd quite forgotten that St. Michel required a *male* heir. It's been so long since we've needed a crown prince, and King Philippe and Celeste seemed to have a fruitful future, and then with the shock of Philippe's untimely death…well, it simply never occurred to me to tell you the truth, until moments ago."

"Surely you'd had opportunity and motive to tell me before now. Why wait?"

"Until now, it didn't matter! Don't you see? Now, without you, St. Michel is in danger of becoming reabsorbed by Rhineland! I had to step forward. As patriots, we simply cannot allow that to happen!"

Sebastian watched her hands clutching and tearing at her hair and dressing gown in a most theatrical fashion. The performance was certainly meant to convince. But could this possibly be true? He did not speak, though thoughts thundered through his mind.

Could he be Philippe de Bergeron's son?

Could this explain the connection he felt to Philippe? The nearly surreal familial bond that had kept him from feeling fatherless at such an early age? Could Philippe have felt some sort of subconscious connection himself? Was that why he'd taken such an interest in Claudette's son? Was that why he'd been so included in palace politics? Given such a position of prestige and power in St. Michel's business world? Was Claudette speaking the truth?

No.

Never.

Then again…

Her story was just left of center enough to be true.

Numb with shock, he tried to reason how this new turn of events could affect his life. He stared at the fire, and watched the flames devour the last of a good-sized chunk of wood. A chill had descended on the room and vaguely, he considered stirring the flames and adding another log. But he was too paralyzed at the moment. Too deep in thought to move.

Not wanting to lose the momentum she'd built, Claudette plunged ahead before he could distract her train of thought.

"Sebastian, my darling, before now, there was no reason to bother you with the sad details of your birth. You were far better off with us. Your…your…" Claudette trumpeted into the wad of tissues she held and bubbles of saliva formed on her lips as she bawled. "Katie died. Most likely of a broken heart. I keep her death certificate and other papers in…in…a safe-deposit box. I haven't seen them in years. It all seems like a…" she waved her tissues, "…dream. You were safe with us. You were our little boy. But now, you are a man. And the very future of the kingdom rests on Philippe's son stepping in and taking the crown. You are crown prince, and, as such, you can save our country from Rhineland, especially since, as far as I know, their marriage was never really annulled!"

She was right on that count.

Overhead an explosion of thunder rattled the windows as Sebastian made a sickening discovery that he suddenly knew was about to ruin his life.

If he was indeed Philippe de Bergeron's son, then he was at the same time Marie-Claire's brother.

Marie-Claire burrowed deep under her feather bed and watched with awe the spectacular storm that had rain sluicing over her windows in sheets. Glowing veins of light branched the sky and thunder boomed in a show that was quite rare for St. Michel.

Especially for March.

She couldn't remember ever having seen anything quite so violent in her twenty-one years in this country. Before now, she'd only read about such things. As the waffled shadow of her French panes flickered on the wall, she wondered how people in less sturdy abodes were faring.

She wondered how Sebastian was faring.

Sebastian.

Nature's wrath only augmented her turbulent feelings since she'd seen him that afternoon. She'd had no idea how powerful their reunion would be for her. When she'd been in Denmark, she'd missed him, to be sure. But just how much became apparent only after he'd liquefied her knees with his kiss.

Eyes closed, she tugged her covers higher and groaned.

Even now she could still feel his warm lips over hers, open, prodding, insistent, his hand around the back of her neck, pulling her closer and she, wilting against him. As they'd stood alone together in the pond that evening, it had been perfect. His kiss had been as warm and wet and sultry as the weather that had rolled in over them.

Fingertips against her mouth, she swallowed a giddy squeal. She was in love. Untamed, stormy, tingling, thrilling love that stole her appetite and robbed her of any rational thought. She couldn't imagine ever feeling more blissful. Happier. More in tune with life.

Though her eyes drifted shut, Marie-Claire knew she'd never be able to sleep. Images of her and Sebastian running for the shore, struggling to pull dry clothing over wet skin, more kissing, riding home just ahead of the storm....

Her earlier worries had seemed light years removed with

his arms around her waist. Only Sebastian knew how to soothe her. To make her chaotic world seem right again. He was the only man for her, and she was sure that he was a gift straight from God himself.

Murmuring to the rhythm of the rain that pelted her windows and balcony, Marie-Claire drew up her knees, clasped her hands beneath her chin and sent up a prayer of thanksgiving for such a perfect match. When she was finished offering her gratitude, she asked the good Lord to tell her Papa not to worry. Everything would eventually work out. Rhineland would drop its ridiculous bid to overtake St. Michel. Her long-lost sibling would be found. Papa's annulment to Katie Graham would be found.

And soon, as all good princesses did, she would marry Sebastian and live happily ever after.

A knock at the door startled Marie-Claire out of a deep, dreamless sleep. She sat up and peered through the darkness to numbers that glowed from her nightstand. Way after midnight. What on earth could anyone want in the wee hours of the morning?

"Just—" She cleared her throat and fumbled for her robe. "Just a minute."

Padding across her room, she pulled open her heavy oak bedroom door and squinted against the shaft of light from the hallway. The security night doorman stood at attention.

"Yes?"

"Your Highness, you have a visitor in the library. Mr. Sebastian LeMarc."

Sebastian? A bubble of joy surged into the back of her throat. It was an effort to maintain a businesslike facade. "Tell him I'll be down in a moment."

"Yes, ma'am."

Marie-Claire rushed to her bathroom, jammed a toothbrush in her mouth, dragged a comb through her hair, spat, fluffed, spritzed, puffed, applied a dash of makeup and finally declared herself ready.

He cut a striking figure, standing in the middle of the massive library, staring at the fire that flickered in the hearth. Before he became aware of her presence, she watched him, and her heart swelled with love.

He was magnificent. Rangy legs spread for balance, he stood, his powerful arms folded over his chest. A long, black trench coat hung to his knees and accentuated the breadth of his shoulders. His hair was damp from the weather and curled most appealingly at his nape and just above his ears. A pensive expression graced his perfectly chiseled mouth, and his gaze was clouded with some unreadable emotion.

Something had happened.

Fear leapt in Marie-Claire's heart. She glanced at the clock that ticked away the hour on the mantle. Nearly two in the morning. What on earth could be wrong?

As if he sensed her presence, Sebastian turned.

The tortured look in his eyes had her flying across the room and finding solace in his embrace. Her hands sought to cup his cheeks and she pulled his mouth to hers, knowing that whatever it was, they could handle it together.

His lips grazed hers and then—oddly—he pulled back. There was stiffness in his countenance that worried Marie-Claire. Eyes flashing, he searched her face and she cast him a tentative smile. She could feel the heat in his hands as he clutched her arms and his breathing came in labored puffs. His hand shook as he traced the barely discernable cleft in her chin with the pad of his thumb.

''In so many ways, you are the feminine version of him.''

''Papa?'' Marie-Claire's brow furrowed at his strange comment.

"Yes. You have an expression…I don't know…when you smile. It leaves no doubt that you are his."

"Mama would have agreed with you. Although, to her way of thinking, the resemblance was not a compliment." Again, she smiled, hoping to lighten his somber expression.

"It must have been why he favored you."

"What?"

"This resemblance. None of your siblings seem to have inherited so much from him."

"None of us inherited what he'd hoped." Her laughter was dry. Rueful. "The similarities would have been much easier to spot in a son."

"Maybe."

"Sebastian, what is it? Surely you did not come here at this hour to discuss my relationship with my father."

He swallowed and glanced away. "No."

"Then what? You're scaring me."

"I'm sorry." His eyes slid closed and with a heavy exhalation, he rested his head against hers. "I came here to talk to you."

"At this hour, it must be grave."

"I don't know."

"Sebastian, please." Her heart was pounding. Again, he held her apart from his body and scrutinized her face in a most unnerving manner. "Have I done something wrong? Said something?"

"No."

"Then what?"

She lifted a finger and rested it on his lower lip and the simple gesture seemed to scald him. Roughly, he grasped her hand and reared back. Hurt, white-hot in its intensity, crowded into her throat, this simple rejection rendering her speechless.

On the mantle, the clock ticked, and, beneath it, the fire

crackled in the hearth. Outside, the sounds of a dying storm whispered through the trees.

"I have to go." Sebastian released her hand and took a step back. And then, another.

"What? But you just got here. And you needed to talk to me."

"I...no. I was wrong."

His simple words held a deeper nuance that she could not fathom, but she knew that something had happened. Something that would change the course of her life. Marie-Claire suddenly knew a fear of loss that overshadowed the death of her father.

"Now. I have to go now." His eyes were cloudy and almost anguished as he backed toward the door. "Goodbye, Marie-Claire."

Marie-Claire's lungs froze in midbreath.

Good-bye?

Why did this usually breezy parting hold such an echo of permanence? Wordlessly, she watched him stride through the massive palace foyer, past the guards, and out through the several sets of double doors that led to his freedom.

Just outside Sebastian's bedroom window the next morning, the sky was a brilliant blue, showing no sign of last night's freak hurricane. The news had reported damage in the millions and more than a dozen fatalities connected with the unusual spring storm. Now, the sun belied the devastation of the night before and streamed into his room, warming great patches on his bed and the floor. The dust had been settled and the air had a scrubbed-fresh quality that Sebastian usually reveled in.

But not this morning.

This morning, he noticed none of the splendor in the world beyond his window, for he was focused on the cracks in his heart. Woodenly, he forced himself to go through the motions of dressing. Preparing for the day. The day after the world had ended.

He hadn't been able to tell her.

He hated himself for his weakness, but it had been beyond his ability when she was so close. Even forcing himself to leave hadn't helped build his courage. Neither had the whiskey he'd drunk when he'd come home, hoping to lull himself into a forgetful stupor. That stupid stunt had only managed to drive what felt like a rusty ax through his brain, leaving his head pounding, his mouth a dust bowl, and his heart a bloody ball of hamburger.

What the devil was he going to do now?

It seemed his only recourse was to meet with Simone and get to the bottom of this mess. The…truth. Then he'd either continue his path with Marie-Claire, or pick up the pieces and do his duty for his country.

It was that simple.

And that horrible.

Sebastian's hands stilled as he buttoned his collar and stared at his haggard reflection in the full-length mirrored doors of his closet. He hadn't slept a wink all night long for lying there and calling himself every kind of fool. It had been lunacy to see Marie-Claire. He should have known that he had no willpower where she was concerned. Her understanding expression and willingness to soothe him without even knowing the problem only endeared her to him further. Made what had to be done between them—temporarily or permanently—only that much harder.

Bracing his palms on the back of a chair, he hung his throbbing head and, squeezing his eyes shut against the brilliant sunlight, thought over his life. He'd grown up with wealth and privilege. Even his high-powered career in St. Michel's fast-paced world of import/export had been essentially handed to him because of his social status. Although, why on earth such status should have been afforded his mother was a mystery indeed. She was uneducated, brash, charmless.

It was common knowledge that she'd married into her social position. Claudette was a social climber. But her husband was deceased now. And her eccentricities were becoming more pronounced with age. Surely, she had to sense that high society would eventually move on. Without her.

Then again, Claudette lived in a dream world. Blissfully, she ignored her dwindling bank account and the signs that pointed to her eventual economic failure. She craved prominence in St. Michel's upper echelon, needing to see and be seen. Her lower class upbringing was an albatross about her neck that she routinely glossed over, fancying herself—because of her aristocratic marriage—to be above the common folk. After all, her husband had been a royal consort and a count. And her son...

Sebastian's head jerked up and he scrutinized the face that had stared back at him these thirty-two years. Could there be any truth to Claudette's fantastic story? Truth be told, there were certain similarities between him and Philippe. Some physical, but there were other things.

Both loved to golf. To ride horses. In fact, all manner of sport had them more than intrigued. They shared a common sense of humor, a passion for life, and intolerance for stupidity and cruelty. A complete dedication to St. Michel and her politics. A loyalty to the monarchy, to history, to destiny. A belief in God and the power of love.

But did these things add up to a blood relationship?

Claudette swore they did.

Sebastian dragged his hands over his face, rubbing his painful temples and forehead. Knowing Claudette as he did, he knew she was not beyond lying. But he'd never known her to fabricate anything to these lengths.

Even so, until he knew the absolute truth, he had to stay away from Marie-Claire. Should the public catch wind of this rumor and suspect anything deeper in their relationship, it could be catastrophic for everyone involved.

Sebastian dropped into the chair that sat at the end of his bed and reached for his shoes. He allowed a loafer to dangle from his fingertips and stared into the mirror as he mulled over his identity. Just who the hell was he? One day, he was a successful playboy, wooing the king's daughter and the next, he was heir to the throne and was dating his half sister.

Confused didn't begin to describe his state of mind.

Even so, several things were becoming dismally clear. Now that his identity was in question, he was shocked at how he'd allowed the life he'd been handed to dictate who he was.

Well, no more.

Soon enough, Sebastian would find out who his parents really were. And in the process, he hoped, he'd discover exactly who he was. Filled with a sense of purpose, Sebastian jammed his feet into his shoes, shrugged into his coat, and strode to the door.

Time to get to the bottom of this mess. As much as he hated the idea of Marie-Claire learning the truth, he knew that there was no time like the present.

He'd swing by and pick up his mother on the way to the palace.

Chapter Six

As the head of security for St. Michel, Luc Dumont knew he must squelch the urge to squirm under the Dowager Queen Simone's intense scrutiny. Because he'd already been hired by Prime Minister Rene Davoine to locate the missing heir, he knew this interview with Her Royal Highness was simply a formality. Nevertheless, it was nerve-wracking. His dealings with some of the world's most hardened criminals suddenly seemed a breeze in comparison to this social interrogation.

The old woman sat, shoulders square, hands clasped in her lap, both feet planted firmly on the floor. Over the years, her severe expression had etched censorious creases into the corners of her mouth and between her eyes. And these eyes, like blue laser beams, missed nothing as they bored into his soul.

It was not every day he spent the morning chatting with royalty in the throne room. Especially crotchety, old royalty, poised like a buzzard, ready to pounce and peck away at even the slightest lapse in the dedication of the police to her case. It was times like these that Luc wished he'd gone into sales, like his father before him.

Luckily for him, Simone preferred a comfortable pair of overstuffed chairs in a grouping by the window to the throne itself, which, to his surprise, actually sat on a small stage in the middle of the room. On a low table before them, a tray laden with fresh pastries lay untouched. Luc knew he'd never be able to chew, let alone swallow in front of such unabashed scrutiny. He shifted in his seat, touched his tongue to his dry lips and glanced around the intimidating room. With the exception of the ever-present security people stationed at the far doors, they were alone.

He glanced back at Simone, wondering where to look. Her shoes were very plain. Functional. There seemed to be a bit of tissue stuck to the bottom of one.

"Are you looking at my legs?"

"Wha…what?" Dazed, Luc snapped his head up from his introspective pose and felt every drop of blood in his body rush to his cheeks.

"My legs. You seem to be staring at them." She picked a bit of fluff from her pencil skirt.

"No! No, I was…" The old bird thought he'd been *checking out her legs?* Mortified, his gaze dropped to her legs, which weren't that bad, all things considered— Good heavens man, *don't look at her legs!* He glanced around for a focal point, any focal point, found it in an exit sign and wished he were on the other side.

"Don't be embarrassed, young man. I pride myself on keeping my figure trim."

"But I was just noticing—" Needing vindication, he gestured to the tissue on her shoe, but she paid no heed.

"Daily walks. I can do a fourteen-minute mile. Pretty good for an old broad pushing eighty, don't you think?"

"Yes, but—"

"You look vaguely familiar to me, and I'm not saying that as a pick-up line." Simone stared at him, her dry, rather flirtatious humor at odds with the permanent scowl on her face. "However, I don't believe we've met before today?"

"I—" Because the moment had passed, Luc gave his head a clearing shake and decided to let the leg issue drop. "You may have seen me interviewed on the local news last month, in a case connected with a French smuggling ring."

"Perhaps. Though I'm not much on TV, unless it's that *Iron Chef* thing. You ever see that?" She chuckled, not caring if he answered. "And *The Antiques Road Show*. Oh, and *Biography*. I'm waiting for them to call me anytime now, as my childhood would make a riveting story… At any rate, where were we?"

"Have we met before?" he prompted.

"Are you flirting with me, young man?"

Again, Luc was at a loss, but she seemed not to notice and instead chuckled at her private joke.

"Oh, yes. Now then." Simone gathered her thoughts. "Before you tell me how you plan to find my missing grandchild, tell me a little about yourself. I like to know who I'm working with."

Anxious to get out of there, Luc decided it best to plunge in at the beginning with an abridged version of his thirty-something years.

"I was born in the United States, but grew up in France. My maternal grandparents died when I was four and my mother died when I was six. When my father remarried, I was sent off to study in England. First at Eton and then at Cambridge. The father of a friend of mine at Cambridge suggested that I go for a career in Interpol, which I had for eight years. I was then brought in as head of the Security Force for St. Michel."

"Why?"

The sharp question took Luc off guard. Why indeed? The fact that he felt that he belonged nowhere in particular was hardly the answer of a professional. "Uh, well, because I was qualified."

"And, exactly what is it that qualifies you to find my grandchild?"

"Other than my education and experience?"

Simone issued a curt nod.

Luc shrugged as he pondered his answer. "I think, in this case, it's because I feel a bit of empathy toward your missing heir. He or she lost their father when they were very young. I lost my mother. I spent time living in both the United States and France and have an understanding of both cultures and...I know what it's like to—"

"To what?"

"—to long for family."

Simone's probing stare warmed a degree or two and for a moment there, she looked nearly maternal. Luc bit back a grin. When she was young, he imagined that she'd been a handful. Probably kind of pretty to boot.

"Very well, then. Tell me what you've discovered so far."

Luc swallowed a sigh of relief. Apparently, he'd passed muster. "As of yesterday, we know that Katie Graham gave birth—"

An odd explosion at the far end of the room drew their attention.

The massive mahogany double doors to the throne room flew open and Sebastian LeMarc burst through, pausing only to issue an urgent apology to the understandably agitated security guards. A wailing Claudette trotted at his heels. Arms outstretched and fingers fluttering, she begged him not to cause a scene.

Sebastian rolled his eyes and tossed a feral frown over

his shoulder, willing her to shut up, but it was futile. Claudette was on a roll.

Recognizing Sebastian and his mother as Marie-Claire's sometime special guests, the guards looked to the Dowager Queen. The slight bob of her head gave them permission to relax and resume their posts.

Before meeting with the queen, Sebastian had wanted to stop and speak with Marie-Claire. Unfortunately, Marie-Claire had been indisposed when they arrived and Claudette's highly distraught emotional state would not allow them to tarry.

Perhaps it was better this way.

First, he could meet with Queen Simone and his mother and then talk to Marie-Claire in private, later, when he had all of the facts. She needed to hear about this debacle from him, and in private. Although—Sebastian's jaw tensed at the thought of that tortured conversation—he'd rather face a firing squad than lose the other half of his soul.

Intent on quickly getting to the bottom of this mess, he strode across the room to Simone. In his hands he carried the paperwork Claudette had collected from a friend of a friend who didn't mind going into the government offices at the crack of dawn to collect documents. For a generous fee, of course.

The noisy interruption tugged Queen Simone's lips down at the corners. "*Mis*ter LeMarc, what is the meaning of this unscheduled visit?"

"I beg Your Highness's forgiveness in this terrible breach of etiquette, but some important information has suddenly come to light that I think you will find most interesting."

Diamonds flashing, Simone waved her spotty, blue-veined hands about and made proper introductions. "Sebastian LeMarc, I'd like you to meet Luc Dumont, head of St.

Michel's Security Force. Luc, the red-faced woman sniveling behind him is Claudette LeMarc, Sebastian's mother.''

Knees popping, Claudette bobbed in an awkward curtsey.

Sebastian took Luc's proffered hand. "Please, forgive my intrusion, but I believe I might save you both some valuable time.''

"Go on.''

"I have reason to believe that you can dismiss Mr. Dumont—my sincere apologies, sir—as the missing heir is no longer…missing.''

Simone stiffened. "I do not take kindly to word games, LeMarc. If you have an heir, produce him. Now.''

"I have, Your Highness." Sebastian glanced without sympathy at his mother, who looked ready to faint. "Apparently, you are looking at him.''

Marie-Claire stood in the doorway, not sure that she'd heard correctly. Sebastian's words hung in the air, flash-freezing the group by the window into a tableau of shock and wonder.

Sebastian was claiming to be the missing heir?

Her brow creased as she puzzled over this odd announcement.

Why had he never told her this before? And, if he were the missing heir, wouldn't that make him crown prince? And, if he was the crown prince, wouldn't that make him Philippe's son with an American woman named Katie Something-or-other? And, if he was Philippe's son wouldn't that make him—

As she staggered into the throne room, Marie-Claire's ears began to buzz. Her face caught fire and the bile rose in her throat. Okay. She was going to faint. She groped about for something, anything to keep her upright, but there was nothing. Only sparkling, shimmering air and swirling walls.

At the door one of the guards glanced at her with concern. Her weak smile and glazed expression had him rushing to her side to offer his assistance. Marie-Claire fought the wave of hysterical laughter that threatened to run amok. She must look quite insane. She certainly felt that way. Although the throne was normally off-limits to anyone but the king himself, the guard led her to it, as clearly, this was a special occasion. Upon arriving at the garish gold and bejeweled chair, she fell most gracelessly upon the velvet cushion and did battle with the urge to vomit. Head between her knees, pasty face cradled in clammy palms she listened as across the room, the stunned dowager found her voice.

"*You* are Philippe and Katie's son?" Simone stared first at Sebastian, then at his mother. "Claudette? How could this be true?"

Claudette stumbled forward and sank without invitation to a seat near the queen. Head bowed, hands clasped beneath her chin, she assumed an ingratiating position. "I...I...was there. At the wedding." She turned her watery gaze to Luc. "Look it up. You will see it's true."

Though suspicion marred his expression, Luc nodded. "This much is true. The signature of a Claudette LeMarc is on the wedding license as a witness."

Again, the room fell silent for a moment as everyone digested this startling turn of events. Marie-Claire allowed herself a miserable peek and seeing Sebastian standing there, so handsome, so strong, so regal—

She ducked her head back into her lap to shut out the horrible image of him as her possible brother.

"Sebastian," Queen Simone barked and pointed, "do sit down. You're making me quite nervous. Would anyone care for a cup of coffee? Perhaps something stronger? It's early," her expression was wry, "but I could use a cocktail about now. Or perhaps an IV drip of something poisonous." Soundlessly, a young servant girl moved to pour coffee.

Her dry wit pushed a small smile to his lips as Sebastian moved to take the empty seat on Simone's other side.

China rattling, Claudette accepted her cup of coffee with shaking hands. "She couldn't keep him."

"Pardon?" Simone stared with undisguised distaste at the overwrought Claudette and her roundabout way of reaching the point.

"Katie and Philippe were told by someone in authority that their marriage was not legal."

The old queen glanced from Claudette to the floor and had the grace to color ever so slightly.

"Katie could not face going home and subjecting her poor child to the shame of being born out of wedlock. So, she stayed with my husband and me in France for seven and a half months, until the baby was born. Then, after…" Claudette paused to honk into her handkerchief before she was able to continue, "after a heart-rending decision, she left him in our care."

Simone exhaled and peered over the rim of her glasses, pensive thoughts drawing her fine brows together. Slowly, her head moved from side to side. "I can scarcely believe that Philippe would never have confided this part of the story to me."

"Because he did not know! Katie's father told Philippe that she had left the country and that the baby was to be adopted out to an American family. Philippe was but a child himself. He had no experience. No recourse." Lost in her tortured reverie, Claudette stared out the window in a dramatic pose, searching her memory for the finer points of the story.

"Do go on," Simone ordered, growing impatient with the theatrics.

"My husband and I were childless at the time. As aristocrats, closely affiliated with royalty," she tilted her chin back and sniffed, "Katie felt that we were the perfect parents for her child, imbued with the proper pedigree with which to give her son everything she could not. Needless to say, we were overjoyed at the prospect of finally becoming parents. Shortly after the birth, we filed for adoption—" She blinked at Luc. "Sir, you may make copies of the legal paperwork I have uncovered and brought with me today."

"You can be sure I will."

"Yes. Yes. Of course." A bright smile stretched across her teeth, and quickly fell away as she continued with her story. "Katie then returned to Texas to resume life with her father. Several years later, my husband and I moved to St. Michel with Sebastian and raised him as our own. Philippe never knew that Sebastian was his son."

Marie-Claire leapt to her feet, swung off the throne and staggered dizzily across the room, one hand outstretched, one cupping her aching head. "*No!* No, I don't believe it. She's *lying!* This cannot be true! Sebastian, don't believe her!"

"Marie-Claire?" Sebastian snapped around at the sound of her voice. The life seemed to leak from his being as his head fell back and his eyes slid closed.

"It's *not true,* I'm telling you," she shouted. "Claudette." Marie-Claire turned on the older woman. Claudette stared warily up at her. "Why are you *doing this?*"

"I'm sorry if this news unsettles you, my dear, but it is the truth."

"I—" Marie-Claire opened her mouth to argue, but was interrupted by yet another tortured shriek.

"*No!*" All heads—including Marie-Claire's—swung to

the far door as this piercing scream reverberated from ceiling to wall and back again. Borne on fury, Celeste swept across the room. The veins bulged at her slender throat and her fists bunched at her sides, poised to strike.

"This," Celeste shrieked and pointed at Claudette, "is outrageous! Are you going to believe this...this...social-climbing *maggot?*"

Affronted, Claudette gasped. "How *dare*—"

"Shut up!" Celeste's hostile gaze swung to Queen Simone. "You *dotty old bat!* There is *no...missing...heir!*"

As the fractious hubbub ensued, Marie-Claire wanted—for the first time ever—nothing more than to believe her father's hateful widow.

Rushing to investigate the commotion from where they'd been brunching in the salon down the hall, Lise and Ariane appeared, followed by Georges and Juliet. Upon learning the latest, their voices rose and the chaos escalated. Soon, everyone was hurling recriminations and casting aspersions in a free-for-all.

Sebastian climbed upon the pastry table and with steely eyes, surveyed the pandemonium. *"Silence!"*

Everyone, the dowager queen included, froze at his command. Not a sound could be heard as he stood, hands on hips, eyes glittering, muscles working in his jaw.

An eon seemed to pass before he spoke again, and when he did, his voice was dangerously low. All eyes focused on him, and everyone, whether they wanted to admit it or not, wondered if they were truly hearing from the crown prince, for he certainly fit the part.

"I have never wanted to be a prince, let alone king. I have no desire whatsoever to fill the position now, or ever. I am as stunned by this sudden revelation as the rest of you."

He turned his gaze upon Marie-Claire for a long, sorrow-filled moment, and the tension radiated between them, causing eyebrows to lift.

With a valiant effort, Marie-Claire attempted to stem the tide of her emotion, but it was useless. Tears streamed down her cheeks. She would never, ever buy into this pack of lies that Claudette was foisting upon her own flesh and blood.

Marie-Claire's gaze flashed between Claudette and Sebastian.

Was she the only one who saw the familial resemblance? The same thick, wavy dark hair, the same slight cleft in the chin, the same cobalt eyes, the same strong jaw. She turned her attention to Claudette—loathing the woman who was attempting to ruin her life—and squinted. Thankfully, physical appearance was where the resemblance between mother and son ended.

Claudette was a swirling mass of insecurities and self-doubt. Her son, on the other hand, was the complete antithesis. Where Claudette was weak, Sebastian was strong. Where Claudette was cloying and manipulative, Sebastian was forthright and honest. Where Claudette needed the approval of others, Sebastian was secure in his own skin.

Her gaze traveled to Sebastian's and locked. Silently, Marie-Claire implored him to come to his senses.

He stared at her, reading her mind, anguishing with her, but unable, for many reasons, to do her bidding. Finally, he tore his glance away, destroying her heart in the process.

"Luc," Sebastian said, "I want you to investigate further into this matter. Find out what you can about my..." he shot a look of derision at Claudette, "...*real* parents, whoever they are. And, Your Highness," he turned to Simone, "I will leave the next step in this calamity to your discretion and to the royal protocol regarding such matters."

Simone nodded.

Marie-Claire stared.

Celeste shrieked.

Once again, all hell broke loose.

Sick to death of the bickering, Sebastian strode out of the room.

Marie-Claire caught up with Sebastian where the corridor ended at the top of one of the four different fantastic de Bergeron Palace staircases. Breathless, she called to him, and it was only the desperation in her voice that halted his rapid escape.

The banister supported his weight as he stopped and turned to face her, even though it was the last thing he wanted to do. Knowing what they had shared together and knowing that there was the possibility—however slight— that she could be his half sister, nauseated him. Heartsick, and suddenly very ill at ease in her presence, he took a deep breath and unwillingly met her eyes with his own. He tried not to flinch as she reached out to touch his arm.

"Sebastian." Lips quivering, her smile was filled with uncertainty.

"What?"

"Surely, you don't believe this crazy story."

The air whooshed from his lungs at her pitiful plea. It took a Herculean effort to stand so near and yet not reach for her. He rubbed his aching head and stared over her shoulder to the wall.

"Why not? She has proof. Legal documents." He snorted derisively. "I'm the right age and there is no denying that there are other similarities—"

"Coincidence!"

He shook his head. "Marie-Claire, don't."

"Sebastian—"

"Marie-Claire, you have to admit there might be a grain of truth to all of this."

"Never!"

"You can't say that. I wouldn't put it past Claudette to have lied to me all these years. Though she is a loving mother, she is basically selfish."

"Exactly! Which is why *she is lying now!*" Marie-Claire moved to stand against him and, with the ornate railing at his back, there was no escaping her touch. She grasped the placket of his shirt and pressed her wet cheek against his chest. Hot tears scalded his flesh and her voice came in muffled bursts. "This cannot be happening."

His arms at his sides, Sebastian stood helplessly as she wept, her body quaking with emotion. Torn and miserable, he did battle with himself and willed her not to cry.

But she did. Pitiful, body-wracking sobs that jarred him to his very soul. She swiped at her tears with the edges of her hands, and tried valiantly to pull herself together, only to have the pain escape again in great gasps of sorrow that echoed throughout the cavernous marble hall.

Sebastian closed his eyes, feeling the lump of lead in his own throat swell to unbearable proportions, cutting off his oxygen, leaving him impossibly weak where she was concerned. He wished he could say something, anything, to take away her agony, but there were no words.

She continued to sob against his chest, clutching his shirt to keep from falling to her knees.

Knowing he must hold her or die, Sebastian circled her waist with his arms and pulled her tight. "Marie-Claire," he murmured into her hair, savoring the taste of her precious name on his lips. "Marie-Claire, please, don't cry, sweetheart."

The endearment seemed to shatter her and she clutched him ever closer.

He ran his hands up her back, filled his hands with her

hair and, cupping her head, tilted her face back, and kissed her mottled cheeks.

"Please, Sebastian." Eyes flashing, she beseeched him. "Don't let this happen. Please believe me when I tell you that Claudette is lying. What mother withholds this kind of information for thirty-two years?"

"What good would this knowledge have done me?"

"Sebastian, she sees opportunity."

"Maybe." He wished he could be completely sure that she was right. But he couldn't. Not yet. Perhaps not ever. "Maybe not. But no matter what the outcome, Marie-Claire, this has put us both in an extremely awkward situation. Especially with the press."

"To hell with the press! I'm sick of the public running my life."

"No, Marie-Claire, think about it from the public's point of view. Lovers, or siblings? Or even worse, *both?* News of our relationship and this birth scandal could cause no end of heartache to everyone involved until we sort out the truth."

Marie-Claire buried her face in his shirt and a keening wail came from deep within her soul. *"No-o."*

He wanted to die.

"Oh, Marie-Claire." He held her tight, cradling her in his arms, rubbing her back and rocking her as he would a small, frightened child. "Marie-Claire, no matter what, I care far too much for you," he swallowed against the grief that burned, "and your father, to ever take a chance on hurting you with this."

"But you are!" She reared back and stared up at him, her gaze imploring. "Sebastian, it's simply not possible that you are my brother! Don't you see? You are a gift from God to me! We were made for each other. We belong together, not as brother and sister, but as husband and wife!"

As much as it tortured him, Sebastian knew it was up to him to be strong. "Marie-Claire, right now, I don't even know who I am."

"I do."

"Tell me."

"The other half of me."

His own words came back to haunt him as she quoted what he'd told her just yesterday. On impulse, Marie-Claire pressed her mouth to his, and for a moment, Sebastian lost all rational thought, his heart tumbling with an avalanche of forbidden desire. Marie-Claire was persistent, pressing his lips open with her own, warming his cheeks with her breath, nipping, tasting, urging.

It was too intense.

"No."

Fearing that he might be losing himself in his sister's kiss, he thrust her roughly away and—heart hammering, breath coming in labored puffs—took several steps down the stairs.

Clutching the balustrade, Marie-Claire sank to her knees.

"We can't do this, Marie-Claire. We can't." Without daring a backward glance, Sebastian left her sobbing at the top of the stairs.

Chapter Seven

It had been twenty-four hours.

Just enough crying time to bruise Marie-Claire's usually peachy complexion and swell her almond-shaped eyes to veritable walnuts. A demonic dance troop had taken up residence in her brain, fox-trotting on her temples and doing the rumba on her eardrums. She knew she needed an aspirin or two, or perhaps—heavy sigh—a dozen, and would have slogged into her bathroom to find some, if she could only be sure she'd live long enough for them to take effect.

Outside her window, a tiny songbird landed on her sill and proceeded to serenade her with its lyrical warble.

"Oh...*shut up!*" she moaned and flopped about in her bed until she located a decorative pillow and flung it at the pane.

Life was over.

She had no reason to go on. She'd lost her one true love and the color had eked from her existence, leaving her emotionally monochromatic.

Black.

White.

And shades of eternal, dismal…

Gray.

A long, unrepressed hiss leaked from between her lips. Her eyes slid shut and she clutched her head as the nightmare of yesterday morning's hideous proclamation revisited. Claudette's shrill voice reverberated in the back of her brain, crying *"He's Philippe's son,"* over and over, and driving Marie-Claire half mad with panic.

After Sebastian had left, she'd sped to her suite, locking herself inside and refusing to eat or drink or speak to anyone, sending family and servant alike away to wonder and worry. She had no desire to eat. To drink. To speak.

Why bother?

Everyone, with the lone exception of herself, had bought into a ridiculous lie. For the love of St. Michel, they need only look at Claudette to see the blessed truth. They were *blood-related.* The town idiot could have figured out that much.

All right, so King Philippe had also had mesmerizing blue eyes and a tiny cleft in the chin.

So what?

And, yes, a little dimple too, and perhaps the same silver-tinged dark hair. And…that resonating vocal timbre that Marie-Claire loved so well in both of them, but that did *not* make him Sebastian's father.

Did it?

No!

"No, no, *no!*" Marie-Claire scraped a knuckle beneath her eyes and pressed her mouth to the satin hem of her blanket. *Sebastian was not her brother!*

They were meant to be lovers. Mates. Parents together. Fate would not be so cruel.

With the speed and dexterity of a three-legged tortoise,

Marie-Claire threw back her covers, dragged herself to a sitting position and surveyed her shocking reflection in the vanity mirror across the room. A poster child for "America's Most Wanted" stared back at her. Her hair stood away from her head like the great, tangled dreads of a shedding golden retriever. Black circles, one part mascara, two parts anguish, circled her red-rimmed eyes and her face appeared to have—she leaned closer and squinted—tire tracks imbedded in her cheeks, no doubt from having been run over by a pack of lies.

Cold and stiff as rigor mortis, Marie-Claire slowly scooted to the edge of her massive canopied bed, and sat for a moment to catch her breath from the exertion.

A knock at the door set the cranial demons to dancing again.

"Go away."

"Marie-Claire, honey, we are concerned. Please. Let us in."

She could hear Lise and Ariane whispering in the hallway.

"Go away." No way was she up for the double dose of sisterly pity that waited.

"We have cinnamon rolls and coffee."

Marie-Claire sat up a little straighter. Then again, some sympathy might be just what the doctor ordered. She stumbled to the door, fiddled with locks and yanked it open.

Her sisters gasped at the grim reaper incarnate standing before them and, with a roll of her bloodshot eyes, Marie-Claire waved them inside and staggered back to bed.

"She looks like Jonah after the whale spewed him out," Ariane observed.

"Should we call the doctor?" Lise wondered.

"Stop talking about me as if I'm not here."

Lise bustled to the window, pushed back the blackout

drapes and threw open the windows to freshen the stale air. Ariane set down a tray, poured Marie-Claire a steaming mug of coffee, then grabbed a brush and sitting down on the bed, began working out her sister's tangles.

"Ouch!"

"Too hot?"

"No, you're tearing my hair out of my head."

"Sorry."

"So." In the shaft of light that now flooded the room, Lise turned and smoothed her hands over her crisp slacks. At only three months pregnant, she still had no need of maternity wear. "It's a broken heart, I see."

Marie-Claire cast a droll look at her sister. "What was your first clue?"

Smiling sadly, Lise joined Ariane and perched at the edge of the bed. "Sometimes it takes an older sister some time to realize that her baby sister is all grown up and capable of such deep emotion."

"I'll say," Ariane groused.

"I'm still waiting for *you* to grow up," Lise retorted.

"I beg your pardon? Just because you're married you seem to think that you can impart advice on all subj—"

"Don't blame my marriage for the fact that you won't mature—"

"Uh… Excuse me?" Marie-Claire stared back and forth between her sisters. "Could we please focus on *my* problems for once?"

Suddenly contrite, they nodded. From Lise, "Of course, Marie-Claire. What can we do to help?"

Jaw set with determination, Marie-Claire puckered her lips and blew at the steam rising from her mug. "I need your best advice on how to win a man's attention."

"Would this man be…" Lise placed a flat palm against her chest and swallowed, "…Sebastian?"

"Duh."

"Our new big brother, Sebastian?" Ariane stared at her agog.

"Yes."

"You want to win the affections of a man that could be...our...our..." As if she were trying to expel an olive pit, Lise pursed her mouth against this assault on her delicate sensibilities. "...*brother?* Marie-Claire, honey, that's just plain—"

"Gross!" Ariane supplied.

"He's *not our brother!*"

"You can't know that for sure," Lise told her.

"Yes! I do!"

"How?"

"Gut instinct, sixth sense, I don't know! Women's intuition! Call it what you will." With her free hand, Marie-Claire gripped the rails at the end of her bed and hauled herself to her knees, tilting her mug at a dangerous angle. Animation chased the fatigue from her features. "Watch his mother's eyes when she talks about adopting him from Katie. A mother's eyes cannot lie. Sebastian is her birth son."

"But what reason could Claudette possibly have for saying he's her adopted son?"

Marie-Claire snorted. "Hello? Crown prince?" Wild gesticulations sent her coffee sloshing over her hands. "Oww." She set the mug back on the tray and sucked the suddenly rising welt on her thumb. "I think Claudette sees herself as some kind of step-dowager-mum-person. I bet she's got her tiara all picked out and everything."

"But Marie-Claire, surely Sebastian can see that she is lying?" Ariane said.

"I think he does."

"Then why is he going along with her?"

"Think, Ariane! She has planted a seed of doubt in everyone. If there is even the remotest possibility that he is my half brother, he knows that our relationship could ruin us both. He would step away from me, even if he knew Claudette was lying, just to protect me."

Lise and Ariane gave this angle some serious consideration and Lise admitted, "I've seen Claudette from time to time down at the country club with her cronies. She *is* a bit of a name dropper."

Ariane said, "And Sebastian shares her startlingly blue eyes. A different hue, really, than Papa's were."

"Now that you mention it, I do see a certain familial resemblance between Sebastian and Claudette."

"It's about time," Marie-Claire groused.

"And it is quite odd that she would wait until now to unveil Sebastian as Papa's son. Why wouldn't she have told him all this before, if it were really true?" Lise stared out the window, pondering.

"Opportunity. Before now, there was none." Marie-Claire's head swiveled back and forth between her sisters. They were beginning to see the light. Even so, Lise was ever practical.

"But what if you are wrong?"

"*I'm not!* Will you trust me on this? Sebastian is no more a member of this family than…than…" she pointed to Lise, "Wilhelm!"

"True." Lise's tone was dry.

"Sorry, honey, I didn't mean it that way."

"I know."

"Anyway, Claudette is up to no good. Don't ask me how I know, I just do. She's the type who will say anything to get what she wants. And she wants power."

"Prestige." Ariane agreed.

"Position." Lise agreed, too.

"We can't let her get away with this. I have to do something. Now! And I need your help. She is ruining my life. And Sebastian's."

"You are really very much in love." Lise reached out and lightly stroked Marie-Claire's hand. A poignant look of longing flashed behind her eyes and was gone.

"Yes."

"Then you cannot chance losing it."

"No," Marie-Claire whispered, aching for her older sister. It would seem that Lise's love life would be next on their "to-fix" list.

Marie-Claire studied her sisters and could tell that they were finally on board and believed, as she did, that Claudette was double-dealing her son's history for personal gain. Gratitude for them both welled, prodding a bubble of joy to rise in her chest. Besides, they both knew that once she set her sights on something, it was far easier to join in on her wacky schemes than to try and beat them.

"I'll help," Lise said on a sigh.

"Me, too."

"Okay." For the first time in twenty-four hours, Marie-Claire grinned. She crawled to the nightstand and found a pad of paper and a pen in the drawer. "You guys talk, I'll take notes. Lise, you have a man. You go first."

A slight grimace graced Lise's face. Marie-Claire darted a concerned peek at Ariane who returned it with one of her own. Even the news of her pregnancy hadn't seemed to draw Wilhelm any closer to his wife.

They watched as Lise tapped her chin with a forefinger and blinked away her melancholy. "Uh…well, I should try to make myself as desirable as possible, I guess."

Marie-Claire began writing. "Desirable. Check." She rubbed the end of the pen against her lower lip. "How?"

Lise wrinkled her nose. "I'd begin by taking a bath."

"Funny. What else?"

"A makeover might be fun. Distracting if nothing else. Why don't we make a day of it, sometime? In Paris? New hair, the latest clothes, the works. For all of us." She looked eager and not just for Marie-Claire's sake.

"Hmm. Yes. That's good. Okay. Makeover. Check. If I can get appointments for tomorrow, you're saying that you'll both go with me?"

Lise lifted a dainty shoulder. "I'd love to. Wilhelm is out of town again and I have nothing better to do."

Again, Marie-Claire and Ariane exchanged worried glances.

Ariane said, "I can go. I need to go shopping anyway. I'm planning a little vacation and I've already made a list. Count me in."

"Okay. Where are you off to?" Marie-Claire asked as she made herself a note to call the hairdresser. When Ariane didn't immediately answer, she looked up. "Ariane?"

Ariane gave an artless shrug. "Rhineland."

"*Rhineland?*" Ever maternal, Lise clutched her bosom. "Whatever for?"

"I've been invited."

Marie-Claire stared. "By whom?"

"Etienne."

"*Etienne?*" Lise gasped.

"Prince Etienne Kroninberg of Rhineland, *that* Etienne?" Marie-Claire blinked. "Etienne the enemy?"

Ariane nodded.

"Are you *insane?*"

"No more so than you."

"Touché." Smile wry, Marie-Claire asked, "When are you going?"

"I'm leaving Sunday morning."

"Sunday? But this is already Friday. Why so soon?"

Marie-Claire and Lise watched their sister color.

"I prefer not to discuss it yet."

Marie-Claire glanced at Lise and whispered, "She prefers not to discuss it."

"We are chopped liver."

"I spill my guts to her about my innermost thoughts and feelings, yet she prefers not to discuss hers."

"We can't be trusted."

"Will you both put a lid on it?" Ariane's mouth quirked in annoyance.

"Sure." Marie-Claire feigned a deep emotional wound. "We don't care what you are doing with Etienne."

"Not in the least." Lise also pouted.

"Good."

"Great. Now then. Ariane, since you will be eloping this week with Etienne, what about some advice from you?"

"I'm not eloping!"

"Whatever."

Ariane rested the brush in her lap and tugged at some of the golden strands caught in the bristles. "I don't know. Why don't you ask Sebastian?"

Mouth twisted in disbelief, Marie-Claire cocked her head. As she spoke, sarcasm oozed. "Oh, that's brilliant."

"I'm serious." There was a gleam of mischief in Ariane's eye. "Treat him like a brother. That's what he says he wants, isn't it? If it were me, I'd confide all my juicy secrets in my 'big brother.' Ask his advice on things like dating and what men look for in a woman and what kind of perfume they prefer and where you might find a new boyfriend—"

For a contemplative moment, Marie-Claire stared at her sister, digesting, and then fell back on the bed and her gleeful hoot bounced off the high ceiling. "Oh, Ariane, that *is* brilliant!"

"Take note then, as I have a number of ideas for you."

* * *

Sebastian pulled his Peugeot into his usual spot at the de Bergeron Palace and set the brake. He considered removing his sunglasses, but then thought better of it. The dark circles beneath his eyes were a testament to his sleepless night. This morning, he'd added a lifetime of church and repentance to his "to-do" list because if hell was even half as bad as this last twenty-four hours, he wanted no part of it.

He'd heard through her sisters that Marie-Claire had sequestered herself, refusing to eat or drink or speak to anyone and that had him worried. That, and the fact that she'd ignored his countless phone calls of apology for the way she'd discovered the shocking truth.

Or the shocking pack of lies.

He unfastened his safety belt and stared up through his tinted windshield at her window. Just as soon as he'd attended the emergency meeting that Simone had called this morning—to put a plan of action together for future announcements and to come up with a politically correct spin on his somewhat mystifying ascension to the crown—Sebastian planned on forcing Marie-Claire to answer her door.

Whether she wanted to or not, they eventually had to talk. To figure out their game plan, when it came to talking to the press. When it came to treating each other with careful dignity whenever they were in the public eye together. When it came to surviving the black cloud of devastation that seemed to have settled in his gut and left him feeling like a walking corpse.

He knew she felt the same way.

Maybe, somehow, they could bring some measure of comfort to each other. Sebastian groaned and propped his elbows on his steering wheel and wondered when he'd taken this left turn into eternal damnation.

The sound of voices had him opening an eye and peering out of his tortured reverie.

Two parking spots down, Luc Dumont had just arrived and was greeting the shy Juliet, Philippe's stepdaughter. She looked to be on her way out to run errands. They were smiling and laughing and conversing, as if the very sun hadn't been snuffed out only hours ago.

Sebastian scowled.

Didn't they realize that this dump of a planet had stopped revolving? Bring on the global warming. Use aerosol cans. Stop recycling. Buy a box of Blubber Helper and have the whales for lunch. Why not? Nothing mattered anymore.

Nothing.

Sebastian disembarked and trudged toward the guest entry to check in. Behind him, his car squawked as he shot the locks with his remote. With a brief nod and an exhausted grunt, he acknowledged both Luc and Juliet and absently wondered how the bookish Juliet knew Luc. He could feel them watching him as he moved and decided he'd better get used to it.

Very soon, the world would be watching every move he made.

Marie-Claire watched Sebastian get out of his car from behind the curtains where she sat perched on her bedroom's window seat. At the sight of his handsome face, her heart went into a free fall. Craning her neck, she followed his rangy stride with her eyes, drinking in the sight, memorizing the little details; the way the sun mellowed his usually coffee mane to a deep honey color, the fluid animal-like way of his gait, the blatant masculinity he so unconsciously exuded, the powerful self-possession that made people stop and stare.

As Luc and Juliet were now.

Cheek resting on the back of her hand, Marie-Claire's thoughts traveled back to that morning after her sisters had left so that she could dress. That she hadn't mustered the wherewithal to pick out an outfit was beside the point.

Within moments of Lise and Ariane's departure, she'd overheard Francie, Ariane's gossip-mongering, addle-brained, man-eating—and these were her better qualities—lady-in-waiting, out in the hall regaling several of the chambermaids in a most conspiratorial, ''in-the-know'' tone, with big news.

''—and a press conference has been called here at the palace for tomorrow night. They say it's to calm fears that Rhineland is on the verge of overtaking St. Michel. But, I think the *real* reason is to cover up a big secret.''

''What?'' The breathless chambermaids were hanging on Francie's every word.

''Promise you won't say anything to anyone?''

Marie-Claire rolled her eyes.

''We promise. Yes, of course.''

''Well, all right. You know I'm dating one of Simone's security guards? Well, *he* said that *Sebastian LeMarc* is…*Philippe's son!*''

A guttural groan welled in Marie-Claire's throat. With Francie on the job the news would spread like greased fire.

''*And,*'' Francie gushed, ''I'm also dating the son of Simone's personal assistant, and *he* says, until they can figure out how to tell the world, they are using the Rhineland take-over thing as a distraction to keep the paparazzi away. Can you believe it? Sebastian LeMarc as…'' the harebrained Francie paused for dramatic effect, then shrieked, ''*the crown prince!*''

''*Eeeeee!*'' The high pitch of their cries surely had St. Michel's canine set yowling in harmony.

''*Isn't he fabulous?*''

Just beyond her door, Marie-Claire heard the ecstatic cavorting of happy feet.

She was going to be sick.

Nevertheless, she couldn't seem to tear herself away from this morbid fascination she had with learning more of Sebastian's future.

Francie was only too delighted to fill in the missing details. "Plus, another man I am dating from the kitchen crew—"

Marie-Claire stared in wonder at the door. Was there anyone on the staff that Francie was *not* dating?

"—*he* says that this morning, Simone is meeting with her secretary, a slew of press and political advisors, the prime minister, Rene Davoine, and *Sebastian LeMarc*—"

"*Eeeeee!*" the groupie maids couldn't contain their glee. "George Clooney's better-looking little brother will be living *here,*" one of them screeched.

"Yes! And," the man-hungry Francie went on, "they've hired Luc Dumont, some cute guy from St. Michel security who I'd like to get my hands on. Is this the most exciting thing to hit St. Michel in years, or what?"

"*Eeeeee!*"

"There will be a big party in the Crystal Ballroom immediately following tomorrow night's press conference, to celebrate St. Michel's continued independence from Rhineland. Everyone who's anyone will be there."

Their hysterical hubbub told Marie-Claire that they all hoped to be called upon to work this party, as it was sure to go down in history as St. Michel's finest hour. Marie-Claire's head thunked against the door, scattering the magpies in the hall.

It had taken her several hours and a half bottle of antacid to recover from that blow.

The double squawk of Sebastian's Peugeot locking

snapped Marie-Claire from her morose ruminations and back to the present.

This "pre-press conference" meeting, she decided, must be the reason he was there. A raw yearning filled her belly as she watched him nod at Juliet, and then disappear into the palace.

Her gaze drifted back to her reserved stepsister, and Marie-Claire briefly wondered what she had to chat about with that guy from security. Marie-Claire knew that Juliet was spending some time comforting their young half sister, Jacqueline. But beyond that…a twinge of guilt niggled because of what she didn't know about Juliet. Really, the woman was so shy and bookish, one scarcely noticed whether she was present or not.

Marie-Claire watched as Luc handed her stepsister into her car, closed her door, then leaned against it and continued to visit through the open window.

Hmm.

Luc hadn't seemed convinced that Claudette was telling the truth yesterday, either. With a thumbnail, Marie-Claire rubbed the edge of her lip. Perhaps she should meet with him, and compare notes.

Perhaps Juliet could introduce them.

Marie-Claire's eyes narrowed. Was he probing Juliet for information? Or was he flirting? Marie-Claire couldn't imagine Juliet flirting with anyone, let alone a sophisticated, rather mature guy like Luc Dumont. She couldn't help but feel a little bit sorry for Juliet, and hoped that she didn't go and do something stupid like fall in love with an older man.

A handsome older man.

A handsome older man who might turn out to be some damned member of the family…

With a grimace, Marie-Claire pushed off the window seat and back onto the floor where she'd been sprawled all afternoon doing "homework" of sorts. Armed with a pile of pillows, a bowl of popcorn, a pitcher of lemonade, a stack of fashion magazines, library books, genealogy websites, nail polish, cotton balls, a television remote control and a notepad and pen, she'd been digging like an archeology student during dead week.

And it was hard work, this. She'd already spent some time on the Internet, reviewing what she could find of Claudette's history, researching the subject of pathological liars—Claudette fit the profile to a T—and trying to find something, anything on a woman named Katie Graham who'd fallen in love with her father, thirty-three years ago.

Since she'd run into some dead ends, she decided to change tack and concentrate on her quest to help Sebastian see that she was the woman for him.

Aiming the remote, she turned the sound back up on the television. As far as she was concerned, the Americans cornered the market on pushy sexuality. At Ariane's prompting, she'd begun her studies with American TV that very morning and would branch out to other cultures, once she got some answers.

So far, she'd flipped through several hundred cable networks making notes here and there, and she had just now landed on *The Jerry Springer Show*. Leaning forward, she peered at the screen to decipher today's topic. A jolt of excitement skittered down her spine as she realized that— oddly enough—the subject was: Men who have married their cousins, and the women who love them.

Microphone in hand, Jerry spun to face his first guest, a Mrs. Lula Parnell, twenty-eight-year-old mother of seven. Marie-Claire stared at the poor thing in astonishment. Gracious sakes, the woman looked *eighty*-eight.

Jerry glanced at his note cards and then affected a sympathetic expression. "Lula, you married your first cousin,

Junior Parnell, when you were thirteen years of age. Is that correct?''

"Yessiree. Thirteen and a half, actually. He was full-growed, though, and already out of the fifth grade."

"Together, you and Junior have seven children?''

"And a little bun in the oven." Lula gave her tummy a maternal pat.

"Junior is unaware that you are pregnant?''

"He's gonna find out right here, on your show."

"Yes. Junior is waiting backstage with his current wife and stepsister, Ona.''

The veins in Lula's neck suddenly bulged. "Yessir. That *bleeeep* stole my *bleeeeping* man from me and when I get my hands on that *bleeping bleep,* I'll *bleep* her *bleeping bleep* until she can't tell her *bleepity bleep* from a gopher hole!''

Marie-Claire frowned. These sound effects made it difficult to keep up, but the gist of the matter was clear. Lula was upset with Ona.

Jerry arched a brow at the camera. "Let's bring out Ona.''

The audience hissed and jeered as the twenty-one-year-old Ona pranced out, looking three or four times her own age, but decidedly fighting the aging process kicking and screaming. Her leather bustier was two sizes too tight, squeezing her generous cleavage out the top.

And bottom.

Her nails were several inches long and festooned with racecars and tobacco slogans. Her wild hair was as brash as her makeup and her spiky heels had her towering over Lula. She shook her fist in a menacing fashion at the audience and then made a gesture to Lula that Marie-Claire figured had a more regional significance.

Nostrils flared, Lula lunged at Ona and Jerry smiled serenely at the camera. "Don't go away. We'll be right back with Junior, after these important messages."

Marie-Claire slowly nodded. Clearly, she needed to toughen up, if she was going to fight for her man. Perhaps she should practice her pithy expletives as well. A Tae-Bo class wouldn't hurt either, if Lula's high-kickin' style meant anything. And definitely she needed to reexamine her choices in clothing. She considered her wardrobe and realized she was far too conservative. Marie-Claire furiously scribbled some notes on her pad. Get in shape. Outrageous clothes.

Okay. Tongue protruding, she flipped through the channels till she landed on *The Ricki Lake Show.*

"Ricki, we used to think that men were from Mars and women were from Venus." The guest author gave her head a smug little wobble. "Wrong."

"Wrong?" Ricki leaned forward and frowned.

"Yes. We now know that men are really from Uranus."

"You're kidding."

"I know, it sounds far-fetched, but the key to success in a relationship with any man is knowing that *Real Men Are From Uranus.*" The expert held up her new book and smiled.

Marie-Claire stuffed a handful of popcorn into her mouth. Uranus? Which one was that? She should have paid more attention in astronomy, she decided as she scribbled, find copy of *Real Men Are From Uranus* in palace library.

Pointing the remote, she next landed on *The Sally-Jesse Raphael Show.*

"Marsha," Sally-Jesse adjusted her signature glasses, "you realize that by not telling your son that he was adopted until he was a teenager, you were risking alienating him emotionally?"

"Sally, there just didn't seem to be any reason."

"Yes, but Marsha, clearly you and your husband are Caucasian. Chuck is African-American. Surely, you knew that someone would eventually let the cat out of the bag."

Marie-Claire scribbled, lies about adoption lead to alienation and again pointed the remote to pause at CNN.

"And in other international news, government officials in Rhineland today announced that they are making plans to reabsorb St. Michel, a tiny province just north of France. The two countries have existed independently from one another since the seventeenth century. A crucial water route leading from inland ports to the North Sea has been the subject of contention for years, more so now that St. Michel has recently upped the usage tax. In a statement made earlier today, St. Michel's Prime Minister Rene Davoine revealed that he has not met with Rhineland's Prince Etienne Kroninberg on this matter and has no immediate plans to do so. In other news…"

Marie-Claire snapped off the TV, feeling that she'd reached saturation with this venue and picked up a magazine. She peered at the cover she held. Why, in no time at all, according to this, she'd be ten pounds lighter and have her man eating out of her hand.

A sudden and loud pounding woke Marie-Claire with a start. Confused, she peeled her face from the shiny cover of the magazine upon which she'd been napping and blinked at her door.

"Marie-Claire?"

Sebastian! Flustered, she rolled over, rubbed her eyes and pushed her hair out of her face. A glance into the bottom of a full-length wall mirror told her everything she needed to know. Bad hair. Bad face. Bad mood.

Bad timing.

"Uh, who is it?" She hoped she sounded breezy. Cool.

Indifferent. Not as if she'd just been snoring and drooling on the cover of *Glamour*.

"It's me, Sebastian."

"Who?" Like a dog chasing its tail, Marie-Claire crawled in tight circles and wondered what to do first. What on earth was he doing here? He couldn't be here. She wasn't ready. She hadn't done all of her homework. Her order from Victoria's Secret had yet to arrive. And she still hadn't gotten through to Dr. Laura.

Okay, think.

She had to change her clothes. What would Ona wear? Certainly not the flouncy pink baby dolls that she sported now. No, Ona would wear something tight. Something made of leather and sheet metal screws. And she'd carry a whip.

"C'mon, Marie-Claire. Open up."

Up on her haunches, she gave her cheeks a couple of bracing smacks and glanced around the room. It looked as if a rebel faction bent on mass destruction had visited; self-help materials, books on adoption and genealogy and half-tested beauty products littered every spare area.

He could not come in here. No way.

Hands forming a plow, she shoved the mountain of magazines she'd been highlighting under her bed. Then, breathing hard, she clutched her comforter and attempted to haul herself to her feet. Unfortunately, the comforter came undocked and Marie-Claire fell back, pulling the great, downy monster over her head, where she grappled about, searching for terra firma. All nature of library books slid to the floor, along with some spicy lingerie catalogs and a volume on the history of the polygraph test.

"Marie-Claire, may I come in?"

Marie-Claire froze. Was that her door opening? He sounded awfully near.

The door closed and the sound of Sebastian's footsteps came from inside the room.

Chapter Eight

Rats. This was *not* the picture of sophistication she'd planned on exuding the next time she and Sebastian met. Static electricity had her hair standing on end as Marie-Claire peeked out from under the comforter. His shoes came into view first and she noted with chagrin that he was standing on a book whose title blared, *Combat Love*.

Her gaze traveled up his powerful legs, over his barrel chest and to his face. She saw thankfully that he was looking at her and not the book. Blood rushed up her neck and flooded her cheeks. Her heart pounded and she began to sweat.

She couldn't let him see that idiotic book.

"What are you doing?" he asked.

Her mind raced back to the vast sea of information and advice she'd collected over the last hours and came to a screeching halt at Ariane's pearl of wisdom. *Treat him like a brother. Isn't that what he wants? Do all the things a kid sister would do with a big brother.*

With a defiant toss of her head, she stared up at him,

nostrils flaring. "Me? Well, since you're here, I was hoping we might, uh," she cast a panicky glance at the book beneath his feet, "wrestle."

She bit back a mortified groan.

Could she *be* any more idiotic? Her eyes slid closed at the image of her and Sebastian going for it, right there in the middle of her room, thumping and hollering and whatever it was kid brothers and sisters did when they were horsing around.

He gave his temple a quizzical scratch. "Wrestle?"

"Sure." She could tell he thought she was nuts. Oh well, better nuts than a sobbing jilted lily, she guessed. "Like this." Charging at him, headfirst, she collided with his shins, knocking him off balance and giving herself a dilly of a headache in the process.

"Owww." Their protests harmonized. She was going to kill Ariane.

As he fell to his knees, Marie-Claire launched the incriminating *Combat Love* book into her closet with a move she'd learned in soccer camp, back when she really was eight.

He stared at her, the disbelief in his voice warring with irritation. "Are you crazy?"

Yes. Crazy in love. With a grunt, Marie-Claire clutched him around the thighs and tugged him completely off balance. They rolled around on the floor, Sebastian with bewilderment and Marie-Claire with purpose. Feet frantically scrambling, she winged the lingerie catalogs, along with a copy of a wedding magazine under her bed with the rest. Sebastian caught an errant fist in the process.

"What the hell? Owww! Marie-Claire, dammit, what are you doing? I don't want to wrestle with you."

"What's wrong, pretty boy? Afraid I'll win?" Elbowing her way over the top of his chest, she flailed about until she could flip her extremely private journal and a well-padded

WonderBra beneath her armoire. In this rather enjoyable
process of tidying up, she accidentally managed to knee him
in the jaw. The sound of his teeth crashing together gave
her a twinge of sympathy, but really, she hadn't invited him
to come snooping.

"Ouch! Damn! Auughh!" One hand flew to his jaw, the
other to her ankle. "I think I just broke a tooth!"

"If you are very good, maybe the tooth fairy will leave
some money under your pillow tonight."

An ominous growl suddenly had Marie-Claire question-
ing Ariane's logic. Perhaps this kid-sister thing was the
wrong tack. Before she could ponder the issue further, Sebastian yanked her by the leg and she found herself flipped
onto her back and lying beneath his body. After some heavy
breathing and a lot of struggle, he managed to pinion her
wrists together over her head. Her flouncy pink baby doll
had tangled around her waist in a most provocative manner.

"I don't think this is a legal wrestling move." Marie-
Claire grunted, wriggling about, trying to escape just far
enough to pull her pajamas back down where they belonged.

"Tough," he growled and locked his feet around hers.
Noses just a thumb's-width apart, he stared at her, and
Marie-Claire could feel his lungs laboring and his heart
pounding in tandem with hers. Their breath mingled, and
Marie-Claire felt a yearning envelop her, nearly rendering
her unconscious.

"Marie-Claire, why are you doing this?"

Hoping and praying she appeared casual, she breezed,
"Isn't this what brothers and sisters do? I'm just trying to
feel my way into our new relationship." Eyes wide with
innocence, she blinked up at him.

He dropped his head. "Marie-Claire, you are making this
very hard for me."

"Oh, and it's a walk in the park for me."

"I didn't say that."

"No, but you expect me to shift gears from lover to sister in less than a day. I'm trying to work with you here," she lied.

Misery flashed behind his eyes, and, though she felt for him, she took this as a good sign. He was no more ready to accept her as a sister than she was to receive him as a brother. Steeling herself against the powerful urge to give the poor guy a break, she gritted her teeth and continued her course.

"We have years of wrestling and jumping on the bed and tickling to make up for. Personally, I think we should do it all. It might bond us as siblings."

Aggravation pulled his mouth into a more severe curve and his eyes narrowed to slits of fury. "I don't think getting anywhere near the bed would be such a good idea." The frustration and impatience with her goading was palpable.

Her breathing became thready. Shallow.

He shifted, bringing his body into contact with hers from ankle to fingertip and Marie-Claire suddenly stilled as she realized that she now had him exactly where she wanted him. Even so, it was a hollow victory.

Come on, she silently urged him. You know the truth. We are not related.

"Okay." She gave a little shrug and angling her head so that her lips nearly touched his, she whispered, "Forget wrestling. How about a pillow fight instead?"

"How about a spanking?"

"Fine. I'll get the spoon. You drop your drawers." All right, she had to admit the bratty sister routine had gone too far. She needed to extend an olive branch, but it was hard to come up with the words with him looking at her as though he'd like to throttle her and then kiss her senseless.

Their eyes locked and attraction grew until the air between them seemed to crackle and burn. Marie-Claire could see that he was battling a fascination he found taboo. Forbidden.

Abruptly, he rolled onto his side and sat up. "I have to get back to the meeting." Tossing the comforter aside, he gripped her bedpost, hauled himself to his feet and stalked across the room.

She knee-walked after him. "Sebastian, wait!"

Head falling back on his shoulders, he paused in her doorway.

"Can you do this?" She rolled her tongue into the shape of a taco shell.

He turned and stared. "Marie-Claire, I don't know what you are—"

"Just do it!" she shouted.

Sebastian heaved a sigh of disgust and stuck his tongue out. However, try as he might, it lay there like a pink potato.

Marie-Claire grinned excitedly. "You're not my brother!"

"What?"

"You can't roll your tongue."

"What the hell does that have to do with anything?"

"It proves you are not related to me." Marie-Claire leveled an accusatory finger at him and fairly vibrated with victory. "The ability to roll your tongue is inherited!"

Sebastian's gaze darted at the ceiling for an instant, and then settled back on her face. "From whom? Your mother or your father?"

Marie-Claire frowned. "What?"

"When you are ready to grow up, we'll talk." The heavy slam of the door reverberated for a full minute after he left.

So. Marie-Claire flagged. Ariane's plan hadn't worked as quickly as she'd hoped. But she had sensed a chink in his armor. It was simply a matter of finding it.

* * *

With a resounding crack, Sebastian's club made contact with the ball. He watched, head back, eyes slit, as the golf ball took flight against the deep azure sky. If nothing else, this new twist in his relationship with Marie-Claire was improving his game. Straight as a builder's plumb line, the tiny white missile arced down the fairway. He picked up his tee, loaded his club, shouldered his bag and headed after his ball.

Golfing alone had never been Sebastian's style, but the last thing he wanted this afternoon was company.

He needed to think.

Marie-Claire had launched a deliberate offensive strike against his moratorium on their romance. She was doing everything in her power to thwart his stalwart efforts to protect her. To protect herself. From him. From the press. And, if she thought he couldn't see through these half-baked efforts, she had another think coming.

He felt a slow grin begin in his gut and spread up into his face as he remembered her antics earlier that day. Man, she was nuts. And that was precisely why he loved her. He shook his head, thinking a lesser woman would be content to give up the fight. To wallow in self-pity.

But not Marie-Claire de Bergeron.

No, Marie-Claire would lasso her man and flip him to the ground in record rodeo time. He laughed out loud, loving her more for loving him so fiercely. As his feet carried him across the grass, he remembered the teenaged banshee he'd first seen diving headlong into the pond. Then and there he'd known that he needed a woman with her pluck as his life partner. He'd never be content with a milquetoast type who had no fire in her belly.

On the other hand, she was causing a bit of a fire in his own guts, for heartburn was becoming a way of life these days. The very reasons he loved her beyond rational thought were the reasons she was driving him mad. Marie-Claire was trying to make him see why they should weather this conflagration together. Yet, he knew from years of experience that to do so would only put them further under the scrutiny of the public eye.

For now, he had to make her see that they couldn't be together.

Yet Sebastian knew that Marie-Claire was not out of wacky schemes. He rubbed the grin on his lips with his fingertips. The idea challenged him. Excited him. Made him feel like a player in the great game of life.

He slowed, then stopped. Clanking, his bag fell from his shoulder to the grass. Five iron in hand, he rocketed off another beauty. Yes, if he was going to win at the game of life with Marie-Claire, he was going to have to stay alert.

That evening, still sequestered in her room, Marie-Claire continued to study, though she was a bleary-eyed, emotional wreck from her skirmish with Sebastian. Gathering her hair and pushing it over her shoulder, she cast a tired glance around at the mess on her bedspread. There was so much advice. And so much of it was conflicting. Beside her lay a stack of yellow pads, filled with notes she'd compiled. Last on her list of self-imposed homework assignments for today was searching the Internet for newspaper advice columns that dealt with situations like hers.

Her head ached as she shifted her gaze onto the screen of her laptop. When she'd finished she would call Sebastian, apologize profusely, and then set the second part of her plan into motion.

Mouse in hand, she clicked and scanned and finally came upon a letter to Dr. Martha. Marie-Claire knew she'd find solid answers to difficult questions in her famous column.

Dear Dr. Martha:

My boyfriend of six years has suddenly decided that we need a break. Martha, I don't want a break. I'm desperately in love with him and hoping that someday soon, we'll marry. I know he loves me too, but something has him spooked. Any advice? I'll do whatever you say as I'm at my wit's end.

Signed,
Heartbroken in Hoboken

Empathy welled in Marie-Claire's throat as she plucked the last tissues from her second box of the day.

"Oh, Hoboken," she murmured into the screen of her laptop. "I know exactly how you feel." She scanned Dr. Martha's answer and realized that the general consensus from most experts seemed to come from the old adage: If you love someone, let him go. If it was meant to be, he will come back to you. If not, you're better off without him.

Better off without Sebastian?

No, she wouldn't be better off without him, but she'd never know if he was truly hers until she let go.

Or, at least until she gave the appearance of letting go.

She reached for the phone and punched in Sebastian's cell number. If she was going to apologize and then set him free, she had to do it now, before she lost her nerve. Waiting just one more minute would thwart all of her hard work and have her groveling at his stoop before sundown, begging him to come back the Lula Parnell way. And that was hardly attractive. Why did life have to be so bloody hard? She was a princess, for heaven's sake. Shouldn't she be living happily ever after just about now?

He picked up on the first ring.

"Sebastian?"

"Marie-Claire?" He sounded tentative. And thrilled. Tentatively thrilled, she guessed. Like her.

"Yes." The word sounded gushy. She cleared her throat. She closed her eyes. She needed to sound emotionally in control. A powerful woman, in charge of her destiny.

With her free hand, she clutched her teddy bear.

"The, uh, reason I'm calling is…" Why exactly was she calling? Oh, yes. To set him free. But then, hadn't he already taken care of that by setting himself free? Oh, this was so confusing. If one set oneself free, would one eventually come back?

"Marie-Claire?"

"I'm here. Sorry, I uh… Okay. I…I've had some time to think it over and I just wanted to tell you, that I think you're right."

"Right?"

"Yes. Absolutely right."

There was a silence on his end.

"Sebastian?"

"Yes, I'm…here."

"Oh. Good. Now then. I also wanted to apologize for my idiotic behavior this afternoon, and to beg your forgiveness. After all, if you are going to be my," the bile rose at the very word, "brother, we will be seeing a lot of each other, around the house, at parties, at our…" she choked, then continued with strangled gaiety, "respective weddings and such."

"Marie-Claire, if you would just—"

"No, no, no. Please. Just let me finish. I wanted to let you know, that it's taken some time, but I've come around to the idea that we are…uh…siblings…and I embrace it. Really. In the most mature sense of our…relationship. For Papa's sake. For your sake."

For heaven's sake, she thought, feeling the panic rise. This had sure as hell better work.

"So," she continued brightly, "I promise to make you proud. You don't have to worry about me...er...fawning after you anymore—"

"I don't?"

"No, no," Marie-Claire hastened to assure. "I realize that none of this is our fault. We couldn't have known. And, so, the best thing would be to...to...to...to...carry on as if nothing had ever happened."

"Nothing? Marie-Claire, for pity sa—"

"Right. To become just one big, happy family. It's for the best. And...and...and...I think that we should—" again, a surge of stomach bile threatened to choke her. She took a cleansing breath and was glad she was lying down. "—I think that we should begin dating other people as soon as possible. For appearances' sake, wouldn't you agree?"

"For...appearances' sake?"

"I'm sure it's the only way. For me, anyway. I need to get you out of my system. Now. And the best way I can think of would be to move on."

Silence.

"Sebastian?"

"You want to move on?"

"Yes."

"So soon?"

"I must. I can't take this stress anymore. It's not like I can sit around and wait for the opportunity to marry my own brother, now, can I?"

"You know damn good and well that's not what I want—"

"That's...that's wonderful. In that case, you won't mind if I bring a date upon occasion to the dinner table. For the sake of appearances, of course."

He snorted. "Of course."

"And, to further my emotional healing, I thought I might start by inviting a date to accompany me to the press conference party tomorrow night."

"Marie-Claire, you do what you have to do."

Was that the tiniest trace of a smirk in his voice? Did he think she was bluffing? Well, she most certainly wasn't. Irked at his arrogance, she said, "Okay. I will."

"You do that."

"Fine."

"Fine."

"Good-bye."

"Good-bye." Marie-Claire hung up then slapped her forehead so hard she saw stars. Oh, great. Now she had to come up with a date. A quick glance at the clock told her that she had less than twenty-four hours to achieve that particular lunacy.

"I don't know why they didn't announce *you* as crown prince during that ridiculous excuse for a press conference today." Expression sour, Claudette fussed at her reflection in a giant gilt-framed mirror that hung just outside the Sapphire Salon in the de Bergeron Palace. It took a number of amazing facial gyrations to get her lipstick and mascara just so, while Sebastian stood impatiently by. "All this inane chatter about Rhineland plotting against us," she muttered, "when we know the only story worth telling is the fact that my son will soon be king!"

Myriad cosmetics were snapped shut and tossed into her bag and with a flutter of her lashes, Claudette declared herself ready. Not wanting to give her time to linger before the mirror, Sebastian took her arm and led her into the crowd that streamed toward the Celebration of Independence Gala that was to begin momentarily in the Crystal Ballroom.

For the last hour, Claudette and Sebastian had been honored guests at the Saturday afternoon press conference, sharing box seats with the royal family in the spacious auditorium designed for just such events. Prime Minister Rene Davoine spoke at length about plans to negotiate with Rhineland to circumvent a crisis situation between the two countries over water rights.

Embarrassingly, Claudette had nodded off during part of the speech and even managed to time her snores during the dramatic pauses. The titters of the audience had jolted her awake and she'd laughed with the crowd about a joke that was upon herself.

And that was only the beginning of this miserable night, Sebastian feared. This was a ''game face'' party, designed to prove to Rhineland that they were not quaking in their boots about the threats being handed down. Though Sebastian was not attending in an official capacity, he knew he was being ''test-driven'' by Simone. She wanted to see if he had what it took to be king someday.

Although, according to the laws that made this a male monarchy, if he was indeed Philippe's son, he already had the stuff it took.

Stomach churning, Sebastian continued his grip on Claudette's arm and marched stoically toward what would no doubt be one of the most trying nights of his life. That Claudette had been invited to attend had his head throbbing and his eye twitching. But the knowledge that Marie-Claire would be there, with a date no less, made him want to beat up one of the statues standing poised for battle in the gargantuan hall.

Puffing to keep pace with Sebastian's lengthy stride, Claudette was still clucking like the snubbed hen. ''A word from Simone, introducing you to the world, wouldn't have killed her. In fact, it would have put Rhineland and its king, that disgusting, impotent Giraud Kroninberg in his proper place, if that's what they really wanted to do. I don't know what they're waiting for.''

Sebastian turned down a deserted side hall and swung on Claudette. Hand-to-wall, nose-to-nose, he hovered over her. ''They are waiting to find out if your version of history is true.''

Claudette gaped at him, expression wounded. ''Why would they even question my word?''

''You tell me.''

''I will not! Don't be ridiculous. St. Michel is in desperate need of a king and you are the man for the job. Who better suited than you?''

''No one,'' Sebastian hissed and raked his hands through his hair as he checked around for the ever-curious paparazzi, ''—*if* I was born to the job. But you'll have to forgive me, Mère, if I'm a little reticent about taking the position. I have never aspired to be the crown prince of this country, let alone king. I still have no desire whatsoever to fill Philippe's shoes. Especially since you waited until the eleventh hour to tell anyone the supposed truth.''

''What are you *saying?*'' Claudette asked, horror-stricken. ''You would pass up a once-in-a-lifetime opportunity because you don't *feel* like taking the job? I have moved heaven and earth to get you to the point you are today and you are going to throw it all away? I'll not have it!''

''*You'll* not have it?''

''You will take your rightful spot! With a simple nod of acceptance we could be set for life. Do you have any idea what that means? *Do you?*'' Her shrill voice caused several heads from the crowd in the main hallway to dip in and look.

Skin crawling, Sebastian stared at his mother. Elevated

blood pressure encouraged beads of sweat on Claudette's brow and, as he stood motionless watching her rant, the suspicion that had begun as a tiny seed of doubt began to take root. Something about the urgency on her part was eerie. A peculiar light would gleam in her eye whenever she talked about him being Philippe's son, and it was almost as if she'd managed to convince herself it was true.

Whether or not it was.

"Mère," he gritted out through a tight jaw, "this is neither the time nor the place for such a conversation. I'll take you home and we can finish this discussion there."

"Are you out of your mind? And miss the Gala Ball?" Her eyes bulged at the very thought. "Never!" With that, chin high, fancy heels a-tapping, Claudette whirled around and stormed off to join the party in progress.

Just one flight up, Marie-Claire stared at the booty spread out across her bed in hapless fascination. She picked up what looked like a punch bowl festooned with faux fruit and wads of sparkly netting and settled it at a rakish angle on her head. What on earth had she been thinking, bidding on this uncertain fashion statement? Must have been swept up in the moment. Her purse, with its tropical birds and authentic "rain forest palm frond weave" was no tamer.

That morning, with her sisters at her side, Marie-Claire had enjoyed front-row seats at a catwalk fashion show for charity in Paris. The spring collection featured haute couture from Milan, London and New York and—she fingered her gaudy new hat—Uranus.

In the full-length mirror across the room she studied the strange apparition that was her reflection. Was she trying to attract Sebastian or scare him to death? The gold lamé dress she wore could surely be detected by radar and, like the ones on Ona Parnell's feet, the pointy, super high-heeled boots could put an eye out. Her new hair, makeup and nail styles also had a space-age quality, all spiky and metallic and—she was assured by her sisters—sexy.

Marie-Claire worried her glittery lower lip with her teeth. She'd made the mistake of telling her sisters she wanted to look a little naughty. Decadent.

Wicked.

In the nicest possible sense of the word, of course. Well, they'd taken the ball and run, and now, Marie-Claire turned and glanced over her shoulder to inspect her backside, she feared Cruella De Vil would look like a nun in comparison. Never mind. Her gaze traveled back to her bed. Surely something from this pile of spare auto parts that passed for the world of fashion's finest would make Sebastian sit up and realize that she was no sister of his.

Anxiously, she fingered the sleeve of a faux zebra coat.

But what if he didn't?

Suddenly depressed, Marie-Claire sagged to the edge of her mattress. She absolutely hated everything she'd bought, and couldn't imagine anyone in their right mind going out in public in any of this stuff. She wanted her old life back. A tear slowly rolled down her cheek. She wanted her Papa back. Her legitimacy back. Her boyfriend back.

With a bang, her bedroom door burst open. Wearing their own purchases from today's Parisian fashion extravaganza, Lise and Ariane swept into her room, full of life and ready to party. She swiped at her tears with her pinky fingers and forced herself to smile. Ariane looked fetching in her micro-mini and peacock feather vest and Lise was all the modern mommy in a tummy-hugging tube gown that had her taking tiny, shuffling steps.

Yes. It took guts to pull off a bold fashion statement, Marie-Claire decided. More guts than she had. Though, she had to admit that her sisters did look chic in a garish, avant-garde sort of way.

"Marie-Claire! You look fabulous!" they gushed when they saw her hunched at the edge of her bed.

"Doesn't she look fabulous?"

"Fabulous."

Marie-Claire harrumphed. "I look like a satellite dish with cleavage."

"No! You're perfect! Isn't she perfect, Lise?"

"Perfect."

"You don't think the hat is too much?"

Lise gave her head an emphatic shake. "No! All that's coming back into vogue, you know."

"No." Heaven forbid. Marie-Claire fingered her crazy headdress. Her neck was killing her and the night had only just begun.

"I have a date all sewn up for you," Ariane announced as she made herself at home at Marie-Claire's vanity and began applying a coat of silver lipstick. "He's not perfect, but on such short notice, it was the best I could do."

"What's wrong with him?

"Well, he's a little young."

"How young?"

"He's not jailbait, if that's what you're afraid of."

Marie-Claire dropped her face into her hands and moaned. "What have you done? Who is this…date?"

"Why worry yourself unnecessarily about who he is? Let it be a surprise. In the meantime, spritz your hair with that glitter spray you paid a fortune for today. We've got a party to attend."

Chapter Nine

The Crystal Ballroom had become an undulating mass of humanity. From where she stood with her sisters at the top of the stairs, Marie-Claire could see a popular British rock band up high on the main stage, their throbbing bass beat underscoring the din of conversation and laughter. Colored spotlights hit the giant Austrian-crystal chandeliers, scattering tiny rainbow prisms like fireflies over the band and revelers.

The party, open to the public at a minimal cost, was designed as a continental nose-thumbing at Rhineland. To show solidarity and independence, as it were, among the people of St. Michel. That being the case, security guards were roaming in abundance. Everywhere, the St. Michel flag was proudly displayed, and the festive décor reflected the country's colors of gold, white and royal purple.

This would be a night to remember.

Hand to banister, Marie-Claire clutched the highly polished wood and attempted to slow her breathing and gather her nerve. Sebastian was somewhere in this room. Like the princess who knew there was a pea under her stack of mattresses, she could feel him in the crowd. Trying to appear blasé, she allowed her gaze to drift like a feather on a light breeze.

"Celeste is here," Lise said, lifting her voice to be heard above the ruckus and, leaning toward Marie-Claire, pointed out their stepmother.

"Mmm."

"Gauging from her outfit, it would seem she is tired of mourning already." Ariane snorted. "She is dressed more ridiculously than we are. What on earth is she trying to prove?"

"And who is that she's flirting with?" Lise squinted over Ariane's shoulder.

"He is paparazzi."

"Oh, great." Sighing heavily, Marie-Claire covered her face with her hands and groaned. "Could my life get any weirder?"

"Is that Luc Dumont?" Ariane leaned back and pointed to another corner of the room. All three heads swung to see.

"Where?"

"Over there…see the woman in that garish, multicolored, retro caftan? Behind her."

Marie-Claire looked in the direction Ariane's finger pointed. "The woman in the garish caftan is Claudette LeMarc."

Sure enough, the ebullient Claudette snagged a drink from a passing tray and seemed unaware that she was the object of such intense scrutiny as she tapped her feet and snapped her fingers to the beat of the music. She was obviously having a ball, surrounded by socialite girlfriends, equally snooty. And equally inebriated.

"And, yes," Marie-Claire said and frowned, "the guy

behind her is Luc. I wonder what he's doing here? I thought Simone let him go?''

''From the way he is staring, I think maybe he has a hankering for Claudette.'' Ariane and Lise giggled.

Marie-Claire relaxed enough to allow herself a smile until she noticed who was standing not five paces from Claudette.

Sebastian.

As if she were dangling from a cliff, her vital functions seemed to suspend with the emotions—supposedly forbidden—that coursed through her. Desire, fright and excitement all warred within for dominance.

He seemed to feel her gaze the second she spotted him. Their eyes met in a collision so jarring, the controlled mayhem faded away and they became the only two people in the room. Head tilted back, Sebastian's thickly lashed eyes were at half mast, slowly perusing her from head to toe and finally settling on her face. His expression betrayed his less-than-brotherly interest. Her bashful gaze dipped and rose again only to have her smile flash-freeze and her rapidly pumping heart crash into her stomach, a leaden, lifeless lump.

Veronike.

How had she failed to notice Veronike Schroeder plastered to his side like a blond body cast? Jealousy sliced through Marie-Claire as she watched Veronike whisper something to Sebastian and then laugh her throaty, husky, steamy-hot, wide-mouthed, disgusting laugh.

''She laughs like a braying donkey.'' Ariane sniffed, and threw a sisterly arm around Marie-Claire's waist. Lise squeezed her shoulder. ''And in that plunging neckline, she looks like a dairy cow.''

Marie-Claire shot them tremulous smiles of gratitude, even as her heart was dissolving. She blinked back the tears.

"Belly-breathe, Marie-Claire," Ariane advised. "You're looking a little pale."

"Don't let Veronike get your goat, honey. She's not worth getting upset over."

Like the managers of a prize fighter, Lise and Ariane rubbed her arms and patted her back and spoke words meant to encourage. Glassy-eyed, Marie-Claire soaked it all in and knew that she had to listen or run. And Marie-Claire never ran.

Her sisters were right. She wasn't going to let some braying bovine get the better of her. She was a de Bergeron! Anger sluiced through her, roiling in her gut, routing out the fear.

"Now, laugh, Marie-Claire. Show them what you're made of."

Obediently, Marie-Claire opened her mouth wide and, shoulders bobbing, hooted.

"Is she laughing or crying?" Lise wondered.

"Can't tell." Ariane peered into Marie-Claire's face. "Are you all right, Marie-Claire?"

"Fine," Marie-Claire gritted and swiped at the tears that swam in her eyes. *So.* It seemed that whatever remorse Sebastian had felt over losing her was short-lived. Well. She clamped her mouth shut. If he could recover from undying love overnight, she guessed she could, too. Sebastian LeMarc would soon see that she did not need him to have a good time. She did not need him to go on living. Breathing.

Standing.

Marie-Claire clutched at Ariane's arm with both hands and, inhaling deeply through her nose, squared her shoulders. She, too, had a date. Somewhere.

"Ariane?" she chirped. "My date?"

"Oh. Ahhh, yes. Your...date."

She followed Ariane's guilty gaze down the long stair to…Eduardo Van Groober.

Marie-Claire's momentary burst of confidence took a direct hit.

"Eduardo?" she asked dully.

"Should I have warned you?"

"You should have shot me."

"Smile," Ariane said, "everyone is looking."

Indeed, everyone was looking. Paparazzi flashes strobed and Marie-Claire was momentarily blinded.

Fumbling, bumbling, stumbling, Eduardo took the stairs three at a time, a mangled corsage in one hand, and a pearl-headed corsage pin in the other. "Oh, Marie-Claire. You look, you look, you're…*très chic!*" When he reached her, he was breathing hard and reeling with zeal. "I brought you a corsage. Here, I can…pin…somewhere…just…"

Unprepared for his effusive welcome, Marie-Claire—still blinded and teetering on Ona-style shoes—was thrown off balance when the tip of Eduardo's three-inch pin found the soft flesh above her breast. Surprised by the stabbing pain, Marie-Claire's ankles collapsed and she rode the sides of her feet down several steps before she managed to grasp the railing.

Ariane and Eduardo rushed after her, while at the same time a concerned Lise hippity-hopped about in her tube dress, trying to catch an avalanche of faux grapes and bananas before they escaped.

Fortunately, it worked.

Unfortunately, a heel had snapped off one of her fancy butt-kickin' shoes.

Fortunately, she never planned on wearing this garish outfit again.

Unfortunately, her rather skimpy gold lamé dress had ridden up her thighs and her hat was now on backwards.

Fortunately, Marie-Claire no longer cared if she lived or died.

Sebastian's heart lurched into his throat as he watched Marie-Claire stumble and then right herself. He took a step forward, but a surge of men beat him to the punch and he could see that she already had plenty of eager assistance. Frustrated beyond belief, he ran a hand over his jaw and around to the stiff muscles at the back of his neck.

Tonight, Marie-Claire was more beautiful than ever before. Her leggy figure was enveloped in some kind of form-fitting, shiny gold dress that accentuated her perfect curves and had every man in the room drooling. Her long, shapely legs appeared even longer in those wild, metallic boots and her hair and makeup were amazing. Trendy. Space-age. Beautiful. She looked like something straight off a Paris catwalk, and Veronike, though she pretended disdain, knew it.

Beads of sweat broke out on his brow and his Adam's apple worked against his bow tie. Searing jealousy, not only of Eduardo, but of every man in the damned room who was fawning over Marie-Claire and helping her right her hat and dress and…fruit, clawed at his heart.

Out of the benevolent bedlam that swirled around him, came a deeply melancholy moment.

How the hell had it come to this? Mere weeks ago, they were the happy couple. And now, here he stood, holding up the limp and clinging Veronike, and Marie-Claire was dating the Van Groober boy.

Certainly, Eduardo was more her own age, but really, was she *interested* in him? It sure looked like it, by the way she was fawning over the corsage he'd just pinned to her breast.

"The children seem to be enjoying themselves," Veronike murmured, gesturing to the stairs. "It looks as if little

Marie-Claire has finally got herself a boyfriend. He's cute. He seems to make her very happy.''

Sebastian had to admit it looked as if she was right. Head thrown back, Marie-Claire was laughing gaily at something witty Eduardo had just said.

''Marie-Claire, I'm so sorry. You're…you're bleeding there.''

Sucking her breath between her teeth, Marie-Claire's head fell back and she winced at the ceiling. She tried to swallow her groans of pain and reassure him, but the pin had plunged deep into the muscle, and it hurt like the dickens. She wondered when she'd had her last tetanus booster. She forced herself to emit some strangled laughter in order to spare his feelings. ''It'll be all right, Eduardo.''

''Oh, good.'' Relief flooded his face, causing his freckles to blend back into his usually ruddy complexion. ''Would you care to dance?''

''Uh, well, Eduardo, actually, I'd like to make it down the stairs in one piece first, and then we'll see, all right?''

''Right! Allow me.'' He held out his arm and miraculously, they descended the stair without further mishap. ''One time, I was working with my dad out in the palace garden, when I was a little kid and I stepped on this nail—''

''Isn't that nice?'' On autopilot, Marie-Claire smiled and nodded, mentally measuring the distance between her and Sebastian.

''—and I had to go to the hospital and have surgery, because it tore up a bunch of ligaments—''

''That's great!'' He was not five meters away. And, he was watching her. Marie-Claire felt her stomach turn to liquid.

''—thought I'd never walk again, but I did! But the only sport I could play was golf—''

Marie-Claire stared past Sebastian as if he wasn't there, even though she mentally documented and categorized every breath he took.

"—because I was so clumsy and so she was really scared after I broke my leg in our school's production of *Les Mis*—"

"That must have been fun." Marie-Claire managed to trump up some more happy-go-lucky laughter and feared that her face would crack with the continual effort. And, though she stared at Eduardo as if his conversation was riveting, she never lost track of Sebastian's whereabouts.

Even across the room, she could feel the raw sexuality Sebastian exuded. Every woman could, it seemed. Even Grandmama Simone, who was currently pestering him for a dance. The gentle way he took the elderly woman into his arms had Marie-Claire smiling in spite of herself. The fact that he was dancing with a queen seemed not to faze him, the way it would have other men in the room. The old girl suddenly looked sixty years younger in his arms.

When the song had ended, Sebastian returned Simone to the sidelines and thanked her for the dance. The entire time they had moved about the floor, he could tell he was being scrutinized. Dissected. It seemed to him Simone thought that if by staring hard enough, she could see the shadow of her Philippe in his expression. She seemed blue and it occurred to Sebastian that on a night not at all unlike this, Simone had lost her only son.

With a squeeze of her knobby hands, he kissed the powdery-soft, paper-thin flesh of her cheek and whispered, "Adieu."

Her smile was half-hearted as she whispered back, "Adieu," with a ring of finality that had him wondering what exactly she knew in her heart.

Alone at last, Sebastian turned his attentions to spotting Marie-Claire. He found her with Eduardo who was asserting his manhood by seizing Marie-Claire and pressing her to his scrawny chest. In a clench that nearly lifted her feet from the floor, he steered her through the crowd, his ill-defined style all jerks and stops like a dog with a rag doll. A lesser woman would have cried whiplash and begged off. Yet, Marie-Claire managed to extricate herself from his clutches and make him look like a halfway decent partner.

Ignoring Eduardo, no doubt out of self-preservation more than anything, Marie-Claire's eyes fell closed and her hips swayed. Sebastian felt his chest tighten. She was a wonderful dancer, seeming to feel the music and letting it flow through her body.

With a groan, Sebastian flexed his hands and fought his never-ending reactions to her. Would it be like this for the rest of his life? If she were indeed his sister, every moment they spent in the same room together would be sheer hell. There was no way on God's green earth that he was going to be able to live like this, wanting something just out of his grasp but never having satisfaction.

If Claudette was telling the truth, there was only one way this thing could go. One of them would have to leave St. Michel.

Forever.

Exhausted from what seemed like an eon of being dragged around the dance floor by the sweaty Eduardo, Marie-Claire beseeched him to find her a cup of punch. Thirsty himself, Eduardo trotted in search of beverages, while Marie-Claire found a vacant chair off in a corner alone. Wearily, she sat, feeling the ache of every bone in her body. Making Sebastian notice what a wonderful time she was having without him was hideous work. Especially in a pair of boots that sported only one heel.

While she waited for Eduardo to bring her a cup of punch, she scanned the room for Sebastian and, unfortunately, found him, dancing once again with Veronike. Morbid fascination held Marie-Claire in its grip and she watched Veronike provocatively thrust her pelvis in time to the music. Like a cat in heat, she strutted in tight circles around Sebastian, rubbing her voluptuous body up against his and smiling a half-awake Marilyn Monroe-type smile. Marie-Claire could practically hear her purr.

In comparison to the flashy, experienced Veronike, Marie-Claire felt like a clunker limping along on a flat tire.

Luc Dumont moved to stand next to Marie-Claire and indicated Veronike with a nod of his head. "I never did learn how to dance."

"That is not dancing. That's the mating ritual of the socially challenged."

"Ah. Looks as if it's working."

"Yes, it does, doesn't it?" Marie-Claire sighed. "We haven't been formally introduced. You are Luc?"

Luc held out his hand. "Dumont. Yes. Forgive my breach of etiquette."

"Of course. I'm Marie-Claire de Bergeron."

"Yes. I'm pretty familiar with everyone in your family."

"So you are. I noticed that you are acquainted with Juliet."

"We met some years ago, yes. She's lovely."

"She is indeed. So. Tell me, Mr. Dumont," Marie-Claire tore her gaze from Sebastian and Veronike long enough to dart him a curious smile, "why are you still hanging around? I thought the case of the missing heir had been solved."

Luc shrugged. "Maybe."

Marie-Claire's brows flew up. "Maybe not?"

"Maybe."

At that moment, Claudette danced by with the prime minister and, with a covert look about to see who was watching, steered poor Mr. Davoine into the path of the paparazzi. Bulbs flashed. Claudette's smile was triumphant. By morning their picture would be splashed across the society pages.

Knowing intrinsically that she could trust him, Marie-Claire decided to confide her fears about Claudette in Luc.

"I think she is lying."

"You, too?"

"So we agree."

"I believe I could unearth enough dirt to fill several books."

"Really?" Marie-Claire patted the chair next to her and when Luc was seated, she leaned toward him. "What do *you* think Claudette's motivation for lying could be? Everyone knows that she's a social climber, but to sacrifice her son? To chance being discovered? To what end?"

"Desperation. From what I've been able to find out, she is in debt up to her diamond earrings. I believe she has her sights set on the royal payroll."

"Really," Marie-Claire murmured, feeling almost sorry for the woman. Claudette had no idea what a treasure she already had in Sebastian. "What do you suggest we do?"

"Tonight? Nothing."

"Nothing?"

"Without the proper proof, there is nothing we can do. But don't fret. Time is on our side."

As Marie-Claire watched Veronike ooze to the beat around Sebastian, Eduardo, cups of punch sloshing, stumbled in her direction. She sighed.

"Mr. Dumont, I'm running out of time."

* * *

Marie-Claire needed air.

Looking a little flushed himself, Eduardo was only too happy to accompany her out of doors. She could feel Sebastian's eyes watching as they swept by, Eduardo chattering about the computer club and chess team, and she limping along and pretending to hang on his every word.

When they got out to the verandah, Eduardo dropped a casual arm around her shoulders. At first, Marie-Claire enjoyed the rather romantic gesture thinking, let Sebastian stick this in his pipe and smoke it.

Then Eduardo grinned at her, and a chill ran down her spine at the quixotic expression on his face. The way his teeth protruded between his lips, gleaming in the moonlight, suddenly struck Marie-Claire as somewhat feral. Vampirish. That, coupled with the fact that his hand had just slid to her bottom, had her wondering exactly what was in that punch he'd been guzzling for the last half hour.

"I can't believe we are finally here, together," he husked, "alone."

Marie-Claire emitted some uncomfortable laughter and pointed out, "Not completely alone. There are several thousand people right back there, in the ballroom."

Eduardo ignored that fact and, nostrils flaring, buried his face in her hair and inhaled. "I've been dreaming of this moment ever since I was in the seventh grade and I saw you ride out to the pond for a swim." He blew several strands of her hair out of his mouth, scratched his face and went back to snuffling. "You were so beautiful. I was going to tell you that I was there, fishing on the other side of the pond, but Sebastian came and told you to get out of the water."

"You…were *there?*"

"Don't worry. I didn't see everything." He chuckled and

his other hand slipped to join the first one at her bottom. "I think that's where I fell in love with you."

"In—" Marie-Claire swallowed, "—*love?*"

"Yes, I have a scrapbook filled with pictures of you."

Uh-oh. A lump of foreboding rose into her throat. Reaching behind her, she gripped his wrists, attempting to keep his boa-constrictor act in check. "Uh, Eduardo? I think we should go back—"

"Marie-Claire," Eduardo rooted around at the side of her neck, "I know that we were meant to be together. I've known it ever since that night."

"Y-Y-You have?"

"Yes." Teeth leading, he traversed her jaw and headed for her mouth.

"Oh, Eduardo." Flabbergasted, Marie-Claire strained back, chin to neck, leaning as far away as his steely grip would allow. She tried to act as if she knew he was teasing. "This is our first date. You can't be in love with me."

As she uttered the words, she knew that wasn't exactly accurate. That same night at the pond was enough time to press Sebastian into her heart for time and eternity. Marie-Claire was losing the battle as Eduardo slowly forced her forward for a little kiss. The confidence in her voice turned to pleading.

"Oh, no, no thank you, Eduardo."

"Just one kiss, Marie-Claire. Then you'll see."

"No, Eduardo, I don't think that would be such a goo—"

Eduardo's lips crashed down on hers and Marie-Claire feared she was bleeding from the collision.

"Mmm….eee…Eduar-dooo, no, please don't. I said…no, Eduardo." Frantically, Marie-Claire squirmed, trying to pry his hands from around her waist, but Eduardo tightened his hold. His hands, incredibly strong now, roved from her hips to the top of her zipper and Marie-Claire feared he was going to disrobe her then and there.

Tears of humiliation welled in her eyes. Damn her foolish pride. She wouldn't be in this predicament if she hadn't been trying to torture Sebastian. Ashamed, she pushed against Eduardo until he suddenly popped away like a cork from a champagne bottle. Her eyes widened as she marveled at her strength.

Until she saw Sebastian.

Holding Eduardo by the scruff of his neck, Sebastian growled, "Eduardo, man, did you hear the woman? She said no. Snap out of it."

Fists flying in the air, Eduardo took a swing at Sebastian and managed to land a solid punch to his gut.

"Owww!"

A kick to the shins had Sebastian gasping with pain yet again.

"Dammit, Eduardo. Stop it, man. That *hurts!*"

"No!" Eduardo panted, still flailing. Though Sebastian held the boy at arm's length by the head, he was just lanky enough to do some pretty serious damage.

"Don't hurt him, Sebastian," Marie-Claire screamed.

Sebastian turned to stare at her. "Do I...*ufff, dammit Eduardo*...do I *look* like I'm hurting him?"

"It's all my fault," she sobbed.

"Leave us alone," Eduardo shouted.

"No," Marie-Claire cried.

Sebastian dropped his head and gave it a disgusted shake. "Will you two make up your minds?"

"She wants me. She cares for me, I know it." Eduardo's protestations grew pathetic. "Tell him, Marie-Claire. Tell him how much we have in common...tell him."

"Oh, Eduardo. I'm so sorry." Marie-Claire sagged

against the concrete railing and pushed her hair out of her face. "I...I'm in love with someone else."

Sebastian's eyes fell closed.

Her words had a sobering effect on Eduardo as well and the boy flagged. His miserable smile was without rancor as he drew himself up and stepped away from Sebastian. "I knew it was too good to be true."

As he ran a hand over his bruised belly, Sebastian said, "Eduardo, no woman likes to be pawed to death on the first date."

"You know—" Eduardo's laughter was mirthless as he dropped his head into his hands and moaned. "I'm such a jerk."

"No more so than I, Eduardo," Marie-Claire said. "I've made such a fool of myself tonight. I'm so sorry if I gave you the wrong impression."

"Don't be." He stood for a long, silent moment, then said, "Maybe tonight was one of those horrible experiences that we will look back on one day and laugh."

"I will if you will."

Eduardo smiled his boyish, buck-toothed smile, and Marie-Claire could see that someday he would grow into a decent man. "It's a date, then."

With a nod at her and then at Sebastian, Eduardo brushed himself off, straightened his cummerbund and shuffled back into the party.

Sebastian watched in silence as Marie-Claire dropped to a concrete bench beside the low row of fat balustrades. Gingerly, she removed her boots, then tossed them over the rail and into the bushes. The hat and fruit followed. With her thumbs, she began to rub circles into the soles of her feet, little mewling moans ushering forth from her throat. He longed to sit next to her and take her feet into his lap, and do that for her, but prudence allowed him to come only as far as the end of the bench.

"Sebastian." She didn't look up as she spoke, seeming more interested in her feet than in the message she began to impart without emotion. "I've been such an idiot. I've been letting other people tell me what to do as far as you are concerned, and that's been a terrible mistake."

The concrete was cold and rough against his palms as he backed up to the railing and stood, ankles crossed. "It hasn't been easy, Marie-Claire. For either of us."

"No. But I have to tell you that I can't go on like this. I will never be able to accept you as a brother. It's simply impossible. And, since you won't accept me as your love—"

"I can't right *now,* Marie-Claire! You know why!"

"Do I, Sebastian?" She stopped rubbing and looked up at him.

Hands flexing, Sebastian wrestled with his frustration. Even if Claudette was not telling the truth, the very hint of doubt hanging over their relationship would be devastating. Marie-Claire had no idea how damaging a rumor of incest would be. She thought she could handle the fallout, but until they had to face that particular disgrace, she couldn't begin to understand.

Marie-Claire dropped her feet to the ground and standing, padded to stand directly in front of him. Laying her cheek on his chest, she circled his waist with her slender arms and sighed a light sigh of homecoming. Her familiar scent enveloped him: soap and something floral in her hair and perfume and fresh air, all combined to produce a powerful aphrodisiac for him.

She tilted her face up to his. "I refuse to let other people run my life. Why don't you?"

Like a martyr on his way to slaughter, Sebastian wilted,

his eyes dropping shut. *Because I'm trying to protect you,* he wanted to shout. Instead, he said, "Because we can't always have what we want, when we want it."

"Not even when it's right?" Marie-Claire whispered, her lips a hairbreadth from his, the taboo quotient holding him motionless except for their labored breathing.

Never had he wanted to kiss anyone more than he wanted to kiss Marie-Claire at that moment. Never had he been more tortured. But, until there was conclusive evidence, the return of the DNA tests that Luc had covertly sent off to the lab in Chicago, there was no way he could chance her reputation. And, even though it was killing him, he could not even give Marie-Claire the slightest hint that she might be right. To do so would only invite disaster.

"Sebastian, I don't care what your mother says. I don't care what the world thinks. I love you. Shouldn't that be enough?"

"It should. But it's not."

"Sebastian, please."

Unable to take another second of this torment, Sebastian did the only thing he knew how. The only thing that could save her from herself. From scandal and public humiliation that would haunt her for the rest of her life.

He withdrew her hands from around his waist and stepped back. "Marie-Claire, stop it. We cannot be together. Not now. Maybe—maybe not ever." Though it was killing him, Sebastian turned and walked away without looking back to see her reaction.

For to do so would only have him running back to carry her off. And he loved her too much to do that.

Just inside, he found Veronike waiting for him. A sixth sense had her offering her mouth to his for a kiss and though he was loath to do so, he took her up on her offer, then led her to the dance floor.

Chapter Ten

Numb with grief, Marie-Claire couldn't even cry. For hours now, she'd been sitting by her window, staring at the twilight sky. Outside, the sounds of dawn reached her through an open window and the whisper of a cool breeze caressed her face. On the ground below, the servants who'd cleaned up after the gala were leaving for home. Voices murmured their partings, car engines rumbled to life. Off in the distance, a rooster heralded the advent of a new day and, at a table by her side a lone candle burned low, hissing.

Dully, Marie-Claire shifted her gaze to the flickering flame and saw her life.

It was over.

Even if Sebastian was not the crown prince, she knew that her foolishness had lost him forever to Veronike. Or, if not Veronike, some other woman who wouldn't go to such ridiculous lengths to prove her love.

She blinked once, then shifted her unseeing stare back out the window. Why would she and Sebastian harbor such intense feelings for each other for five long years only to have it come to such a disastrous end? It simply did not make sense.

A light tapping at her door interrupted her wretched ruminations. Ariane appeared, carrying a valise and dressed in a sensible wool traveling suit. Quite a change from the last time she'd entered the room, Marie-Claire reflected, lifting a hand in despondent greeting.

Ariane set her purse and bag on Marie-Claire's bed and then silently moved across the room. Gently, her fingers combed through Marie-Claire's hair and she whispered, ''I just stopped by to tell you goodbye.''

''Already?''

''It's Sunday morning.''

Marie-Claire nodded. ''So. You are off to Rhineland.''

''Yes.''

''Why?''

Ariane's chuckle rang false as she fussed with a small tangle of strands. ''Why? Because Etienne invited me, of course.''

''He *invited* you?'' Marie-Claire briskly rubbed her face with her hands. Life just kept getting curiouser and curiouser, as Alice would have said when confronted with Wonderland. ''Ariane, in the past, you've found Etienne to be arrogant and overbearing. Why the sudden change of heart?''

With a careless shrug, Ariane moved behind the chair and began to twist Marie-Claire's hair into a French plait. ''Things change.''

Cheeks puffed, Marie-Claire exhaled long and slow. ''Um-hmm. Don't I know it.''

''Are you going to be all right?''

''Eventually.''

''Marie-Claire, I don't think Sebastian cares a fig for Veronike. After you left last night, he didn't speak a word to her.''

''Before he kissed her or after?''

Marie-Claire could fairly hear Ariane grimace. ''He *kissed* her?''

''On her big, bloated…bulbous…*bulging* lips.''

''*Really?*'' Surprised, Ariane stilled her hands and then she tut-tutted and once again began to weave her efficient braid. ''Well, it couldn't have been that great because every time I saw him, he was by himself and looking miserable. Eduardo on the other hand, mixed it up rather well on the dance floor with a number of young local ladies.''

Marie-Claire lifted her shoulder a notch. ''It doesn't matter. I've lost him.''

''Eduardo?'' Ariane tried to inject a little levity.

''Well, I've hurt him, too. I have a lot of apologizing to do.''

''When you do, you must bring me with you. Most of that kooky stuff was my idea.''

''But I was the one with the fruit on my head.''

''Yes, well, we all make mistakes. Especially when it comes to love.''

''Is that what you are doing now, by heading off to Rhineland?''

''Perhaps.'' Ariane secured Marie-Claire's braid with a clip and bent to kiss her cheek. ''Call me?''

''Mm-hmm. I'll be calling from Tatiana's house in Denmark. For some reason, when my life falls apart, she is the only one able to step in and mother me.''

''Give her my love.''

She covered Ariane's hand with her own. ''I will.''

As Marie-Claire watched her sister gather her belongings

and slip into the hall, she wondered listlessly at Ariane's sudden interest in Etienne Kroninberg, prince of Rhineland. For a while now, she'd noticed that Ariane had been acting rather more secretively than usual, and her motives for going to Rhineland were weak. After all, just six months ago Ariane seemed to have no feelings for Prince Etienne whatsoever. What had changed?

Fingertips wet from a touch to her tongue, Marie-Claire snuffed her candle, crawled into bed and assumed a fetal position. Her eyes drifted shut and she decided to worry about Ariane after she woke up.

Over a week later, Marie-Claire was just now able to lift her head from her pillow and venture out into the world again. She pulled her scarf more closely about her face and hunched against the blustery wind that nudged her down the busy streets of Copenhagen. Tatiana needed eggs and milk for a dessert she was making, hoping, no doubt, to put some weight on her granddaughter's skinny bones.

Marie-Claire snorted into the furry collar of her coat. Fat chance. Since she'd arrived in Denmark, she'd already lost five pounds. In all the wrong places. Story of her life.

Like a salmon fighting upstream, Marie-Claire navigated through the crowded sidewalk, faces coming, going, all strange, all a blur. Horns sounded, people shouted. Typical, these sounds of life in the city. Marie-Claire was glad for the anonymity. Being able to come and go without the intense scrutiny of the security guards was a rare and wonderful privilege.

As she drew near the market, she passed a newsstand and paused to catch up with life.

Her heart caught in her throat and her head began to buzz as she stared at the blaring headlines:

St. Michel's Royal Daughters Illegitimate?
Late King Philippe of St. Michel a Bigamist?

And even worse yet:

Sebastian LeMarc Crown Prince of St. Michel?

Clutching the sales table for balance, she perused the articles and her heart shifted from a dead standstill to overdrive. Icy with shock, Marie-Claire spun about and forced her legs to carry her all the way back to Tatiana's house, forgetting her errand in the process. She rushed inside, turned on the television and searched for a twenty-four-hour news station. After several misses, she hit upon the story being discussed on a Paris network.

"What is it, darling?" Concerned by Marie-Claire's frantic return and anxious demeanor, Tatiana moved from the kitchen to her parlor. She dusted her flour-coated hands on her apron, then perched on the couch beside Marie-Claire and adjusted her glasses.

"Listen, Tatiana. It's in the papers, too." Tears rose with the television's volume.

"—and this report is fueling further speculation about the sex of Queen Celeste's baby and whether this child will eventually take the throne.

"Recently, there has been speculation that Sebastian LeMarc, import/export mogul from St. Michel, is the missing heir apparent. However, Mr. LeMarc could not be reached for comment at this time. Palace officials in St. Michel also continue to have no comment, except to say that, quote, 'We are running the government smoothly and the people of St. Michel can be assured that when the crown prince comes to light, he will fit the DNA profile and all other criteria. These things take time. Speculation is not helpful at this juncture.' End quote.

"A reliable source close to the royal family does tell us that King Philippe married when he was only eighteen to an American named Katie Graham. The marriage was never annulled, making Philippe de Bergeron's subsequent marriages invalid, and his offspring illegitimate. And, in a related story, the government of Rhineland—"

Tatiana gasped. "Who would do such a thing?"

Remote in hand, Marie-Claire turned off the television and stared at the black screen, remembering what she'd just read in the paper.

"Wilhelm."

Luc Dumont heard the ring of his phone just as he was lathering his hair with shampoo. Typical. He slammed off the faucet and listened to the ring. Not his cell. Not the pager. Not the regular phone. Must be the fax. Good. He turned the water back on and ducked. The water sluiced over his head, hot and refreshing. He'd worked late last night at Interpol's satellite office in St. Michel and had used the better part of the wee hours researching the materials his men had spent this last week collecting on Claudette LeMarc and her late husband, Henri.

Seems that if there had been two sets of railroad tracks in St. Michel, Claudette would have been born on the wrong side of the wrong set. She'd grown up in abject poverty, her father a drunk and her mother bedridden after a stroke. Together, they'd had eight children, and Claudette, being the oldest, was no doubt expected to shoulder much of the parenting load.

A twinge of pity struck Luc as he lathered his body. If he had to guess, that was the reason Sebastian had no siblings. Claudette was tired of mothering by the time she got to him. Which raised several other good questions, including why she would bother to adopt so early in her marriage.

With both hands, Luc leaned against the fiberglass wall

and let the hot water pound on his back. Ah, well. The answers would surface all in good time. The pieces were certainly beginning to fall together.

Claudette had dropped out of school with a third-grade education and had met her husband Count Henri LeMarc in a pub where she worked as a cocktail waitress. His pedigree as a descendent of a twelfth-century line of French aristocrats, had impressed her and they were married just four weeks later. Sebastian was born in a hospital in northern France nine months after that.

Once again, Luc shut off the water and, grabbing a towel, mopped himself off and tied it around his hips. He moved to the fax machine, picked up the sheet that had fallen to the floor and began to read. Finally. The DNA test results had arrived at the French offices of Interpol that morning. And, as he flipped through the subsequent pages, he realized with a start that Sebastian LeMarc's fate had been sealed.

Tatiana Van Rhys had always been a rebel. Photos of herself and her young daughter, Johanna, were scattered around her living room, always depicting them doing something adventurous. One photo was of them sky-diving. Another of them mountain-climbing. And yet another of them smiling on a sailboat, holding up fish nearly as large as they were. On the end table beside the couch where Marie-Claire sat was a particularly beautiful picture of Johanna skiing in the Swiss Alps.

Marie-Claire peered closely at her mother's blissful smile and felt stirrings of melancholy for that mother-daughter relationship. Now, more than ever, she needed her mother, even though Johanna had never really had a maternal bone in her body.

Rebellion seemed to run in the family, Marie-Claire thought wryly, as she regarded her grandmother's simple cottage. Having lived her entire married life in a palace, Tatiana, as a widow, now preferred this simplicity and the freedom that came with it.

Outside the curtained windows a March wind blustered, but inside by the fire, it was cozy. Safe from the injustices of life. The small living room was tidy and furnished with odds and ends and souvenirs of Tatiana's many travels and the kitchen always had the smell of something freshly baked, as it did now.

Marie-Claire could see Tatiana withdrawing Danish pastries from the oven and drizzling icing on them. The kettle whistled and cups clanked. Upon her arrival in Denmark this last time, Marie-Claire had decided never again to leave this homey haven, especially since there was no real reason to return to St. Michel anymore. She'd stay here and take care of Tatiana, when and if the tiny dynamo ever needed caretaking, and then, when Tatiana passed on, she would be the next old lady to love this house.

Fragrant tray in hand, Tatiana swept into the room and pressing an ottoman into service as a table, poured them each a cup of tea. Gooey and warm, the Danish would tide them over until suppertime. All afternoon, she and her grandmother had been deep in a conversation that had Marie-Claire regaling a softly clucking Tatiana with the details of Philippe's secret marriage that, until now, had been known only to Simone.

"—and he was three years younger than I am now. Can you believe that? I guess, when they found out she was going to have a baby they ran away to France to get married. They were very brave, I think, to buck convention and marry."

Tatiana had held her tongue for the better part of an hour, which for her, was a minor miracle. But now, she had to unleash her opinions or burst.

"Child, do you want to live your life with a man you do not love?"

"What? No."

"Well, that's just what your mother did, poor thing. And I was partly responsible. I encouraged the marriage between your mother and father, because my husband—God rest his soul—convinced me that it would be a good political alliance. But from the minute your mother said 'I do,' I could see that the child was miserable. I have always carried a terrible load of guilt over that. She was never cut out to be a wife. Or, unfortunately for you lovely girls, a mother. But thank God she had you, no?"

Marie-Claire swallowed hard and nodded.

"Even so, I can never encourage anyone not to follow their heart again."

"But Sebastian is convinced that he is my brother."

"Stuff and nonsense. You have a very good feel for character, my child. If your gut tells you that Claudette is lying, then I don't doubt that she is. From everything you've told me so far, it would only stand to reason."

Marie-Claire set down her teacup then flopped back and rolled her head toward Tatiana. "Thank you for your vote of confidence, Grandmama, but last time I saw Sebastian, he was lip-locked with Veronike Schroeder."

"I'm going to hazard a guess that he kissed her for a very good reason."

"Which is?"

"Why, how better to protect you from the unknown? My darling, if he were to have thrown caution to the wind and declared his undying love to the public that night, where do you think you and he would be right now?"

Marie-Claire gestured limply at the television. "On that show?"

"Precisely. Now, my sweet, as much as I hate to do this,

I'm going to kick you out of my house. I want you to go home and get to the bottom of this. Certainly, the truth will surface soon. And, when it does, you need to be there to fight for your man.''

Sebastian was fighting mad. Blood pumping like the bellows that fanned the flames of hell, he stared at the papers Simone had just faxed to him at Claudette's house. He could taste murder in the bile that rose in his throat as he swung around to face her. His mother cowered in the corner. He advanced on her, brandishing the faxed papers.

''Why?'' he shouted.

''Why…what?'' Claudette cringed more deeply into her calfskin club chair.

''Don't play dumb with me, Mère. I have papers here that spell out the unfortunate fact that I am indeed your flesh and blood. Though it seems that we are both reluctant to admit that.''

''What is that you have there?'' Holding out one last hope that her dreams of becoming the next dowager queen were not crashing down around her, Claudette gestured to the pages he held.

''This is news from Interpol in France. DNA results that state unequivocally that thirty-two years ago, in a hospital in France, the woman who bore me, was you. Claudette Alexandra LeMarc. Not Katie Graham, in some tragic story that you concocted.''

Now that Sebastian knew the truth, Claudette shifted into an offensive mode and sitting up straight, did her best to smoothly backpedal. ''Sebastian, surely you could not have learned to be such an ingrate from me! I did all of this *for you*. In your best interests.''

Jaw slack, Sebastian stared at this illogical woman he once thought he knew. ''You think that *lying* about my parentage and slipping me into the royal family like some...*cuckoo's egg,* was in my best interest?" Sebastian advanced to the edge of her chair and, gripping the edge until the wood frame cracked, leaned down. His voice was low. Menacing. Deadly. "What kind of crazy are you?"

Hand to throat, Claudette leaned away from him, afraid. "I thought that after you were in place, all the questions would die down. They would see, as I do, that you are the one who should wield the power in this country. You would make a wonderful king."

"Not if I am not *born to the position!*" Sebastian strode several paces away from her. "Do you realize what you have cost me? Do you have any idea at all, what your selfishness has done?"

Her stare was blank.

"No. I see that you do not. Mère—" Nose to nose again, Sebastian inclined his head to the mass of clutter in her parlor. "It is time for you to grow up. I have just two suggestions for you. First, you need to take back everything you have purchased in the last month, and then have an estate sale and get rid of everything else. When you have finished that gargantuan task, I suggest," his gaze stabbed into hers, "that you get a job."

"A..." Claudette looked as if she'd just swallowed something rancid, "a job?"

"If you wish to continue eating, yes." Sebastian pushed off her chair, reached for his overcoat and tossed it over his shoulder. "I'm going to the palace to beg forgiveness for your temporary insanity. I'll tell Simone to expect you soon so that you can do the same. Then, if she can even still look me in the eye, I'm going to ask for her granddaughter's hand in marriage."

Forgetting the hot water within which she was boiling, Claudette leapt to her feet and clasped her hands in a rapturous manner. ''You will be joining the royal family after all?''

''If I am lucky, yes, I'll be joining the royal family. You, on the other hand, will be joining the work force. Good luck, Mère.''

Once back at home in St. Michel, Marie-Claire was anxious to discuss the headlines she'd seen with Luc Dumont. After stowing her bags in her suite, she was told he was in one of the palace's comfortable salons. She found him sitting with the dowager queen, flustered over some sharp remark the old woman had just made. Upon spotting Marie-Claire, Simone beckoned. ''Come here, darling girl, and save me from this boy's endless flirtation.''

Flushing crimson, Luc opened his mouth to protest but thinking better, instead heaved a resigned sigh.

Simone ignored him. ''How was your trip to Copenhagen?''

Marie-Claire grinned in sympathy at Luc, then turned to Simone.

''I heard the news. Saw it in the papers, even there.''

''I was hoping we could spare the world our dirty laundry, but Wilhelm—'' Simone's eyes clouded over and she swallowed hard.

''I know. How is Lise holding up?''

''As can be expected. Depressed about Wilhelm. Morning sick with the baby. Still grieving Philippe. Trying to cope with possible illegitimacy. Other than that, she's in fine fettle.''

''I'll go see her in a moment. But first, I heard that the palace is still officially denying Sebastian as crown prince. What are we waiting for?''

''You haven't heard? Oh, darling, I'm so thoughtless. I should have called you first! Luc here has discovered through a series of DNA tests, that there is no way that Sebastian is Philippe's son.''

''What?'' Marie-Claire whispered as joy surged into her throat.

''Yes, it seems that Claudette was lying to save her spendthrift hide. Although I forgave her and assigned her a job in the palace kitchen, slicing onions. Which reminds me. I must check on her now.'' Before she could struggle to her feet, Luc leapt to assist. ''I'm too old for you, son,'' she groused and slapped his hand from her arm.

''But—''

''Why don't you focus this energy on someone your own age. Tell this child about Claudette's deception and leave me be. Marie-Claire, you can ask him the finer points of the case, but suffice it to say, we are still searching for the crown prince.''

Relief lifted her out of her chair and Marie-Claire stood watching her grandmother totter out of the room. ''She's a tease,'' Marie-Claire said once her grandmother was out of earshot.

''I'm finding that out.''

Hands clasped under her chin, Marie-Claire looked deeply into Luc's eyes. ''So it's true. Sebastian is not my brother.''

''No. In fact, I'm in the process of tracing Katie Graham's marriage certificate to Texas. So we're back to the drawing board.''

Laughing, Marie-Claire rushed forward and, grabbing him round the neck, stood on tiptoe and soundly kissed his cheeks. Pleased, he made no effort to back away.

''Oh,'' she breathed, ''thank you, thank you!''

''My pleasure. Anything else I can do?''

''Yes. You can let her go.'' Sebastian's voice, like the voice of an angry mythical god boomed fire from behind them and before they could even protest, he'd grabbed Luc by the scruff of the neck and landed a neat right cross to his face.

Surprised, Luc reeled, and falling to the floor, clutched the welt that was forming at his jaw. "What the *hell?*"

Astonished, Marie-Claire emitted a strangled scream. *"Sebastian!"*

"This time," Sebastian roared, "I'm not getting hit." He dove down and lifted Luc off the floor by his shirt. Luc dangled, still too shocked to register the fact that Sebastian LeMarc was preparing to beat him to a bloody pulp.

"Sebastian," Marie-Claire rushed to grab his arm, "stop it! Luc is simply telling me the truth! That you are not the crown prince! That you are not my brother! That we can," she burst into tears, "be together."

Sebastian dropped Luc with a thud.

"For crying out loud," Luc moaned from the floor, "what is it with this family?" Dragging himself to his feet, Luc stood swaying and pointed at them. "I keep getting accused of flirting and dammit, *I'm not!*" With that, he straightened his shirt and staggered out of the room.

"Dumont," Sebastian called after him, "I'm really sorry—"

Luc waved a hand behind him. "Yeah, yeah," he muttered and left.

Slowly, Sebastian turned and stood, watching Marie-Claire, and she was reminded of that night at the pond, when his eyes saw into her soul. His hands settled at his narrow hips, and, breathing hard, she thought how masculine he was, always charging in to save her from herself.

"So you know." Boyishly, he pushed the fingertips of one hand through his hair, straightening it.

"Yes." Marie-Claire nodded, her pulse drumming crazily, and she fought the urge to move to him and tousle his hair.

"You were right."

"You will have to learn to live with that, as I usually am."

Sebastian rolled his eyes.

A slow smile tugged at the corners of her mouth.

They stood, transfixed with helpless wonder at their sudden freedom.

"Come here," he whispered.

Marie-Claire need not be told twice. She ran the few steps it took to fling herself into his powerful arms and fill her hands with his hair.

Noses bumped, chins collided, but it only took an instant for their mouths to come home. Marie-Claire's laughter turned to a liquid moan as he gave her the kiss she'd been wanting for weeks. Wilting in his arms, she could feel her heartbeat pounding against his and hear his breath coming in labored pants.

"Ahh, Marie-Claire," he whispered. "How I've missed you."

"Mmm." He swallowed her heartfelt reply.

How long they stood like this was anybody's guess, but the clock chimed the quarter and half hours. The kisses ebbed and flowed, entwined with whispered endearments, ripening to perfection like fine wine. Marie-Claire draped her arms over his shoulders and fell back, dangling in his embrace, loving the onslaught.

"I missed this."

"Yes," she murmured.

"You have certainly helped me realize three very important things in this life."

"Mmm. And what would they be?"

"Well, for one thing, that life is very short, and to waste even a moment is a sin."

Her head snapped up and her eyes flew to his. "That's just what I learned from you!"

"Ahh, good. Then you won't refuse me, when I ask you to mar—"

"Yes!" Marie-Claire's squeal was gleeful as she pulled his face low for another kiss.

"I don't want to wait," Sebastian said, when she let him up for air.

"Neither do I."

"Good. You have two weeks."

"Two weeks?"

"Just enough time to let the public digest the fact that we are not related. Yet, anyway."

Marie-Claire nodded, the cogs in her mind already grinding into motion. "Two weeks is not much time, but I'm up to the task. There are cable shows and advice columns dealing with just such emergencies...."

"God help us all," Sebastian moaned.

Marie-Claire giggled and buried her fingers into his back pants pockets. "Sebastian?"

"Hmm?" He was busy kissing the back of her jaw, directly under her ear.

"What else have you realized?"

"Uh...I forgot."

Her laughter was lazy. "You did not. Think."

"I can't."

"Tell me."

Eyes heavy with desire, Sebastian paused and thought. "Oh. The second thing is that I have no desire ever to live above my means. So. If you'll agree to live with me at my house in the—"

"Yes!" Again, Marie-Claire cut him off with a long, soulful kiss.

"And last, but certainly most important of all, I love you more than any man has ever loved a woman."

"Oh, Sebastian. I love you."

Sebastian loosened his collar. "You know, it's still going to take some adjusting, to get me over the idea that you are not my sister."

Marie-Claire growled and tugged his lower lip between her teeth.

"Okay. I'm adjusted," he said, and angled her mouth beneath his.

Epilogue

Through a wide arched doorway made of stone, an ethereal gold light, courtesy of the setting sun, streamed into a small garden niche. Just outside the palace walls, it housed a large glass gazebo, erected just for this special occasion. The site was perfect for a twilight wedding in the middle of April.

Fragrance from the spring flowers that crowded the formal gardens wafted about on the light breezes and into the open windows. Gentle spring rains misted the leaded panes on the roof, refracting light and dazzling the guests. Pea-stone paths wended through pine trees and thickly flowered rhododendron bushes and bulbs of hyacinth and tulip, all culminating at the arched door.

Inside the glass house, candles burned and light harpsichord music played as Marie-Claire moved, escorted by a smiling prime minister, toward Sebastian. Made of French silk and Italian chiffon, Marie-Claire's dress swished along the satin floor runner and Sebastian thought he'd never seen anything so beautiful in his life.

The audience was small, only Marie-Claire's family and

a few friends. A much chastened Claudette sat in the front row, crying real tears at the beauty of the occasion. Ariane had flown home from Rhineland for the ceremony and stood with Lise as maid and matron of honor.

As all weddings do, this one moved to its swift conclusion with an exchange of vows and a kiss that lingered nearly as long as the ceremony had. The minister, having pronounced them husband and wife, held up his hands to still the applause.

"Ladies and gentlemen, it is my privilege, for the first time ever, to introduce Mr. and Mrs. Sebastian LeMarc."

Over the din, Sebastian leaned in to better hear Marie-Claire.

"So," she said, "we are family after all."

He nodded and whispered back. "So we are, my wife. But our family is way too small, to my way of thinking."

"Are you suggesting that we skip the reception?"

"If we leave now, we can be starting on that baby in less than an hour."

Losing a slipper as she went, Marie-Claire grabbed his hand and together, they ran into happily ever after.

*   *   *   *   *

SILHOUETTE®

DESIRE™

joyfully presents

ROYALLY WED:
The Missing Heir

Who can succeed the throne of St. Michel?
An heir—a son—may exist!
Now a desperate search is underway for...
the missing heir.

May 2003
OF ROYAL BLOOD
by Carolyn Zane
and
IN PURSUIT OF A PRINCESS
by Donna Clayton

June 2003
A PRINCESS IN WAITING
by Carol Grace
and
A PRINCE AT LAST!
by Cathie Linz

IN PURSUIT OF A PRINCESS
by
Donna Clayton

DONNA CLAYTON

is the recipient of the Diamond Author Award for Literary Achievement 2000, as well as two Holt Medallions. She became a writer through her love of reading. As a child, she marvelled at her ability to travel the world, experience swashbuckling adventures and meet amazingly bold and daring people without ever leaving the shade of the huge oak in her very own back garden. She takes great pride in knowing that, through her work, she provides her readers the chance to indulge in some purely selfish romantic entertainment.

One of her favourite pastimes is travelling. Her other interests include walking, reading, visiting friends, teaching Sunday school, cooking and baking, and she still collects cookery books, too. In fact, her house is over-run with them.

Please write to Donna care of Silhouette Books. She'd love to hear from you!

In loving memory of Doris Montgomery,
my mom, my friend

Chapter One

"Let the mission begin." Princess Ariane de Bergeron glanced around, her heart pattering like the wings of a hummingbird as she made her way through the maze-like halls of the castle. Anyone overhearing her talking to herself would dub her a simpleton. But wasn't that just what she wanted? Let the citizens of this foreign country think she was silly. That fit her plans perfectly.

Yes, she was in a foreign land. And although the lush and hilly terrain of Rhineland was nearly as beautiful as her own neighboring country, she had to remember there were enemies here. Enemies who were plotting to seize her beloved St. Michel.

Ariane was so concerned for her countrymen, in fact, that she was here under the guise of responding to the interest of Prince Etienne Kroninberg. Just a little over six months ago, the prince had traveled to St. Michel to present her with a formal invitation to the opera. Everyone realized the significance of this visit. Etienne had clear intentions on Princess Ariane. And her father, King Philippe, had been in full agreement that the two royal families should unite.

Royal protocol had forced Ariane to accept the date, but if the truth were to be known, she found the opera to be the most boring pastime ever invented. And if the prince of Rhineland enjoyed opera, then he must be boring, as well. In order to entertain herself, she'd invited plenty of attendants and friends along for the evening. So many, in fact, that she'd spent little time alone with the prince. And if the complete truth were known regarding her conduct that evening, the crown prince would not only have been insulted, but downright outraged.

She grinned even now as she thought about her wicked behavior. The poor man. He'd obviously had no idea what he'd been up against. Now, had he invited her to go rock climbing or parasailing, maybe then she'd have wanted to get to know him. As it turned out, she returned to the opera house before the performance had ended…with Prince Etienne none the wiser, thank heavens.

However, it had been pure luck for her—and the whole of her country—that Etienne had shown an interest in her. Under the pretense of responding to his attention, she planned to keep her eyes and ears open, to collect all the information possible about who was plotting against her country.

As she descended the curved staircase, she glanced at the massive grandfather clock standing on the landing. Twelve minutes past the hour. Perfect. Ariane's grandmother, Dowager Queen Simone de Bergeron, had advised that when one was attending a party given in one's honor it was polite to arrive fashionably late, allowing time for the other guests to have assembled themselves.

Her name was announced and she paused inside the doorway of the ballroom as she'd been taught to do since she was a child. All eyes turned to her.

She was confident that her attire befitted her position. The soft silk of her strapless, form-fitting gown was the same midnight blue of her eyes. Her hair was swept off her shoulders with the perfect amount of wispy tendrils framing her face. The jewels in her tiara glittered, as did the diamonds gracing her earlobes and throat. Her father would have been proud....

Grief rushed over her, but she quelled the tears that so suddenly scalded the backs of her eyelids. Now was not the time to succumb to emotion, not with a room full of nobility scrutinizing her every move. Forcing her mouth to spread into a gracious smile, she made her way toward her host and hostess.

"Your Highness." Ariane greeted the king of Rhineland, offering the man a curtsy. But it was the queen who reached out to her.

"Oh, Ariane," the woman said, "we'll have none of that formal behavior from you. This is Giraud." She indicated her husband. "And I insist that you call me Laurette."

The king chuckled jovially. "You'll have to do as she says," he told Ariane. "I may wear the bigger crown, but Laurette runs the place."

They laughed, and Ariane was keenly aware of the fondness this couple obviously shared. All her instincts told her that she was going to like these people. She hoped she didn't discover they were involved in the conspiracy.

Laurette's expression turned somber. "I was so

sorry to hear about the passing of your father. King Philippe was a wonderful man.''

Sorrow welled up in Ariane. She had yet to come to grips with her grief. She smiled through the pain. ''Thank you. No one knew Father was having heart problems.''

''If there is anything we can do for you while you're here with us…''

The king's kind offer touched Ariane's heart.

Suddenly, Queen Laurette looked pained. ''I'll have to apologize for my son. I don't know what could be keeping him. He's always in some meeting or other.''

''I've sent out a search party.'' Giraud patted Ariane's arm. ''Don't worry. He'll turn up soon enough.''

''I'm sure he will.'' But even as Ariane stood there with her back to the crowd, she became cognizant of the low murmur rushing through the room. Surely the guests were discussing the prince's faux pas.

As she made her way across the polished marble floor, Ariane's smile didn't wilt in the least; however, she could feel annoyance spark inside her like the striking of a match. Of all the pompous, egotistical things for the prince to do! Arriving *after* her at a party given in her honor was not only arrogant, it was downright rude.

Like the loyal and trusted friend she was, Francie, Ariane's lady-in-waiting, stood nearby, the frown on her brow blatant proof of the aggravation she felt.

''He's an oaf to have done this to you,'' Francie said in a rush.

Ariane sighed, knowing exactly about whom Francie was speaking. "It's all right. I'm not concerned with the prince, anyway. You know that."

The words rolled off her tongue easily enough—and they *should* have been nothing but true. So why, she wondered, was she feeling so perturbed?

"Yes, but no one else here does," her friend reminded her. "And now everyone's talking. They'll all be thinking—"

"Keep your voice down." Ariane picked up a flute of champagne from a tray and nodded her appreciation to the servant who offered it. Once the man was out of earshot, she said to Francie, "I know what they'll be thinking—*and saying.* That I'm a desperate woman who is hankering after their prince."

Maybe that was the cause of her irritation. She didn't like being thought of as desperate.

"But *he* was the one who made first contact," her lady said, her ire obvious.

Francie got herself worked up easily and it never failed to tweak Ariane's humor. A grin curled the corners of her mouth. "It's going to be all right. Yes, I had hoped that my arrival would go smoothly, but I can surely handle a bumpy start." She smiled a genial greeting to an elderly man who strolled by. "Maybe the prince has taken ill. Or he's been detained with affairs of the state."

"At eight o'clock on a Saturday evening? Nothing could be more important to the prince of Rhineland than to be *here*." Francie's expression displayed her indignation as she firmly added, "Ten minutes ago."

"Okay, you've made your point. So the prince is an arrogant lout." Ariane sipped her champagne. "Speaking of affairs of the state…what do you say we find a likely candidate and talk politics? That *is* why I'm here.''

Francie's nose wrinkled. ''Political talk bores me. You know that.''

Yes, Ariane did. ''Then you go find a handsome man to dance with.''

The woman started to go, but paused long enough to warn, ''You be careful.''

''Careful is my middle name. Besides—'' Ariane let her eyes go wide with feigned naïveté ''—as soon as I show them that I'm empty-headed and harmless, every official in the castle will be clamoring to impress me with all they know.''

Etienne slipped into the ballroom using a side door. His parents would have his head for being late. But the matter couldn't be helped, he thought, his mouth firming into a grim line. He could only meet with the most trusted members of his Intelligence Service when everyone else was otherwise occupied.

Ruthless rumors were afloat. It had been reported to him that a person—or persons—within his father's cabinet wanted to seize control of the neighboring country of St. Michel. Etienne was appalled that someone wanted to take advantage of the de Bergeron family when they were still in mourning over the loss of King Philippe. The idea was barbaric in this day and age.

Granted, the unexpected death of the king left the country with no male heir—and it was common knowledge that the law of St. Michel declared that females could not rule. It was an archaic edict, but legally enforceable, nonetheless. No war would be fought. Not a single Rhineland soldier would march across St. Michel's border. This battle would be waged in the international courts. And all of this would take place in a civilized and peaceful manner. Yet it would be nonetheless barbaric in Etienne's mind.

He paused when he caught sight of his parents who were waltzing out on the dance floor. His mother was just getting over a serious bout of pneumonia. She'd been ill for some time now and his father had been worried that she may not recover completely. It was good to see them enjoying themselves.

He let his gaze travel slowly over the guests in the ballroom. It didn't take but an instant to find who he was looking for. She stood out in the crowd, his princess did. Ariane was that stunning. Heat spiraled like liquid smoke low in his gut.

Her honey-blond hair was twisted into an intricate coiffure, a few loose and softly curling strands falling to brush against her sexy bare shoulders whenever she moved her head. The line of her milky neck was long and graceful and delicate. She had the kind of throat that enticed a man to press his nose against warm skin, to inhale the distinct and subtle womanly aroma that would be hers and hers alone. Ariane, he silently surmised, would smell of sunny summer days and flowery meadows.

He had to admit, Princess Ariane's visit had him more than a bit perplexed. He'd made his intentions known prior to her father's passing. King Philippe had let Etienne know that he was quite in favor of a match between himself and Ariane. Etienne's own father was in favor of such an alliance as well. However, Princess Ariane hadn't seemed the least interested in Etienne as a suitor.

He'd returned home feeling rebuffed. He wasn't a quitter, though, by any means, and he'd had every intention of having another go at the beautiful Princess Ariane. However, his mother had taken ill, and Etienne had stood in for his father so he could be with his mother. Then King Philippe had died. Contacting Ariane during her time of mourning simply hadn't seemed appropriate.

No one had been more surprised than Etienne when the de Bergeron royal envoy had arrived announcing Princess Ariane's intentions of visiting Rhineland.

He started across the floor. Surely, the princess would be feeling affronted by his tardiness. He had some groveling to do. He may as well get it over with.

When he approached, all conversation stopped.

"Your Highness." He bowed deep, wanting to express his profound apology. He straightened, leveling his gaze on her beautiful deep blue eyes. "Please forgive me." He pressed a light kiss, first to one cheek, then the other, taking full advantage of the old-style traditional greeting. Her skin was warm satin against his lips. "I hope you believe me when I say my late arrival couldn't be avoided. I do apologize for my absence."

He'd been wrong. Her scent didn't bring to mind summer days and wildflowers. She smelled of starlit nights washed clean by fresh rain.

Her lovely gaze went round and she said, "You've been absent?"

The two men standing in the small group did their best to stifle the humor incited by the Princess's cutting question.

Touché, Etienne thought. He deserved that. She had every right to put him in his place.

Her smile was dazzling enough to steal away a man's thoughts.

"I've been having a wonderful conversation with the reverends here," she told him.

What she'd said took him aback. Surely the lords had introduced themselves. Unable to quell his surprise, he queried, "Reverends?"

"Yes," she said. "The pastors here were just telling me about your beautiful country."

"Princess," Etienne felt compelled to correct, "Lord Hecht is minister of the interior. One of his many duties includes suggesting policy for our parklands." The man named Hecht offered Ariane an indulgent smile. "And Lord Bartelow is deputy minister of trade. He advises the king on issues of commerce." When Ariane's gaze still didn't seem to register understanding, he allowed himself to go a little further. "These men have been appointed by my father to help him run our government."

Ariane's chuckle sounded like tiny bells as she focused her attention on the two elderly men. "Oh…and here I thought I'd been talking to men of the cloth. I heard the word 'minister' and…well, I just naturally assumed…"

Again, she laughed. Daintily. Infectiously. And although the lords politely joined her, Etienne could tell from the quick, covert expressions that passed between them what they were thinking: if brain cells were dynamite, the lovely princess apparently wouldn't have enough to blow her nose.

This exchange was Etienne's first inkling that something about the de Bergeron princess seemed…well, shifted just a little bit left of center. Her behavior was somehow…off. And as he stood there listening to her talk, this deviation from what he thought should be the norm became more and more pronounced. He wasn't too proud to admit that the situation had him highly perplexed.

At one point when Lord Hecht was explaining his plan to create more nature sanctuaries, Princess Ariane suddenly snagged a passing female guest by the arm and exclaimed, "I simply must know where you bought that dress. The fabric is heavenly."

The three men stood speechless at the sudden shift in the conversation. However, the women seemed happy enough discussing clothing designers.

As the evening progressed, Etienne became downright amazed at how the princess would ask seemingly coherent questions regarding someone's political position only to make a frivolous comment that left her looking, well, less than intelligent.

Etienne honestly didn't know what to think. Maybe Ariane wasn't the woman he'd believed her to be.

Being the crown prince of Rhineland, the one who would next succeed to the throne, Etienne had realized early in his life that he couldn't chose a wife purely on whim. For several years now, the king himself as well as the king's most trusted advisors had been discussing the subject of Etienne's taking a wife. No man liked the idea of others offering input on who he took as a life mate, but, well, that was just the way things were done when you were of royal blood. Especially so when you were in line to become king.

From what he'd learned of Ariane de Bergeron, he'd had high hopes that she could very well be the perfect woman for him.

She was poised, there was no doubt about that. Having this woman gracing his arm would make any man proud. She was most certainly beautiful. The kind of woman who stirred the most primitive instincts in a man. He was experiencing that just being near her now, he realized, feeling the embers of desire smoldering even as he stood next to her. She was of the royal de Bergeron bloodline, a stately and well-respected family. And he'd been told she was an educated woman, having studied in Switzerland, acquiring a degree in political science.

Several women had gathered round them now, and he frowned as he listened to the conversation at hand. Had Ariane just compared the running of a monarchy to shopping for shoes? This evening was becoming more bizarre by the moment.

Sources had informed him that the princess had a head on her shoulders…a head supposedly filled with an impressive brain. However, if he were to believe what he was seeing—and hearing—this evening he'd have to say there was nothing more than a big air bubble between her ears.

"Oh, my," Ariane exclaimed suddenly, "but it is warm in here, don't you think?" She batted her innocent eyes at Etienne, clearly expecting him to make all things right for her.

"If you'll excuse me for a moment—" he let his gaze touch upon hers and then glanced at the group at large "I'll have the doors opened and fetch a cool drink for the princess."

The women standing within earshot hid their smiles and the men's gazes slid awkwardly from his. Normally, it wasn't Etienne's place to do such menial tasks as seeing to the temperature of the room or arranging for guests' refreshment. On any ordinary evening, he would have handed the chore over to one of the servants who hovered nearby. However, with complete and utter bewilderment spinning his thoughts into a dozen different directions, this was turning out to be no ordinary evening he'd ever experienced.

He gave quick orders to push open the doors leading to the garden to the first servant he saw, then he scanned the room in search of someone carrying a tray of drinks. He stopped short when he caught sight of his mother looking wan, and he immediately made his way through the crowd toward her.

"Are you feeling all right, Mother?" he asked. "You look done in."

Her smile was tired. "I think I've just had too much fun this evening, is all."

"Where's Father? He should see you to your room." Etienne glanced around him. "Would you like me to escort you?"

"No, no." Laurette's brow puckered. "You go back to Princess Ariane. Are you seeing to it that she's having a good time? Have you asked her to dance?"

The queen's tone held a mild inflection of accusation and censure. Etienne couldn't stop the smile that spread across his mouth. "Yes, I've asked the princess to dance. So have half a dozen other men. However, so far she hasn't been so inclined to accept."

His mother looked utterly scandalized. "She *has* to dance. *With you.* What will everyone say? You see to it that you get that young woman out on the dance floor."

Dutifully, he said, "Yes, Mother." Then he gave her a small, teasing salute.

"Oh, now," she said, "stop that. I'm not trying to mother hen you. I just want—"

"I know exactly what you want," Etienne gently interrupted. "You want Princess Ariane's visit to go well. And so do I."

The elderly woman glanced toward the crowd that had gathered around Ariane at the far side of the ballroom. She murmured, "She's probably upset. If only you had been on time...."

"Mother, trust that I'll make everything right."

"You always do, dear."

Just then, Etienne's father joined them, reaching up to clap his son on the back.

"That's one beautiful woman who has come to Rhineland to see you, son," he told Etienne. "Don't let her get away."

Etienne grinned. "I don't plan to."

Well, he hadn't planned to. But after spending a couple of hours in her company, he wasn't so sure anymore.

"All my top advisors say she's self-assured, humorous and well-educated—"

From his father's opinion, Etienne could tell the man hadn't spent much time this evening in the princess's company.

"—and that she's just perfect for you."

Etienne remained silent, his mind churning with troubling thoughts.

Giraud's gray eyes softened as they leveled on his wife. "You'll have to see to things for the remainder of tonight's festivities, Etienne. I'm going to retire for the evening with my lovely wife. She might be feeling better, but I believe she's not fully recovered just yet."

This protective behavior warmed Etienne's heart. He hoped to someday make a match as loving as the one his parents shared.

That thought had his gaze drifting across the room until it latched onto Princess Ariane. The deep blue silk of her dress hugged the curves and valleys of her luscious figure. The soft light turned her blond hair to glistening honey.

"She's perfect," he softly murmured his father's opinion aloud.

Self-assured, humorous, well-educated. The description haunted Etienne's mind.

Something wasn't right here. All the information he'd been given pointed out the fact that things were not adding up. Ariane *was* all of those things, Etienne was sure. And if he was sure of that, then her behavior had to be some sort of put on.

He sighed. But that just made no sense to him. No sense at all.

However, for some odd reason, it seemed as though the princess wanted the people of his country to think she was naïve and…well, dim-witted. She was putting on a show. And quite a show it was, at that.

But the question was…for whom? And why?

Chapter Two

"As long as capitalism remains what it is," Rhineland's prime minister, Arvin Schmidt stated, "then surplus capital will never be utilized for the purpose of raising the standard of living of the masses in any country boasting free enterprise."

Oh, how Ariane desperately wanted to comment. She'd have loved to tell the man that capitalism was commodity production at the highest stage of development, when labor power itself becomes a commodity, and if it raised the standard of living it could not be capitalism because uneven development and wretched conditions were fundamental states where free enterprise reigned.

Arguing politics was her passion, but she bit her tongue and remained silent. Some of the silliness that had spewed from her mouth tonight had utterly mortified her. It seemed to her that she'd talked to everyone, and every person in the room must think that her brain was made of marshmallow fluff. She didn't like making herself look stupid, she was quickly learning. But it couldn't be helped. She needed the government officials to feel safe in expressing their political views in her presence. How else was she to learn who among them were working toward the annexation of her beloved St. Michel?

Just then Prime Minister Schmidt remarked, "There are rules to be followed for every form of government."

Something in the man's tone drew her attention as sharply as if she were zeroing in on a bull's-eye.

"No matter the type of leadership that rules," he continued smoothly, "laws *must* be followed. No matter how difficult that might prove for some citizens."

Was the man sending out a cryptic message? Ariane wondered. Or was he merely trying to impress her with his opinions. Keen interest buzzed through her veins like adrenaline and she allowed it to show on her face with the hope that Schmidt would elaborate a little more. However, before he could, she felt a light touch on her forearm.

"Pardon me, princess."

She turned to see Etienne, and she stared into his handsome face, realizing for the very first time the startling color of his eyes—pewter-gray. Fringed with dark lashes, the effect was enough to steal her breath away.

Ariane had been so miffed at the man earlier in the evening that she hadn't been able to control the urge to put him in his place. She had forced herself to ignore him when he'd first arrived, wanting to convey how insulting his tardiness had been to her. She'd focused the whole of her concentration on the two "ministers" she'd been talking to…she nearly grinned now as she thought of the complete genius of *that* sham. Surely after that silly assessment the prince and the lords thought her to be a total idiot.

But now her anger was gone as she really and truly saw Prince Etienne for the first time this evening.

She fumbled for words. Stumbled over her thoughts. And there wasn't a single ounce of deception or pretense in her behavior. She simply couldn't get her tongue and the notions in her head to properly jive. Something strange was taking place…it was as if she'd been a train barreling down a track and suddenly found herself completely derailed.

"May I have this dance?" he asked.

The wheels in her brain turned, but she couldn't seem to get her larynx to utter a single sound. He cupped her elbow in his palm, obviously expecting her to accept his invitation.

Panic welled up within her. No, no! she wanted to shout. It was bad enough that she'd made herself look stupid to the upper echelon of Rhineland society. She certainly didn't want everyone to discover that she also had two left feet!

It wasn't that she hadn't tried to learn to dance. She'd suffered through two full years of torturous dance classes. Although, the fact that the instructor had been a snooty little man who had made her feel nothing short of a lumbering elephant out on the dance floor when all her other siblings—full, step and half—had blossomed into elegant swans under the man's tutelage. And her stepbrother Georges, a man who hated to fail at anything, had finally thrown up his hands in utter frustration when he'd attempted to teach her.

With her heart pounding so hard that blood whooshed dizzyingly through her head, she was finally able to sputter, "C-can't you see I'm in the middle of a c-conversation with the prime minister?"

The question sounded abrupt even to her own ears, and Ariane was horrified that she hadn't tempered her tone.

Having been born a princess, Ariane had attended many balls and parties in her twenty-three years, and she'd become skilled at turning down invitations to dance. Her grandmother, Dowager Queen Simone, wanting to help her granddaughter work around this little problem, had trained her extensively on just how to decline a request to dance without hurting the feelings of the party offering the invitation. In fact, Ariane had succeeded in doing just that at least seven or eight times this evening.

But the way Etienne's dove-gray eyes sparkled had thrown her for a loop. Why hadn't she noticed before this moment how amazing—how mesmerizing—his gaze was?

The prince's grip on her elbow tightened gently but insistently, and he guided her away from the group. He murmured, "Our prime minister could talk the ears off a brass monkey. But I have orders from none other than the queen herself who threatened me if I didn't get you out on the dance floor."

The dread churning inside Ariane didn't abate a bit, but the humor playing around the handsome prince's mouth lulled her into querying, "And what did she threaten you with?"

Etienne chuckled, and Ariane could tell from the look on his face that this man was very fond of the woman who had given birth to him.

"Oh, she didn't specify the hazards I'd face if I didn't follow her instruction," he told her. "She didn't have to. She's been my mother for twenty-nine years. I know better than to disobey her wishes."

"Sounds like Queen Laurette is quite a tyrant," she teasingly surmised.

The prince grinned, and she felt as if the summer sun were shining full on her face.

He whispered conspiratorially, "Don't let this get about...but I've got my mother wrapped round my pinkie. However, I do like to keep her happy. So help me out here, would you? Just one little dance is all I need from you, and Mother's mind will be put to ease."

Maybe it was the fact that her own mom had died when she was seventeen, or maybe it was because she had such a terrible relationship with her current stepmother, the jealous and oh-so-insecure Queen Celeste, but Ariane found it very endearing, indeed, to discover that the prince had formed such an open and loving bond with his mother. And the fact that he didn't mind Ariane knowing how he felt about the queen, well, that was just icing on the cake.

The heels of her shoes clicked on the smooth marble floor that was fairly swarming with couples who had already begun swaying to the breezy orchestral melody.

She hesitated, then decided she'd better do what she could to warn him what he was in for. "Etienne, please..."

He stopped and looked down at her, apparent curiosity puckering his high, intelligent brow.

Oh. She'd made herself out to be foolish enough tonight, she hated the notion of divulging further faults. Finally, sheer desperation had her softly admitting, "I'm afraid I'm about to embarrass you."

Again, he chuckled and Ariane was bombarded with the sudden outrageous urge to place her palm against his chest to feel what she instinctively knew would be the sexy tremor of his laughter. Her eyes widened at the astonishing thought.

"You could never embarrass me," Etienne told her. "In fact, I'm sure I am already the envy of every man in the kingdom."

She knew he meant to flatter her with the compliment, but she was too anxiety-ridden to even smile at him. "You don't understand…"

Before she had time to explain, he whirled her around to face him, deftly snuggling one palm at the base of her spine, enveloping her hand in his free one.

The closeness of him, the heat of him, made her feel as if she were suddenly thrust into a vacuum from which she couldn't draw breath. Yet as soon as they began to move, she automatically craned her neck in an attempt to watch where she was going. She panicked at the thought of bumping into another couple, of stepping on his feet, of slipping on the smooth, polished marble. She imagined what a sight the two of them would make if they were to go tumbling to the floor. Her apprehension hitched up another notch.

Funny thing about the waltz, the leader was the one who moved forward. As long as she was stepping away from Etienne, she didn't think she'd mash his toes with hers. She could place her foot first and he was responsible for not trampling on her. However, the dance also involved a great deal of turning, and the very first time the prince guided her toward him every muscle in her body tensed up—and she planted her foot directly on top of his.

His handsome face registered more surprise than pain. Ariane chucked him a quick look of apology before dipping her chin to once more stare at her feet.

Etienne had been graced with the princess's regretful expression for only a moment, but the vulnerability he'd read in her eyes, on her furrowed brow, affected him in the most amazing manner. He felt this immense urge to soothe her turmoil, to protect her from the eyes and opinions that she feared, to sweep her away from the crowd…to ravage that perfect pink mouth of hers with fierce kisses.

Without another thought, he waltzed her right out the huge double doors and onto the flagstone veranda that overlooked the formal gardens. The music spilled out into the night right along with them, but they stopped dancing and walked in silence to the stone half wall that edged the area.

Moonlight washed across the trees and shrubs, dusting them in a soft, pallid radiance. The unusually warm spring had caused the flower bulbs to burst from the ground and send forth their heady scents. It seemed as though a million stars glittered against the velvety night sky.

''Thank you.''

The gratitude in her sweet voice tugged at his heartstrings.

He couldn't keep the smile from curling the corners of his mouth. ''How was it you missed Dancing 101?''

Etienne knew dance instruction was common practice for all children of royal lineage, so he was certain she'd understand his question.

Her sigh was as soft as the night air. "Oh, I took the class," she admitted despondently. "And I flunked it. Twice." She gazed up into his face. "I thought the second time round I just might get a passing mark...but then I fell right on my behind during the last session of learning the foxtrot. After that, the instructor—a mean and unforgiving little man, I might add—refused to have me in his classroom."

His grin widened, but Etienne turned his head away until he succeeded in snuffing out the chuckle that rose up in his throat. It was obvious that she felt bad enough about her plight without him laughing at her.

Keeping his expression just as straight as he could, he said, "When is the last time you saw anyone dance the foxtrot?"

"That's the same thing I said to—"

She paused, seeming to realize the humor he found in her story.

"Okay," she told him. "Go ahead and laugh. It *is* pretty funny."

"Oh, no." He shook his head. "I wouldn't dream of laughing at your expense."

Her nose wrinkled, and Etienne thought it was the cutest thing he'd ever seen in his life.

"It's just that I have no rhythm," she complained.

He felt compelled to say, "That's not it at all."

Her perfectly arched brows lifted a fraction in silent question.

"It's the fear you have to conquer," he told her.

"Fear? Why, as far as I know, I'm not afraid of much of anything."

Before full insult could set in, he rushed to further explain, "It's clear to me that you don't trust your partner. You're afraid you're going to be led into disaster. The moment you realize that your partner is competent in his role, then your concerns will dissolve like sugar in water. Here, let me show you.''

She balked, but he took her into his arms. Immediately, her spine arched and she stood tall, just as she'd been taught.

He settled his hand low on the curve of her spine, murmuring, ''You have great form.''

Great form, he wanted to repeat. He felt heated tendrils sprout and curl in the deepest depths of his gut.

When they were in position, her gaze unconsciously dipped downward.

''Oh, no,'' he softly chided. Tucking his bent knuckle gently under her chin, he tipped up her jaw. ''Look me in the eyes. Relax. Don't even think about the steps. Don't give your feet—or mine—another thought. Just listen to the music. Let it roll through you. And trust me.''

Iridescent moon rays cast half of her features in shadow. Her prominent features were highlighted by the pearly glow: cheekbone, brow, chin, nose. And what a perfect nose it was. Etienne had to force himself not to plant a quick kiss on its tip.

He gazed down into her beautiful face, their gazes locking…and something extraordinary happened.

''Trust me,'' he repeated in a whisper, pushing off into the first step of the dance.

The next few minutes seemed laced with magic. A mysterious je ne sais quoi that he'd never before experienced in his life. He couldn't tell if it was the silky night air, or the soft strain of the orchestra…or the gorgeous young woman who stared up into his face.

Her dark eyes never left his. Not for a second. And the atmosphere seemed to heat up with each step they took, each dip and sway and turn they made. They may have been under the open sky, but Etienne had the strange sense that time itself was drawing around them like a warm and protective blanket.

The waltz they performed on the stone terrace was nearly flawless. There could be no other way to describe it.

Finally, the music faded, and the two of them stood there in that dancers' stance seemingly hypnotized. She studied his face as if she was seeing him for the very first time. The heat of her penetrated the silk of her dress, and he was sure his fingertips would be scorched. The muscles of her elegant, milky throat convulsed as she swallowed. Still they stood motionless, silent.

Of course, what seemed a hushed eternity couldn't have been more than the span of five or six heartbeats.

There was an intensity in the moment that called to Etienne. And it would have been so very easy for him to bend toward her. To place his lips against hers. To taste what he thought must be the delectable honeyed sweetness of her mouth.

But the part of his brain housing his common sense flickered to life. Doubts about this woman flooded into his thoughts. He was certain she'd been playacting all night. Pretending to be something she was not. And he couldn't help but wonder why.

In the end, he released her, clasping his hands behind his back so as not to surrender to the overwhelming desire he felt to kiss her, to touch her.

When he released her, she blinked slowly, once, twice. There was a lethargic sleepiness in her expression, and Etienne got the feeling that she was waking from a trance. He knew exactly how she felt. Then he noticed that her chest rose and fell as if she were out of breath...or physically reacting to the high intensity of the moment. Heaven could attest to the fact that he certainly was.

"I can't believe it."

The awe expressed on her face only made her all the more beautiful.

"I can't believe I waltzed without crushing your toes."

Her chuckle was filled with both giddiness and delight, and Etienne had to make a conscious effort not to reach out to her, then and there.

"Dancing won't ever be my favorite pastime," she remarked. "But at least now I know I can do it." Seemingly without thought, she added, "With the right partner, of course."

Her aside only seemed to heighten the thick atmosphere that swirled around them in the night air. He couldn't help wondering if she was as conscious of it as he was.

"I-I'm suddenly feeling exhausted," she whispered abruptly. "I hope you'll forgive me if I bid you goodnight."

He nodded a single, silent farewell, but she strode away from him so quickly that he doubted she even saw it.

The rusty quality of her voice coupled with the blatant fact that she was so obviously fleeing the scene told him that—yes—she had realized the magic that the two of them had conjured in those short few minutes under the stars.

* * *

Ariane came awake slowly, stretching on the luxurious bedding like a languid kitten. Sunlight streamed into the airy room and the warbling of birds, muffled yet melodious, could be heard even though the windows were closed against the morning chill.

All through the night she'd been plagued with dreams of pewter-gray eyes so fiery that she'd become consumed by them, of an embrace so secure that it had robbed her of all thought, of skin so hot that she felt burned by its touch, of a jaw so strong it was mesmerizing, of a mouth so perfect and kissable that she'd become thoroughly obsessed by the idea of tasting—

Stop!

Opening her mouth, Ariane gulped in a head-clearing breath as she pressed her palm flat against the base of her throat. She didn't want to think about what had happened between Etienne and herself at the ball last night. And she certainly didn't want to dream about the man.

Okay, so they had shared a few minutes together out under the silky night sky.

A few surprising—no, *amazing*—minutes.

Ariane did all she could to ignore this more precise description of the time she'd spent on the terrace with the prince.

Her trip to Rhineland held a solitary purpose. To glean political information for the head of her country's security force, Luc Dumont, who had been none too happy that she'd insisted on coming on this mission. But insist she had. She must remember her goal. She must remember that Etienne was a convenient motive for her visit. That was all he was. She refused to allow him to become anything more than that.

To allow fanciful thoughts to frolic around in her head would be useless. She and Etienne would never—could never—be anything more than they already were—mere acquaintances.

And the reality of her life was the reason.

Not only remembering, but focusing on the practicality of this fact made it all that much easier to clear the sweet but hopeless dreams from her head.

Movement at the window drew her gaze, and Ariane smiled as she watched the goldfinch that sat on the deep stone sill. The bird searched and pecked, then sang a few resounding notes, then went back to searching and pecking.

It felt so nice to be away from the tension that had built up in her home back in St. Michel. Her stepmother, Celeste, had never been the easiest person to live with, and luckily the palace was big enough that avoiding the woman was quite easy. However, since King Philippe's death, the queen—as Celeste preferred to be called these days—had become downright cantankerous.

Granted, the woman was nearly seven months pregnant. And the stress over worrying about the gender of the child she carried was probably contributing to her ill humor.

Ariane turned over onto her side and adjusted the pillow under her head.

The only way for her stepmother to retain even a modicum of her power was if she gave birth to a boy. A male child who would be in line for the throne. Of course, Celeste had professed to have taken a test that proved the gender of her baby, but Ariane wasn't the only one in the palace who thought it strange that the queen had yet to produce the medical documents to confirm that fact.

Smoothing her hand over the soft Egyptian cotton spread, Ariane sighed.

Even if her stepmother bore a baby boy, that child might not be first in line to be the next king. That honor would go to the child conceived during the marriage of Philippe, then crown prince of St. Michel, and an American woman named Katie Graham.

The young couple had fallen madly in love when Philippe had been eighteen. They had married without their parents' consent, and because Katie had been under the legal age to do such a thing, Philippe's parents had tricked them into believing that their union was null and void, that their marriage certificate wasn't worth the paper it was written on.

Philippe's mother, Ariane's grandmother, Simone, had expressed a deep regret over her deceitful actions of all those years ago when she'd recently relayed the story. She'd told Ariane and her two full-blooded sisters, Lise and Marie-Claire, that she and her husband had only been acting in what they truly believed to be their son's best interest.

So all those years ago the young couple parted. Philippe resumed his education and the training he'd need to act as king, and young Katie had left St. Michel brokenhearted—*and pregnant.*

If the child Katie had delivered was male…and if he was still alive…then *he* would be the next de Bergeron king of St. Michel.

However, Simone had told them all that as far as she knew Philippe had never heard from Katie again.

And no one had any idea if the child the woman gave birth to was male or female.

What worried Ariane more than anything was the future of St. Michel. Hundreds of years ago, those wonderful, loving people had fought long and hard to form their own realm, for the right to pledge themselves to the de Bergeron family. Yet it seemed that keeping their country intact was hinging on the discovery of the whereabouts of one little baby, hopefully now a grown man.

The de Bergeron missing heir.

Ariane placed her fingertips to her mouth to stifle a yawn.

Of course this turn of events—this fantastic story brought to them by Simone—affected Ariane and her sisters. But the fact that her own parents' marriage had been invalidated and that Ariane and her sisters had been deemed illegitimate should have upset Ariane more than it did. She should be terribly distressed by the idea of having her title stripped from her, of losing her position in society. Ariane couldn't quite put her finger on why the notion didn't ruffle her more.

It could be that the calm she felt over her situation was possible because she knew no one but her sisters, her country's prime minister, close family members and Luc Dumont, the head of St. Michel's security force—trusted family members and friends, one and all—were privy to her and her siblings' predicament. Once the rest of the world learned of the fact that she was misbegotten, then it could be that she'd fall completely to pieces.

What would Prince Etienne think when he learned

the news? The question flitted unbidden through her head like a leaf tossed on the wind.

Ariane threw back the blanket and sat up on the edge of the mattress. She shoved the silly query from her mind. What did she care what he thought? What did she care what *anyone* thought?

A nice hot cup of tea was what she needed to clear away all these unpleasant doubts and questions.

The guest suite in the Kroninberg Palace was spacious and sunny. It consisted of two en suite bedrooms, one for her and one for her lady-in-waiting, connected by a delightful high-ceilinged sitting room. That's where she found Francie munching on a piece of buttered toast.

"What time is it?" Ariane asked, surprised to see that breakfast had been served on a large tray. "Shouldn't we be taking the meal with our hosts?"

"Everyone's sleeping in this morning." Francie wiped her fingers on the crisp, white linen napkin in her lap. "The maid told me when she delivered the tray, so I decided not to wake you."

Ariane poured a steaming cup of tea from the porcelain pot. "So how did you sleep?" she asked. After dropping in one sugar cube, she stirred and then eased herself down in the velvet armchair flanking Francie's.

"Just fine."

Her lady looked as if she were the proverbial cat that had swallowed a canary.

"Okay," Ariane said, "out with it. What's on your mind?"

"Oh, nothing."

Francie's voice had a sing-song quality to it that relayed that the opposite was the real truth of the matter.

"It's just that I watched you go outside with the

prince…and not too much later you came rushing back through the doors and right out of the room. Your face was flushed and you looked…well, you looked as if something had happened." She swept a few nonexistent crumbs from her lap. "When I followed you up here, you'd already shut yourself up in your bedroom. Which was a clear sign to me that you didn't want to talk about what happened. Which tells me that something *did* actually happen."

"You're deluding yourself, my friend." Ariane took a sip of her tea, but she was cognizant of the slight tremble of her fingers. The last thing she wanted to talk about was her time out on the terrace with Etienne. "Nothing happened. Nothing at all." When Francie's eyes rolled expressively, she reasserted, *"Nothing."*

Her friend chuckled. "What is that old saying? The one about the princess protesting too much? I think that just might fit you to a *T.*"

Ariane let her gaze settle on the ornate teacup and said nothing.

Evidently not getting the message that Ariane didn't want to discuss the matter, Francie boldly asked, "What did you talk about when you were with Etienne? And how come you rushed away from him and left the party?"

"You don't take a hint very well, do you?" Ariane quipped.

Just remembering those pewter eyes, and how she'd seemed to fall headfirst into them…Ariane's heart tripped an unsteady beat and she felt all shaky inside.

She had no idea what had happened to her during those moments. Etienne's arms had enveloped her securely. She'd become almost entranced by his steady gaze. The heat of him had swathed her like a warm and protective cloak. Somewhere in the back of her brain she's been aware that the spicy scent of his cologne held a hint of citrus. The combination had been utterly enticing.

Trust me.

Even now, the mere memory of his rich, resonant voice sent shivers coursing down her spine like a shower of cool spring rain.

She'd been enraptured. By his gaze. His scent. His touch. By *him.*

Never before had she been so stirred by another human being.

When Ariane failed to rise to Francie's bait, the woman remarked, "Etienne is awfully handsome."

She waited, and Ariane remained stubbornly silent.

"He looked awesome last night."

More silence.

Finally, Francie blurted, "And those trousers he wore accentuated his nice, tight butt, too."

Ariane gasped, tea splashing over the rim of the cup. "Francie!"

Her friend giggled. "Well, I'm glad to see you're alive and well. With all the silent treatment I'd thought you'd died right where you sat."

Sighing, Ariane pursed her lips for a moment. Then she said, "I am alive and well. And I agree with everything you just said. The prince is a handsome man. And he looked delectable last night." She grinned. "And I did notice his butt. Are you happy now that I've bared my soul?"

Francie grinned with clear delight.

Then Ariane's shoulders drooped a fraction and she lifted her chin determinedly. "But tell me something…what is the fabulous prince going to say once he learns that I'm no longer a princess?''

The pleasure slowly slid from Francie's expression.

"I'm here on a mission," Ariane continued firmly. "I'm on an assignment that just might help our countrymen. *That's* what I have to focus on."

Francie looked contrite. "Yes, but there was no royal proclamation that said you couldn't have a little fun while you're here."

Ariane shook her head in disagreement. "That kind of fun will only lead to hurt and heartache. For everyone involved."

Chapter Three

Etienne sat at the end of the long table, making a great effort to appear interested in the story being recounted by the man sitting next to him. No matter how hard he tried, he simply couldn't seem to spark an interest in the gentleman's escapades of starting a coffee bean plantation in Kenya. In fact, it was all he could do not to doze off into his raspberry sorbet.

It could have been because the man's adventure had taken place nearly a half century ago, or that he kept losing track of the storyline which caused him to repeat some portions of the tale several times over. Still, Etienne did his best to chuckle at all the right places and raise his brows to show he was impressed when the exploits required it.

All through dinner, though, his gaze kept skimming down to the other end of the table where Ariane sat at his father's left. For the past several evenings Kroninberg Palace had been a hive of activity. First had been the ball welcoming Ariane to Rhineland. Then for three nights running, the formal dining room had been filled with government officials, dignitaries and special friends of the family who wanted to spend some time with the princess.

Etienne would have given his eyeteeth to have been seated next to Ariane. But since she was the guest of honor, her place was near his parents. And as a member of the Kroninberg family, Etienne had to do his part by sitting at the opposite end of the table and entertaining the guests who were not fortunate enough to sit nearer the princess.

During each lingering meal, Etienne had had a hard time giving the dinner guests his full attention. And the reason was simple.

Ariane.

Tonight she wore a sleeveless, figure-hugging dress in a captivating shade of burnt orange. The hue of the shiny-looking fabric set off both her deep blue eyes and her tanned, curvy body. Her honey-blond hair fell, sleek and loose, just past her shoulders, and Etienne kept daydreaming about combing his fingers through those soft tresses.

Ariane's easy smile flashed now at something his mother said, and he felt as if someone had stirred a pile of slow-burning embers inside him. Heat coiled in his belly and his jaw unwittingly tightened against the yearning that was kindled.

He wanted this woman. In the worst way.

Etienne still suspected she was playacting. That the empty-headed persona she was presenting was just that. A mask. A guise.

However, he had to admit that he wasn't quite sure. If she was putting on a show, she sure was good at it. Not once in the days that she'd been in Rhineland had she slipped up. Time and again, she'd draw the government officials into political discussions only to make some outlandish remark that made her seem downright silly.

But why did she continue to choose a topic on which she seemed to know so little? Did she not realize how dense it made her appear? Maybe she really *was* flighty and shallow.

No. Etienne refused to fall for that, no matter how hard the princess was working to make everyone around her believe it. There was an intelligence in those midnight eyes of hers that just seemed to be screaming for release.

What he needed to do was force her to show her true self. To somehow trip her up. And he didn't want to do that in the company of anyone else.

Suddenly a plan formed in his head. He'd invite her to dinner in his private suite, talk to her about world governments. She certainly seemed interested in the subject. He'd make some purposefully erroneous remarks about different political principles and then he'd see if she rose to the bait. He nearly chuckled at the perfection of his plan. No woman could resist correcting a man who was blatantly wrong. Ariane would be no exception.

But what to do about the princess's lady-in-waiting? Simple good manners dictated that he invite Francie along to dinner, too.

Then he thought of Harry, his equerry. The two of them were close friends…Etienne suppressed a grin…they'd even been partners in crime a time or two when they'd been students together at Eton. Berkshire, England hadn't known what had hit it after the two of them had pulled a couple of their harmless pranks.

His friendship with Harry had been what had prompted Etienne to ask the Brit to move to Rhineland as his personal assistant.

Harry's ornery streak was still thick enough that he could easily come up with a scheme to coax Francie out of Etienne's apartments, leaving Etienne alone with Ariane for a while. Better yet, Harry could waylay Francie even before the two women were to arrive for dinner.

Etienne could hardly contain his mirth as he realized that his own ornery streak hadn't faded much over the years.

The plan set, he nodded enthusiastically at something the old gentleman beside him said, and when everyone around him laughed, he followed suit. However his mind was focused on tomorrow evening…when he'd succeed in getting Ariane alone.

Where in the world was Francie? Ariane paced the sitting room of the guest suite. She'd been dressed and ready for half an hour.

Dinner with the prince. In his apartments.

Ariane trembled inside.

Her case of nerves had a twofold cause. First off, she was uneasy about her ability to keep up this brainless façade. So many times over the past few days she'd nearly blurted out her true opinions to the administrators and bureaucrats she'd talked with. She'd discovered just how much she abhorred looking like a senseless idiot.

And secondly, she'd done everything she could to keep from being alone with Etienne. Those mesmerizing moments they had shared on her first night in his country had really thrown her for a loop.

Before arriving in Rhineland she'd thought of Etienne as nothing more than a means to an end in her goal of discovering who was plotting against her country. But she'd quickly discovered that the prince was an alluring man. A sexy danger to her mission. Like flint against steel, he sparked feelings in her that she wasn't up to dealing with right now.

When she'd received his dinner invitation this morning, her first reaction had been relief. All those formal meals were beginning to get to her. She'd smiled so much that her cheek muscles were becoming sore.

Fretfulness had Ariane actually opening the door of the guest suite and peering down the hallway one way, then the other, in search of Francie. She stepped back inside and shut the door.

She glanced at the beautifully carved German cuckoo clock on the wall. Being fashionably late was one thing, but this was bordering on nothing short of bad manners.

What was worse? she wondered. A terribly tardy arrival? Or visiting the prince's private apartments without her lady in tow?

Certainly, Etienne would have staff members in attendance to serve the meal. And surely Harry, his personal assistant, would be present, as well. There should be plenty of people milling about to act as chaperones.

Not that a princess needed a chaperone in this day and age. However, Ariane almost smiled as she thought of how her elderly and quite conservative grandmother, the dowager queen, would respond. It was never seemly, Simone would say, for a single woman to visit a bachelor's private rooms unescorted.

Finally, with a frustrated sigh Ariane decided she could wait no longer. She took a final look at herself in the full-length mirror, giving a small nod at the thought that her black trousers and apple-green sweater fit the casual dress requirements stipulated for tonight's date.

Adrenaline surged through her. This was not a *date*, she silently chided herself. She had simply accepted an invitation for dinner. She had to eat, didn't she? And so did the prince. They were simply going to share a meal together. That was all.

She'd told Francie the honest to goodness truth about her feelings regarding her chances of a real relationship with the prince. The man wouldn't be interested in her in the least once he found out that she'd lost her title. Dabbling in the allure he stirred in her would be fruitless. And wrong.

She was smarter than that.

The center of the hallway leading to Etienne's suites was covered with a plush peach-colored carpet that muffled the sound of her steps. Like all the other doors in the palace, his was massive and constructed of some dark, rich wood that glowed with an aged patina that only hundreds of years could produce.

She knocked, and the door was opened almost automatically by none other than the prince himself.

"Good evening," he greeted. "I was beginning to think you weren't coming."

"I'm sorry. I was waiting for Francie, but she never did show up." She entered the room, impressed by its masculine design. The furniture was oversized and upholstered in leather. The color scheme was dove-gray and burgundy. It was easy to conclude that the masculine furnishings fit Etienne.

"Why, she's with Harry," he said easily. "I thought you knew."

"No, I didn't." Ariane frowned. "Francie's usually very good about keeping me informed on such matters."

Etienne lifted one shoulder. "Harry told me he invited Francie riding."

Now she was really confused. "But she's afraid of horses."

He grinned. "That's what Harry said. And he was appalled by the idea. He talked Francie into letting him give her a riding lesson."

His smile quirked up one corner of his mouth, and Ariane's knees went weak at the sexy sight.

Etienne raised his dark brows. "Harry has a way with women."

She blinked, shaking her head, and she couldn't stop herself from smiling. "He must." Almost to herself, she murmured, "I can't imagine Francie going within twenty yards of a horse, let alone sitting in a saddle."

"I hope you don't mind their missing dinner."

He led the way further into the room. Ariane followed.

"Have a seat—" he indicated the ornately carved table in the dining area just off the living room "—and I'll go ahead and plate up the food."

She made her way to one of the chairs, taking in the covered silver servers sitting on the sideboard. "You're going to serve?"

He nodded even though his back was to her as he uncovered the first silver server. "That's okay, isn't it?'' he asked, steam wafting heavenward. ''With Harry and Francie busy, I thought I'd take advantage of this…privacy. I had the meal delivered and told the maid she could have the evening off.'' He paused long enough to look at her over his shoulder. ''What better way for us to get to know one another?''

Something danced in his pewter gaze. Something she couldn't quite make out. Was that a teasing glint? Or something more serious? Before she could decide he pivoted back to the sideboard and reached for a soup bowl.

Ariane listened, suddenly aware of how very quiet the apartments were. No maid. No Harry. No Francie. The two of them were truly alone.

Her already jittery nerves became positively frayed at the ends. Pointing out that it wasn't proper for them to be alone in his quarters might please her grandmother to no end, but it would make Ariane look like an old-fashioned stick-in-the-mud.

Her gaze settled on his broad shoulders and the play of hard muscle and sinew under his soft cotton shirt as he ladled out the soup. Her mouth watered and she swallowed, blaming her overactive salivary glands on the delicious and distinct scent of the lobster bisque rather than the delectable sight of Etienne's toned body. Her gaze slipped lower, even. To the taut derrière that she and Francie both had complimented not so very long ago. And that's when he chose to turn around and face her.

While he carried the soup to the table, Ariane frantically avoided his gaze by focusing on unfolding her napkin and fumbling to place it in her lap.

''Thank you,'' she murmured as he set the bowl before her.

The bisque was creamy, and it should have tasted luscious on her tongue, but Ariane was too antsy to take much note of it. Etienne sat across from her. He'd lighted a set of three short, chunky candles and the flames flickered and danced, reflecting in his intense gray gaze.

They made small talk over the roasted capon with sage dressing and braised endive. He told her a little of his childhood. How the king and queen hadn't let their royal duties keep them from being loving parents who were very much hands-on with their son. Whenever possible they had taken their evening meal together. They'd attended his school functions, cricket matches and riding events. They had vacationed several times a year as a family.

Ariane thought Etienne's upbringing sounded picture-perfect. Just what she wanted for her own children…were she to have any, that was. She was too embarrassed to talk about her own youth. What in the world would she say? That her family was nothing short of dysfunctional? That her own parents had divorced when she was only three years old, and that her jet-setting mother hadn't really seemed to mind all that much about leaving her children behind? That the only "mother" Ariane really remembered was a nanny who had left the palace as soon as her ward had turned sixteen? That her father had married twice more over the years in some warped attempt to sire a boy child who would inherit the throne of St. Michel? That her current stepmother, her father's pregnant widow, could barely stand the other children her husband had fathered during his previous marriages? That the tension in the palace since the king's death often bordered on explosive?

She stifled a mournful sigh. For some odd reason, she didn't want Etienne to know just how off-the-wall her family situation was, or just how abnormal her upbringing had been.

It wasn't as if she hadn't been loved. Even though her father was very concerned with producing a male heir to inherit his kingdom, he'd loved his daughters very much. Showered them with attention when his duties had allowed it. Whatever parental affection she lacked had been made up for in the tight-knit bond of devotion she and her sisters had formed. And she felt close enough to Georges and Juliet, her father's second—actually, third—wife's children from a previous marriage, to be able to warmly call them her brother and sister. And twelve-year-old Jacqueline, Ariane's half sister, was the light of her life.

It was her father's fourth wife, Celeste, who had become the dark cloud hanging over the palace these days. The woman was just—

Ariane forced the shadowy thought from her head. She didn't want to spend time contemplating such unpleasantness.

Dabbing her napkin to the corners of her mouth, she smiled at the prince. ''Dinner was wonderful.''

''Marjorie will be happy to hear that,'' Etienne said. ''But then I knew she'd outdo herself. She studied at all the best French culinary schools. She's been with us for as long as I can remember. She's getting up there in years and does more supervising in the kitchen rather than cooking these days, but she told me she prepared this meal with her own hands.''

''She must be very fond of you.''

''And I of her.''

A light sparkled in his eye, telling Ariane just how

much he liked the elderly woman who ran the Kroninberg Palace kitchen.

Her shoulders drooped a fraction and her gaze slid from his as the place she called home once again failed dismally in comparison. With Celeste in charge of running the de Bergeron household, staff never seemed to stay for very long. It was impossible for Ariane or anyone else in the family to strike up the kind of affectionate relationship that Etienne obviously shared with Marjorie.

"Let's take our coffee out on the patio," Etienne suggested.

He rounded the table and helped her from her chair. He had exceptional manners. She'd expect nothing less from a noble, yet his attentive behavior made her feel very...special. The scent of his cologne, an enticing mix of warm spice and citrus, swirled on the air, and she fought the urge to close her eyes and savor it in a deep inhalation.

She paused at the set of French doors while he went to the sideboard to pour two cups of coffee.

"I noticed," he said when he came toward her and handed her a cup, "that you haven't said much about your family."

Ariane murmured, "I haven't, have I."

The soles of her shoes grated softly against the ancient stone underfoot that had been worn smooth and shiny with time. The fragrance of lilac hung, ripe and heavy, in the silky night air.

"You warm enough?"

His query was automatic, and his concern for her made her insides grow snug and cozy with appreciation. She'd thought the man would be boring...stuffy, even, but she was learning that he was very caring. And he stirred something in her. Something mysterious. Exciting.

"I'm fine, thank you," she said.

He sipped his coffee, and Ariane wondered what it might be like to taste the rich liquid that glistened on his moist, full bottom lip. The unbidden thought made her start. Immediately, her gaze flew to the cup and saucer she held and she was relieved to find that she hadn't sloshed any coffee over the rim.

"I guess it's hard for you to talk about it," he said. "Your family, I mean. It must be terribly hard. Mourning the loss of your father."

His mention of her bereavement had tears springing to her eyes. She missed her father. Terribly. Pined for his laugh. His loving smile. She missed the attention he used to bestow on her and her sisters. Albeit, the attention he gave them was sporadic—he did have a country to run—but when he came to the playroom to visit them, they always had a lovely time together.

He'd been a good man. A shrewd and judicious ruler. The country had prospered under his reign. The people of St. Michel had respected Philippe de Bergeron. Ariane could always be proud that he had developed such a good reputation among his people.

However, it hadn't been the grief she suffered over her father's sudden passing that had kept her from talking about her family, about her childhood. It had been fear of humiliation. Pure and simple. She didn't want Etienne comparing her motherless upbringing to the ideal childhood he'd experienced. No way, no how.

"You know," Etienne said, "I've been thinking about the changes I'll make when I become king of Rhineland."

She was both surprised and relieved at this abrupt and unexpected change of topics.

"Changes? You think your father's ruling philosophy needs amending?" Her curiosity piqued, she turned to face him fully.

Moonlight turned his thick head of hair to a rich chestnut and his angular jaw threw a shadow across his corded neck. She knew if she were to run her fingertips down the length of his throat that his skin would be hot to the touch.

The thought was so vivid that she automatically tightened her hold on the coffee cup to make certain she hadn't acted on the notion. A hemmed-in feeling began to creep over her. Ariane desperately tried to shrug off the odd sensation and focused on the interesting conversation at hand. Etienne might be about to give her some great clues regarding who might be plotting to annex her country. She'd best pay strict attention.

"I'm thinking it's time for a hike in taxes," he stated boldly. "But I haven't decided if I should implement a luxury tax—" he grinned "—demand a levy on the toys bought by my richest citizens. Or apply a smaller tax that will affect the middle-class populace."

What he said surprised her to such a degree that she set down her cup and saucer on the nearby glass-topped table.

"Why?" she asked. "Rhineland's economy is very stable. And has been for years."

"I equate stable with stagnant. We haven't had a tax increase since my grandfather's reign. Change for the pure sake of change could be a good thing."

"It could be a bad thing, too." A stupid thing, was

what she really wanted to say. "You couldn't impose a tax increase without the backing of your officials, and without a solid reason to back up your proposal, I don't see how you'll get them to agree."

A strange expression lit his gaze, but before Ariane could come to terms with what it might mean, he turned his head and looked out over the vast manicured lawns.

Softly, he said, "Who was it who said, *'L'etat, c'est moi'*?"

"I am the state," Ariane repeated. Without thought, she added, "Louis the XIV coined that phrase. But he was an oppressive tyrant."

Etienne nodded, grinning slyly. The look should have set off warning bells in her brain, but she was too concerned with the unsuspecting citizens of Rhineland to notice.

"Ever heard of the divine right of kings?" he asked.

She nearly snorted, but thankfully suppressed the reaction. "You don't honestly believe that sovereigns are direct representatives of God, do you?" Derision laced the edges of her tone. "That's ancient doctrine. And if you remember, it's what led to the French Revolution. No one in their right mind would consider—"

Her jaw snapped shut as she realized just how far down the path of this intellectual conversation Etienne had led her. Her gaze caught and held his, and she saw that odd expression…that dancing light…flashing humorously in his cool gray eyes.

Hoping to cover her blunder, she chuckled with as much delight as she could muster. "You're teasing me.'' She let her chin dip and she shot him a coy look. ''You ought to be ashamed.''

Now her mind worked frantically. Could she salvage the situation? What could she say to make herself look less erudite? She shouldn't have reacted so rashly to his insinuation that he intended to govern under autocratic rule, but she'd become so riled at the suggestion that he intended to take advantage of his own subjects that she hadn't thought before speaking her mind.

Marshaling a serious tone, she proclaimed, ''But I'd think that the woman you take as your wife…the queen of your country…would *love* the idea of a tax hike.'' She smiled prettily. ''It would mean more money for jewelry and ball gowns and shoes. A queen can never have enough shoes, you know.''

She was breathless as she waited to see if he fell for her ploy, yet at the same time she felt utterly mortified to think that he might. Appearing so darned superficial galled her to no end.

Etienne set his cup down next to hers and approached her. His gaze was as silvery as the moonlight. Enthralling. The night air seemed to heat up and swirl slowly, sensuously around the two of them.

''Now that you've brought up the subject,'' he said smoothly. ''Let's talk about who I might take as my queen.''

The sumptuous tone of his voice stunned all thought from her head.

''I'm so happy that we're finally alone,'' he continued.

His whispered words sent a shiver coursing across every inch of her skin.

"I'm so happy that you've come to visit Rhineland." He clarified, "To visit *me*."

He ran the backs of his fingers down her jawline, then traced her bottom lip with the pad of his thumb.

She couldn't seem to pull her gaze from his, and she anticipated that if he were to press his lips to hers, his kiss would be laced with the flavor of rich French roasted coffee. She'd have given her best diamond tiara to taste what she guessed would be a most luscious experience.

Oh, heaven help her. Ariane felt sluggish. Drugged with the sudden desire that welled up like tidal water, filling ever nook and cranny of her being. Threatening to drown her. What a wonderful way to go!

But her self-preserving instinct had her fighting the fog that enveloped her brain. She could offer up a silent prayer, but she knew no deity would come to her aid. No angels were going to swoop down to save her. If she was going to be rescued from this thick, sensual air Etienne had conjured with his mere nearness, his gentle touch, she'd have to be the one to do it.

Think, Ariane. Think. The silent order was firm and it resonated through her head.

All this mannerly attention and romantic interest could be a strategy meant to lull her into a false sense of security. Etienne could be the person leading the faction of his government that wanted to seize St. Michel. If that were so, that made him the enemy! If that were so, it also made him an arrogant conniver!

Planting her palm firmly against his chest, Ariane dragged a lungful of head-clearing air into her body. She stepped away from him.

"I-I'm not feeling well all of a sudden," she blatantly lied. "I've come down with a terrible headache."

His expression was a strange mixture of concern and…was that *triumph?* But that made no sense. Her brain was whirling with too many overwhelming thoughts to figure out what he might be thinking. This entire evening had her dizzy with confusion.

All she could think about right now was getting away from this situation. Away from those silvery eyes. Away from the heat of him. Away from the desire that pulsed in her. Throbbed through her veins.

She turned from him. "I need to go to my rooms and lie down."

"Wait," he said. "I'll be happy to walk you back—"

"No!" Ariane hurried through the French doors. "I'll be fine. I know the way. All I need is a rest, I'm sure."

She rushed through the sitting room and out the front door of his apartments.

Etienne stood on the patio staring out at the night, seeing nothing, his mind, his every thought on his beautiful princess.

He couldn't stop the chuckle that rumbled to the surface. He'd chosen the right bait to catch her when he'd suggested taking unfair advantage of his people. She'd been clearly incensed by the idea. And when he inferred that he planned to make Rhineland an autocratic monarchy with that mention of the divine right of kings, she'd fallen for the lure—hook, line and sinker—and he'd reeled her in.

And what a catch she was! His grin widened further and he felt a tug of desire pull at his insides.

Oh, she'd tried to salvage her ruse. But she'd nearly choked on her ditsy comment about higher taxes affording a queen more material wealth. She loathed looking like the village idiot. Realizing that amused Etienne immensely.

He wasn't the kind of man who liked to play games with people. But he felt justified in the laying of this trap for Ariane because it was so obvious to him now that she *was* playacting. In reality, she was an intelligent woman with quite a head on her shoulders. Especially where politics was concerned. And the inanity she'd been presenting to all and sundry was just a mask she wore.

This realization had his curiosity working overtime. Why on earth would she want everyone to believe she was brainless? he wondered for what felt like the thousandth time.

Before he could come up with a guess to the question, he was overwhelmed with an amazing sense of relief. He was delighted to learn that she was, indeed, an intelligent woman. For he feared that the lovely Ariane had stolen his heart. And no man wanted to think he'd fallen in love with a twit.

Chapter Four

Ariane pushed the brush through her hair, and once it was smooth and tangle-free, she made neat parts and began plaiting the strands. Francie was more adept at making a French braid than she was, but her friend had found something much more interesting to occupy her time lately than acting as Ariane's lady-in-waiting. Not that Ariane minded. The whole point in taking Francie on as her lady was to afford her friend the chance to meet eligible and suitable young men. Francie came from an old and well-respected family. Marrying just anyone was out of the question.

It seemed Francie meant to explore the possibility of a relationship with Harry. The couple had spent a great deal of time together ever since he'd succeeded in persuading her to climb into a saddle last week. They'd had daily rides and taken driving excursions into the small nearby towns. Seemed that Francie didn't have time for Ariane all of a sudden.

Being on her own had left Ariane feeling panicked.

Since their arrival in Rhineland, Francie had been a great excuse for Ariane not to have to spend time alone with Etienne. But since Francie and Harry had become something of an item, Ariane had pretty much lost that excuse.

However, she continued to succeed in sidestepping the handsome prince. One day this past week, Queen Laurette had taken her on a tour of Rhineland's finest medical centers. Ariane had enjoyed the opportunity to visit the children's wards. On another day, King Giraud had insisted Ariane tour some of the country's vineyards. They had tasted various wines: Riesling, Pinot, Viognier, Chardonnay, and an Auslese that had proved to be deliciously sweet.

She had discovered that Etienne's father was so interested in his country's vinters that he visited them often, always bringing his very own tastevin. The small saucer-shaped cup was made of highly polished silver, its ridges and crevices allowing him to inspect the color and clarity of the wine. Ariane had enjoyed her outing with the king, and he'd evidently enjoyed it, too. The next morning he'd sent her a gift. Her very own silver tastevin.

Two days ago, Ariane had slipped from the palace, unnoticed, for a day of shopping, and yesterday she'd ridden all around the countryside on a docile mare she'd borrowed from the royal stables.

How could she keep herself busy today? What excuse could she come up with to—

Staring into the mirror now, she recognized the desperate look haunting her eyes. Her fingers fumbled suddenly and she let her arms relax at her sides, the braid she was working to create slipping into a loose mess as she was struck with a terrible realization.

She was expelling more time and energy *avoiding* Etienne than she was in gathering political information for the head of St. Michel's security force. Luc would be upset when he discovered that she'd found out almost nothing about who in Rhineland might be plotting against her country. Rhineland's prime minister delivered cryptic messages that seemed laced with hidden threats about government, laws and rules, and Ariane found that mighty suspicious. And she'd overheard an oil tycoon named Berg Dekker complaining about having to pay to dock his barges at St. Michel. But she'd learned nothing concrete about who might be behind the actual conspiracy or to what lengths the rogues were planning to go.

Why was it that evading the prince had taken precedence over fulfilling her royal mission?

Well, darn it, Etienne was too good-looking for common decency. And he stirred in her emotions and feelings that were most *in*decent. She'd only been alone with the man twice…and both times she'd been overtaken by some strange dazed-like stupor. She hadn't been able to draw breath. She hadn't been able to think straight. She hadn't been able to speak properly. And the urges that had tugged at her…driving her to act…well, in a manner that was *not* befitting her position.

All she wanted to do when she saw him was—

Her heart thudded and heat rose to flush her face as shocking thoughts bombarded both her brain and her body. However, she wasn't able to stem the devilish grin that pulled at the corners of her mouth.

She should be so ashamed at the wicked and wanton notions rolling around in her head.

"And what are you smiling at so early this morning?"

Ariane's gaze rounded as she caught site of Francie's reflection in the mirror. Her friend stood in the doorway of her bedroom, and Ariane had been so preoccupied with her naughty thoughts that she hadn't even heard the door of the guest suite open or close.

Grabbing up the hairbrush, Ariane busied her hands. "I might ask you the same thing," she said, hoping to put Francie off. "Your cheeks are full of color and your smile is a mile wide. What have you been up to this morning?"

It was clear that Francie had lost her heart, Ariane thought, because a woman in love was too easy to distract.

"I have never met a man quite like Harry."

Francie's words were spoken on a euphoric sigh as she approached Ariane.

"Here, let me do that," she said, taking the brush from Ariane's hand. Then her eyes misted over as she continued, "He makes me all tongue-tied, and when I'm with him I can't seem to breathe."

Ariane grew still. Weren't those the very thoughts she'd just had about her own reaction to Etienne?

Francie ran the brush distractedly through Ariane's hair. "Harry is sweet. And sensitive." She caught Ariane's gaze in the mirror and whispered, "Is it too soon to say I think I'm in love?"

Shocked, Ariane let her brows shoot toward the ceiling. "My first instinct is to say yes. Francie, you've known the man for a week."

"Oh, but what a week it's been."

With nimble fingers, Francie parted her hair and began to plait the strands, over and under. Ariane noticed the dazed look in her gaze—the same dazed look Ariane had been stricken with both times she'd been alone with Etienne. Could it be that she was falling in love with the prince?

No. No! She would not allow herself to think such silly thoughts.

How in the world could she fancy herself in love with the prince? She barely knew the man. People in love knew everything about one another. Favorite songs. Favorite foods. Favorite activities.

"Last night, Harry took me for a walk in the garden. He said it was the place he loved best in all of Rhineland. He said it reminded him of the countryside of England where he grew up. However, then he said that he'd never enjoyed it as much as he did with me. He brought a bottle of champagne." Francie giggled like a schoolgirl. When she continued, her tone was hushed. "He kissed me, Ariane. Under the moonlight." She sighed, and her voice was awe-filled as she added, "I've never experienced anything like it before in my life. It was so romantic. He is so romantic!"

She fastened the end of Ariane's braided hair. The poor woman looked utterly overwhelmed with emotion.

Ariane felt the need to speak her mind. "Are you sure he's…well…suitable? You don't want your parents finding fault with your choice."

A smug gleam twinkled in Francie's eye. "He's in line for a dukedom."

There was pride in her voice, Ariane could hear it. "He must not have much money if he's working for Etienne."

Francie waved off the thought. "My family has

enough money for the both of us. I'm not worried about that. Harry will charm Mother, and Father will love the idea of having a British duke in the family.''

"But—"

"No more buts, Ariane." Francie plunked her fists on her hips. "I want you to be happy for me."

Ariane stood up and turned to face her friend. "Oh, Francie, if Harry makes you happy, then I'm delighted."

So why didn't she feel delighted? she silently wondered as she hugged Francie to her tightly. What was this sensation sitting in the pit of her belly like a brick?

Stifling a groan, Ariane finally recognized what it was.

Envy.

She was envious of Francie's good fortune.

Once it was discovered that she was no longer a princess, no man would have her. Not a duke. Not even a court jester.

And certainly not a prince.

"I'd better go down to breakfast," she told Francie. "I don't want to keep everyone waiting."

"I won't be down. Harry and I had breakfast in town." Her gaze glittered with excitement as she added, "And we plan to have lunch out. After we've visited some antique stores. Harry loves antiques."

Ariane smiled. She knew her friend was a fiend for antique furniture.

"You have fun," Ariane called as she left the suite.

Making her way down the stairs, she wondered if she'd ever find someone with whom she could explore commonalities. She wondered if she'd ever meet a man who loved the outdoors or who enjoyed adventurous activities as much as she did, herself.

The image of an intense gray gaze flashed, unbidden, in her mind.

Did Etienne love to feel the wind blowing through his hair? Did he get excited at the mere thought of taking a hot air balloon ride? Would he climb to the top of a mountain for the sole purpose of seeing if he could do it?

Ariane came to a dead stop on the stairs. When, exactly, had the nebulous "man" in her thoughts become Etienne?

Her inhalation was suddenly shaky. She had better be careful. There was no chance of a relationship between her and Etienne Kroninberg. No chance whatsoever.

He might find her attractive now—and he *did* desire her, just as much as she desired him, that had been clearly evident both times they had been alone—but as soon as he discovered that she had the stain of illegitimacy on her name, no amount of allure would be enough for him to continue pursuing her.

He was the crown prince of Rhineland. It was important for him to make a good marriage. One that brought respect, privilege and wealth to his royal house. Doing so was his honor-bound duty.

Chasing after a woman with no title, no social standing, no land, no money save a small personal trust fund, would be the last thing Etienne would do. In fact, she wouldn't be surprised if the man actually ran from the very sight of her once he discovered the truth.

The instant she stepped into the breakfast hall, Ariane knew something was amiss. The room was narrow, and nearly forty-five feet long, with huge windows that let in the sun and allowed a spectacular view of the formal gardens and the rolling hills of the Rhineland countryside in the distance.

During her visit here, she'd learned that King Giraud conducted most of the affairs of state in a set of offices located in the east wing of the palace, so it was not unusual to see some of his ministers, cabinet members and advisors sitting at the table or serving themselves from the vast array of delicious smelling food offered on several sideboards.

Everyone nodded at her in greeting, but not one of them offered her a smile. It was almost as if they had a difficult time meeting her gaze. Even the servants seemed to avert their eyes, giving her a wide berth as they carried their trays in and out of the room.

Ariane's steps slowed as her thoughts swirled like a tornado. What on earth was wrong with everyone? Had she somehow disgraced herself and the de Bergeron name by breaching etiquette in some way? Granted, she'd stayed away from the castle most of yesterday, but she'd sent word to the queen of her intentions. Had she missed some meeting? Had she forgotten some important invitation? What indiscretion had she made that would have everyone treating her as if she'd contracted the plague?

Holding her head high, Ariane walked straight for the regal couple who sat at the head of the table.

"Your Highness." She smiled at the king and dropped a small curtsy. The greeting was a tad formal for breakfast, Ariane realized, but she wanted Etienne's father to understand that if she'd hurt him or his wife in any way, if she'd somehow embarrassed herself, she wasn't above accepting responsibility and offering humble apology.

It was Queen Laurette who spoke. "How are you this morning, my dear?"

"I'm fine," she replied, observing that both of their expressions seemed taxed. "However, I couldn't help but notice…"

Letting the rest of her sentence fade into oblivion, Ariane glanced around the room, then back at the king and queen. "There seems to be a great deal of tension in the air," she said. "Is everything all right?"

She'd always heard that it was the silent seconds that took the longest to pass. Ariane discovered the truth in this. The awkward stillness seemed to echo off the walls. Giraud and Laurette were obviously uncomfortable about something.

The king's gaze slid to his tea cup, and when he looked at her again, there was a sadness in his eyes that had Ariane's heart hammering in her chest. He had something to say, that much was clear. And it was obvious to her that he was trying valiantly to find the right words to speak his mind.

Bustling movement had all heads turning toward the door at the far end of the room where Ariane had entered the hall. Etienne strode toward her with purpose in his brisk steps. His mouth was bracketed with stern determination.

"Princess Ariane—"

He fairly announced her name, so booming and forceful was his voice.

"I've been looking everywhere for you," he said. "We're late for our ride. The stable hands have our horses saddled and ready."

Knowing that she hadn't accepted an invitation to

ride with the prince this morning, Ariane instantly realized that he must know what was going on and it was his intent to rescue her. From what folly, she hadn't a clue. But she thought it was sweet of him to come charging in like a white knight to sweep her away from the obvious unpleasantness she had been just about to encounter.

His smile was bright and in direct contrast with the staid faces of everyone else in the room, including the king and queen. His strong, tapered fingers slid over her forearm, and his touch sent electricity jolting over every inch of her skin.

"You'll need to change," he told her easily.

It was evident that he wanted her away from here. Away from the covert stares. Away from the friction that fairly crackled in the air.

For the span of a single heartbeat, Ariane hesitated. She really should stay to find out what the king had been about to say. But then she relented, turning to Etienne with a quick, flashing smile.

"I'm sorry if I kept you waiting," she told him.

She took his arm, and the two of them made their way down the length of the breakfast hall and out the door. Midway up the staircase, she asked, "Okay, what's happening?"

"Happening?"

She grinned. "Your tone tells me you're stalling. And you aren't doing it very well, either. You'll have to tell me eventually, you know. I can't apologize until I know what I've done wrong."

His hand covered hers, and his skin was warm against her own. She felt oddly protected.

Etienne's voice softened as he assured her, "You've done nothing to apologize for."

"Well, something was going on in there. Why else did you rush in to save me?"

By then they had reached the door to the guest suite.

Etienne looked uncomfortable, his handsome face taking on the same strain she'd seen in the expressions of the king and queen just moments before.

"What is it, Etienne?"

Just then a maid rounded the corner, a small stack of pristine white bath towels in hand.

"Let's go inside," he murmured the suggestion. "You're going to need a little privacy."

As Ariane pushed her way through the door, she said, "Francie's probably still here...."

But her eyes immediately swept the room and she could tell from the quiet that the two of them were alone.

"She and Harry are out and about again," Ariane told him. She turned to face him. "So what's this all about?"

For as long as she lived, she wouldn't look back on this moment without wanting to kick herself. She should have guessed what was coming. She should have known what had churned up the storm clouds.

"Ariane—"

He moved in closer, and she saw that his gray gaze contained flecks the color of slate. His hands slid up along her forearms and again she felt enveloped with a peculiar protectiveness.

"Your brother-in-law, Wilhelm Rodin, came to see my father late last night."

Fear spiked through Ariane like a bolt of lightning. "Lise? Is my sister okay? Is the baby all right?"

The panic she experienced regarding her pregnant sister's welfare had her trembling uncontrollably.

"He didn't say anything about Lise's health," Etienne told her. "I assume she's fine. There's no reason to think otherwise. From what I was told, she's on her way home to St. Michel."

"But why would she…" Confusion stole away the remainder of her query.

His beautiful mouth pursed into a firm, straight line. He sighed. "Ariane, there's no easy way to say this. Wilhelm came to my father requesting a decree of divorce from your sister."

Ariane gasped. "*What? But why?*"

Again, Etienne paused, and she got the distinct impression that he was steeling himself for the telling. What on earth could have happened between Lise and Wilhelm?

"He had some fantastic story," he said. "He told father that King Philippe had married when he was eighteen. To an American woman. And that he and this woman had a child together. He told us that there is a search being conducted. If the child is found, and if the child is male, then Philippe's first son will take over as king of St. Michel."

His pewter eyes looked pained, and Ariane had to let her gaze dip to the floor. She wasn't supposed to know this information. She had to act as if she were hearing it for the very first time. But, dear Lord in heaven, why would Wilhelm go to King Giraud with what was supposed to be a de Bergeron family secret? Why would the man divorce his pregnant wife? None of this made sense.

She knew the story couldn't stay hidden forever, but she never imagined it would be revealed like this.

"Wilhelm told my father that your father's first marriage to the American was never properly annulled." He leveled his gaze at her. "Ariane, if all this is true, then your father's marriage to your mother wasn't…legal. And that means, well, that you and your sisters are…"

He let the thought wither away as he was evidently unable to utter the word.

"Illegitimate," she finished for him. Her voice grated as she said, "My sisters and I are illegitimate."

Etienne's exhalation was so miserable sounding that Ariane got the impression that he had more to relay. And he did.

"Father has no choice but to grant Wilhelm his divorce," he said. "Wilhelm is claiming that his marriage to Lise took place under false pretenses. Of course, father will stall for a couple of days, however, Wilhelm was quite insistent." His tone quieted, intensified. "But you should also know that your brother-in-law went to the media. He sold the story to the highest bidder late last night. An article ran in one of those trashy gossip rags this morning. Other European papers are picking it up. I even heard a report on the BBC news this morning. The whole world is being alerted to what's taking place in the St. Michel royal house."

Ariane would never have guessed that this was how the story of her father's previous marriage would break. St. Michel was a small monarchy. There were several gossipy newspapers printed in her country, and the paparazzi were relentless in their pursuit of some tidbit of information on any member of the de Bergeron family. But she couldn't imagine that the people of the outside world would be the least bit interested in the St. Michel royals, or what took place behind their palace door.

She had imagined that she would be the one to tell Etienne about the plight that had befallen her and her sisters. And she'd planned to do it before leaving Rhineland. Well, that plan was worthless now.

Poor Lise! Her older sister must be devastated! She must be feeling lost and alone and scared to death. And Celeste wouldn't make her sister's homecoming an easy one, that was for sure. Wilhelm Rodin was a dirty, rotten scoundrel and that was all there was to it.

A dark cloud gathered as Ariane thought of her brother-in-law. The man had always been cold and calculating. Wilhelm had used the fact that he was a member of the royal house of Rhineland to convince King Philippe that a match between himself and Lise would unite their two countries. Ariane had felt uneasy about the marriage that their father had arranged for Lise. However, Lise had seemed content with it, so Ariane had kept her opinions to herself.

Pregnant and abandoned by her husband, Lise must be beside herself. At least Marie-Claire would be nearby. And Juliet and Georges. And sweet little Jacqueline would surely brighten Lise's days.

Even though Ariane worried about her older sister, she couldn't deny the utter joy that shot through her at knowing that the truth was finally out. She should be terribly distressed at the thought of losing her title, her social standing. But she wasn't. She felt…well, she felt liberated. No more official duties to perform. No more restraints on her behavior. She would very soon be able to start a whole new life for herself. One without official obligations or limits on her activities.

But first things first, she silently realized. She was in Rhineland on a mission. Just because the truth was out about her no longer being a princess didn't mean she stopped loving her country. She had a job to do. And she had every intention of doing it.

Etienne looked confused by her silence.

Finally, he softly asked, "You do realize what this means, Ariane? You do understand, don't you?"

Rather than jumping up and down in sheer delight as she wanted to do, she knew she had to once again clothe herself in her costume of shallowness and frivolity. And she had to do it quickly. For if she didn't, Etienne would certainly realize she'd been duping him all along. No princess in her right mind would be happy about having her title stripped from her.

"Oh, Etienne—" she collapsed against his chest, resting her head on his shoulder as she desperately tried to conjure some tears "—what in the world am I going to do? I've lost everything. *Everything*. I'm so humiliated."

She felt his body tense, and he moved in a manner that let her know he meant to lean away from her. Allowing him to look into her face now was out of the question. She had to summon up some real distress first.

Ariane clutched him to her, hugged him tight, all the while doing what she could to build up her anxiety.

"My friends will surely abandon me! I'll be shunned. I'll be a laughingstock."

With her body pressed so tightly against his, Etienne battled the desire chugging through him like a runaway locomotive. There was no stopping it. He should be ashamed of himself. Ariane was suffering a terrible torment. He should be comforting her…not imagining her naked in his arms.

But her breasts were firm. Her tummy, flat. Her hips, soft, curved. And she was so close. So very close.

Etienne closed his eyes. The insanity of passion pressed in on him just as tightly as she was, fogging his brain, stealing away his common sense.

He gulped in air. Fought the yearning that surged like liquid fire through his veins.

The defenselessness in her voice. The silkiness of her hair brushing against his neck like warm silk. The trembling of her body.

He wanted her. And, heaven help him, but he feared that submission was inevitable.

The hunger seething in him became greedy. It built in him like a frenzy until he thought he would go crazy with it. Finally, he did the only thing he could do. He surrendered.

Gently, he inched away from her. He tipped up her face until her anxious midnight eyes locked with his.

And then he covered her mouth with his own.

Chapter Five

Her lips were hot as brimstone and candy-sweet, just as he'd imagined they would be. He was vaguely aware of hearing a groan and instinctively knew it had originated deep in his own throat. He didn't even attempt to quell the sound of it, but let it rumble, low and sultry, a clear sign of all he was feeling.

His every thought had been consumed by this woman since her arrival in Rhineland. His sleep had been plagued by shadowy, sensuous dreams in which he'd touched and tasted, kissed and fondled. He'd become nearly obsessed with the hot and needy yearning she kindled in him.

She was playing some kind of game. He'd discovered that for certain the night they'd had dinner alone together. He'd pondered her behavior until he'd become scatty with bewilderment and frustrated beyond belief. But at this particular moment none of that mattered to him. *None of it.* All that filled his mind was his need. Right now, the need pulsing through him was a palpable thing. A living entity. To savor this moment was a necessity. To treat the here and now as if it might be his one and only chance to get this close to her.

The kiss was electric. Jolting. Shocking. Heat licked at every part of him like fiery flames. Engulfing him, consuming him. This was the kiss that filled every man's fantasy.

The thought made him balk…no, this kiss was *better* than any fantasy because it wasn't imagined or dreamed. *It was real.*

His tongue skittered along her luscious, velvety bottom lip. The taste of her ignited a fervor low in his gut. Blistering vines sprouted to life, a burning bush, curling, swirling inside him, stems and buds and leaves smoldering with heated desire. Growing. Spiraling. Until he was filled to the brim.

Nothing could extinguish the fire raging within him. He was helpless against it and knew that all he could do was let it blaze until it spent itself. Until it reduced itself to ashes.

Etienne lifted his hands, cradling her perfect face between his fingers. She felt so tiny. So vulnerable.

He kissed her mouth, her cheekbone, her eyelid, her temple. He pressed his lips against the silkiness of her hair. The faint scent of fresh rain filled his nostrils, fanning the wildfire of his passion to even greater heights. He wanted to get lost in her, to let the heat and the longing devour him, absorb him— *become him.*

His breath came in ragged gasps, and then he drew his head upright, dragging open his heavy eyelids in order to look down into her angelic face.

Her expression was like a douse of icy water against feverish skin.

There was desire in her indigo eyes, yes. Embers of it glowed white-hot, he could clearly see that. But there were other emotions, as well. Emotions that shook him to the core.

Confusion. Turmoil. And some other emotion that was inscrutable and impossible for him to decipher.

"Oh, Lord, Ariane—" he emitted a remorseful groan, his hands falling from her face to her shoulders "—what have I done? Forgive me. Please."

She tried to look away, but he lifted her chin, urging her gaze back to his.

"I've just delivered news that is sure to make you feel as if your whole world is about to crumble," he whispered. "And do I comfort you? Do I reassure you? No, instead I take full advantage of your weakness. I act like a—"

Disgust sliced through the rest of his thought, and he fell silent from the weight of the guilt that descended on him.

This morning, when his father had told him about Wilhelm and what was happening in the de Bergeron family, all Etienne could think about was how devastating this news was going to be for Ariane. Saving her from being hurt and disgraced had been his only thought as he'd rushed to reach her before anyone else could. But when he should have been strong for her...when he should have been a firm shoulder for her to lean on, all he had succeeded in doing was crumbling under his own plaguing desire for her.

He swallowed, and all he could bring himself to say was, "I'm sorry, Ariane. I truly am."

Silence, leaden and sluggish, turned the air hanging between them heavy with awkwardness.

Finally, he said, "I know what you must be feeling."

What he interpreted as a sad smile shadowed the corners of her mouth.

"No," she told him, her voice soft as a sigh. "I don't believe you do."

Self-reproach shot through him like a piercing arrow. Of course, he suddenly realized, he had no idea what she was feeling. How could he? Nothing like this had ever happened to him.

"You're right," he admitted. "All I can do is guess. And I would say that you have to be feeling overwhelmed. And afraid. Anxious about what the future will hold for you."

An intense yet unreadable expression crept across her beautiful features.

Something deep inside him compelled him to say, "This turn of events doesn't change who you are, you know. I mean that."

Now her deep blue gaze clouded, still indecipherable.

"Yes," he sadly admitted, "some people will turn their backs on you. There are those who will be unfeeling, even contemptuous of your predicament. You'll have to prepare yourself for that. But your friends…your *true* friends will stick by you, Ariane. You'll see."

He hoped she understood the silent implications behind his words. He wanted her to understand how he felt. Maybe he should just spell out his feelings. Maybe he should tell her in simple, no-nonsense language that she could count on him. But he didn't.

Whether the reason for that was the doubt he'd felt over the mask of shallowness she'd insisted on wearing since her arrival, or his own overwhelming confusion and uncertainty over how all this would or should affect his intentions toward her, he couldn't say.

His fingers firmed reassuringly on her shoulders. "Everything's going to be all right. That's the honest truth. Now, I want you to go put on your riding gear. I wasn't lying to you when I said the stable hands had saddled up some horses for us. As soon as Father told me the news about Wilhelm requesting attendance with him, I thought it would be best if I could save you from facing all those people at breakfast. I wanted to be the one to break the news to you, and my parents agreed that would be best. I called the stables to have the horses saddled and waiting, then I called your room, but you'd already left. I rushed to fetch you as quickly as I could."

She looked the epitome of innocence, and that ripped at the very heart of him. He wanted to gather her up in his arms. He wanted to protect her from this awfulness. But he dare not. He couldn't trust himself to do the right thing by her. Not with his passion still simmering just below the surface.

"Go on now," he told her, this time more firmly, and he let his hands fall to his sides. "Go get changed. All this will look less threatening after a nice, quiet ride."

He watched her turn and walk away from him, her bedroom door closing behind her.

Ariane couldn't have settled for a nice quiet ride even if her very life had depended on it. Wind whipped through her hair and her thigh muscles burned as she pressed them against the powerful body of the chestnut mare beneath her. Leaning forward over the animal's mane, she fairly stood in the stirrups as she tore across the Rhineland countryside. She could hear the hoofbeats of Etienne's horse just behind and to her left.

Overwhelmed. Afraid. Anxious.

Etienne had told her he imagined that these were the emotions she must be experiencing. And he was correct. However, he'd been completely wrong about the motive behind those feelings.

He'd been sure that her devastated expression had been due to the news he'd imparted. That the whole world now knew about her father's previous marriage—the marriage that made her and her sisters illegitimate and stole away her title of princess.

But that hadn't been what had rocked her world to its very foundations. Not at all!

She had been nearly knocked off her feet by that unexpected kiss he'd planted on her lips.

Her reaction to his touch had terrified her. Fearful that she wouldn't be able to suppress the passion that had exploded inside her like a blast from a flare gun, flickering and sparkling, rising heavenward at lightning speed.

She had been riddled with angst—was *still* riddled with it—over why he would show her such sweet and precious attention when he'd just discovered that she was illegitimate. That she was baseborn. That she had no royal title. That she no longer could offer him a thing: money, lands, social standing, reputation… nothing.

His behavior made no sense to her. Having had

weeks to anticipate his reaction to the news, she'd expected him to have nothing else to do with her once he found out she wasn't a legitimate de Bergeron...once he discovered that she could bring him no fortune, no lands. That she could bring his country no special economic favors. The loss of her title meant the loss of everything he—the crown prince of Rhineland—might find desirable in a marriage union with her.

So *why* had he kissed her? Why had he shown her such kindness when she'd predicted that he'd coolly yet politely disengage himself from her, inform her in no uncertain terms that there would no chance of their forming any kind of relationship?

The questions echoed mockingly through her brain as the horses' hooves pounded across the meadow.

There could be only one answer.

Pity.

Etienne felt sorry for her, for this plight she was facing. And he was just being nice. He'd consoled her. Assured her. Showered her with kind benevolence. That's all there had been to that kiss.

That conclusion stabbed through her heart like a double-edged knife, slicing her to the very soul. It was also what had her racing, hell-bent, over hill and dale.

She didn't want any man feeling sorry for her. She didn't want any man consoling her out of pity! Least of all Etienne!

A tiny ray of light shined through the frustrated darkness invading her mind. Maybe...just maybe, Etienne had kissed her because he was truly attracted to her. Maybe he didn't care that she could bring his kingdom no assets. Maybe he was simply a man who wanted a woman.

A man who wanted *her*.

He'd said the loss of her royal title didn't change who she was.

Come on, Ariane, a small, mean voice silently scolded. *You are not a stupid woman. You must realize that the disguise you've been wearing has made you look like a total idiot.*

There was no way on God's green earth that a man as intelligent and sophisticated as Etienne could feel attracted to a woman as addlepated as she'd led him to believe she was. The thought was utterly ridiculous.

So why *had* he kissed her? And why *had* he acted so intensely allured by her the night they'd dined together in his suite? If romance hadn't been the motivating factor behind his behavior—and it surely couldn't have been given the way she'd been forced to act—then what had been his intention?

Nothing good, that was for certain.

Pity could have spurred the kiss they had just shared, once again feeling sickened by the mere idea. But what about the other instances when they'd been alone and he'd become so tender and amorous? The times before he'd known about her illegitimacy?

The man was up to something. Of that there could be no doubt.

Had he known all along of the trouble brewing in St. Michel? Had his intention been to bombard her with romantic attention in order to get the scoop on what was happening in the de Bergeron Palace? Was he scouting for firsthand information on the search for the de Bergeron missing heir? Could it be possible that Etienne had been using her to get information just as she'd been using him?

The doubts and questions only further solidified her suspicion that Etienne himself might be behind the Rhineland plot to annex St. Michel.

But his kiss had just about melted the very soles of her shoes. His touch had stirred her desire in a way that she'd never before experienced. This man had some strange power over her. She hated to admit it, but it was true.

He touched her, and she became pliable as clay in his deft fingers. He kissed her, and she sizzled like the sun itself.

She'd have to fight the feelings this man brought out in her. She'd have to put her personal wants and desires aside. She might find her handsome prince alluring as the devil himself, but she must remember that he was most probably her worst enemy.

Etienne galloped up close, reached over and touched her forearm. Automatically, she reined in the mare.

"Whoa," she murmured as the animal slowed. "Whoa there."

He looked flushed, and more striking than ever before.

"I realize that you're upset," he told her with a grin. "But I'd rather you didn't run the legs off my best horses."

Ariane slid her hand down the mare's neck, patting it affectionately. "I'm sorry," she told him. "I just got caught up in my thoughts."

He caught hold of her reins. Their gazes clashed.

"I meant what I said before, Ariane. I totally understand your being upset by what's happening, but this won't matter to your true friends." His gray gaze intensified, as he added, "And I hope that's how you think of me. As a true friend."

He's lying. He's lying. He's lying.

Reality reverberated through her head like a chant. She had to keep telling herself the truth. No one else was here to do it. Yet at the same time she couldn't help admitting that all she really wanted to do was believe each and every one of his lies.

Aside from being outright rude, there had been no way for Ariane to escape the king and queen's invitation to the opera. Giraud and Laurette were proud of the famous European theater troupe they had lured to Rhineland for the season. The actors were talented enough, but the tragic opus had Ariane so bored that her eyes had begun to glaze over. She'd sent a silent prayer of gratitude heavenward when the lights of the theater had gone up, announcing intermission. The king, queen and their huge entourage of guests made their way to a private refreshment area where everyone feasted on a variety of champagne and other wines, caviar, cheeses and an assortment of imported exotic fruits.

"Are you enjoying the performance?" Queen Laurette asked her, flashing a bright and expectant smile.

"It's wonderful."

It wasn't a lie, Ariane decided as she watched the queen move on to converse with her other guests. The stage had been professionally transformed to replicate an eighteenth century Italian town square. The costumes were flawless in their historic design. The orchestral music and operatic songs were performed to utter perfection. It was just that Ariane found the opera—*all* opera, not just this one—tedious enough to bring her to tears.

She made small talk with several groups of people and sipped at a flute of sparkling pale champagne. Finally, she made her way toward the secluded alcove where Francie, Harry and Etienne stood talking.

The prince was dressed in his formal evening attire. The charcoal-gray jacket made his shoulders look broad and invited a woman's fingers to rove over them. Ariane was drawn to him like a moth to flame.

"He's going to leave her," she overheard Harry state. "That woman deserves to be abandoned to her fate."

Ariane knew Etienne's personal assistant was predicting the outcome of the opera's second act.

Francie gave his shoulder an intimate little push. "No woman deserves to be completely abandoned."

"This one does," Etienne agreed. "At best, she's a horrible mother. At worst, she's a murderer. Abandoning her is exactly what her husband should do. Get out while the getting is good, I say." Then he gave a small chuckle.

The sound of his laughter sent chills coursing down Ariane's spine. Why, oh, why did she find this man so alluring?

Nearly a week had passed since the news of her father's previous marriage had broken. In that time, Etienne had treated her as if she were made of delicate bone china. He'd insisted that everyone in the palace, servant and dignitary alike, treat her with the utmost respect, even angrily demanding that one government official take his leave from dinner when the man intimated that Ariane was no longer deserving of the royal treatment with which the Kroninbergs continued to present her.

Etienne had been kind and honorable toward her, and fiercely protective of her. And all the while, Ariane had been on her guard, watchful of some slipup on his part that would reveal to her the motives behind his wonderful behavior.

Oh, yes, he was very good at playing this game of cat and mouse. Much better than she, Ariane had to admit. All the pretense between them—he, acting the caring guardian and she, feigning the brainless wonder—had her nerves pulled taut to the breaking point every single day. She hoped to discover some fantastic piece of information about the Rhineland plot against St. Michel so that she could return to her country as soon as possible, for she didn't know just how long she could take the stress of this tremendous tension.

There was another reason she wanted to return to St. Michel. One that had nothing whatsoever to do with political intrigue.

Every time Etienne fought a battle for her—no matter how small, and no matter that she realized he must have ulterior motives—she felt her hold on her heart slipping a little more. She fought the tender emotions and the heated desires that raged inside her. She fought them hard. But it was a campaign she feared she was losing. If she didn't get away from this man soon, she was going to end up a casualty of war.

Francie saw her then, and waved for her to join them. "Ariane, tell us what you think. Does Cassandra deserve to be abandoned by her husband?"

Etienne turned, and there was something in his pewter gaze that made Ariane feel flushed with delicious heat from the roots of her hair to the tips of her toes.

"It does appear," Ariane said, "that Cassandra would never win a prize for Mother Of The Year. But raising six sons would be an overwhelming task for *any* woman, you have to agree. Her father died under mysterious circumstances, yes. However, no one but a crazy person commits murder without cause. And if you ask me, Cassandra isn't mad. If she killed her father, she must have had just cause. And if she's a murderer, think of the guilt she must be carrying around. Like baggage. Sometimes, a person's baggage can become so heavy that she—" Ariane shrugged one bare shoulder a fraction "—well, she just has to do something to lighten her load. Even if that something looks a little strange to everyone else." She grinned.

Francie and Harry laughed. Etienne just looked at her intently.

Finally, he murmured, "A very wise observation. I hadn't thought to delve into Cassandra's psyche to that extent."

Ariane's heart hammered. The manner in which his gray eyes pressed her, coupled with the realization that she'd stepped completely out of her role of inane behavior, had her feeling suddenly light-headed.

She chuckled gaily and decided to do what she could to cover her tracks. "Or our Cassandra could just be a spoiled little girl at heart. Maybe she killed off her father because he refused to give in to her every whim, and she intends to do away with the other men in her life because…well, because she's simply decided she hates the male of the species."

"Gruesome." Francie shuddered. "I hope she's

completely innocent. That's what I'm rooting for anyway.''

"*You're* the innocent one, if you believe that,'' Harry said.

The four of them laughed, but Ariane didn't miss the curious light in Etienne's gaze as he studied her. Thankfully, the lights overhead flickered to signal that the second act was about to begin and everyone automatically gravitated back into the theater.

"Let's go find out what happens to Cassandra,'' Francie said to Harry, setting down her crystal flute on a nearby table. The couple left the alcove.

Ariane couldn't stop the smile that curled on her lips when she watched Francie stop long enough to share an intimate little tête-à-tête with Harry right there in the hallway, their heads together as they laughed.

"They certainly look happy,'' Ariane couldn't help commenting to Etienne.

"Harry seems to have fallen head over heels for Francie.'' One corner of his mouth quirked upward as he softly added, "And to think I was the one who set up their first date.''

The remark had her looking at him quizzically.

A delighted twinkle lit his dove-gray gaze when he explained, "The night I invited you to have dinner with me in my rooms I asked Harry to waylay your lady.''

Ariane actually gasped at the admission.

Etienne chuckled, lifting his hands palms up. "What can I say? I wanted to be alone with you.''

Her blood raced at an alarming speed. Partly due to his flirtatious remark—she loved the idea that he'd wanted to be alone with her—and partly due to suspicion about why he'd admit to having Harry intercept Francie. The man was bent on keeping her off balance and in total confusion, it seemed.

Before she could think of an appropriate response, his expression took on a mischievous air. He looked around the nearly empty reception area. "Listen, would you mind too much if we missed finding out how the opera ends?"

"No. I wouldn't mind at all." Stung by self-consciousness over how quickly she answered, she purposefully slowed her speech, asking, "Why? Are you feeling ill? Do you need to go home?"

"I'm fine." He tossed a keen look her way. "It's you I'm worried about."

"Me?"

Etienne's grin was so sexy that Ariane felt her knees growing weak beneath her long flowing gown.

"Yes, you," he said. "Midway through the first act, you looked like you wanted to fidget and squirm right out of your seat."

Affronted, her spine straightened as she firmly pointed out, "Why...I've never fidgeted in my life."

His grin widened. "And as the performance continued, I was sure you might start snoring at any moment."

Shock had her mouth actually dropping open, her brow puckering. "I *do not* snore, Etienne Kroninberg!"

The teasing glint illuminating his gaze melted away her indignation.

"Hmmm." She rolled her eyes, suppressing the humor building up in her chest, tugging at her mouth. "Sounds to me as if you haven't been watching much of the opera, yourself. You've been spending your time watching me.''

''Indeed,'' he murmured. Then he took her hand. ''Come on, let's get out of here.''

Ariane felt like a kid as the two of them rushed down the carpeted stairs and out the front doors to make their escape.

The restaurant they entered was gorgeously decorated in rich, dark woods. The wainscoted walls, the floors, the chairs, the tables, everything glowed with a polished patina that reflected the soft overhead lighting. Catering to the after-theater crowd, the establishment was nearly empty and would remain so until after the performance.

When the waitress showed them to a private table near the back, Etienne murmured something to the woman that Ariane couldn't quite make out. Ariane raised her brows at him as he held her chair and then slid into the one across from her and he explained, ''I was ordering something special for us. A surprise. I hope you don't mind.''

''Not at all,'' she told him easily, doing what she could to quell the thrill that shot through her to think that he'd want to surprise her with something special. She also couldn't deny that she was curious beyond measure.

Feeling the need for a diversion, she surrendered to the overwhelming urge to try to make him understand her feelings about tonight's entertainment.

''It's not that I don't like opera,'' she told him, looking guiltily down at where her hands were clasped on the tabletop. ''I understand that the singers and actors work hard to perfect their craft. That it takes an army of people to accomplish all the tasks required to put on a performance of that magnitude. But, well, it's just that…'' The rest of her thought faded and her shoulders sagged. She lifted her gaze to his. "Okay. I'll admit it. I don't like the opera."

Etienne rested his elbows on the table and his chin on his fists. "It is the most boring pastime ever invented, isn't it?"

Her eyes widened. She breathed, "You think so, too?"

He nodded. "A better word for how I feel about it might be tedious."

It was then that the waitress arrived with cups of steaming espresso for them both. And she placed a heavy porcelain custard cup in front of Ariane.

One look at the scorched sugar coating had her entire body reacting with glee. "Crème brûlée!"

Immediately, she checked her reaction. She sounded like a kid in a candy store. Even though she suffered a twinge of embarrassment over her childish squeal, she couldn't keep the delight out of her voice as she rationalized, "It's my favorite."

His gaze lit with merriment. "Well," he said on an exaggerated sigh, "if you have to miss the opera, you should miss it for something absolutely wonderful."

She'd already placed her napkin in her lap and picked up her spoon. But his words—the peculiarity in his tone—had her pausing. Her gaze found his, and when she realized to what he was referring, she felt her face flush hot with mortifying embarrassment.

"You know!" His expression told her she'd guessed correctly. "Oh, Etienne, I'm so sorry. You must think I'm positively horrible. You came to my homeland all those months ago and offered to take me out and I repaid the kindness by acting atrociously. I never meant for you to know that I left the opera house that night. I do hope you believe me." In an attempt to salvage at least some of her dignity, she pointed out, "I *did* get back before the end of the performance."

"That you did," he admitted with a chuckle. "And I appreciated the effort. Very much."

Of course, they were talking about the night when he'd traveled to St. Michel, before her father's death, to ask her to attend the opera with him. Feeling bored stiff with the performance, Ariane had talked Francie into stealing away for a bit. The two of them had left the theater for a quick snack. Ariane had ordered crème brûlée.

"But how did you know?" she asked, spooning up some custard and taking a taste. She closed her eyes to better enjoy the cool creaminess on her tongue.

"You had invited such a crowd to accompany us that night," he told her, "that I had completely lost sight of you at intermission. But Harry just happened to notice how you and Francie hung back after the break. He followed you when you left the theater. And like all good equerries, he reported everything to me later on."

Her groan was filled with self-loathing. "You must think I'm a terrible person. I *am* a terrible person." But then she groaned again, this time from sheer enjoyment as she swallowed. "Mmm. This is so good."

He laughed as he added a dollop of cream to his espresso and slowly stirred. Suddenly cognizant of her conduct, Ariane laughed, too. She put down the spoon in order that he might understand that she meant what she was about to say.

"I really am sorry, Etienne. It's just that, well…"

"It's just that crème brûlée is your favorite. And you dislike the opera." His tone was both matter-of-fact and filled with forgiveness.

She sighed. "Exactly."

They shared a warm chuckle, and then Ariane picked up her spoon and dug into her dessert with eager yet dainty relish.

He watched her, obvious pleasure curling his sexy mouth. Ariane couldn't help but recall the pleasure that mouth had given her not so very long ago. His kiss had been titillating. Arousing. Captivating.

Then she thought of Francie and Harry. Of the budding relationship the two of them were free to explore. Would she ever find that kind of happiness now that she'd lost her place in royal society? Who would want her now? Certainly not someone with a position as important as that of the man sitting across from her.

Etienne noticed that she'd stopped eating. "What's wrong? Is the—"

"No, no," she assured him. "The custard is delicious. Thank you very much for ordering it for me."

"What is it, Ariane?" he asked, refusing to be put off.

Never would she dare admit to him the reason for her sudden melancholy.

Instead, she softly replied, "I want to thank you for something else, too."

He looked at her with obvious interest.

"I want to thank you for the way you've treated me all week. You didn't have to, you know. Everyone would have said you were well within your rights to send me packing back to St. Michel."

He reached across the table and slid his hand over-top hers. Sparks seemed to zip and sizzle over her skin.

"Ariane, you've got to stop allowing this little problem to depress you so," he said.

"Little problem?" She wanted to laugh, but it stuck in her throat.

"I mean it," he continued firmly, the pad of his thumb roving back and forth across her flesh. "Look, for all you know the American woman your father married when he was eighteen could have met with some ill fate all those years ago. If she died before your parents married, then your title would be rein-stated, wouldn't it? I know it's a long shot, but..."

Her spine straightened. "I never thought of that."

"And St. Michel is going to be just fine," he told her. "They'll find the missing heir. And if your half sibling is male, then they'll bring the gentleman back to reign as your father's successor."

She tilted her head just a fraction. "And if he's a she?"

Etienne lifted the fragile cup to his lips, took a sip, then replaced it on the saucer. "Then," he told her, "there's always the baby that Queen Celeste is car-rying."

Ariane shook her head. "Yes, my stepmother does claim she's had tests that prove she's having a boy."

"See there—"

"But she's mean and conniving," she added, doing all she could to curb the bitterness she felt toward Celeste. "It wouldn't be beyond her to lie about a thing like that. And up to now she's refused to show anyone the actual test results. She won't even provide them to our prime minister."

"Well, she can't lie once the baby is born, now can she?"

Ariane didn't answer. There wasn't much that Celeste wasn't capable of.

"I think we need to change this gloomy subject," he said. And doing just that, he asked, "Since you've made it quite clear that you don't like the opera, what do you like to do for fun?"

"I enjoy riding."

His dark brows raised. "Every time you saddle up you nearly exhaust my horses."

"I like physical activities. Anything adventurous. Exciting." Her mind churned with possibilities. "Like, say, skydiving."

"I was afraid you were going to say something like that."

"It's not something I've ever tried," she admitted. "Yet."

He remained silent as he shook his head.

"I like hiking. Especially to places I've never seen before."

"Now there's something more my speed."

Ariane finished the last bite of her custard and dabbed the white linen napkin to her lips. "It's hard to have fun, though, when the security people are dogging your every move. I know it's their job to protect me, but it would be great to escape them. Just for a bit."

It had been an offhand remark. One that she and her sisters had repeated to one another many times over: their wish to be free of the watching eyes of security personnel, and the ever-present reporters who forever seemed to be looking for the scoop of the century. With so many people following and harassing a body, it was nearly impossible to go anywhere or do anything without everyone and their mother knowing about it.

However, her complaint prompted something in Etienne. It was clear that his mind was churning, his thoughts spinning. Finally, he leaned toward her, his cool gray eyes glinting with mischief, and said, ''I'm up for a little adventure and excitement.'' One dark brow lifted, inquiringly. ''Are you?''

Chapter Six

He'd learned something tonight, Etienne decided as he shrugged out of his formal jacket and tossed it onto the bed. Ariane wasn't like any other woman he'd ever met.

Yes, he'd suspected it. All those months ago when he'd gone to St. Michel, and even more so since her visit to his own homeland. The thought had even flitted in and out of those hot, shadowy, increasingly erotic dreams that featured her every time he fell asleep. However, the fact that she was amazingly and wonderfully different from any other female he'd encountered had been solidified in his mind when he'd witnessed the gleeful light in her gorgeous deep blue gaze when he'd suggested that the two of them slip away from the opera tonight. Like a power switch that had been suddenly thrown, an impish energy seemed to palpitate from her.

The absolute wicked naughtiness that had curled the corners of her sexy mouth as they had left the theater, hand in hand, had had Etienne silently vowing that, if Ariane enjoyed breaking the rules as much as she seemed to, then he was willing to become a fun-loving rebel right along with her. She was like a breath of fresh air. And being with her filled him with a robust exhilaration.

He'd so enjoyed her display of shock in the restaurant when he'd revealed he'd been privy all along to her behavior when he'd taken her on that fiasco of a first date. He believed her apology had been sincere. His heart had been touched by her earnest appeal. She really hadn't meant to hurt or embarrass him that night. He realized it. Her exuberance for life—and her love of crème brûlée—had made it impossible for her to sit through the tragic opera he'd taken her to see.

A man couldn't hold a grudge over something like that, now could he?

Etienne chuckled as he changed out of his suit and into jeans, a sweater and a pair of sturdy hiking boots. Then he hurriedly tossed a change of clothes, a comb and his toothbrush into a knapsack. He wasn't certain where he was going to take her or exactly when they'd return, so he decided to go prepared. He'd told her to do the same.

Feeling like an errant youngster flushed with the excitement of running away from home, he slung the pack over his shoulder, shut the door of his suite and went to fetch Ariane.

His knuckles had barely touched her door when she opened it to him.

''I'm ready.''

Her midnight eyes danced with an exhilaration that was utterly beguiling and it was all he could do not to tell her she looked ravishing. However, he knew he'd best focus on his goal of getting them out of the palace unnoticed by the security personnel or else he just might give in to the desire that sat smoldering in his belly like glowing embers.

In that instant, Etienne paused, wondering exactly what he was doing. It had been his intention in pursuing Ariane to land himself a wife who was a princess. A woman of royal blood. A noblewoman who could rule Rhineland by his side when he became king. However, although Ariane had been born and raised as an aristocrat, she'd lost her royal standing. He should be putting distance between them, not running off on an adventure with her.

Ariane picked up her canvas knapsack, but after taking one look at his face, she asked, "You okay?"

He smiled. "Fine," he said. "I'm just fine. Let's go." Taking her hand in his, he tugged her out into the hallway.

They laughed like kids and talked about every topic under the sun on the drive to Rhineland's largest national park. He told her of some of his and Harry's exploits when they'd attended Eton together. And she recounted some of her own teenage misadventures with her sisters. She told him about attending school in Switzerland and how she'd missed her family.

Etienne knew from a college psychology course that middle children were usually quiet, self-conscious overachievers who strived for attention that was typically showered on either the older or younger siblings. However, it didn't seem that Ariane fit that mold at all. She was self-confident, outgoing and clearly unafraid of taking risks. Etienne discovered that those qualities appealed to him. Very much.

"Right after my stepmother, Helene, died," she

said, seemingly eager to recount another escapade from her youth, "my sisters and I slipped down into the wine cellar with my stepbrother, Georges, and my stepsister, Juliet. All of us got a little tipsy before we were discovered."

Her chuckle chimed like soft bells in the darkness of the car. Then he heard her sigh.

"Georges was eighteen," Ariane continued. "He was old enough to know better. So was my oldest sister, Lise." Again she laughed and admitted, "So was I, actually. But all of us had been grief-stricken for days and days. The whole household was morbidly silent. Father had been desolate over Helene's death. And the loss of another stillborn son."

Etienne felt her eyes on him.

Her voice softened as she admitted, "I guess all of us kids were just looking for some way to break out of our sadness. We were giggling like monkeys when the housekeeper found us."

After a moment, Etienne asked, "How did your father feel about the method you used to…er, overcome your sorrow?"

White teeth flashed in the shadows when she smiled. "Oh, we'd only opened two bottles, so we hadn't imbibed all that much." Then she whistled. "But Father's neck veins began to protrude when he learned we'd opened two of the rarest wines in his collection."

"Angry, was he?"

She was quiet for a moment, and he sensed rather than saw her shake her head. It was then that he realized she was recalling what must be a vivid memory from her past.

"Yes, but in the end he forgave us all. We had a secret weapon, you see."

Etienne was silent as he waited for her to elaborate.

"We sent Marie-Claire to plead our case for us. She was Father's favorite." Again, she paused. "It wasn't the first time, or the last, that she got us out of trouble. She had Father wrapped around her little finger."

Being an only child of parents who enjoyed a stable and loving relationship, he couldn't imagine what it must have been like to grow up in a family that consisted of siblings, stepsiblings, half siblings, stepmothers and nannies.

"Did that bother you?" he couldn't help but ask. "Your father having an obvious favorite, I mean?"

She exhaled softly. "I'd love to be able to say it didn't bother me in the least. But I believe there isn't a little girl alive who doesn't want to be the apple of her father's eye."

Ariane's soulful tone did something odd to him, and he made a silent vow there and then that if he were to have children he'd never give one child more esteem than another. He'd love each and every one of his children just as exuberantly as the next.

"The fact that Marie-Claire was Father's pet didn't affect my relationship with my sister," she said. "Luckily, I realized early on that it wasn't her fault. And I loved her dearly for getting me out of trouble when she could." She grew still suddenly. "But I did learn something from it."

Etienne pulled the car into the empty parking lot and cut the engine. He sat in the quiet darkness, hoping against hope that she wouldn't make him ask the question that rolled around in his mind.

Thankfully, she put his curiosity to rest.

"I learned that love shouldn't be treated like a pie. The pieces shouldn't get smaller with each portion that's served. And no one deserves a bigger slice than anyone else."

Softly, he said, "I agree." He marveled that their thoughts were so much in tune.

There was a forlornness in her tone that made him believe that there had been times during Ariane's childhood when she'd felt lost—and very hurt—by her father's preferential treatment of her younger sister. Oh, Ariane was attempting to handle the matter maturely, and Etienne found that quite an engaging attribute, but it was clear to him that she was bothered by it, nonetheless.

He'd have loved to pull her to him, to hug away all the bad feelings that might be festering inside her, to convince her somehow, some way that she was just as lovable as Marie-Claire. But all he did in the end was to gently reiterate, "No one deserves a bigger slice of love then anyone else."

They were quiet for some time, and the air seemed to crackle and rumble with a stormy awareness. However, before things had a chance to become uncomfortably awkward, Ariane focused her gaze out the windshield at the forest ahead.

"So, where are we?" she asked.

"Byron Park. Named for my great-great-great-great-grandfather." He looked at the dark path and wondered now if bringing her here had been the wisest choice. "I haven't been here in years, but I camped here as a boy. I had a great time on that mountain, and I remember this place was simply awesome at night." He eyed her thoughtfully. "But I'm having second thoughts about this adventure. Maybe we should wait until daylight—"

"Are you kidding?" She opened the door and exited the car as she spoke. "The moon is full. Just like a huge flashlight." When he didn't get out immediately, she leaned over and peered at him. "I love hiking. And I've never done it at night. This will be fun. Come on!"

He had no recourse but to get out of the car, too. Hesitation had him saying, "But what about—"

"No buts," she cut in. "We'll be perfectly safe. This is Europe, remember. The most dangerous animal we're likely to meet is a hungry chipmunk."

He laughed. "The danger I was thinking of is all those tree roots out there waiting to trip us up. One of us is bound to break an arm or leg."

Waving off his dire prediction, she grabbed her backpack from the rear seat, shrugged into it and set off toward the path. Etienne reached for his pack and followed her.

"Wait for me!" he called.

Ariane had been right, he soon realized. The moon illuminated the path in most places, but he grew to look forward to the areas that were thickly wooded and deep in shadow for those were the times when he took her hand. Solely for safety reasons, of course.

"What are you chuckling at?" she asked, when he slid his palm against hers on a dark part of the trail.

"Oh, nothing." A conversation was what he needed now. His mind whipped through possible topics. Finally, he said, "You've spoken of your father, your stepmother, your siblings. But you haven't said anything about your mother. What kind of person was she?"

For a moment, all he heard was the rustle of the leaves overhead.

Then she said, "There's not a whole lot to tell. I don't remember much about her. You see, my parents divorced when I was three. Over the course of her marriage to my father, my mother gave birth to three girls. The story goes that she wasn't interested in having any more children. My father was desperate for a male heir, so they decided it was time for their relationship to come to an end. He says he really didn't have a choice."

She tugged her hand from his, reaching up to her shoulder to grip the harness of her knapsack. Her whole body seemed to tighten, alerting Etienne that the end of the story wasn't going to be pleasant for Ariane.

"My mother was what you might call a jet-setter, and apparently eight years of marriage were more than enough for her," she said, seeming to pay close attention to where she planted her feet on the dirt path. "She couldn't wait to get out of St. Michel." She quietly added, "Away from her family." Ariane sighed deeply, almost as if steeling herself. "She spent her time skiing in Aspen, gambling in Monte Carlo, sailing the Riviera, soaking up the sun in Fiji. She never missed the America's Cup finals, or the running of the bulls in Pamplona, or the Wimbledon tournaments, or a dozen other events in a dozen other countries. Her lifestyle didn't leave her much time to be a mother to her children. But that didn't seem to bother her. Lise, Marie-Claire and I remained in our father's custody after our mother left. We were raised by nannies for the most part. We did see our mother occasionally. A couple of times a year. But…"

Whatever else she was going to say vanished like a thin night mist and Etienne was sorry he'd broached the subject in the first place.

Ariane continued, "She died many years ago. In a scuba diving accident somewhere near the Great Barrier Reef."

So essentially Ariane had grown up without a mother...and often feeling as if she were playing second fiddle to her youngest sister for her father's affections. She must have experienced many lonely and confusing times as a child. Etienne's heart broke for her. Yet he marveled that the experiences of her youth didn't seem to have had any adverse effect on her personality.

The instinct to protect her welled up in him something fierce. In answer, he reached out, and sliding his palm up her forearm, he gently pried her fingers loose from the strap of her backpack and held her hand firmly in his even though the pathway ahead was brightly lit by the fat full moon that hung in the silky night sky.

The smile she offered was small, and sad, her face luminous in the reflected light, and he felt as if his heart were some kind of powerful engine *thub-thubbing* in his chest.

"My father's second wife, Helene—"

Suddenly Ariane stopped speaking, then tilted her head as if an idea just occurred to her.

"—I guess Helene was Father's third wife. I'm having trouble remembering that." She shook her head. "Anyway," she went on, "Helene tried to be a good stepmother to me and my sisters. Of all of Father's wives, Helene is the one I hold closest to my heart. She was the widow of an old friend of Father's, and after she and Father married, she was very preoccupied with trying to give my father the baby boy he so needed. It was almost as if Helene and my father had some sort of arrangement, or agreement. She was looking for a father for her children, Georges and Juliet, and father wanted an heir. ''

''A marriage of convenience,'' Etienne murmured.

Ariane nodded.

''Those kinds of relationships are quite routine in our world, you know,'' he quietly pointed out.

If the truth were known, he'd actually thought of offering Ariane the same sort of arrangement when he'd first traveled to St. Michel all those months ago. Save himself a lot of trouble by cutting through all the formalities and offering the woman a deal. A union between their royal families that would afford both their countries some benefits. Ariane's father, King Philippe, had hinted that he would be open to such an offer.

However, after having met Ariane, after having experienced firsthand her feisty nature, he simply hadn't been able to bring himself to make the proposition. He'd liked her. From the first. And although putting forward a bargain was the route he probably should have taken, he hadn't wanted to stilt any possible future he might have with Ariane with awkward official offers that would surely lead to something less than the real thing. And his gut had told him Ariane wasn't the type of woman who would react favorably to an offer of marriage that was based on political or economic reasons.

After that first meeting, he'd planned to visit St. Michel again just as soon as Ariane had had time to grieve for her father and his mother had had time to regain her health. But then Ariane had arrived in Rhineland—and he'd been ecstatic about the idea that she might be responding to his interest in her. Until her odd behavior had him guessing there were ulterior motives behind her visit.

"Well, even if Father and Helene married because of some kind of bargain they made," Ariane said, "I still loved the woman. It was she who brought Jacqueline into my life."

"Your youngest sister?"

Ariane nodded. "My half sister, really. She's like a ray of sunshine in that house, Etienne. You'll have to meet her. She's just a wonderful little girl. Curious and bold. Full of spirit."

He grinned. "A little like you, huh?"

Her mouth pulled back warmly. "I don't know about that. I just know that she and I share a strong bond. Jacqueline is the reason I've stayed at the palace. I could have moved out. Would have preferred to, actually, since Father's death. There are several summer cottages and town houses for the choosing, but I just couldn't leave my baby sister to fend for herself against Celeste. Jacqueline is only twelve. She's needed a protector since Father passed away."

Again, she grew still, vulnerability fairly pulsing from her.

"I've worried about her since I've been gone. I've talked to her several times on the phone. Grandmama and Marie-Claire both promised to look after her."

She glanced up at the stars as if offering up a silent prayer.

"I hope she's okay. I hope Celeste hasn't crushed her spirit." Ariane sighed glumly.

Etienne gave her hand a reassuring squeeze. "I'm

sure she's doing just fine. Come on, now,'' he chided, the poignancy expressed in her deeply furrowed brow clawing at the very heart of him. ''We're here to have fun, remember?''

''You're right.'' Her chin tipped up suddenly and she seemed to shake off the bad thoughts. Suddenly, she paused, her head tilting a fraction to one side. ''Listen. What's that?'' Before he could answer, her whole face lit up like a hundred-watt bulb. ''A waterfall! I can hear it. Come on!''

Without releasing his hand, she broke into a jog, lugging him along with her.

The falls was what he'd brought her here to see. As a boy, the sight of the rushing water had never left his mind. He'd wanted to share this with her.

''Oh, Etienne,'' she breathed almost reverently, ''the water looks just like liquid silver. It's just beautiful.''

The cascading water was beautiful yes, but not nearly as beautiful as her face. Her dark eyes shined, her full, perfect lips were partially open. The awe she so obviously felt was clearly articulated on her face. He realized at that moment that he'd like to experience every aspect of life with her…through her eyes. He loved the way she become so caught up in the moment.

''A Rhineland poet once described the falls as 'tumbling moonlight,''' he told her.

''The description fits perfectly.''

''The river is spring fed. The water bubbles up from deep inside the mountain. It's crystal clear and perfectly safe to drink.''

She blinked, then turned her gaze on his. Her eyes glittered with renewed excitement. ''The pool is just lovely. I'm sure the water's freezing now. But if it were summer, I'd love to have a swim.''

He remained silent, but made a mental note of her remark. If it was at all possible, he'd bring her back once summer arrived.

''Can we climb to the top?'' she asked.

''Of course.'' He answered quickly, catching the fever of her delight. He'd have given her the stars if she'd asked for them. Now, he only hoped he had the stamina to back up his promise and make the steep climb. ''Wait for me,'' he found himself calling again, and he trotted after her.

Later, they sat on the mossy ground, completely spent from the strenuous ascent. He studied her perfect profile.

There were other ways in which he'd rather tire himself out, he couldn't help but think. Ravishing her luscious lips with his own would be high on his list. As would peeling the clothing off her delectable body and touching her, loving her, all over.

''What are you thinking about?'' she asked. She lifted the bottle of water to her mouth and took a swallow.

Etienne actually felt his face go ruddy and hot, and he was relieved that her attention was focused on the swift current that carried the spring water bubbling over rocks and boulders on its way to the falls rather than on him. He took a deep breath and did what he could to banish the erotic images from his mind.

But doing so, he promptly discovered, proved a difficult task.

''Not a thing,'' he said at last. ''I'm just trying to recover. It isn't easy keeping up with the likes of you.''

She grinned. "You're earning lots of points by the mere fact that you're trying." Her smile faded then, and her tone grew whisper soft as she added, "But for the life of me, I can't understand why you would."

The reasons were mounting, he thought to himself. Yet at the same time, he had to admit that the thought wasn't ever too far away that reminded him there were serious reasons why he shouldn't. Luckily, though, he didn't have to respond because she chose that instant to stifle a yawn.

"It's late," he told her. "And we're both tired. We should get back to the car."

"I'm not just tired. I'm exhausted." She stretched out, laid her head on his lap. "Can we just rest for a bit first?"

"Sure."

Etienne reclined against the massive tree at his back and gazed down at Ariane. Her chest rose and fell in an easy, rhythmic motion. Her honey-blond hair glowed golden in the bright moonlight, her dark lashes cast fan-shaped shadows high on her milky cheekbones.

Desire quickened inside him.

He'd learned many things about Ariane tonight. She hadn't had the best of childhoods. Over the years her family had consisted of a conglomeration of step-mothers, siblings and stepsiblings. Yet she'd grown into a confident, vivacious woman. She cared deeply about her sisters and her brother. She couldn't sit through an opera without becoming bored to tears, and she'd risk an international incident in order to enjoy a crème brûlée. He grinned. He'd also learned that she looked just as good in jeans and hiking boots as she did in silk and high heels. The yearning he felt for her swirled low and hot, warming him to the marrow.

Etienne had discovered some things about himself, too. First and foremost, he liked Ariane. No, he more than liked her. And he sure as hell desired her.

In fact, he'd realized that he was falling hopelessly in love with the woman.

Sighing, he closed his eyes and tried to relax. But the notions eddying in his head made that next to impossible.

All of these realizations posed a huge problem for him.

He'd gone out seeking a wife. A princess. His parents fully expected him to fulfill that goal.

Yet here he was at the top of Byron Mountain after having run away in the night with a woman who had no title, no fortune, no lands…not even a social standing to offer him and his country.

Had he totally lost his mind?

Or just his heart.

Chapter Seven

Ariane opened her eyes, inhaling a deep, sleepy breath. The scent of Etienne wrapped her in a snuggly blanket and had her releasing a contented sigh. The sound of his heartbeat against her ear made her lips pull back in a drowsy smile. His chest made a wonderful pillow. She should feel self-conscious by the intimate manner in which her palm was splayed against his flat abdomen, the way her body was pressed up close to his, but her brain was much too fuzzy to give the notion more than a fleeting thought. All she wanted to do was lower her eyelids and slip back into her restful slumber.

A moment or two later wakefulness nudged at her. She extricated herself from Etienne's cozy embrace, marveling at how they had become so entangled on the mossy ground during the night. She'd only meant to rest her eyes and her tired body for a few moments, but she saw that the sky was turning pink with a new day.

Ariane realized that she'd never spent the night under the stars before. She'd never slept in a man's arms before, either.

She sat up, stretching the kinks out of her muscles. She didn't think she'd ever roused with such a feeling of peacefulness. Was the feeling brought on by her having slept outdoors? Or because for hours and hours she'd been cuddled in Etienne's arms? It wouldn't take a rocket scientist to figure this out, she silently surmised.

Reality slowly seeped through her sleep-fogged brain, churning up her thoughts and her emotions, and dragging her into the fully conscious world.

As she stared down at the gorgeous prince in slumber, she couldn't decide if this outing made her delirious with happiness or crestfallen with utter misery. Elated that Etienne would abscond from his royal duties, she realized that he possessed a bit of an adventurous spirit that closely matched her own. She'd enjoyed the trek up to Byron Falls. She'd been enchanted by the stories of Etienne's past. She'd taken great pleasure in telling him about her own. Their time together seemed to sparkle like the stars in the predawn sky. All in all, the evening had been soul-stirring.

So had Etienne.

However, the wretched facts remained: he was the crown prince of Rhineland, and even though he could play at courting all the women he wanted, he could never settle down with any female who didn't have an impeccable name and reputation.

She didn't fit either category. She'd known that even before arriving in his country. And now he knew it, too.

Ariane watched him sleep, his features relaxed, the

rustic shadow of whiskers on his jaw making him devastatingly desirable. It was all she could do not to reach out and run her hand over his flat stomach. She wondered what it would be like to slip her fingers underneath his sweater and tangle them in the springy hairs of his chest peeking out from the neckline.

After getting to know him, she found it difficult to envision him trying to do something as unscrupulous as usurping a neighboring country. He had a strong character, yes. He would make a great king someday. But there was a difference between a man who was powerful and one who was heartlessly ruthless.

The cool morning breeze had her unwittingly rubbing her hands up and down her forearms. Snatching up her pack, she walked to the creek and then along the gurgling water until she found a spot private enough to refresh herself. She splashed cold, clear spring water over her face, then pulled her toothbrush out of her pack and cleaned her teeth.

The sun was just coming up over the horizon, turning the sky a glorious crystal blue, when she returned to the spot where they had slept together and found Etienne and his backpack gone. Before she had time to feel even a moment of concern, however, he broke through the trees and smiled at her.

The manner in which her heart lurched at the mere sight of him hinted that her feelings for this man were more serious than they should be. That thought was worrisome.

"Good morning," he said. "I was just cleaning up a bit…and answering the call of nature."

Ariane grimaced. "Nature's calling me, too, but…" She glanced around, disliking the idea rolling around in her head.

He chuckled. "Not to worry. There's a public rest-room just twenty yards or so down that path. That's where I've just come from." He pointed in the direction from which he'd just come.

Her shoulders sagged with gratitude. "Thanks." And she toddled off to use the facilities.

When she returned, he said, "I hadn't expected to spend the night outside. How'd you sleep?"

"Fine, but I am feeling a little stiff," she admitted.

"Were you cold in the night?"

Ariane simply shook her head in answer, remembering how she'd had to untangle herself from him. He had kept her toasty warm all night long, but she didn't feel comfortable making that confession.

"D-did you sleep well?" she asked, unable to meet his gaze.

"A soft mattress would have been nice." He looked at the horizon, stretching his broad back and shoulders this way and that. "But the walk down to the car will surely loosen us both up, don't you think?"

She nodded, realizing that he, too, sensed the awkward air that had crept over them. It was clear that he was doing all he could to avoid mentioning the fact that they had slept together. Granted, they hadn't shared a single sensuous touch or one whispered word of want, but there was still something amazingly intimate in the notion that they had spent the night in each other's arms.

"I'm starved," she blurted, feeling the sudden need to fill the silence that surrounded them.

"Then our first order of business is finding some breakfast."

Worry wrinkled the bridge of her nose. "It's a long drive back. Maybe we should return to the palace. If you don't show up for breakfast everyone will be up in arms.''

"Nonsense," he said, waving off her concern. Conspiratorially, he whispered, "I don't know if you've noticed, but I'm all grown-up. It'll be okay if we spend the day together.''

She cast him a dubious glance. "Being grown-up is one thing, but worrying your parents by disappearing without a word is quite another.''

"Okay, okay," he appeased. "I'll call home as soon as we can find a phone. Will that make you happy?''

The smile with which she graced him was clear evidence that it did.

He took her hand in his like it was the most natural thing in the world, and the unwieldy moments seemed to scatter like the darkness of night chased away by daybreak.

It would be lovely to forget, just for a little while, that he was a prince and she was a woman who had lost her title—and with it every chance she might have had with a man like Etienne.

Yes, forgetting reality would be lovely, indeed.

The tiny roadside café catered to tourists, a prime source of Rhineland's revenue, and the place was buzzing with travelers even at this early hour. However, because Etienne and Ariane were dressed as they were in jeans, jackets and heavy hiking boots, and the fact that they both looked a little rumpled from their night spent at Byron Falls, they were able to sit at a table right next to the window and enjoy their coffee while gazing out at the beautiful view of the rolling hills without being recognized.

"So," Ariane said to him, "your parents were okay with us slipping off?"

He nodded. "Everything is fine. Father was a tad miffed that we slipped away from the opera last night. But he was happy that I called. I want to thank you for encouraging me to get in touch with him. That was very thoughtful of you."

She gazed at him over the rim of her cup, some unreadable emotion clouding her beautiful eyes.

"They really don't mind your spending the day with me?"

"Absolutely not," he said. "Father told me to show you a good time. He knows you've been under a great deal of stress lately."

The sigh she expelled had him asking, "What is it, Ariane? Something's bothering you. Tell me what's on your mind."

"It's nothing."

But her tone was whisper soft and she'd averted her gaze out the window. When she looked at him next, a smile had returned to her lips.

"This is nice," she said.

He knew without asking that she meant the picturesque town he'd brought her to, the charming café, being out in public unnoticed, the freedom from personnel whose sole goal was to protect and defend, being away from the prying eyes of the press.

"It *is* nice," he agreed. "In fact, I have to admit to feeling a bit envious of your new beginning."

A confused frown bit into her delicate brow. "My new beginning?"

"Your life is going to burst forth with color and freshness and fragrance—" he grinned "—like spring bulbs erupting from the earth. Just think, no protocol to follow, no etiquette to worry about, no official duties to perform.'' Although he could actually hear the covetousness in his tone, he didn't feel the least bit self-conscious when he added, ''No rules to follow. No one to answer to.''

She just looked at him.

''Oh, what I wouldn't give to be in your shoes.''

Wasn't it funny? he thought. He'd planned this spur-of-the-moment jaunt of theirs as a means of getting Ariane to open up to him. Being the high-spirited woman he had come to know her to be, he realized that she'd never be able to turn down an opportunity to experience a little adventure, and she'd agreed to run away with him without a moment's hesitation. However, rather than coercing her to reveal her deepest thoughts and feelings to him, here he was exposing his own wishes and desires.

Finally, she tilted her head and grinned at him, and he thought the expression was sexy as the dickens.

''Come on now.'' There was chastisement in her tone. ''No rules and no one to answer to is a great concept, but you can't sit there and tell me that you're envious of my illegitimacy.'' She moistened her lips, and when next she spoke, her voice grew serious. ''I may have gained some freedom, Etienne, but my father's actions—and the fact that my grandparents kept all of it a secret—have cost me everything.''

Ariane was a strong woman, Etienne knew. But whenever she displayed any sense of vulnerability, all he wanted to do was scoop her up into his arms and protect her from the world.

He slid his hand overtop hers. Her skin felt hot against his. And silky smooth. Little zips of current seemed to stick him like tiny needles.

"I've said this before—" he leveled his gaze on her so she'd realize his utter sincerity "—the news regarding the circumstances of your birth doesn't change who you are inside."

She swallowed, her midnight gaze growing haunted. Softly she said, "But it sure does change a lot. For me and my sisters. Look at what's happening to Lise. Wilhelm has left her high and dry, Etienne. And she's pregnant. I talked with Marie-Claire yesterday morning and she told me that our wonderful stepmother has refused to allow Lise to move back into the palace."

"She can't do that."

"Oh, can't she? You don't know Celeste." Ariane could only shake her head. "I'm sure the woman isn't interested in having any more competition around her. That's how she always saw us, you know, as competition. For everything. My father's affections. The royal coffers. Even the public's fondness, interest and attention." The sound she made was filled with disgust. "Just everything."

Myriad emotions seemed to ooze from her in waves, yet all he could do was sit there and listen.

"There is so much controversy surrounding the baby Celeste is carrying," she continued. "There are even doubts being expressed by some over who fathered this child."

Lord above, Etienne thought silently. He'd known St. Michel's royal house was in an uproar, but he hadn't guessed the family had been experiencing this kind of turmoil.

"Do you think your stepmother is capable of doing something like that?"

"Is she capable? Yes."

Ariane's voice sounded small, and he was hit yet again with the urge to protect her from harm, from all negative emotion.

"But I sure hope she didn't," Ariane added. "She couldn't get away with a thing like that. Not with the DNA testing that's available today. And government officials will eventually require it. I know the prime minister won't let Celeste get out of it, no matter how she fights it."

"I would think proving the legitimacy of her child would have her running to take the tests."

She nodded. "Now you can better understand why there's so much controversy swirling around her pregnancy."

The waitress arrived with their platters of food, and Etienne smiled as he watched Ariane pick up her fork and dig in with enthusiasm. For some reason, he thoroughly enjoyed the idea that she loved to eat a good, healthy meal. He'd never been attracted to wafer-thin women, and although she could never be described as overweight, her body was luscious and curvy. Like a warm, ripe peach just waiting to be plucked. And savored.

He allowed himself a moment to close his eyes and imagine biting into a juicy piece of fruit, dream of the heady taste as syrup dribbled down his chin unchecked. Desire quickened inside him and his eyelids flew open, his gaze zeroing in on Ariane's full, rounded breasts, his salivary glands working overtime. He forced his eyes to her pink lips. He'd kissed her mouth. Had sampled the sweetness of her. Oh, how he'd love to relish the whole of her.

Etienne was besieged with a strange shakiness. This woman did things to him that no other had.

"Is something wrong?"

"No," he lied. Picking up his fork and knife, he focused his attention on his plate. He inhaled a deep breath in a vain attempt to quell the throbbing of his blood through his veins. Once again, he was amazed by how she stirred his libido. But his desire for her wasn't purely lust alone. He wanted to get inside her head, to know what she thought about life. He wanted to discover what made her laugh, what made her sad, what made her angry, what made her proud. He wanted to know all there was to know about her.

In an effort to make some forward strides in this quest, he asked, "How do you feel about the law your government has that states only male heirs can sit on the throne?"

Her eyes grew hooded. Was that distrust he saw clouding her features? But before he could decide, her gaze cleared somewhat. As she chewed, her shoulders lifted in a small shrug. Finally, she swallowed. "Of course, it's an archaic law. One that's demeaning to all women, not just the females of the de Bergeron royal family. If I could do something to change it, I would." Again she shrugged. "But I can't."

Although she was presenting a face of casual indifference to something she could do nothing about, Etienne sensed that she was deeply hurt by her government's inability to acknowledge that women were capable of acting as sovereign leader.

He found it impossible to still his tongue on the matter. "I think someone ought to change the idiotic law. Can't the officials of your country see that it could have a devastating effect on St. Michel?"

Etienne pressed his lips together. He hadn't meant to bring up her country's governmental problems.

During the weeks she'd been in Rhineland, he'd had his top intelligence agents scrutinizing every member of his father's cabinet. Time and again, his people reported hearing stories and plans, but no one could pinpoint with whom the heretical campaign to seize neighboring St. Michel was originating.

Again, he noticed how her dark blue eyes became shadowed with what looked to him to be suspicion. For the life of him, he couldn't figure out what he'd said to make her look so guarded. He'd only told the honest truth. The edict of male-only rule *was* idiotic.

Ariane's eyes lowered to her plate. "Even if my father hadn't been involved in the marriage that left me illegitimate, and even if females could reign St. Michel, I'd never be that ruler." The corners of her mouth pulled back. "I'm second born, you know. I have an older sister." The sigh she expelled was purposefully melodramatic. "It's like that phrase 'always a bridesmaid…never a bride.'"

Her chuckle seemed lighthearted enough to have Etienne figuring he'd misconstrued her doubtful expression of a moment before. He felt warmth creep over him and he smiled.

"Somehow," he told her, "I don't see that old adage fitting you at all."

Ariane had never experienced confusion to this degree. One moment, Etienne seemed like a knight in shining armor ready to sweep her away from the sad reality of her life. Then out of the blue, he talked about the devastation St. Michel was surely headed for.

Had the comment been an innocent opinion? Or had he finally slipped up and revealed his true intention? The last thing she wanted right now was to discover that Etienne was behind the plot against her country. However, if that's what she learned, she sure didn't want to hide her head in the sand.

The two of them finished their breakfast and drove to Rhineland's largest lake, a landlocked body of crystal azure water. Etienne rented a boat from an old man who was fishing from a pier, and rowed them across the flat, calm lake. She lifted her face to the warmth of the sun, wishing she could remove the brick-like apprehension sitting in the pit of her belly.

Suddenly she realized that Etienne had stopped rowing and she dipped her chin to look him in the face. Ariane felt her heartbeat flutter. Why did he have to be so gorgeous? Why did she have to be so attracted to him? Why did they have to be thrown together when her country was going through such turmoil?

She'd have loved to simply ask him if he was planning to annex St. Michel. She wished she could come right out and tell him she was working to discover who was plotting against her country.

But that was impossible.

Then she noticed the humor lighting his gray gaze.

"Now that we're in the middle of nowhere," he said, "I can tell you what's on my mind."

Ariane blinked once, her brows raising in surprise. What in the world was he about to suggest?

"I want to take this opportunity to say that I'm on to you," he said. "Not once since we left the opera last night have you made any kind of silly observation. Each and every thought and opinion you've expressed has been completely intelligent. I want it noted that I've known all along that you're not as beef-witted as you've wanted everyone—including me—to think.''

His grin was captivating enough to charm the trout right out of the lake, and although panic at having been found out had the blood whooshing through her ears, she had to admit that she was beguiled. Dazzled. Enthralled. By his charm alone.

''Now,'' he softly continued, easing himself closer to her, ''all I have to do is figure out why you'd do such a thing in the first place.''

Ariane couldn't seem to think straight with him so near. Had she really discarded her mask of stupidity? Had she let down her guard so completely?

Before she was able to answer the silent queries, Etienne cupped her face between his warm, strong hands. The air seemed to heat and churn and swell with some mysterious—

No, there was nothing mysterious about what tugged at her.

Desire.

Passion.

Yearning.

As if pulled by some invisible surge of magnetic energy, Ariane felt herself leaning toward Etienne at the same time that he drew closer to her. Her gaze was riveted to his perfect mouth. The moist, swarthy skin of his full bottom lip was a shade darker than the rest of his flesh. She wanted to taste it. She wanted to feel the roughness of his whiskers against her cheek, her neck. She wanted to run her fingers through his thick hair.

When he finally did press his mouth to hers, his kiss was sweet, almost chaste. And it left her wanting more. Much more.

He whispered her name against her lips, nestled his nose up next to hers as if he wanted to inhale the very same air as she. Ariane found this to be a most sensuous act.

Etienne kissed her again, lightly. Ardor shuddered through her body from head to toe. She wanted nothing more than to surrender to it. But something made her hesitate.

Swallowing, she forced her eyes to open. She looked at the face of her handsome prince and knew that she'd never forget this moment all the days of her life. When she was a wrinkled old woman, she'd think of the time she'd run away with Prince Etienne Kroninberg of Rhineland, and she'd smile.

But now she had to think of her country. She had to remember to whom she owed her loyalty.

Her people.

Etienne could very well be the enemy, her brain silently whispered.

Gently, she inched away from him. Out of his loving embrace.

"I can't," she told him softly. "I just can't do this."

His brow furrowed, and she could clearly see that she'd wounded him with her rejection. Something in her had her saying, "Your parents have been wonderful to me since the news of my..." The rest of her thought faded. She knew he understood. "But we both know that they wouldn't approve of this. We both know that it's your job to make a good marriage. It's your job to wed a woman who can bring something good to Rhineland." A lump formed in her throat, but she forced out, "We both know I'm not that woman."

Chapter Eight

Ariane stared out the car window only vaguely aware of the lavender and wild thyme that covered the rolling hills in a carpet of dusky purple. The tomb-like silence between herself and Etienne had been more than she could bear so she'd finally reached down and snapped on the radio. Anything, even the babble of a news broadcast, was better than this unsettling quiet.

She'd messed up something terrible over the past eighteen hours or so. Dropped her guard. Completely blown her cover. When she and Etienne had escaped from the opera last night, she'd peeled off the simpleton costume she'd so painstakingly designed over the weeks since arriving in Rhineland.

It would be nice if she could blame absentmindedness for this blunder. However, she was too practical to lie to herself. Sitting here now she had to admit that each and every time she'd led Etienne to believe her brain was made of nothing more substantial than air bubbles, she'd been appalled down to the soles of her feet! She'd hated him thinking she was a brainless wonder. So now he knew she wasn't a complete idiot.

When he'd gleefully exclaimed that he'd suspected all along that she was putting on a show, she'd actually had to tamp down her joy. The elation that had shot through her was just one more indication of how much Etienne had come to mean to her. However, that delight had died a quick death just as soon as he'd expressed his determination to discover just why she'd do such a thing. The last thing she wanted was for him to learn that she'd been using him in order to spy on his government.

Making him privy to what intelligence she did have hadn't been the only way she'd blown her cover. In telling him that she wasn't the woman for him, she'd pretty much destroyed the disguising motive she'd been using for visiting his country. That was not to say that her masquerade had been going all that well since the news of her illegitimacy had broken, but at least she'd had a small thread of an excuse to hang onto regarding why she'd remained in Rhineland when everyone fully expected her to return to St. Michel in disgrace.

Now, even that thin thread had snapped by her own hand. She'd have no recourse but to return to her homeland. And she'd be leaving with very little evidence to present to the St. Michel security force. Luc Dumont, head of security, would surely be disappointed when he learned that she couldn't point a finger at who was plotting to take over their country.

Even with all this turmoil spinning in her mind,

unwittingly, she darted a quick glance at Etienne's tight profile. It should be deemed against the law for a man to be so attractive.

Again, contradictory emotions roiled inside.

No one had ever affected her the way this man had. He'd ignited something in her. A light. No—*a fire*.

A flame that flared brightly, burned white-hot.

She wouldn't regret the weeks she'd spent with him. Yet at the same time, she was relieved that she was being forced to go home. She was calmed by the knowledge that she was through with all this game playing.

Not one to toy with anyone's feelings or affections, she was content that her stint as a spy was over. Ariane frowned when the radio newscaster's report caught her attention.

"…it is not known if Prince Etienne went off willingly with the ex-princess of St. Michel or if Ariane de Bergeron kidnapped him. The royal spokesperson stated today that King Giraud plans to hold a press conference this afternoon just as soon as Luc Dumont, director of St. Michel's security force, arrives at Kroninberg Palace. The royal spokesman went on to say that rumors of Queen Laurette's collapse are true. But he rejected the suggestion that it was due to the fact that her son had gone missing. The royal physician is currently at the palace. For BBC news, this is—"

Etienne turned off the radio.

All Ariane could think to do was whisper, "I'm so sorry, Etienne. Your mother has—"

"It's hype," he stated, slicing through her sentence with his knife-sharp words. "The media are sensationalizing this thing. I talked to my father. He knows I'm fine. He'll alert your security people.''

''But they just said the queen collapsed,'' she couldn't help pointing out.

''Yes, I heard that.''

She knew that a rush of stress was to blame for his sudden brusqueness. In an effort to assuage his anxiety, she said, ''I'm sorry if I've caused your family any harm. Bad press is one thing, but if your mother has taken ill because of something I've done—'' She broke off the sentence and simply shook her head.

Intensity turned his eyes to slate-gray. ''If something's happened to my mother, it's health related. You had nothing to do with it, I assure you.''

She remembered then that he'd told her Queen Laurette had been gravely ill with pneumonia prior to Ariane's arrival in Rhineland.

For some reason, Etienne's reassurance didn't lighten the load that seemed to fall on her shoulders like a wet woolen cloak. She'd caused the royal family of Rhineland enough trouble for one visit, she gloomily surmised. First, the news of her father's teen marriage had hit the newspapers, radio and television broadcasts while she was visiting the king and queen's home. The Rhineland media had had a field day with the fact that an illegitimate princess was trying to sink her claws into their one and only son. And now those sharks of the media were in a feeding frenzy over the fact that she may or may not have kidnapped the crown prince of Rhineland.

Everyone—the king and queen, Etienne, even the Rhinelanders themselves—would be much better off if she were to go away.

Far, far away.

* * *

She'd expected to meet confusion when they arrived at the palace, but what she saw when she entered the elegant royal reception parlor would have been better described as unqualified pandemonium.

A group of diplomats, several from Rhineland and at least four from St. Michel that Ariane could recognize, were shouting, facial veins bulging on some, others waving their arms in anger. Servants scurried silently in and out of the room, bringing the ambassadors various messages, carrying refreshment, or hovering discreetly in case their services were needed. A mob of security personnel from both countries was working with electrical technicians in setting up what looked to be a center of operations complete with several pieces of high-tech computer hardware, a recording device and two telephones.

The king was not in attendance. Neither was the queen. The absence of Etienne's parents concerned Ariane to a huge degree. She could see that Etienne was experiencing an identical reaction.

"I'm sure you wouldn't mind excusing me while I go find my father," he murmured in her ear.

"Of course."

The stiff, formal nod they exchanged brought Ariane's mood another notch lower than it already was.

When she next glanced up, her gaze connected with Luc Dumont's vivid blue one. She could tell from the expression on his face that he was not happy with her.

The other men didn't even look up from their work when Luc left the group and came directly to Ariane.

"What's that all about?" she asked him lightly, pointing to the control center being set up and hoping against hope that she could lighten Luc's stern disposition. She rallied a smile as she quipped, "Did everyone honestly expect me to be calling in a ransom demand for the prince? I know I've been known to do some crazy things in my day, Luc, but..."

The man didn't crack a smile. "You know it's common procedure to prepare ourselves for any situation. The king did tell us he'd heard from his son early this morning. But that was hours ago, Ariane. We had no way of knowing what could have happened to the two of you. You could have met with—"

"Some extremely nefarious characters. Yes, you've warned me a hundred times over the years." Ariane forced another smile, but still Luc's mouth remained stubbornly grim. Finally, her shoulders sagged and she muttered, "Anyone ever tell you that you take your job much too seriously, Dumont?"

His lips pressed together in an obvious effort to suppress a hint of humor. "Yes," he answered unhesitatingly. "You." The glint in his eye was the only other signal that the gravity he was conveying was softening.

Now that his irritation had abated somewhat, Ariane felt safe to offer her heartfelt apology for slipping away without telling anyone. Tilting her head, she looked up into his face. "Would you believe that this was all Etienne's idea?"

The doubt in Luc's blue eyes told her that her long, adventure-loving reputation was going to have her shouldering the blame for this fiasco no matter what the truth of the situation really was.

At that moment, one of the St. Michel diplomats shouted, "We will not agree to issuing any kind of formal apology until it is certain Ariane de Bergeron returns unharmed and it is learned that she is at fault.''

Ariane sighed. Even her own government was willing to allow her to take responsibility for this mess.

''Gentlemen.''

Although Luc hadn't raised his tone, Ariane plainly saw that he commanded the attention of the entire room. The hubbub ceased and all eyes turned to him.

''As you can see,'' he told them, ''Ariane and the prince have returned, safe and sound.''

However, it was clear that the men weren't going to give up their argumentative attitudes easily.

''I don't see Prince Etienne.'' The Rhineland diplomat's tone was heavy with suspicion.

''What has she done with him?'' another asked. ''That woman should be taken into custody.''

A flash of fear arrowed through Ariane, and she felt an overwhelming compulsion to defend herself. ''But Etienne is fine,'' she insisted. ''He was just with me. Luc saw him. So did everyone standing around the doorway here.'' She indicated the nearby servants. ''He went to find his father, and to check on his mother.''

Only after Luc and two of the domestics had proclaimed Ariane to be telling the truth did the Rhineland dignitaries back down.

Acute awkwardness fell over everyone in the room, and it seemed that no one knew quite what to do now that the emergency had passed. Luc told his men to break down and pack up the communications center they had been setting up. Then he said to Ariane, ''Would you mind coming with me? We need to talk.'' To the dignitaries in the room, he said, ''I need to debrief Ms. de Bergeron. We won't be long.''

Once they were alone in the library, Luc gently chided, "What were you thinking, Ariane? Going off like that was—"

"But I'm okay," she said. "You didn't have to come running to my rescue."

Frustration had Luc lifting his hands, palms up. "Slipping away from security in St. Michel is one thing, but to do so on foreign soil, not to mention the fact that you were working undercover. For me. Is it any wonder that I flew here just as soon as—"

"But it really *was* Etienne's idea," she interrupted, hoping to put him at ease. Then she sighed. "I realize it was foolish of me to have agreed to go along with him." She tilted her head, her face screwing up as she explained, "But his parents took me to the opera, Luc. *The opera.* When Etienne suggested we escape the dull evening, I just couldn't resist."

She hoped her dire tone would convey to him her dilemma—and her need to flee. She knew he did when one corner of his mouth tipped up and he simply shook his head in silence.

"What can you tell me about Queen Laurette's condition?" she asked, unable to quell her concern any longer.

"We haven't been given very much information." Luc reached up to worry his chin between his thumb and index finger. "Apparently, she's fallen ill. But the doctor won't say yet if she's having a relapse of pneumonia or if it's her heart. If it was truly serious," he finally surmised, "they'd have taken her to hospital."

Common sense alone told her that much was true. Still, concern knitted Ariane's brow. Lowering her eyelids, she whispered a quick, silent prayer for good health for Etienne's mother.

The moment she opened her eyes, Luc said, "You need to return home."

"I'm ready." Ariane realized that she'd answered too quickly and concisely when she saw Luc's gaze narrow, but thankfully he kept his curiosity in check.

"I'll arrange for you to say your goodbyes to the royal family."

"That won't be necessary." She kept her tone firm.

"But protocol dictates—"

"Luc," she softly asserted, "I no longer need to concern myself with protocol."

Again, Luc looked at her askance, but remained silent.

She sighed. "Etienne and his father need to be with Queen Laurette. This is not the time for me to be bothering them with silly goodbyes."

Ariane's throat felt desert dry. She didn't want to face Etienne. Everything that needed to be said had been said out there on that lake earlier today.

"I'll send them all personal thank-you notes the moment I arrive home." Meaning to veer him away from asking any uncomfortable questions, she composed herself, nonchalantly tucked a wayward strand of hair behind her ear and asked, "How is everyone at home, anyway? Marie-Claire? Jacqueline? Has anyone heard from Lise? Wilhelm left her and has requested a divorce from King Gir—"

"Slow down. I'll tell you all the news." Luc took a seat on the overstuffed russet armchair and motioned for Ariane to sit on the adjacent couch. As soon as she was settled, he continued, "Marie-Claire and Jacqueline are fine. So is your grandmother. Everyone is staying out of Celeste's way." His jaw tightened. "That woman is turning into a veritable shrew. She's flying into rages at the least little thing."

"Has she produced the results to those DNA tests?"

"No. But those results aren't as critical as they used to be."

Ariane gasped. "You've learned something about my father's firstborn child."

"I have," Luc admitted. "I discovered that Katie Graham, King Philippe's first wife, gave birth to a boy. Your half brother."

"But this is wonderful, Luc." Joy rushed through her. "That means that—"

"Rhineland can't annex St. Michel."

Ariane felt utterly weak with relief. Her grin couldn't have gotten any bigger.

"Well," Luc said, "that is *if* I can find Philippe's son. And if he's willing to take on the job of ruling a country." He chuckled. "I can't imagine any man turning down that job, can you?"

She shook her head. This news couldn't have been better.

"Katie Graham, or Katherine as she was better known," Luc continued, "was killed in an automobile crash." Before hope could flicker in Ariane about having her title reinstated, he added, "After your father's marriage to Johanna. So your parent's union never was legitimate, Ariane. I'm sorry. However, your father's first wife died before he married Helene, so that means that Jacqueline's royal title has been restored."

Joy rushed through Ariane on her youngest sister's behalf.

Luc's gaze flattened. "Of course this validates Celeste's marriage to Philippe, as well. It also justifies her claims that her unborn child could be the heir to St. Michel's throne. But only if Katherine Graham's child can't be located. Finding your father's first son is top priority. He'd be thirty-two now." He grew pensive, seeming to mull over his thoughts. "I only hope I can find him."

"You'll find him," she insisted. "I have faith in you. What more did you find out?"

"Well, before her death Katherine married an American by the name of Ellsworth Johnson. I've turned over documents to Prime Minister Davoine that prove all these facts."

Ariane trusted Rene Davoine, St. Michel's prime minister. He'd continue with the search of the de Bergeron missing heir no matter what Celeste had to say about it.

"So I guess the documents you dug up prove that Sebastian LeMarc isn't my father's son."

"Exactly," Luc told her.

"Claudette's claims were pretty outlandish from the beginning." Ariane shook her head. "That she befriended my father's first wife, took her in and housed her until her baby was born. That Katie Graham returned to Texas without her child. That Claudette raised the boy. And that the boy was Sebastian. Truth is often stranger than fiction, but come on."

Luc shrugged. "We had to take the story seriously. That birth certificate Claudette produced sure looked legit."

"Poor Sebastian," Ariane said on a sad sigh. "He must have been left reeling. Having been told that the people you'd always thought were your parents weren't, and that you were next in line to be king…"

She exhaled in a rush. "He had to have been bowled over."

Luc nodded. "He was. But all is well now. And I have good news. News that will make you want to pack your bags and head home to St. Michel."

Ariane's brow lifted in interest.

Luc's face lit up with pleasure. "Marie-Claire and Sebastian have, er...how can I say this delicately...taken a shine to each other. They're getting married. Immediately."

"You're kidding! My youngest sister never mentioned a word when I spoke with her on the phone." Ariane knew she'd have to think up some kind of devious punishment for the ornery Marie-Claire who had so callously left her in the dark. Then she realized what all this meant. "We're going to have a wedding! Grandmama must be thrilled, I'm sure."

Remembering the plight of her oldest sister, Ariane asked, "What of Lise? She's home, isn't she? Is she okay?"

"Lise is fine. And she's home. In St. Michel."

Luc's expression grew hooded.

"What?" Panic washed over Ariane. "What is it?"

"It's just that Celeste has become petty, almost unbalanced these days. No one can predict what she might do next." He shook his head, admitting, "She's refused to allow Lise to move back into the palace."

"Marie-Claire did tell me that." Concern knit Ariane's brow. "Lise is pregnant. And surely she's feeling depressed about Wilhelm leaving her. And she's scared, I'm sure, about the future. Lise needs to be near her family. How can Celeste force her to live by herself right now? The woman really is a witch."

He heaved a sigh. "It's not really all that bad. Lise is living in a cottage on the palace grounds. She's safe and warm and dry."

"Poor thing." Ariane's ire ruffled when she thought about her stepmother's treatment of her sister. "Celeste would have us all out on our ears if she could."

Softly, Luc said, "I'm afraid you're right."

She asked about her stepsiblings, Georges and Juliet.

"Georges is great. He's doing what he can to hold down the fort. And Juliet—"

Hmmm…the way his eyes misted over, Ariane thought, one would be led to believe that Luc had some real sentimental feelings for Juliet.

"—she's fine as well."

But the smile that shadowed the corners of his mouth continued to rouse Ariane's curiosity.

After a moment of silence, he asked, "What have you found out during your visit? Did you learn who might be plotting against us?"

Her brow wrinkled and agitation had her sitting up straighter on the couch. "Making everyone think I'm a blubbering fool was a great way to get people to disclose information to me that they might not normally. They thought I was too stupid to understand the ins and outs of government. I've heard bits and pieces of gossip. Prime Minister Schmidt made some very cagey remarks about governments needing to follow the laws of their forefathers. And I heard that a man by the name of Berg Dekker is complaining long and loud about paying fees to use St. Michel's docks. I know it's not much. I'm sure there's a faction within the Rhineland government who want to seize

St. Michel, but…'' She let the rest of her thought fade as she absently worried her thumb back and forth across the opposite palm.

Before she could subdue her tongue, words began to tumble from her mouth. ''During the weeks I've been here,'' she said, ''I've gotten to know Etienne pretty well. He's a formidable man. He's going to make a great ruler once his father decides to step down. But I just can't see him taking possession—taking *hostile* possession—of St. Michel. He's just too—''

''Whoa. Hold on, Ariane.'' Luc reached over and discreetly placed a calming hand on her knee. ''When you came here, we had no one on our list of suspects. And that remains the case. No one believes that Etienne—''

He stopped, his back straightening. His eyes narrowed suddenly. ''Oh, my,'' he softly whispered, reclining against the chair back. ''I think the prince has stolen your heart.''

The fact that someone other than herself was privy to her secret had a lump rising up in her throat. She had difficulty breathing, and sudden, hot tears splintered her vision into a thousand shards of light. Her chin trembled.

Displaying this kind of emotion was taboo according to all the training she'd received. A royal never let people see her cry. Ariane was a complete disgrace to the de Bergeron name.

Well, what did it matter? She wasn't a legal de Bergeron, anyway. Still, she should try to show a bit of dignity. This kind of pitiful exhibition would surely make Luc uncomfortable.

But to the contrary, the head of St. Michel's security force rose to his feet and came to sit next to her. He even put a comforting arm around her shoulders. It was then she realized that this strong, protective man would make some woman a great husband someday.

"It'll be okay, Ariane," he crooned. "Just because things look bad at the moment doesn't mean that this situation will be in the forefront of the news forever. There will be other catastrophes. Soon someone else's misfortune will take the limelight off of you and Lise and Marie-Claire. You'll see."

"Don't feed me a bunch of fairy tales, Luc." A teardrop scalded its way down Ariane's cheek. "No matter where the limelight shines next, the fact remains that my sisters and I have been proved illegitimate. *Illegitimate.* No titled man will have anything to do with us. Look at Lise. Her husband left her without a backward glance."

"Yes," he whispered, "but look at Marie-Claire. She found a good man who loves her. You will, too."

But she didn't want just any man. She wanted Etienne. But the loss of her title meant that they could never be together. Never.

Pure agony swelled in her chest. If she didn't get out of this room she'd end up sobbing like a big baby. And that wouldn't be fair to Luc. His job was to protect her, not mend her broken heart.

She pushed herself to a stand. "I've got to find Francie so we can pack. I want to go home, Luc. I want to go home now."

Chapter Nine

"It was a beautiful wedding, wasn't it?" Francie leaned closer to the mirror and applied powder to her forehead and chin with small, quick pats.

"It was," Ariane agreed. "Marie-Claire looked lovely in grandmother's wedding dress. All that white satin and chiffon. She looked like she was floating down the aisle. And there must have been a hundred tiny buttons. Just gorgeous."

Lise had worn Simone's wedding dress when she'd married Wilhelm. And Marie-Claire had worn it today. A tinge of sadness shot through Ariane when she realized that her chance to wear her grandmother's gown would surely never come.

Then she turned her attention to her half sister, Jacqueline. "And you, my sunshine, made a beautiful candle lighter."

The twelve-year-old wrinkled her nose prettily. "I tried to tell Marie-Claire that I'm old enough to be a real bridesmaid.'' She exhaled a long-suffering sigh. ''But she just wouldn't listen.''

An affectionate smile was Ariane's only response. Jacqueline had been lodging that same complaint for the full two weeks that Marie-Claire had been planning her wedding.

''Would you look at that,'' Francie commented. ''The child is cute even when she pouts.''

''Oh, Francie,'' Jacqueline grumbled. ''I am not.''

Ariane laughed. ''You are, too,'' she insisted, planting a kiss on her youngest sister's forehead.

Laughter and smiles on the outside. That's what Ariane had strived for. She desperately wanted to cover the turmoil continuing to rage inside her.

Ever since her return to St. Michel, Ariane hadn't experienced a single moment when thoughts of Etienne weren't hovering around somewhere in her head. She often visited with her older sister Lise at the cottage, offering her comfort, an ear, and many days a sturdy shoulder to cry on. Ariane had thrown herself into the wedding preparations, going to seemingly endless dress fittings, attending rehearsals, helping to choose music and shopping with Marie-Claire and her other sisters, full, half and step, as all the females eagerly offered opinions as the bride picked out her trousseau.

But on the inside Ariane had felt like an automaton. A walking zombie.

She wanted to be a good and strong presence for all her sisters so she did all she could to hide the sadness that filled her. Thankfully, Marie-Claire was too much in love, too preoccupied with wedding plans to notice the agony Ariane was feeling. And Lise, pregnant and alone, had too many worries of her own and was doing what she could to allow Marie-Claire the attention she deserved at this most happy time. In fact, everyone at the palace seemed caught up in the festivities.

Except for Celeste. Ariane's stepmother spent her days vacillating between agitation, grumpiness and out-and-out anger. But despite the woman's bouts of ranting, the de Bergeron sisters had banded together to throw together a beautiful wedding for Marie-Claire.

However, even in the face of the joyous occasion Ariane had felt stiff as a board and utterly emotionless as she'd walked down the aisle.

Until she saw him.

Etienne had been in the church this afternoon.

Her step had faltered when their eyes met. And held.

Always a bridesmaid, never a bride, she'd recalled telling him.

Somehow I don't think that old adage fits you at all, she'd remembered him replying.

She had departed Rhineland knowing that she'd left her heart behind—in Etienne's possession. But as the two of them stared at one another in the dimly lit church, Ariane realized the depth of her love for her prince. Etienne had done more than win her heart— he'd captured her very soul.

Knowing that nothing could ever come of the love that filled her to the brim had been devastating to her. Luckily, she'd been able to garner enough of her wits together to complete her trek down the aisle. But she'd barely heard a word of the ceremony, she had been quaking so terribly inside.

"You're a beautiful bridesmaid." Young Jacqueline smoothed her hand over her sister's loose, shoulder-length hair, pulling Ariane back into the here and now.

"Thank you, love."

Always a bridesmaid. That phrase would always have a poignant memory attached to it, Ariane realized.

She blinked, thinking once again of the intensity of Etienne's pewter gaze as he'd stared at her in the church earlier. If she hadn't known better, she'd be compelled to believe he was trying to communicate some profound message to her.

Foolish woman, a silent voice scorned.

Always a bridesmaid. Again, the axiom whispered through her mind.

Yes, that's just what she'd be.

Just then the door opened and the dowager queen entered the powder room. "Is this a private party? Or can anyone join?"

"Grandmama!" Jacqueline jumped up from the dainty stool and raced to the elderly lady. Simone met the child's warm enthusiasm with open arms.

"I can't wait," Jacqueline said to the elderly woman, "to get my chance to borrow your wedding dress."

"And you'll make a lovely bride. But you must give yourself time to grow up first." Simone's smile shined love down on her youngest granddaughter. "You were fabulous today, my dear. I'm very proud of you."

"Thank you," Jacqueline said primly.

Ariane's mouth quirked when she noticed that her young half sister didn't repeat her objection about being old enough to be a bridesmaid. Jacqueline evidently knew that complaining to Simone would warrant nothing more than a lesson in royal etiquette.

A noble never groused.

"Francie," Simone addressed Ariane's lady-in-waiting, "would you mind taking this young lady to the reception?" To Jacqueline, she said, "They've set out the dessert."

Jacqueline's eyes lit with delight, and she and Francie left the powder room.

Ariane fished a comb from her beaded bag and ran it lightly through her hair. "Marie-Claire looks lovely, doesn't she?"

Simone said, "She does. And so do you. You've always looked wonderful in deep purple. Your skin just glows."

A silent smile of thanks was Ariane's answer.

If it hadn't been for her grandmother, there had been times during her life when Ariane had thought she'd lose her mind living in this hodge-podge of a family. Simone was a loving and caring constant in what often seemed an extremely chaotic world. Of course, she was also very prim and proper, the picture of self-control.

"Or, hmmm, I wonder—" Simone's tone took on a teasing lilt "—if there could be another reason behind that glow."

Her whole body going taut, Ariane held her breath as she waited for her grandmother to offer more details. Simone didn't disappoint her.

"There's a handsome prince at the reception who seems to be on the lookout for someone." The elderly woman's face wrinkled with a soft smile. "Could it be you he's searching for?"

Ariane's heart pounded like a hammer.

"Etienne's looking for me?"

Simone beamed. "Is there another prince that you've fallen in love with?"

Unable to contain her surprised gasp, she gawked at her grandmother, knowing full well doing so was most unladylike. "But...how did you know?"

"Oh, dear child," Simone cooed, "at the ripe old age of seventy-five if I can't spot someone wearing their heart on their sleeve, then I may as well open the gate and put myself out to pasture."

Ariane's spirit plummeted. Had she really revealed her feelings for Etienne so openly in that split second of hesitation when walking down the aisle?

"You weren't the only one who was blatantly expressing your feelings." Simone's laugh was soft as goose down.

The room felt as if it were devoid of oxygen. Ariane couldn't seem to inhale, so she waited. Breathless.

"From what I could see," the elderly lady continued, "that man is just as smitten with you as you are with him."

Hope soared inside Ariane as if it had sprouted the powerful wings of eagles and taken flight. But the reality of her situation had despair weighing down the fleeting anticipation.

"Even if he does feel something for me," Ariane said, unable to get her voice above a whisper, "nothing could ever come of it. He's the crown prince of Rhineland. I'm just—"

"A kind, caring and clever young woman with plenty to offer," Simone asserted stubbornly. "Not to mention the fact that you're terrifically beautiful to boot."

Ariane fell silent, not knowing how to respond. She loved that her grandmother would come to her defense so fiercely. But reality was what it was. And there could be no changing it.

As if tuned into Ariane's thoughts, Simone's brows arched regally. "My dear, do not underestimate the power of love. It can move mountains. Just look at what it did for Marie-Claire and Sebastian." Gazing off, Simone reached up, lightly touching her index finger to her lips as she suddenly became lost in thought. Finally, she said, "Words can't express how happy I am that she married for love."

It was common knowledge that Simone's marriage to Ariane's grandfather, Antoine de Bergeron, had been an arranged one.

"Oh, I'm not complaining," Simone continued softly. "Antoine and I grew to love each other over the years." She grinned at Ariane. "But in the beginning, things were pretty rocky. The love Marie-Claire and Sebastian share will save them that much, at least."

The warmth of her grandmother's velvet touch on her shoulders had Ariane meeting Simone's gentle gaze.

"You don't look convinced that love is a mighty force."

A knot of emotion swelled in Ariane's throat until it actually grew painful. "Oh, what I feel for Etienne is powerful, all right." She sighed. "But I feel so guilty. I've wronged him, you know. I've wronged him in more ways than one."

Simone didn't speak and loving patience seemed to palpitate from her as she waited for Ariane to unburden herself.

"First off, I misjudged him terribly. All those months ago when he first showed an interest in me, I was angry that Father seemed to be forcing Etienne on me. Father seemed determined to make a union between the de Bergeron and the Kroninberg houses, and it infuriated me that I was his bait. Pure stubbornness had me believing a bunch of preconceived notions about Etienne. I convinced myself I wouldn't like him. Surely he was boring, I thought. Surely he was stuffy. Surely he was high-minded. Not the kind of man who would interest me at all. But what I took for arrogance, wasn't arrogance at all, Grandmama. It was a seriousness regarding who and what he was—a prince with a future filled with duty and responsibility.

"And I wronged him, too," she continued, "by suspecting he was behind the plot to seize St. Michel. I have no rock-hard evidence that he isn't involved, I just know in my heart that he's not the kind of man who would do something so ruthless."

Her grandmother smoothed a satiny hand down Ariane's cheek. "Follow your heart, child. Listen to what it tells you and you'll never be led astray."

Agony had tears springing to Ariane's eyes. "But my heart is telling me to go to Etienne right now. To tell him how I feel, title or no title. And all that will do is force him to reject me."

"There you go again," Simone tenderly chastised, shaking her head. "Underestimating."

There was that hope again. New wings budding to life.

Ariane blinked. "You really think I should go to him?" Anxiety wrinkled her brow. "But won't he think I'm…forward?"

Simone waved away Ariane's fears. "This is a new age, my dear. These days, women go after what they want."

In that instant, Ariane felt light as air. Almost buoyant.

What do you have to lose? a silent voice soughed through her mind.

Nothing. And everything.

Fear clawed at her.

What do you really *have to lose?* the voice insisted.

Well—Ariane's mind whirled like a dervish—if she revealed her heart to him, he could politely turn her down, using his princely duty as a perfectly acceptable excuse. However, if she were to reveal her feelings for him…he just might take her in his arms and tell her he felt the same way.

The attraction that had hummed between them like an electric current couldn't be denied. By either of them.

But if she didn't bare her soul to him, she would spend the rest of her life wondering what Etienne's response might have been. Could she live with that regret for the remainder of her days?

She knew that simply wasn't an option.

Her decision made, she couldn't keep the smile from her lips as she said to her grandmother, "I want you to know I love you. And I'll be forever grateful to you for urging me to—"

Simone silenced her with a soft index finger against her lips, her eyes shining as brightly as Ariane's.

"You're wasting time, my child. Go get that man and make him yours."

Giving her grandmother's hand a quick squeeze, Ariane raced from the room to seek her destiny.

Whatever fate had in store, regret over remaining silent about her love for Etienne wouldn't have a part in it.

The quick loop she'd made around the reception hall hadn't turned up her prince. Ariane's gaze darted from face to face. She had to find him. He couldn't possibly have left without seeing her, could he?

Suddenly, she came upon Luc and Juliet. The couple looked positively secreted away in the secluded niche and they parted as soon as they saw her. Was that guilt she felt emanating from them? But her mind was too preoccupied to give the matter much thought.

"Have you seen Prince Etienne?" she asked them.

"He was asking for you earlier," Juliet said.

The ever-vigilant Luc replied, "I saw him go outside. Toward the gardens."

Of course. The formal gardens. Why hadn't she thought to look there rather than become panicked that Etienne might have taken his leave without saying goodbye?

"Thank you," Ariane said to Juliet and Luc, and then she rushed toward the wide, arched stone doorway that led to the gardens.

The pungent scent of pine mingled with the aroma of hyacinth and lupine as she made her way along the pea-stone path that winded through the trees, shrubs and blooming bulbs. The setting sun had turned the horizon a vivid burnt orange, but Ariane barely noticed it.

She called his name just as soon as she'd caught sight of him.

He turned to face her, and she couldn't keep herself from running the final steps that separated them.

That familiar throbbing vibration resonated, thick and heavy, in the silent moments they spent studying each other. She felt as if she hadn't seen him in months.

Tell him, her brain screeched at her. *Tell him all you feel.*

I will, I will, she silently promised herself. But she was trembling so. With elation. With fear.

Taking a deep calming breath, she decided at last to take it slow. Her dream, her fairy tale, her idea of *rapturous paradise* would begin—or end—tonight. The perfect words would have to be carefully chosen.

"How is your mother?" she asked softly, feeling suddenly shy. "Recuperating well, I hope."

The small smile he offered her spoke of his gratitude that she cared enough about his mother to ask after her health.

"She's improving daily," he told her. "She and my father send their regrets for being unable to attend your sister's wedding. But my mother simply must follow doctor's orders."

"Of course." The air felt so...warm. "It was kind of you to attend in their stead."

He murmured, "I wouldn't have missed it." His gray eyes leveled on her. "I'm sorry we had to part without saying a proper goodbye, and I appreciated the note you sent. In fact—" he deftly slipped his fingers between the facings of his jacket and extracted the ivory envelope "—I've read it at least a thousand times."

Ariane's heart fluttered furiously against her ribs. He'd kept her note. On his person. He'd read it again and again. That had to mean something wonderful...didn't it?

Emotions waged a war inside her. She wanted to trust her intuition, but the panic over misconstruing his meaning was rising like the swell of a great and potentially fatal tidal wave.

Awkwardness had her gaze sliding from his. "I've been so busy since I returned home."

"I understand," he told her, tension pulling his tone taut. "Helping your sister plan her wedding, I'm sure." After a heady pause, he haltingly declared, "It was a beautiful wedding."

He'd strung out the word beautiful, emphasizing it, and that had Ariane's eyes latching onto his once again.

Had that compliment really been meant for her? Was he implying that he thought her beautiful?

Oh, she wished that if that were so, he'd come right out and speak his mind. It certainly would make her intentions of revealing her feelings for him a little less frightening.

"I've been busy, too," he told her.

"Oh?"

Etienne nodded. "With Mother so ill, I've been fulfilling Father's obligations."

He grinned then, and she thought her heart would melt right down into her shoes by how appealing she found it.

"And I had to make my own travel arrangements," he continued. "Seems I'm about to lose my equerry."

"Harry is leaving his post?" she asked.

Etienne nodded. "Seems he's about to ask your lady-in-waiting to marry him. Harry approached Francie's father to ask permission and the man not only granted it, he also asked Harry to come work for him."

Placing her palm against the purple satin bodice of her gown, Ariane released a poignant sigh. "Oh, Francie must be ecstatic. I wonder why she hasn't told me? That woman couldn't keep a secret if her life depended on it."

"She hasn't told you because she doesn't know yet."

Happiness for her friend had Ariane smiling warmly. "I won't say a word. I'd never dream of bursting her bubble."

Do not underestimate the power of love. It can move mountains.

Her grandmother's words gurgled through her mind like a fountain of fresh spring water.

Follow your heart, child. Listen to what it tells you and you'll never be led astray.

Still, fear of rejection paralyzed her tongue. But then her mind was bombarded with all of Etienne's kindnesses: he had done everything he could to save her from humiliation after Wilhelm had sold the story of the de Bergeron scandal to the media, and in the weeks that followed Etienne had insisted that everyone treat her with respect. She also recalled how he'd taken her away from that boring old opera, and how he'd shown her such a wonderful time at Byron Falls. He was a good man. A caring man. And she loved him. Down to the very soul of her being.

She swallowed and garnered every ounce of her courage. "There's something I want you to know."

His gaze glistened with curiosity, and Ariane was certain she observed a keen anticipation in his handsome face.

Footsteps crunching on the pea-stone path had both

Ariane and Etienne turning to see Celeste approaching.

At nearly eight months pregnant, the woman's belly protruded under the pale yellow chiffon. Ariane had wanted to warn her stepmother that yellow wasn't a good color for blondes, that it turned the skin tone pallid, but Celeste had been so on edge lately that Ariane knew the woman would have misinterpreted the advice as pure criticism. So, she had simply kept her opinion to herself.

While Ariane and her sisters had been helping Marie-Claire plan her wedding, they had all steered clear of their stepmother. Celeste had flatly refused to allocate funds for something as frivolous as Marie-Claire's nuptials. Why, the woman had proclaimed for everyone to hear, the three daughters of Johanna Van Rhys weren't even real royalty. In Celeste's opinion, a grand wedding was not necessary.

Of course, the sisters had disagreed. Marie-Claire had spent her life as a princess, Ariane had thought, so she deserved a day of splendor…even if it was on a small scale.

Now, Celeste's eyes narrowed with unmistakable nastiness. ''Well, my, my…what have we here?'' she purred like a spiteful cat. She raked Ariane up and down with a scathing glance. ''Don't tell me the middle by-blow thinks she's going to snag herself a prince.''

Chapter Ten

Her knees went wobbly and dizziness swam in her head. Ariane heard the tiny, far off mew of a weak kitten, and then was overwhelmed with a dark conglomeration of amazement, confusion and anxiety when she realized that the sound had bubbled up from her own throat.

"Do you honestly believe he would want the likes of you?" Celeste's voice sliced to the bone. "He has everything. Land. Money. Status. A kingdom will someday be his. But you…you can offer him nothing. You have nothing. You *are* nothing."

Each slur was like a physical slap in the face. Mortification was too mild a word to describe what was crashing through her like a rock slide. Her stepmother couldn't have hurt her more if she'd taken a rapier and run her clean through. How could Celeste humiliate her so? And in front of Etienne? But the even bigger question was…why would she do this? *Why?*

She and her stepmother had never had the best of

relationships. But then Celeste hadn't bonded with any of King Philippe's children or stepchildren. She simply didn't waste her time with anyone who couldn't offer her something she needed or wanted. And it didn't help that she was a jealous woman. She'd been resentful of Philippe's love for the children living under his roof, she'd been envious of any attention he gave them.

However, the behavior she was flaunting now seemed very strange, indeed. Although she was a woman who, when wronged, would go out of her way to exact revenge, she didn't normally sink her fangs into someone who hadn't injured her in some way.

For Celeste to bombard her with such a degrading attack—with no provocation—just didn't make sense. No sense at all.

Suddenly, Ariane realized she was being propped up by a mass that was warm. Solid. Strong. As if she were moving through a thick, viscous fog, she tilted her head and looked up to find Etienne standing beside her, one arm curled protectively around her shoulders.

"With all due respect, *Your Highness*—"

The manner in which he'd twisted the formal address was clear indication that he was offering the current queen of St. Michel anything but respect.

"There's more to royalty than mere chance of birth."

Ariane tipped up her chin further to get a better look at Etienne who was glaring at Celeste. His facial muscles were taut, his dark brows bunching with the fury that so obviously rolled through him.

"Royalty is synonymous with dignity," he continued. "Goodness. Nobility. These qualities are innate in the aristocracy. They come from within.

"Royalty isn't worn on the outside." The calmness in his tone didn't take the bite out of his words, and his opinion was exemplified by the fact that he took a moment to let his gaze wander over the strand upon strand of expensive pearls draped around her neck, the chunky gold rings flashing with emeralds and rubies that adorned her fingers.

Ariane had never seen his eyes so cold and flat, like dull steel.

"Royalty," he continued, "can't be acquired through marriage."

Celeste's face went ghost white and she was barely able to contain the gasp that rose to her crimson lips. Ariane was certain her stepmother was about to fall to her knees from shock right there on the garden path.

Etienne couldn't have injured Celeste more even if he'd physically struck her. Evidently, he was privy to her past...he must know of her background prior to marrying Philippe.

She'd been a commoner. Not a single nobleman climbed among the branches of her family tree. She didn't even have the privilege of calling herself one of the nouveau riche. She'd simply been an average, middle-class woman chosen to be queen because she'd used her wiles to capture Philippe's eye, and then she'd wielded her powers of persuasion to convince him that she could provide the male heir that the royal house of St. Michel so desperately needed.

Celeste quickly regained her composure. Anger had her cheeks blotched with an ugly red.

Her top lip convulsed in a sneer. "I should just

keep what I know to myself,'' she said to Etienne. ''Ariane is just what you deserve.'' She smoothed her palms over her swollen waistline. ''But I'm going to prove to you how regal I can be. I'm going to forgive your nasty remarks and reveal the truth.''

Her stepmother's gaze leveled on her, chilling Ariane to the marrow.

''You thought I didn't know,'' Celeste said. ''You thought your conniving and spying was a secret. Well, there are consequences to every action, dear girl. And now you're going to face yours.''

Ariane's blood froze in her veins. Her stepmother knew that she'd been in Rhineland to spy on Etienne's government.

No, she wanted to shout at Celeste. *Please stop!* Having Etienne learn what she'd done—like this— wasn't what Ariane wanted. She'd planned to break it to him gently…*after* she'd revealed her heart to him.

Celeste turned her attention to Etienne once again. ''You may have thought Ariane was visiting your country to further develop the interest you showed in her just before my poor husband passed away. But I'm here to tell you that you've been duped.''

Feeling as if she'd been surrounded by a glass bubble, Ariane couldn't seem to draw breath. She was horrified. By the words coming out of her stepmother's mouth. By the look on Etienne's face.

''Ariane was in your country,'' the woman barreled full-steam ahead, ''acting as a spy for our security force. Word had reached us that some faction inside your government meant to annex St. Michel. Ariane's mission was to find out who was behind the plot.''

Her gaze zeroed in on him. "And *you,* Prince Etienne, were at the top of the list of suspects."

Ariane's short, sharp inhalation drew his attention. Slowly, he swiveled his head, and where—just a moment ago—that icy pewter stare had been aimed at Celeste, it was now directed on *her.*

"But that's not true," Ariane said, her tone a mere breathy whisper forced from her aching throat. Without thought, she continued, "There wasn't a list of suspects. There still isn't. Celeste, why are you doing this?"

Her stepmother's gaze was cool and collected. "What can I tell you? I am who I am. And besides that, the shrimp on the buffet table have upset my stomach. I'm feeling a little grumpy. For some strange reason, I feel that it just wouldn't be right for me to stand by and see the crown prince of Rhineland saddled with the likes of you."

After having offered the only excuse she evidently meant to give, Celeste turned on her heel and made her way back toward the wedding reception.

The funny thing was, the parting shot her stepmother had made hadn't wounded Ariane in the least. She guessed that, at that point, she was simply numb.

The hurt, the accusation, the questions radiating from Etienne's gaze forced her to lift her eyes to his.

"Is it true?"

It was such a small question. Just three little words. Yet Ariane knew the query was going to ruin what might have been.

There was so much she wanted to say. So much she wanted to explain. She couldn't answer the question he'd asked without first defending her actions. If she did, he'd resent her forever. He'd be terribly hurt, and he wouldn't hear the really important matters she had wanted to discuss.

Matters of the heart.

"Etienne, before I—"

"All I want from you," he viciously interrupted, "is the truth. Did you come to Rhineland to spy on my government?"

There was only one way for her to answer. So, after only a second's hesitation, she softly admitted, "Yes."

His jaw tensed. "And you used me to do it."

This was not a question. Still, Ariane felt compelled to nod.

"But Celeste lied when she said you were on the list of suspects," she rushed to say. "When I left home, there were no suspects."

Pain flickered in his gaze. "Do you really think that matters to me?"

Sadness welled up inside her. "I guess it doesn't."

His pain seemed to metamorphose into a deep anguish right before her eyes, and she thought her heart was going to rip into two ragged pieces.

"I've got to go," he stated, his voice hard and sharp as slivers of granite. "I must fly to Washington, DC, for my father. With Mother still so weak, he refuses to go. I'm to go in his place. I didn't want us to part again without having the chance to say goodbye." He emitted a sound much like a growl. "I've been a fool."

He'd actually taken a step away from her before she was able to get her tongue to work.

"Etienne! Please. Wait."

For an instant, she thought he meant to walk away

from her. Every muscle in her body quaked as he paused, and then he turned to stare at her in silence.

"I know everything is ruined," she told him. "I understand completely if you never want to see me again."

One moment passed. Then two.

She wanted desperately to bare her soul to him. But her fear was too strong.

But in that moment, she truly realized she had nothing to lose.

"I want you to know—" she paused long enough to moisten her lips and swallow "—that when I returned home to St. Michel…I left my heart in Rhineland. With you."

Emotion burned her eye sockets and an instant later unshed tears blurred her vision.

"I know my actions are unforgivable," she continued. "I should never have used your interest in me the way that I did. But we were desperate, Etienne. My country was in peril. You'd have done the same thing had you been in my shoes. I know it isn't much of an excuse, but the love I feel for my country…the loyalty I have for my father's subjects…those are all I have left."

His pewter eyes didn't soften a bit.

"I never expected to fall in love with you, Etienne. I never in a million years expected you to be so…kind to me. Especially after the news was out that I'd lost everything." She took her bottom lip between her teeth for a moment, pondering just how much she should say. Finally, she could hold back no longer. "Why would you be so kind, so respectful…unless you were up to something yourself? I wondered…I couldn't help but wonder, Etienne…was it possible that you were attempting to remain as close as you could to the de Bergeron throne?''

"So you did suspect me?''

His accusation cut her like a knife.

"What else was I to think?'' Her tone rose in pitch, but she immediately felt contrite. ''But it didn't take me long to see that you're too good-hearted to do something as brutal as seizing a neighboring country that had been friends with yours for so many years.''

She watched his jaw muscle tense and relax, tense and relax. Time seemed to slow until her nerves fairly jittered right out of her skin.

"Now I understand the stupid act you played,'' he said. ''You thought your naïveté would seem harmless...that *you* would seem harmless...while you were steadily pumping my father's government officials for information.'' The magnitude of his ire had his gaze abruptly averting to the pea-stone path. ''I've got to go, Ariane. I've got to go now.''

There was a finality in those words that had tears spilling unchecked down her cheeks, her chin trembling. ''You do forgive me, don't you?'' She heard the reckless urgency in her tone and didn't care one wit. ''I mean, I can live with the fact that we can't be together. It wouldn't have worked anyway. No one in Rhineland would be in favor of such a union. Your parents. Your government. Your people.'' She swallowed. ''You're expected to marry a woman with...''

The rest of the thought faded into oblivion. She didn't have it in her to once again list all she'd lost when she'd been labeled illegitimate.

"But, Etienne, I couldn't stand it,'' she said, heedless of the pleading stance of her body language, ''if

I thought your anger over my actions was so great that you couldn't find it in your heart to forgive me.''

He was silent for some time. Finally, he said, ''I've got to go. My plane will be waiting.''

''Of course,'' she murmured, her heart rending into dozens of pieces. He was going to withhold clemency. He was going to imprison her in walls of blame. ''You have a country to represent. I understand fully.''

''I'm overwhelmed, Ariane. I'm…I'm—''

But he refused to make any further declarations that might weaken him further. She saw that much glistening in his wounded gaze.

Then he cleared his throat against the still awkwardness that had descended upon them. ''I'll be gone a few days. I'll call you when I return from the U.S.''

The desolate sound of his retreating footsteps crunching on the tiny stones as he walked away from her was something Ariane would never forget. Not in all her days.

''Sure.'' The soft spring breeze carried away her whispered response, but it couldn't remove the despair that filled her spirit. ''Sure you will.''

The minutes…the hours…the days dragged by as if something strange had happened to decelerate time itself. Ariane walked listlessly back toward the palace after having spent much of the afternoon with her oldest sister, Lise.

No matter how depressing she found the state of her own life, Ariane did her best to put on a happy, optimistic front when she visited Lise. Pregnant and alone, Lise was filled with anxiety regarding the future for her and her baby.

Ariane had attempted to point out the best aspect of her sister's plight: she was free of Wilhelm, a man she'd never loved, but had married for purely political reasons in order to appease their father. However, Lise didn't seem bolstered by that fact. If the truth were to be known, Ariane fully understood. Lise was a woman alone, just as Ariane now was; however, Lise would soon have a child she would be responsible for. No wonder her sister was fraught with fear.

At least, Ariane thought, Lise had something with which to occupy her time. An expert in appraising objets d'art and jewels, Lise spent her days cataloguing all the royal artifacts owned by the de Bergeron family. In fact, Lise had shooed Ariane out of the cottage door, stating that she needed some quiet time in order to do a little research on one particular original oil painting that hung in the palace gallery.

Tramping over the hilly meadow that separated Lise's cottage from the palace, Ariane wondered what on earth she'd do with the rest of her day. A fresh breeze blew through the glossy leaves of the tree in front of her, the sun causing the foliage to wink and sparkle like metal. No. Like liquid silver.

Immediately, she was transported back in time to the moments she and Etienne had spent together at Byron Falls. They had slept together, his body protecting her from the night's chill. The intimacy she'd experienced had made her feel bonded to Etienne in a very special way. Had started her dreaming about being with him forever and always.

Ariane shoved the image and the notion from her

mind. Reaching down, she plucked a weed that seemed to strain toward the sun.

Etienne was gone from her life forever. She simply had to resign herself to that.

She wondered what she'd do with herself for the remainder of the day. She hated having so much time on her hands. Normally, she'd be out gallivanting over the countryside on a horse, or exploring St. Michel's few caves, or hiking until she was exhausted. But none of these activities seemed to interest her.

Marie-Claire was with Sebastian on his yacht as they sailed the Greek Islands on their honeymoon. Even Francie had abandoned Ariane. Her lady-in-waiting was with Harry in London meeting his family. Francie was taking a full year to plan her wedding, wanting her nuptials to be the talk of St. Michel. And if Ariane knew Francie, the wedding would be stunning.

Indulging in a bit of useless daydreaming, Ariane decided there and then that she would settle for a few loving words spoken in front of a vicar in the tiniest church in all of St. Michel.

A wedding is not in your future, a harsh voice chastised. And it was all her own fault, she knew.

Ariane tossed the weed to the ground, and shoved the thought from her brain. Love and marriage. They were nothing more than whim and fancy. Something she didn't have time for.

She nearly groaned. It seemed that time was all she did have. And time seemed bound and determined to crawl by like an itty-bitty inchworm on a journey of a thousand miles.

Movement at the crest of the hill had her squinting

against the sun. She grinned, thanking her lucky stars. Jacqueline had evidently finished her lessons and was racing to meet her. Ariane knew her youngest sister never failed to divert her attention from all these depressing thoughts of what she'd never have with Etienne.

"What's that you've got?" Ariane called once the child was close enough to hear.

"It's for you!" Jacqueline was so out of breath she could barely speak. "There's…There's—"

"Slow down." Ariane laughed at her antics. "My favorite baby sister has gone into a tizzy."

"But there's a man at the house. Waiting for you. And he brought you this."

Taking the small dish from her sister, Ariane felt the coolness of the ceramic against her palm.

"It's…"

Could she believe her eyes? Could it mean…?

"It's crème brûlé!"

So excited was she at the implication that she dropped the custard cup in the meadow and dashed up the hill toward home, the hem of her full skirt flipping up with each step.

"But what about the pudding?" Jacqueline shouted after her.

"We'll get it later. Come on, Jackie! Come on!"

By the time they reached the palace, Ariane's hair was in tangles. She was panting. And a fine sheen of perspiration made her nose shine. But she didn't care. Her only thought was to discover the identity of her visitor.

Her grandmother was just coming out of the door leading to the parlor. "I was just coming to find you." But after Simone had a chance to get a good look at her, she clicked her tongue against the roof of her mouth. ''You're a mess.'' But as she smoothed her fingers through Ariane's hair her eyes glistened with excitement that couldn't be controlled. ''You've got a visitor.''

''Grandmama,'' Ariane breathed, the thrill she felt making her tone quake, ''he brought my favorite sweet.''

Simone's soft mouth spread into a smile. ''Oh, he brought more than one.''

Ariane's heart tripped against her ribs. He was here. And it wasn't a dream.

''Well, don't keep the man waiting,'' her grandmother gently chided, evidently giving up any attempt to make Ariane look more presentable.

When Jacqueline made to follow her sister into the parlor, Simone caught her by the hand. ''You are coming with me, young lady. You're a mess, too. Your face needs washing and your hair needs a good brushing.''

''But Ariane looks just as bad as I do—''

''Never you mind about Ariane,'' Simone said. ''She's old enough to take care of herself.''

Jacqueline groaned in a most unladylike fashion, whining, ''Why do I always have to miss the good stuff?''

The child was led off toward the stairway by her grandmother. Ariane stood outside the parlor door, her mind racing. She quickly combed her fingers through the tangle of her hair, and after tucking one hopelessly knotted strand behind her ear, she hurried inside the room where the love of her life was waiting.

He stared out the window, his own agitation showing as his hands clenched and unclenched in fists behind his back.

Oh, Lord, but he was devastatingly handsome. Etienne Kroninberg was enough to melt the heart of any woman he came near. He succeeded in dissolving hers into a pulpy mass each and every time she laid eyes on him, that much was certain.

Hoping to capture his attention without having to speak, she smoothed her palms down the waistline of her skirt and shifted her weight from one foot to the other. Instinctively, he turned. And his pewter eyes were on her.

He seemed to devour her with his gaze, and Ariane felt her stomach churn with wild anticipation.

Could she be reading something into his visit, into his gift, into his eyes that wasn't really there? What about his parents? she wondered. What about his princely duty to make a good marriage? What of—

"Hello, Ariane."

The melodic sound in his greeting raised the fine hairs on her arms.

"Hello." Suddenly, she felt like a teenager meeting a boy for the first time. Timidity seemed to wrap her in a silken cocoon, but she'd be darned if she'd let it get the best of her this time.

"I brought you a gift."

She let her gaze follow where he indicated, and she gasped when she saw the trays laden with servings of crème brûlé that covered the top of not one, not two, but three of the tables in the parlor.

Laughter bubbled up from inside her. "You'll have me as fat as a cow."

"It's a bribe, you know."

Her chin dipped automatically at the sound of his

tone, and she found herself looking at him through raised lashes. "A bribe?"

She felt positively giddy with trepidation.

"I'm hoping you'll forgive me," he said. "For walking away from you at Marie-Claire's wedding without...well, without working out everything that was standing between us."

Emotion, dark and thick, flooded through her at the mention of the moment he'd walked away from her, the moment she'd been sure that all her hopes and dreams had died.

"Oh, Etienne," she said, unable to stop the words from tumbling from her lips, "I can't tell you how sorry I am about the way I hurt you."

His gaze turned a soft dove-gray and he nodded a silent acceptance of her apology.

Relief burst like a nova inside her, colorful and liberating. If his only intention in being here was to forgive her for using him the way she had, Ariane felt that would be enough.

"I shouldn't have come to Rhineland—"

"It's okay, Ariane," he said, his voice gentle and full of understanding. "You were right when you said I would have done the very same thing had my government...my homeland been threatened as yours seemed to be." He took a moment to take a deep breath. "I have my own confession to make."

The tiniest of frowns bit into the small space between her brows. What could he have to confess?

"You see," he continued, looking penitent, "I've known all along about the plot to annex St. Michel. So has my father."

Ariane couldn't contain her shock.

"Oh, we don't know who's behind the conspiracy,'' he rushed to assure her. ''But from the moment of your father's death, we've heard rumors that there were some inside our government who would like to see your country seized by our own.'' His expression took on a pained look. ''I'm sure you can understand what's behind it all. It's the port city of St. Michel. It's your access to the river…to the North Sea.''

Now it was her turn to nod in understanding. She was quite aware of why the Rhinelanders might be envious of St. Michel, even though her country was the smaller of the two.

''I've been working with the most trusted members of my intelligence force,'' he told her. ''Father and I were hoping to discover—''

''I wish you'd have told me,'' she broke in.

''I didn't want to worry you. And Father felt it might harm our relations with your country if news of this conspiracy got out. We wanted to take care of this…since we're fairly certain it's someone or some group inside our own government.''

Curiosity had her asking, ''So you haven't discovered who's behind this?''

''No. A lot of people are talking about it, but so far all we're getting is rumor and innuendo. No hard facts.''

She told him her suspicions regarding Rhineland's prime minister and the man named Berg Dekker. Ariane brightened when a thought suddenly occurred to her. ''Do you think that's all this could be? Talk? Maybe…''

She let the rest of her theory fade when she saw him shake his head.

''I believe there is a plan afoot,'' he said. ''And I'm committed to weeding out the extremists. They're planning and plotting against St. Michel. Their actions are unlawful. And I want them punished.''

"You should speak with the head of our security force. Luc Dumont might be able to help you discover the identity of the people behind the scheme. In fact, I'd be happy to help, too.''

He grinned then. ''Well, you've sure proved that you're an excellent infiltrator.''

Embarrassment heated her cheeks.

"Our governments can work together on this," he agreed. "I want these fanatics jailed as soon as possible.''

St. Michel was safe. Etienne was going to see that it was. And he wasn't even connected to St. Michel's royal family or government.

The love she felt for him swelled her heart to the point of bursting.

''Why?'' Her question came out in a whisper. ''Why would you feel so adamant about protecting St. Michel?''

He hesitated before saying, ''Because it's the right thing to do.'' But the words hadn't had time to settle before he was striding toward her. He didn't stop until he was inches away. He took her hands in his. ''That's not the complete truth.''

Leading her to a nearby settee, he silently urged her to sit. He eased himself down next to her.

Something extraordinary was about to take place. She could feel it in the air. Hope escalated, but reality quickly dashed it.

''Oh, Etienne…'' Emotion lodged in her throat and she tugged her fingers free of his.

Fate was so cruel to fulfill her dreams only to steal them right away.

She forced herself to look into his eyes, the sadness she felt emanating from her in waves. "I can't let you do this. I have nothing to offer you, Etienne. Absolutely nothing."

He studied her silently for what seemed like minutes, but she knew must have been only seconds. Long, endless seconds.

"I came here all those months ago," he said quietly, reaching over and taking her hand in his once again, "in pursuit of a princess. A strong woman who could unite our families, our countries. I arrived here with nothing but that duty on my mind."

He oh-so-gently squeezed her fingers. "What I took as my royal obligation might have been what prompted our first meeting. But it was you who stole my heart. All those months ago when I came here to take you to the opera."

Her eyes rounded. "But I behaved abominably back then."

His mouth pulled into a grin that was wide and terribly sexy. "I know. And that's what clinched it for me. The fact that you slipped off…that you just couldn't resist escaping what you felt was a boring evening…that's what let me know that you were the one for me. I knew you'd always keep me guessing. You'd keep my life interesting. It was then I decided I had to have you."

She didn't know what to say. She couldn't believe the words he was speaking. Somehow, she just couldn't trust this was real.

Ariane swallowed. "But what about your parents? What about the duty you told me about? Your father will be furious—"

"Shhh," he said, pressing his fingertips gently

against her mouth. "My parents are quite happy to see me happy." He moistened his lips. "You see, the duty I felt pressured over was coming from me. I thought it was the thing I was supposed to do. My parents' marriage was a love match from the beginning. My mother and father fell in love, and their fate was sealed."

His brows drew together. "When you showed up in Rhineland acting as if you had noodles in your head, I was determined to discover what you were up to. When news of your—" He stopped short, seemingly unable to speak the one word that might bring her pain. His tone softened when he continued, "When news of your father's previous marriage came to light, all I could think of was protecting you. Even though I knew your situation had changed, it didn't change my feelings of wanting to be near you. And when we ran off for our day of fun and I saw that you were just as smart as I knew you were…it really didn't matter to me why you'd want to put on an act. All I knew was that I wanted you."

Intensity darkened his gaze. "I love you, Ariane. Please say you'll marry me."

Just then Jacqueline ran from where she'd evidently been eavesdropping. "A wedding! A wedding! We're having another wedding. Please, Ariane, please, please, please don't make me light candles. I want to be a bridesmaid. I'm old enough. I am!"

"Jacqueline de Bergeron, you little minx!" The regal Simone strode into the room. "Your sister hasn't even had a chance to accept the man's proposal."

Ariane saw the way her grandmother's eyes were shining with unadulterated joy so she didn't have the heart to point out that the elderly woman's obvious snooping just outside the door made her just as much a minx as Jacqueline.

Screwing up her face, Ariane asked Etienne, "You really want to unite yourself with this crazy family?"

In answer, Etienne got down on one knee. "I do."

Ariane's heart filled with love. "Then how can I possibly refuse you?"

Epilogue

As she stood in the doorway of the ancient stone church dressed in all this royal finery, Ariane had never felt more like a princess. Her grandmother's dress fit her to a T. Her hair had been coiffed and adorned with diamond-studded clips that glimmered from beneath the filmy veil.

The love of her life waited for her at the altar. Etienne looked mouth-wateringly handsome in his high-buttoned scarlet jacket and black trousers with razor-sharp creases. He looked eager…and nervous, as if he thought she might suddenly decide not to join him there to exchange vows of love and fidelity.

She smiled softly because she knew in her heart there was a greater chance that the whole of Rhineland would crumble and disappear than there was of her changing her mind about becoming his wife.

Forever and always.

She'd heard it said that a woman would never experience more anxiety than on the day she pledged herself to a man. But Ariane felt no butterflies in her stomach. All she experienced was a heady excitement that was nearly a fever of hope and love. She wanted to race up the aisle, shout her vows for all to hear and then fling herself into Etienne's arms. But she knew the dowager queen would be mortified by such behaviour, and that thought had Ariane suppressing the impish chuckle that threatened to bubble up from her throat.

The citizens of both St. Michel and Rhineland had been in an uproar when they'd discovered that she and her sisters had been stripped of their royal titles. But Ariane had suffered very little tumult from the ordeal. In fact, she'd delighted in the freedom that the circumstances had lent…even though those circumstances had been all too fleeting.

In marrying Etienne, the crown prince of Rhineland, Ariane would once again be an official princess with all the responsibilities and restrictions that came with the title. Did that bother her? Not in the least. Because the benefits of such a position outweighed the liabilities. By far.

The strains of the old pump organ filled the air of the tiny chapel—the only church in all of Rhineland that could accommodate this lightning-fast wedding of hers and Etienne's—and Georges stepped up beside her, offering her his arm.

"Are you ready?" her stepbrother asked softly. "Your groom awaits."

At that moment, she became aware of the exhilarated tension that seemed to pulsate from the wedding guests.

Offering Georges a bright smile, Ariane slid her hand over the crook of his proffered arm. "I'm more than ready. In fact, I'm counting on you to keep me from making a total fool of myself by sprinting up there to him.''

Georges chuckled, cocking a brow at her. ''That wouldn't be very ladylike, now would it?''

Ariane silently shook her head, and trained her gaze forward on the man with whom she would spend the rest of her life. His dove-gray eyes called to her, mesmerized her, lured her like the pulling and tugging of some irresistible magnetic energy.

Automatically, she tightened her grip on her step-brother's arm and forced her steps to remain slow and measured. She was determined to act in a manner befitting her position. Later there would be plenty of time to follow the urges of her heart.

How lucky she was, she thought, her heart pounding in breathless anticipation with each and every step she took closer to her future. How very, very lucky.

Hours later, it took the two of them many long and frustrating minutes to free Ariane from the yards and yards of Italian satin and French chiffon. There must have been a hundred tiny buttons needing to be unfastened. Etienne had taken his sweet time undoing them, following each and every one with a passionate kiss that had her panting for his touch.

Etienne's ceremonial garb was tossed hither and yon, the trousers over the back of the chair, jacket lying in a pile on the floor, while the shoes …well, the whereabouts of his shoes was anyone's guess.

Finally the newly married couple were free of the constraints of clothing and were swathed in nothing more than the cool satin sheets of their honeymoon bed.

"Lord," Etienne groaned into Ariane's hair, "do you know how long I've yearned for this?"

She laughed. "I don't know what you're complaining about." She kissed one corner of his mouth. "I had to wait two whole weeks for this while I planned the wedding."

He grinned, kissing her back. "And it was a wonderful job you did, too."

Ariane lifted her arm, resting it on the pillow above her head. She sighed dreamily. "It was a nice wedding wasn't it? Jacqueline was a beautiful bridesmaid. So were Marie-Claire, Lise and Juliet. Georges was good enough to agree to walk me down the aisle, even though he just did the same for Marie-Claire two short weeks ago. Gosh, even Celeste was almost nice."

Etienne grimaced comically. "Almost."

Grinning, Ariane smoothed her fingers down her husband's jaw. "You've made my grandmother very happy."

"Oh?"

She nodded. "You married me for love," she told him. "That was very important to her...seeing her granddaughters marry for love rather than duty." A sexy chuckle bubbled up from her throat. "And the fact that you've promised to keep me in crème brûlé all the days of my life didn't hurt. She loves knowing I'll be well cared for."

Lowering his head, Etienne placed a hot kiss high on her milky breast. "Can we stop talking about your family? I didn't marry them. I married you. And I'm anxious to make you my wife...in every sense of the word."

"Mmmm." Ariane squirmed slowly until she positioned herself intimately beneath him. "I like that idea. Very much."

Happiness. Contentment. Ecstasy. Love to last a lifetime.

All the things she thought were lost to her, she'd found in her prince. Etienne was her soul mate. The man who made all her dreams come true.

And she would love him for all eternity.

* * * * *

Look out for the next exciting instalments of

ROYALLY WED: THE MISSING HEIR

in June 2003

A Princess in Waiting
by Carol Grace

and

A Prince at Last!
by Cathie Linz—

only from Silhouette Desire.

Turn the page for a sneak preview of
A Princess in Waiting,
Charles and Lise's story,
by Carol Grace.

A Princess in Waiting

by

Carol Grace

Once upon a time in a small country called St. Michel, wedged between France and Rhineland, lived a beautiful princess named Lise de Bergeron. The princess didn't live in the stately palace with its turrets and ballroom and bevy of servants. She lived in a small cottage on the palace grounds. Lise had no crown and no legitimacy since her parents' marriage had been declared invalid. She was not surrounded by maids who waited on her hand and foot. She was attended by her former nanny, the woman who had raised her when her mother deserted her and her sisters. Nanny was old now and afflicted by arthritis and it was Princess Lise who was more caregiver then pampered princess.

A lack of royal trappings did not bother the princess. What did bother her was that her father the king had recently died, she'd been deserted by her husband, Wilhelm of neighboring Rhineland, and she was three months pregnant. All in all, this past year had been a difficult one. The future was unclear. What was in store for her and her unborn child?

Things had been worse when she was married to Wilhelm. Yes, they'd lived splendidly in Rhineland, where he, as a member of the royal family, had money and power. But he was a cold, arrogant, ambitious man who'd been chosen for her by her father for political reasons. If she had one thing to be thankful for, it was that she was rid of the scoundrel. She'd endure any amount of shame if she never had to see him again.

An hour later she heard a car pull up in front of the cottage.

After a few moments, there was a knock on the door of the greenhouse. Lise pushed an errant strand of hair back from her face.

''Yes?''

''Lise?'' It was a deep voice. Vaguely familiar. ''It's Charles. Charles Rodin.''

''Charles?'' Charles, her husband's twin brother? What on earth was he doing here. Anything, anyone connected with her ex-husband was upsetting and an intrusion in her new life. Wilhelm had left her and she wanted no reminders of the biggest mistake of her life.

''Can I come in?'' he asked.

As annoyed as she was, she couldn't help but notice the difference. Wilhelm would have barged in. His brother waited to be invited.

She opened the door. And stared at the man who stood there. He looked disturbingly like her ex-husband and yet the expression on his face was nothing like Wilhelm's arrogance. She barely remembered Charles from her wedding, at which he was the best man, and she hadn't seen him since that fateful day, but she knew this was a man who was self-confident but not arrogant. Still, the resemblance bothered her and brought back unpleasant memories. She wanted nothing to do with Wilhelm or any member of his family. She was doing her best to forget all of them. And now this...

"Can I come in?" he asked again.

What was wrong with her? She'd been raised with better manners than to let a guest stand in the doorway. But he was so big, so broad-shouldered, so startlingly like his brother, she thought he *was* in.

"Of course," she said briskly.

He stepped into the small greenhouse with the earthen floor and suddenly the glassed-in room was crowded to overflowing. She had no space, no room to breathe or think. There was a fluttery feeling in the pit of her stomach. She tried to think of something to say, but her mind was blank. All she could do was to stand there and wait for him to say something.

After a long silence during which he looked her up and down with a shade too much intimacy and she continued to stare at him, she finally found her voice.

"What is it, Charles, what do you want?"

He frowned at her lack of civility. What did he expect, that she'd welcome him with open arms, after what his brother did to her?

"I came when I heard the news, about the divorce...to see if...to see what I could do."

"Nothing. You can do nothing. You can't stop your brother from divorcing me, you can't make my parents' marriage valid, you can't find an heir for our country and you can't bring my father back to life.

So go back to your country and tell your brother I don't need him or his family.''

Charles looked surprised at her angry words. ''I haven't been in my country for months nor have I seen much of my family. Perhaps you aren't aware, but my brother and I have never been close. And now we are hardly on speaking terms,'' he said stiffly. ''We lead separate lives, both professionally and personally. When I ran into Wilhelm last week in Los Angeles he told me about the divorce. I couldn't believe it. It's only been, what…''

''Eight months,'' Lise said. ''Eight months that I am doing my best to forget. So if you don't mind, I'll get back to work.'' She pivoted on her heel and turned back to her frame. If only she'd been wearing a gown and a tiara, she might have pulled off this obvious dismissal and he would have left. She'd used the imperial tone. She had the movement down pat. Those years of training in demeanor came in useful at times. But not today. He didn't leave. He did just the opposite. He stepped forward. He was right behind her, leaning over her left shoulder.

She wasn't quite sure what to make of him. Or why he was there in the first place. She didn't know how to get rid of him. Or if she really wanted to. There were questions she wanted answers to. And she had to admit she wanted to know how Charles felt about her.

Charles leaned back against a stone countertop and studied her for a long moment. He was trying to collect his thoughts, but just looking at the lovely princess caused his mind to wander and his heart to pound erratically. The last time he'd seen Lise de Bergeron had been on her wedding day.

He'd thought at that time that in her white satin gown and diamond tiara she was the most beautiful thing he'd ever seen. He'd been filled with an unbecoming rush of envy for his older brother. As usual, Wilhelm had succeeded in snatching the prize before Charles had a chance to compete.

When his brother found out Lise was illegitimate and would inherit nothing, he immediately divorced her. When Charles heard that straight from his brother's mouth he was stunned. His brother was not known for his kindness or compassion, he'd always had a ruthless streak, pushing aside anyone and anything that got in his way, but this time he'd gone too far. Charles was not only stunned, but he was ashamed on behalf of the family honor. He was determined to do something to make things right.

She didn't know why he was there, but he did. He'd planned his speech. He knew what he had to say, but now that he was there and she was looking at him with those incredible blue eyes, he could only stand and stare.

She'd changed. It had only been eight months, but she was not the same demure princess who'd dazzled him on her wedding day. It wasn't only her clothing, it was her manner. He thought she'd be meek and mild and jump at the chance he was going to offer her. Now he wasn't so sure. She had a stubborn tilt to her chin, a proud look in her eyes and a certain tone to her voice. If he'd been infatuated with her before, he was fascinated now. He didn't know what she was going to say next. He decided to put off his declaration.

"I mustn't keep you any longer, Charles," she

said, glancing at the door. It was plain she was dismissing him before he'd said what he'd come to say.

He'd hoped to establish a mood and set up the appropriate atmosphere. He'd planned to lead up to it gradually, but he no longer had time. It was clear it had to be now. He stood and looked down at her. It was now or never. He took a deep breath.

"I came today to offer my hand in marriage," he said.

* * * *

Don't forget A Princess in Waiting *by Carol Grace and* A Prince at Last! *by Cathie Linz will be on the shelves in June 2003.*

Don't miss this exciting conclusion to ROYALLY WED: THE MISSING HEIR.

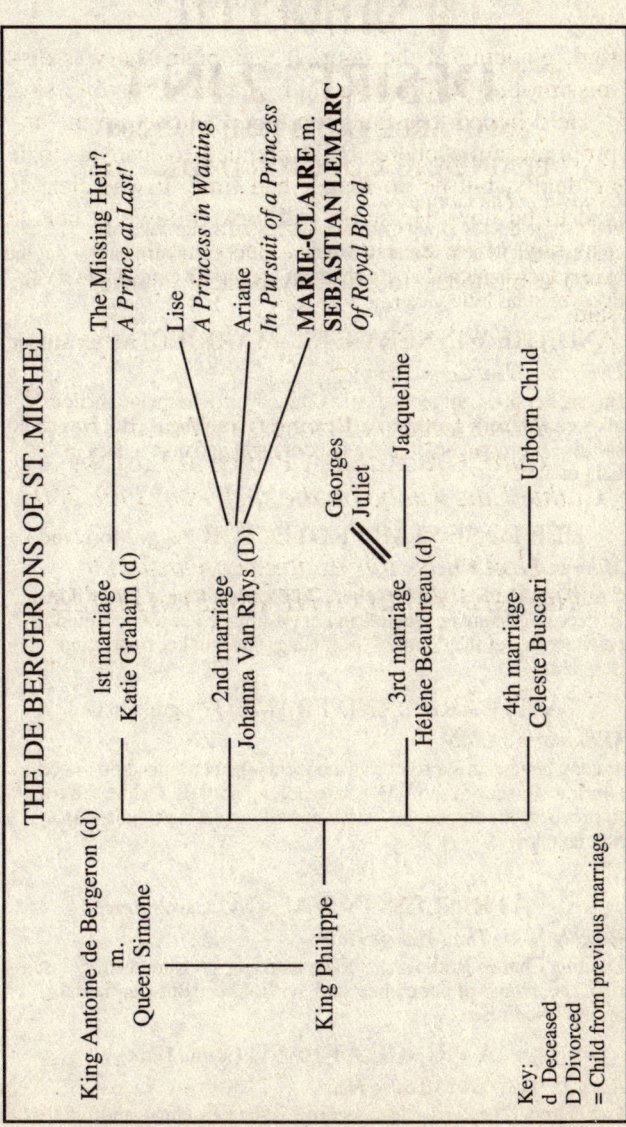

THE DE BERGERONS OF ST. MICHEL

King Antoine de Bergeron (d)
m.
Queen Simone

1st marriage
Katie Graham (d)

The Missing Heir?
A Prince at Last!

2nd marriage
Johanna Van Rhys (D)

Lise
A Princess in Waiting

Ariane
In Pursuit of a Princess

MARIE-CLAIRE m.
SEBASTIAN LEMARC
Of Royal Blood

3rd marriage
Hélène Beaudreau (d)

Georges
Juliet

Jacqueline

4th marriage
Celeste Buscari

Unborn Child

King Philippe

Key:
d Deceased
D Divorced
= Child from previous marriage

0503/51a

◆ SILHOUETTE®

DESIRE™ 2-IN-1

AVAILABLE FROM 16TH MAY 2003

PLAIN JANE & DOCTOR DAD Kate Little

Dynasties: The Connellys

Handsome doctor Doug Connelly suggested a marriage of convenience to help Maura Chambers with her unborn baby—but the hungry look in his amber eyes had her hoping for more. Until she discovered his little secret...

AND THE WINNER GETS...MARRIED! Metsy Hingle

Dynasties: The Connellys

Buying her boss, gorgeous Justin Connelly, in a bachelor auction allowed Kimberly Lindgren to have one fantasy night. But how could she give her virgin heart in the dark of night and take it back in the light of day?

HER LONE STAR PROTECTOR Peggy Moreland

Millionaire's Club

Gruff private investigator Robert Cole was smitten by lovely florist Rebecca Todman, but secrets in her past made her wary. Could he convince her of the depth of his feelings and win her trust...and her heart?

TALL, DARK...AND FRAMED? Cathleen Galitz

Millionaire's Club

Tycoon Sebastian Wescott was innocent—he certainly didn't need alluring attorney Susan Wysocki to defend him! But while she tried to prove his innocence, he found himself increasingly guilty—of falling in love...

A PRINCESS IN WAITING Carol Grace

Royally Wed: The Missing Heir

Dashing Charles Rodin *seems* to be marrying pregnant beauty Lise to right the wrongs of her ex-husband, his brother. But Charles has always loved Lise...

A PRINCE AT LAST! Cathie Linz

Royally Wed: The Missing Heir

Luc Dumont, head of palace security, is the new king—and Juliet Beaudreau is to teach him royal protocol. He's determined to sweep her into his arms, but can he convince her to be his queen?

world's most
Eligible Bachelors

RICH, GORGEOUS, SEXY AND SINGLE!

An exciting new series featuring the sexiest, most successful, dynamic men in the world!

Millionaire to Marry *by Rachel Lee*   18th April 2003

Detective Dad *by Marie Ferrarella*   16th May 2003

His Business, Her Baby *by Dixie Browning*   16th May 2003

That Mysterious Man *by Maggie Shayne*   20th June 2003

Coming Soon!

SILHOUETTE®
SPECIAL EDITION™

proudly presents seven more fantastic stories from

Lindsay McKenna's

exciting series

MORGAN'S MERCENARIES

Meet Morgan's newest team: courageous men and women destined for greatness—fated to fall in love!

SILHOUETTE® SENSATION™

presents

ROMANCING THE CROWN

The Royal family of Montebello is determined to find their missing heir. But the search for the prince is not without danger—or passion!

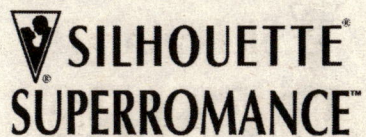

★ SILHOUETTE®
SUPERROMANCE™

is proud to present

THREE GOOD COPS

by
Janice Kay Johnson

The McLean brothers are all good,
strong, honest, men. Men a woman
can trust…with her heart!

HIS PARTNER'S WIFE
May 2003

THE WORD OF A CHILD
July 2003

MATERNAL INSTINCT
September 2003

0503/SH/LC64

SILHOUETTE®
DESIRE™

is proud to introduce

DYNASTIES:
THE CONNELLYS

Meet the royal Connellys—wealthy, powerful and rocked by scandal, betrayal...and passion!

TWELVE GLAMOROUS STORIES IN SIX 2-IN-1 VOLUMES:

February 2003
TALL, DARK & ROYAL by Leanne Banks
MATERNALLY YOURS by Kathie DeNosky

April 2003
THE SHEIKH TAKES A BRIDE by Caroline Cross
THE SEAL'S SURRENDER by Maureen Child

June 2003
PLAIN JANE & DOCTOR DAD by Kate Little
AND THE WINNER GETS...MARRIED! by Metsy Hingle

August 2003
THE ROYAL & THE RUNAWAY BRIDE by Kathryn Jensen
HIS E-MAIL ORDER WIFE by Kristi Gold

October 2003
THE SECRET BABY BOND by Cindy Gerard
CINDERELLA'S CONVENIENT HUSBAND by Katherine Garbera

December 2003
EXPECTING...AND IN DANGER by Eileen Wilks
CHEROKEE MARRIAGE DARE by Sheri WhiteFeather

The Shannon Sisters

by
CJ Carmichael

*The stories of three sisters whose lives
and loves are as rocky — and grand — as
the mountains where they grew up!*

A Second-Chance Proposal
March 2003

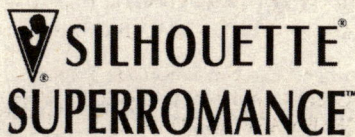

A Convenient Proposal
May 2003

A Lasting Proposal
July 2003

▼ SILHOUETTE®
SUPERROMANCE™

0203/SH/LC56

▼ SILHOUETTE®
SPECIAL EDITION™

proudly presents

CROWN AND GLORY

*Where royalty and romance
go hand in hand...*

April 2003 - Silhouette Special Edition
The Princess Is Pregnant! by Laurie Paige

May 2003 - Silhouette Special Edition
The Princess and the Duke by Allison Leigh

June 2003 - Silhouette Special Edition
Royal Protocol by Christine Flynn

July 2003 - Silhouette Desire 2-in-1
Her Royal Husband by Cara Colter
The Princess Has Amnesia! by Patricia Thayer

September 2003 - Silhouette Desire 2-in-1
Searching for Her Prince by Karen Rose Smith
The Royal Treatment by Maureen Child

November 2003 - Silhouette Desire 2-in-1
Taming the Prince by Elizabeth Bevarly
Royally Pregnant by Barbara McCauley

Silhouette Books
is delighted to present

from award-winning author
MARIE FERRARELLA

The Bachelors of Blair Memorial

Meet—

Lukas Graywolf: lover, healer and hero
In Graywolf's Hands
Sensation – May 2003

Reese Bendenetti: loner, doctor and protector
MD Most Wanted
Sensation – July 2003

Harrison MacKenzie: MD, bad boy and charmer
Mac's Bedside Manner
Special Edition – September 2003

Terrance McCall: secret agent and doctor in disguise
Undercover MD
Sensation – November 2003

0503/SH/LC59

SILHOUETTE®
INTRIGUE™

proudly presents its new Confidential series
with three sexy, rugged agents in

Chicago
Confidential

Men bound by love, loyalty and the law—
these specialised government operatives
have vowed to keep their missions and
identities confidential…

NOT ON HIS WATCH

Cassie Miles
May 2003

LAYING DOWN THE LAW

Ann Voss Peterson
June 2003

PRINCE UNDER COVER

Adrianne Lee
July 2003

SILHOUETTE®
SPECIAL EDITION™

presents three more passionate and adventurous stories from

MONTANA

Welcome to Montana — a place of passion and adventure, where there is a charming little town with some big secrets...

Her Montana Man by Laurie Paige
May 2003

Big Sky Cowboy by Jennifer Mikels
June 2003

Montana Lawman by Allison Leigh
July 2003

FREE!

1 Book
and a surprise gift!

We would like to take this opportunity to thank you for reading this Silhouette® book by offering you the chance to take another specially selected title from the Desire™ series absolutely FREE! We're also making this offer to introduce you to the benefits of the Reader Service™ —

- ★ FREE home delivery
- ★ FREE gifts and competitions
- ★ FREE monthly Newsletter
- ★ Books available before they're in the shops
- ★ Exclusive Reader Service discount offer

Accepting this FREE book and gift places you under no obligation to buy; you may cancel at any time, even after receiving your free shipment. Simply complete your details below and return the entire page to the address below. *You don't even need a stamp!*

YES! Please send me 1 free Desire book and a surprise gift. I understand that unless you hear from me, I will receive 2 superb new titles every month for just £4.99 each, postage and packing free. I am under no obligation to purchase any books and may cancel my subscription at any time. The free books and gift will be mine to keep in any case.

D3ZEB

Ms/Mrs/Miss/Mr ....Initials ....
BLOCK CAPITALS PLEASE

Surname ....

Address ....

....

....Postcode ....

Send this whole page to:
UK: The Reader Service, FREEPOST CN81, Croydon, CR9 3WZ
EIRE: The Reader Service, PO Box 4546, Kilcock, County Kildare (stamp required)

Offer not valid to current Reader Service subscribers to this series. We reserve the right to refuse an application and applicants must be aged 18 years or over. Only one application per household. Terms and prices subject to change without notice. Offer expires 29th August 2003. As a result of this application, you may receive offers from Harlequin Mills & Boon and other carefully selected companies. If you would prefer not to share in this opportunity please write to The Data Manager at the address above.

Silhouette® is a registered trademark used under licence.
Desire™ is being used as a trademark.